C000085781

HIS FIRST HIS SECOND

An Alicia Friend Investigation

A. D. DAVIES

www.addavies.com

ISBN: 978-1782803799

Novels by A. D. Davies

The Sublime Freedom

Shattered: Fear in the Mind

Co-Authored:

Project Return Fire – with Joe Dinicola

Lost Origins Novels:

Tomb of the First Priest

Secret of the Reaper Seal

Curse of the Eagle Plague

For my muse – you know who you are

Prologue

KATIE HAGUE KNEW she was swimming. She just didn't know why. She wasn't a strong swimmer, even though she'd spend hours in the pool on holidays, sometimes even brave enough to dip in the sea. Always with her parents watching, though.

She'd been thirteen on her last family holiday, a self-catering deal to Turkey, not that her dad couldn't afford somewhere more exotic. Turkey was Katie's choice. *Gobble-gobble*, she'd said again and again until the day of departure, and then all through the flight too, where her mother valiantly fought the urge to strangle her only child. Her dad smiled quietly.

Now, eight years after that final holiday with all three of them, Katie swam alone. Somewhere she didn't recognise. Somewhere black.

With her feet unable to touch the bottom, or anything solid, she trod water for a moment, something she always found hard. She never ventured out of her depth, not without her dad nearby or, more recently, unless Brian was with her.

And where the hell was Brian now?

They argued outside a late night bar—not loud, just testy. She was hungry, had suggested a curry, but Brian wanted to go on, "Just for one more, babe, please?" *A taxi.* Alone. That was Katie's last memory, the last she recalled, here, now, in this pool.

Movement caught her attention. Something nearby. She did not see it because of the dark, but a sweeping cold embraced her head and shoulders like an undercurrent flowing in from deeper water.

No, that wasn't quite right either.

All her body below the surface was numb, unfeeling, and now all above felt chilled. She hadn't seen the event, that *something*, but she knew:

A shadow had fallen over her.

"Who's there?"

Her words should have reverberated around the walls of a municipal pool, or a private home in the middle of the country, but the dark ate her voice right up. No echo, no sound coming back at her.

This meant there were no walls.

She was swimming outside.

But even outside there were buildings, trees, rocks. She was treading water, outdoors, with nothing around. No lights. No people.

So why did she get the impression she was not absolutely alone? Other than the invisible shadow, she had no reason to think someone watched her, not here.

Whatever "here" actually meant.

No light...

No buildings...

Was she in the middle of a *lake*?

Her breathing grated in her throat.

No, of course not. There would be light. There's always light. The darkest of freezing British waters still drew moonlight and stars; even when hiding, their light still penetrates. There is no *absolute* dark.

Each breath now hurt. She needed her inhaler. Her throat swelled within. She kicked her numb legs to no avail, and when she flapped her arms, no splashes whipped up.

This can't be.

Alone; swimming; out of her depth; now an asthma attack.

An object wedged in her mouth: hard, plastic, smaller than a matchbox.

She gagged. Tried to spit it out. But it was too big, lodging itself between her teeth.

A hiss.

Then light.

A pinprick, not in front of her but *inside* her head.

Her shoulders grew cold now, as if she were gliding upwards, out of the ... lake? The sea? The pool?

That thing, still stuck in her mouth, gave another hiss.

And Katie breathed.

The item hissed a third time and the cold spread to her chest, her back, down her stomach. Her hips. The light inside her expanded, enveloping her in cold. She wanted to use her arms to wrap around herself for warmth, but found them stuck behind her.

Looking down now, struggling to free herself, she saw her thighs raised, the clothes she was wearing when she argued with Brian still strangely dry. The odour of sweat and booze and a faint whiff of cigarette smoke urged her to undress and shower, but her hands remained bound tight. She couldn't see behind, could not turn at all.

Then, like a spotlight growing, her vision improved: a white-tiled floor, her bare feet bound by handcuffs, stockinged legs moving up into the little skirt that barely covered her underwear. She could not see past her chest, other than to confirm her clothing remained intact.

She was sitting on a hard wooden chair.

"Hello, Katie."

The deep voice penetrated the spotlight—calm, polite even.

"Please stop struggling, Katie, I don't want to hurt you."

From swimming in blackness to being tied to a chair. Nothing. Nothing could explain this.

She tried her voice. "Who are you?"

It hurt to speak. Now her head throbbed also. Like a hangover. She was about to be sick.

A bucket slid into view within the spotlight, a glimpse of a foot that nudged it closer.

"Please use this if you need to vomit. I won't be angry if you miss. Only if you don't try."

The foot peeking out of the dark into Katie's halo of light meant something. A clear fact, a truth that really should not be.

"The spotlight's real," Katie said aloud.

"Of course it's real," came the man's voice. "What a strange thing to say."

"Why am I here?"

"You are my second."

"Your ... what?"

"Please don't make me repeat myself, Katie. It annoys me. You are my second. This..."

Another spotlight cracked to life. It illuminated a girl five feet away, dressed similarly to Katie, like she was going clubbing, with long dark hair like Katie's, about Katie's age.

And then it all fell away: the swimming, the light, the dark, this disembodied voice from the blackness all around. But the girl frightened Katie the most. This girl, bound to a chair, gagged, blindfolded, looking so much like Katie they might have been sisters.

"This is your new roommate," the man said, now behind Katie, hands on her shoulders, his breath on her neck. "She is my first. You will be my second."

And, doing her very best to aim for the bucket, Katie vomited. She was pleased that a lot of it missed.

"Hmm," the man said. Then footsteps. An arm flashed into the light and tossed Katie's inhaler onto her lap. The footsteps receded.

And both lights went out, leaving nothing but pitch black.

Chapter One

IN MURPHY'S WORLD, the darkness meant peace. There was a beauty to the air that returned him to childhood visits to the seaside, like passing through an almost a physical barrier; one minute breathing thickly in the city, the next opening a car door and luxuriating in crisp, clear air. Here, with his eyes closed and his breathing steady, Murphy could almost have relaxed and fallen into a deep, solid sleep.

"Murphy?"

He could all but hear the waves swelling and breaking, a soft whoosh and crash, whoosh and crash. Sand kicking up in the wash, pebbles hurting his soft feet as he skipped over them.

"Sir?"

Saltwater spray on a windy day, walking atop clay cliffs, wind roaring in his face.

"Detective Inspector."

Murphy opened his eyes and turned to the clean-shaven constable and exhaled through his nose. "I'm thinking."

"Of course, sir. But Chief Superintendent Rhapshaw is..." The constable shivered, still soaking wet in his uniform, a blanket wrapped around him, doing his best to appear professional.

"Son," Murphy said, "do I frighten you?"

"Sir?"

"Do I frighten you? Am I an intimidating presence?"

"I'm not sure how to answer that, sir."

Murphy studied the boy's face. Probably popular with the ladies, a flat stomach, strong arms. He even had those hard man-boob things that seemed so desirable in the station changing room. Men—kids, really—tensing and showing one another their new muscles, lumps they never realised they had until their latest gym session popped them out of their dormant state. He had heard a word come to life over the past few years and it seemed to fit here: *homoerotic*. It used to be "metrosexual" when a guy took good care of himself with preening and skin lotion, but nowadays it had taken a step toward the norm, with men on display to other men, without a hint of self-consciousness or irony. Yes, *homoerotic* was more appropriate. But hey, each to their own. Soft skin and low body fat didn't make a kid a bad copper.

"I mean," Murphy said, "when you talk to me you sound like you're expecting me to yell at you, or give you a spanking."

"Sir?"

Okay, Murphy was officially bored now. "Where's the Chief?"

"Parking up near the cordon. He'll be about ten minutes."

"You were first on scene?"

"Yes, sir. I followed every rule. All of them."

"Gold star to you. In fact..." Murphy handed the constable a pound coin. "There's a newsagent down the road. Get yourself a whole bunch of gold stars."

The constable stood there looking at the coin in his hand. He closed his fingers around it, put it in his wet pocket, and looked back at Murphy, confused.

Murphy closed his eyes but opened them again quickly, unwilling to be dragged back into his peace, knowing he would have to return here all too soon.

He said, "The body, constable. Tell me about the body."

The constable led Murphy down a soggy, green hill to the edge of the lake where the scene of crime officers—SOCOs— mooched about in their white, papery suits. Their feet squelched and Murphy's footing loosened and then gripped again, while the kid leading him was firm and sure. Murphy decided he, too, would be firm and sure and not be shown up by a junior in front of the SOCOs. Murphy was surprised the constable talked so confidently.

"I responded to a triple-nine call at approximately oh-eight-thirty. Caller reported a drowning at Roundhay Park. I entered the park eight minutes later and cycled to the point where the caller said he would be waiting. I met Mr. Hudson—who had been walking his dog—and he pointed out what appeared to be a body floating—"

"What's your name?" Murphy asked.

"Er, Duncan. Duncan Powel."

"Okay, Constable Powel, we're not in court. Tell me about *the body*."

"Oh. Okay. Here. She was dead when I got to her ... bruised, cut up, her nails..." Powel looked at the ground.

The corpse lay on a wooden pallet beneath a white tarpaulin.

"I thought putting her on here would be better than the soil," Powel said.

"Good." Murphy nodded to Powel's uniform. "You said you followed every rule."

"Yes, sir."

"Does that include jumping into a cold lake when you couldn't know what dangers lurked under the surface?"

"Sir?"

"You're not a complete retard, Powel, so I assume you read up on the section that tells you not to place yourself in danger even when trying to help someone. Is my assumption correct?"

"Yes, sir, but—"

"And so you saw someone face down in a lake, jumped in without a thought to your own well-being and dragged that face-down someone back to shore hoping to resuscitate them? That about what happened, Constable Powel?"

"Yes, but when I realised she was long-dead I followed procedure to the letter..."

"Give me my pound back." Murphy held out his hand, eyes on the white sheet.

"Sir?"

"My pound. Give it back."

Powel placed the pound in Murphy's hand and Murphy held it tight. He bent down to the tarpaulin, lifted it a little, and then gently lowered it. He was aware of Powel standing over him and imagined the kid's bottom lip sticking out. Murphy felt a bit shitty about that.

"Powel?"

"Sir, I thought I was doing the right thing. If she'd been alive..."

Murphy stood to his full height so he was an entire head above the young constable. He put the pound back in his pocket, placed a hand on Powel's damp shoulder, and said, "Don't tell anyone, but ... promise you won't say anything?"

"Promise, sir."

"I would have done exactly the same thing."

"Sir?"

"I'm saying well done, Powel. Unofficially, you did a good thing here. If I were first on scene, I'd have gone swimming too."

A grin flickered briefly but Powel stifled it. "Thank you, sir."

"Go get changed."

As Powel tramped off, Murphy suppressed a glimmer of respect for the man-child and turned his thoughts to the body at his feet. But something else was about to drag Murphy's day down a little further. Chief Inspector Rhapshaw crested the hill, greeted by the clipboard-wielding crime-scene manager, who would invite the senior officer to sign in, before approaching Murphy and laying out the protocols for what would certainly be a major investigation.

Before the head of Yorkshire's Serious Crime Agency reached him, Murphy ascertained that the body was probably beaten to death and, although he had no medical expertise beyond twenty-odd years of listening to experts, he estimated the body had been in the water no longer than a few hours. He also managed to see through the bruising and cuts and filth, and identify the corpse as Hayley Davenport.

"Murphy," Rhapshaw said.

"Sir." Murphy stood and greeted the officer with a curt handshake. As with most people, Murphy loomed far taller than Graham Rhapshaw, and as with most people, Rhapshaw took a step back before he was comfortable enough to speak.

"Is it the Davenport girl?"

"Looks like it."

Rhapshaw turned from the corpse and paced toward the lake. He wore the uniform that he once told Murphy gave him gravitas when speaking to the press and underlings, and as such he glared at the muddy path as if it somehow offended him. "Lot of rain last night."

"The SOCOs are covering the area. But you're right. I doubt they'll find much."

"And is this similar to the Bradshaw girl?"

"Pippa."

"Hmm?"

"Pippa, sir. Her name was Pippa Bradshaw." Murphy noticed a woman wandering along the shore. She came from out of the woods on the other side of the lake.

"Are you suggesting I'm being insensitive, Detective Inspector?"

The woman was short, blonde, her hair in a ponytail. Probably mid-to-late twenties. Dressed like she belonged in an office. Except for the bubble-gum pink wellington boots.

"No, sir," Murphy said. "It's my own way of thinking about them. First name terms."

"We've talked about that before."

"And I haven't forgotten. Don't worry. I'm fine."

The woman was getting closer now. Murphy excused himself from Rhapshaw and approached over the sodden ground. "Hello? Miss?"

She didn't look up, engrossed in the long grass along the lakeside. She bent down and picked up a Coke can, peered inside, and discarded it.

As Murphy drew closer he saw she was a pretty little thing; petite, he estimated her head would come up to his chest. He called again, "Miss, excuse me."

This time she looked up. "Oh, hi!" She greeted him like an old friend she was surprised to see.

Murphy guided her aside. "Miss, I'm not sure how you got through the cordon, but this is a crime scene. A young woman has been..."

"Murdered, yes, I know." She smiled cheerily at him. "I'm Alicia Friend."

"And?"

"And Graham asked me to come along, see if I could help. Cool, huh?"

Murphy took a mental step back. Cute, blonde, seemed to almost bounce even though she was stood still. "Graham?"

"At your service." Rhapshaw's voice again. When Murphy turned, Rhapshaw said, "You've been pestering DCI Streeter for more personnel and he has been pestering me. Therefore, Detective Sergeant Alicia Friend is now on attachment from the Serious Crime Agency. She's been a damn good copper for me, and worked as a criminal analyst in any number of departments. Seems like a good fit."

"Sir, if by 'analyst' you mean 'psychic'..."

"Murphy, how long have you known me?"

"Ten years, on and off."

"And in those ten years, what exactly could you possibly have seen to make you think for one fleeting minute I'd employ a psychic?"

Murphy saw his point. "She's a shrink then?"

Alicia stood forward. "I'm a psychologist. My brain is like some mini-computer, but you can't switch it off and back on again. I'm also a policewoman with a mean right hook and a pretty decent track record wherever my little feet have taken me."

Murphy stared at her a moment.

Did she just say "little feet"?

"DS Friend, thanks for coming down, but we don't even have the forensics in yet."

"It's okay," she said. "I already have a theory about your suspect. For starters, it's not much of a stretch to start using the fave phrase of Hollywood thriller writers: serial killer."

Murphy shook his head. "*Sir*, what the hell is this? Buffy the Vampire Slayer takes a stroll and she's sure this is a serial killer? That mini-computer of hers needs de-bugging. We have two bodies. Similar appearance, similar age, similar deaths, but it's not enough for a pattern. It's barely a coincidence."

"Really?" Rhapshaw said. "Are you saying she's wrong?"

"Not definitively, no. I mean, there *are* signs it was the same man as Pippa, of course, but..."

Rhapshaw was about to respond but Alicia Friend got in first: "Well, technically a serial murderer needs three kills, but from what Graham tells me, a third girl went missing yesterday in similar circumstances to Pippa and Hayley. Close in appearance, twenty-two years old, which means there's about five days until a third body shows up."

"We still don't know..."

"Are you a betting man, DI Murphy?"

To Rhapshaw, he said, "Sir, I know I asked for extra feet on the ground but I'm not sure this is the answer."

Rhapshaw shrugged.

Alicia said, "Because if you're really into gambling and want to throw one of those little balls onto the roulette wheel—by the way, I'm using the little ball as a metaphor for Katie Hague's life, and the roulette wheel for the chances of finding her alive—"

"I get the imagery."

"Good, because if that's what you're going to do—hope that the forensics turn up a fingerprint or find the name and address of the person who beat Hayley Davenport to death secreted about her person—then I very much doubt Katie's going to make it."

Murphy grew conscious of his breathing, the cool air through his nose far louder than it should have been. The winter breeze blew, the SOCOs' paper suits rustled, and the wind bit at his neck. Alicia Friend shivered but her eyes held his.

Rhapshaw said, "Murphy, your desk is clear as of now. Reporting to Detective Chief Inspector Streeter, *this* is your only case. Find the missing girl, and catch this bastard."

"Fine," Murphy said. "Let's hear the theory."

Rhapshaw smiled satisfactorily. "Let me know when the forensics get in."

While the chief inspector struggled back up the hill, Alicia Friend told Murphy what she'd seen so far.

Chapter Two

ALICIA CONSTANTLY FOUND herself deeply disappointed with human nature. Heck, she'd been studying it for years. And the poor, grumpy man charged with finding whoever killed Pippa and Hayley, he didn't seem to like Alicia at all. That was okay, though. He'd come around. They always did. Five phases was what it usually took for this type of detective to respect her, but they were pushed for time here, so she had to get stuck into him quickly. With DI Murphy about to have his mind blown by Alicia's superior intellect, his reaction would dictate whether she would be an effective part of his team or not.

When the chief ascended out of earshot, Alicia turned to the lake. "Your killer came in that way." She pointed to the heavy woodland on the opposite side. "Probably parked up on the ring road in one of the old horse tracks and came through that way."

"Wow." Murphy stood beside her, rubbed his moustache in a way that Alicia thought looked defensive. She'd know more shortly. He said, "You figured that out, eh? The fact there was a carnival over the hill behind us didn't enter into your little deduction?"

"The carnival is irrelevant. The woods would have been

packed with druggies and shaggers, so he'd have had to come down after midnight when it was quieter. Even then, why take the chance of coming here? These woods are used for all sorts. He had a specific reason."

She smiled up at him. Waaaayy up at him. He pulled his shoulders back, making himself appear even taller. She moved over to the body, beckoning Murphy without looking his way, knelt on a SOCO-approved pad, and lifted the sheet to the girl's filth-streaked naked body. "Okay, firstly she was beaten with far less rage than Pippa. Her injuries are less pronounced. Meaning?"

"I've been doing this for over thirty years, DS Friend. I don't need to be quizzed."

"Then prove it."

"If it *is* the same guy ... it means he's more careful this time. The first was rage, killed her with a single punch. When he realised she was dead, he beat the body almost unrecognisable. This time he took longer. Learned from the first time. With Hayley ... he enjoyed it more."

"Wow, you *have* been doing this a long time. Well done."

"Well, thank you."

"But look at what else he left us. Mud."

"Forensics will confirm whether it's mud or not," Murphy said sarcastically. When Alicia said nothing further, he crouched beside her. "What about the mud?"

"It's special. It's sinking mud."

"Oh. I didn't realise it was special *sinking* mud."

"Bear with me."

She replaced the sheet and thanked the SOCO very much and again beckoned Murphy to follow her. With another rub of his 'tache, he rose to his full height and fell in step behind. He sighed as they walked.

"Are you jealous?" she asked.

17

"Of?"

"My wellies."

"They're pink."

"I keep 'em in the car at all times. You should think about doing the same."

"I'll bear that in mind."

They lapsed into silence again, just the squelching of mud and the light breeze and Murphy sighing yet again.

"You know where we're going?" Alicia asked.

"I presume you're going to show me the magic mud."

"It's not magic, silly. It's sinking mud. At least it used to be."

"Used to be?"

"Here."

They'd arrived at the north end of the lake where it felt colder than back with the body. The path that circled the water staggered a small stream via a footbridge, the stream feeding the lake at a trickle. About twelve feet off-shore sat a mini island, with evergreens and deciduous shrubs growing side-by-side and all over each other. From here they could see through the bare branches to where Hayley Davenport's body lay, but in summer it would have been bright and dense with foliage. Alicia spread her arms in a *ta-daaa* gesture toward the water between shore and island.

She considered saying *Ta-daaa*, but settled with, "Et voila."

"It's water," Murphy said.

"When I used to come up to Roundhay Park with my mum and our dogs, this was the part of the trip where mum would tell me to be extra careful. Especially since I was usually on my bike."

"Because of the sinking mud."

"Right. They've cleaned it up a bit since me and mum and Bonker and Stonker came up, but if you grew up in these parts, you know about the sinking mud. That if you fell in and there was no one with a rope or something to save you, you'd sink in over your head and keep sinking and you'd never be found."

"Bonker and Stonker?"

Alicia jumped and clipped Murphy round the ear. "Pay attention, Inspector." He looked as shocked as if she'd jabbed him with a cattle prod, but she continued. "Bonker and Stonker are perfectly good names for Springer Spaniels. They're getting on a bit, just like my mum, but they're still going strong. Again, just like my mum. Now, perhaps you'd like to comment on my theory."

"You hit me."

"You deserved it. Comments please."

"You grew up round here, heard a story about sinking mud, and you think our killer heard the same story and dumped the body here believing it would never be found."

"Correctamundo!"

"You're mental."

Murphy started striding back toward the body and Alicia had to trot to keep up.

"Oh, come on," she said, walking backwards in front of him. "Why else is she covered in mud like that?"

"There's no mud. You said they cleaned it up."

"It peed down last night. Think harder."

Murphy stopped. He opened his jacket and placed his hands on his narrow hips, breathed out—a bit over-dramatically in Alicia's opinion. Closed his eyes. When he opened them, Alicia could tell she won a minor victory in there.

He said, "It was muddy when he arrived. He dumped her before the rain came, expecting her to sink. The rain swelled the stream which swelled the lake which ... floated the body."

"And the mud—not sinking mud any more, but hey—is still pretty thick."

"Which is why it stuck to her so much. Even the lake wouldn't clean her completely."

Alicia felt good about him seeing sense. But then bad, *so* bad, about the dead girl. "I bet we find mud in all her orifices, in all her wounds, in her mouth ... the killer grew up here in Leeds, he knew about the mud, but he's probably been away, come back."

"Jail?"

"Or a really long holiday. But prison. Perhaps there are more like this one?"

Murphy had his mobile out, in-hand, dialling. He listened until someone picked up. "Cleaver, sorry, I know you've only had a few hours sleep, but for your shift tonight I need you checking parolees for the last year. Violent crimes preferred. Leeds residents. And cross-reference them with similar patterns to our murders, patterns that perhaps stopped for a while ... yes, when our parolees went down. And Cleaver? If you and DS Ball need to buy in a civvie team to help crunch the numbers, I'll authorise the overtime." He hung up and turned to Alicia. "Okay, you're in."

"Cool and the gang." Alicia couldn't help but smile. "What now, boss?"

He stroked his moustache again, eyes wandering to the lake. "Now? Now some officer has to inform Hayley's parents their daughter is dead."

"Should we do that?"

"No. We have a third missing girl. We can't do any more here."

Alicia had left her Ford Focus in Roundhay Park's main car park. As they trudged up the hill in that direction, Murphy filled her in about Katie Hague's disappearance.

She was out in the city centre, clubbing with her boyfriend

Brian and a group of friends. Brian claimed Katie and he rowed about whether to stay out for a bit more booze—he'd wanted to do some shots with his pals from the rugby club—but she was hungry and stroppy and demanding a curry. So he said fine, go, and she had.

1:30 a.m., 10th December.

That was the last timestamp on the nightclub CCTV, the final time anyone, namely a doorman called Duane, could positively ID her. And now, just over thirty hours later—the 11th December—she was still missing.

Why was Murphy so sure it was the same man who'd killed Pippa and Hayley?

Because of the circumstances of their disappearances.

On the 5th of December, Hayley Davenport went ice-skating with two girlfriends, wrapped up in four layers, a bright red scarf and a woolly hat to match. It was an evening in Millennium Square where Leeds City Council had erected a temporary rink next to the German market that pops up every Christmas. When it was her turn to get the hot chocolate in, she told her friends to wait by the stall selling multi-coloured mechanical dolls and delved into the crowded market. She did not return. No drinks stall-owners saw her. Her body turned up in North Leeds, today, the 11th, probably killed yesterday, or more likely—with Katie being taken in the early hours of the 10th—the day before.

Five days in captivity.

On the 27th November—eight days prior to Hayley going missing—Pippa Bradshaw attended her local pub in the suburb of Chapel Allerton, celebrating a work colleague's leaving do. Stella, the small PR firm's HR manager, was being made redundant but was in buoyant mood having booked a six-month trip to Australia on the back of her pay-off. Pippa was so excited for her that she'd turned up holding a huge stuffed koala and wearing a cork-strung hat. Murphy learned she had been planning to make the same trip once she finished uni. That night, though, Pippa—a little drunk—popped to the loo and never returned. She was found dead on the 3rd of December, in a shallow grave, in woodland in the grounds of Harewood House, a beauty spot owned by a relative of the Queen, located between Leeds and Harrogate.

Six days in captivity.

Two days later, he took Hayley. Meaning:

- 27th Dec: Pippa taken.
- 3rd Dec: Pippa found; she died that same day.
- 5th Dec: Hayley taken.
- 9th Dec: Hayley killed.
- 10th Dec: Katie goes missing ... same kidnapper? *Probably.*
- 11th Dec: Hayley found ... *after being concealed.* Did that mean something?

They shelved that for now.

At Alicia's Ford Focus, Murphy said, "They're all between nineteen and twenty-one years of age, they all have dark, shoulder length hair, and they're all..." He trailed off.

"What?" Alicia asked. "What else is it?"

"They're beautiful, Sergeant Friend. I mean stunning. And not air-brushed magazine stunning, I mean with a little extra something ... a sort of ... 'way' about them, as my mother would have said. A ... strength of personality."

Alicia thought for a moment. "You sure you're not a little bit in love with these girls, Murphy?"

He frowned. "I'm trying to say each of them had more to offer than good looks. That to see this he would have had to watch them. *Stalk* them. He waited for the right moment to strike and ... well ... you know the rest."

"I'll drive," she said. "I'll drop you off later."

"You don't know where we're going."

"Katie's house, right?"

"Right. How...?"

"Get in," Alicia said. This was not going to be pleasant.

Chapter Three

THE ANSWER WAS SIMPLE: Alicia knew that's where they were going because she knew Murphy had only spoken to Richard Hague—Katie's dad—once, and that was when he came into the station to report her missing. The description rang a bell with a member of Murphy's team and they called the DI to check the photo Mr. Hague had brought with him. Murphy deduced instantly that he had a big problem on his hands.

Now, with the emergence of a second body, they needed as much information as possible. There was still a chance the killer was acquainted with all three, and this, Alicia hoped, would be what caught him. She doubted it, though.

Once Murphy gave her the address and she gave it to the satnav, they were off to see a distraught father and ask him some awkward questions. Driving, Alicia asked Murphy his first name.

"Donald," he said.

"Donald?" She nodded. "How about Donny? Or Don? Donald 'the Don' Murphy. I like that. The Don."

"Murphy's fine."

"Nah. It's Don."

"Even my wife called me Murphy."

"Called?"

"She's ... gone now."

"Sorry."

"You prefer Friend? Or Alicia?"

"What do you think?"

"I think you're sitting so close to that steering wheel, if we crash and the airbag goes off it'll kill you."

She winked at him. "That's why I disengaged it as soon as I bought the car. Us short-arses have to make these little adjustments. And don't look like that. Yours still works."

"That's not the reason I gave you a look. You're short enough to be cute. Try being a lanky beanpole all your life."

"Aw, diddums. Would ickle Donny Murphy like a hug?"

The grumpy DI almost smiled. "How the hell do you get away with that?"

"With what?"

"This silly little girl act."

"This is an act?"

"It must be. No one's as cheerful as you. Not unless they're medicated. Legally, or otherwise."

"So because I choose to be happy rather than sad, this is a bad thing?"

"In your case? Yeah, a bit."

"Oh, you'll get used to it. On average, it takes five stages. First, disbelief that *moi* could possibly be considered one of the best in my field. Then the second stage is irritation. But when you see how useful I am, you'll reach stage three: acceptance. Stage four is reliance, and stage five is collaboration, where you actively want me around. I don't do this consciously, though. I'll just be my cheery self. You'll fall in love with me and the change in *you* will happen all by itself."

Murphy pulled a jolly serious face with a seriously serious frown. "You don't *choose* whether you're happy or not."

"Actually, you do. Everyone knows how body language betrays what you're feeling, that if you're amused you smile or laugh, if you're angry you look ... frowny. Grumpy, you look like, well, like you. But it works the other way too. Smile. Try it right now. Smile for thirty seconds and I guarantee no matter how miserable or grumpy you are you'll feel better at the end of that thirty seconds."

"It's the next left."

She turned, obeying both Murphy and the satnav. "Smile, Donny-boy. Look." She smiled for him. "Not hard."

"Pull up here."

She parked and turned off the engine, opened the door and got out. Murphy did the same and leaned on the roof.

Alicia mimicked him and said, "Before the end of the day, I *will* make you smile."

"If we find Katie Hague by the end of the day, I'll definitely smile."

"Nuh-uh. Ten pounds. You'll smile, regardless."

"No tickling?"

"No tickling."

"Make it twenty," he said.

"Fine. Twenty. Now which one is Mr. Hague's?"

"Go easy on him. He's a widower, raised Katie alone for the past ten years."

"Hey, who's the psychologist here?"

"Just don't bloody tell him to smile."

Richard Hague lived with Katie in a nice semi in the Shadwell area of Leeds, a place where the moderately well-off and stinking-rich live side-by-side. Older than her by a fair distance, he was still a good-looking fellow; not Ryan Gosling good-looking, more Robert Downey Jr. or Pierce Brosnan. Mid-to-late forties, she guessed, early fifties at the outside. She could have checked, but decided to guesstimate for the fun of it.

Murphy had phoned ahead and told Mr. Hague about the Serious Crime Agency, how they mostly dealt with organised crime, not the murder of individuals. But Murphy insisted—as much to reassure himself as Mr. Hague, Alicia supposed—that Katie was not a murder victim. She was a *kidnapping*. And since the SCA dealt in kidnappings, albeit usually for ransom, they were putting their best man on it.

Detective Sergeant Alicia Friend was now their best man.

"What a pretty name," Mr. Hague said, gently shaking her hand.

The instinctive comment made Alicia smile, without forcing it this time. No wife in the picture, but clearly not attached either. He wasn't *coming on* to her, she was sure of that, but Mr. Hague was only human after all.

"Sorry," he said, and sure enough, the skin beneath his eyes bloomed a little rosier.

"Don't be sorry." Alicia took a deep-cushioned seat in his warm living room. "It *is* a pretty name. I like my name."

"Mr. Hague," Murphy said. "I'm really just here to advise you that Detective Friend is now collaborating with us. She has an excellent record in the Serious Crime Agency and I'm sure we'll make progress soon."

Richard Hague nodded.

"You refused the offer of a family liaison officer," Alicia said. "I'd like you to reconsider. They can be extremely helpful in keeping you informed—"

"I'm sure you'll tell me as soon as you know anything. DI Murphy's communication has been more than enough. I'd rather be alone for now." Mr. Hague's mouth tightened.

Alicia thought, *He doesn't want a police officer to see him at his weakest. Must keep this as business-like as possible. For* his *sake.*

She said, "I could do with a look at Katie's room." She felt bad saying that because she worried she'd have to lie to him in a moment.

"Why is that?" Mr. Hague asked. "It's not like she's run away or anything."

Damn. Now for the lie.

She said, "I like to get a feel for the person I'm fighting for."

He seemed to like that. Fighting for his daughter. Yeah. Alicia would be *fighting*. But she didn't really need to get a feel for her in order to operate. That was the lie. The truth was something she didn't like to talk about, not to a victim's parent.

"Okay," Mr. Hague said. "Right this way."

He carried himself well. Not too tall, but erect. Certainly, next to Mr. Hague, DI Murphy seemed positively shabby. Murphy, despite his height, tended to slump in his walk, while Hague *strode*.

In Katie's room, Alicia tried to keep her face neutral. Mr. Hague stood at the door. His shoulders blocked it so Murphy couldn't get through.

"Do you need to be alone?" Mr. Hague asked.

"No, this is fine." Alicia sat on the bed. She lowered herself to Katie's pillow and breathed in. Unscented. She lifted a small teddy bear from the pillow, too small to cuddle, but enough to have close by.

"Her mother's," Mr. Hague said.

Alicia nodded and replaced the bear. She stood and took in the dresser and its wide mirror: makeup, lipsticks, a hairbrush. There were clothes strewn on the floor, nice ones. Miss Sixty jeans, FCUK crop-top (*FCUK football—what about me?*), a black Donna Karen dress dangling from the bookcase, still on its hanger, a class above the other clothes.

"She was meeting a man," Alicia said.

Mr. Hague's hands found their way to his trouser pockets,

and he slouched. It didn't suit him. He should hold his shoulders back, like when his subconscious was flirting with Alicia.

He said, "We got on okay, but we didn't share stuff. I guessed she had a boyfriend, but I don't know much about him. She said she was going out with friends. That's all."

"Brian," Murphy said to Alicia. "His name is Brian Dawson. We eliminated him as a suspect."

She detected an air of one-upmanship, Murphy eager to remain in charge.

Fine. Let him have it.

She opened the closet and examined Katie's wardrobe. Lots of jeans, a few smart tee shirts, an old England rugby shirt with WILKINSON on the back. Alicia ran her hand along the lettering. "Aww, she likes our Johnny."

"Rugby," Mr. Hague said. "One of the few things the two of us enjoyed together."

His head bowed and Alicia knew—God, she got sick of "just knowing" sometimes—that he was holding back tears.

She said, "You talk in the past tense."

"Hmm?"

"Mr. Hague, you talk in the past tense. Katie *had* a boyfriend. You *got* along fine. Has DI Murphy not told you that *if* this is the same person who took the other girls, he keeps them for up to a week before—"

"I told him," Murphy said.

Alicia stepped closer. "Mr. Hague, do you understand that Katie is in all likelihood still alive?"

Richard Hague came fully into his daughter's room and held Alicia's hand. He smelled clean, without scent. Like Katie. Tears sat in his eyes, like raindrops about to fall from the branch of an oak.

He said, "Do you have children, DS Friend?"

Something bitter caught in Alicia's throat as she replied, "No. No I don't have any children."

"Me neither," Murphy said.

Mr. Hague sat beside Alicia. "It's hard to explain. But I suppose ... if I think of her as already dead, it'll be easier for me when they find the body."

Alicia did not want this. She needed Mr. Hague to be strong.

"I lied to you," she told him. "When I said I needed to get a feel for Katie."

Mr. Hague smiled without humour. "I thought there was something fishy about that line. Bit too Hollywood."

That surprised her, but she said nothing. A prompt for someone else to fill the silence.

"And I didn't think you needed stoking up," Mr. Hague said. "I can see it in you, Detective Friend. You're determined."

"And how, exactly, do you see this?" Murphy asked.

"I used to be a salesman."

"Ah," Alicia said. Then to Murphy, "Best psychologists in the world. A good salesman can read a person," she clicked her fingers, "like that."

"I spent ten years flogging alarm systems in the States. Proper yuppie, I was. I set myself targets and met them. Every time. Made a fair bit of money, but I missed England after a while. The States were too ... I don't know ... it's not the best place to raise kids. Not with all the gun violence."

"And that's what you wanted? Kids?"

"Gillian and I wanted a million of 'em. We had Katie and then a couple of years later Gillian got sick. She got better again, relapsed. Went on for years. She lasted until after Katie's fourteenth birthday, but ... well, she couldn't fight it forever."

Alicia wanted to reach out and touch him, to reassure him that people cared, that *she* cared. She couldn't allow him to lose his daughter, to experience that pain again.

"Sir, let me explain something to you." She went to the pillow. "Katie has no real vanity. Unusual for a twenty-two year old these days. She is clean, but she doesn't primp and preen." Alicia gestured to the clothing and the dressing table. "She likes to look good, but isn't really into fashion. If she hadn't been meeting Brian she'd have worn the jeans and French Connection top. The designer dress was too over the top, so she went mid-way. That shows she's sensible, Mr. Hague, and not given to impulse."

He sat up straight, the slouch now tucked away.

"What's her favourite movie?" she asked.

"Raging Bull."

"And intelligent too. That's a thinking person's movie. Bet she hates Rocky films." Alicia saw in Mr. Hague's eyes she was correct. "Katie doesn't go for pulpy fiction, no Mills and Boon or chick-lit. It's Hemingway and Paulo Coelho and the like on these shelves." She sat next to him and held one of his big hands in both hers. "Mr. Hague, I'd be willing to bet real money that she's the type of person who, if she's afraid of heights she climbs the Eiffel Tower or goes skydiving, right?"

Mr. Hague showed a glimmer of a smile at last. Alicia all but heard Murphy's silent tut. Hague said, "Swimming. She's a poor swimmer, but she'd always go in the pool. Or the sea."

"But never without supervision?"

"Never. She's asthmatic too, so she needs her inhaler nearby."

"See? She's sensible. Now in my experience, the sort of people I think we're dealing with always talk to their..."

She nearly said "victims".

"They *talk* to their captives. And if Katie is half the girl I believe her to be, she'll last as long, if not longer, than the others."

One corner of Mr. Hague's mouth turned up.

"That's it." Alicia poked the other corner so he displayed a full smile. "Mr. Hague, to coin a cliché, it's not over until I say it's over. And until then, I want you to hope. Pray if you pray. But you should try to keep your spirits up no matter what. Watch DVDs, have a drink if you like—"

"I'm teetotal," Hague said.

"Whatever. Do what you do. And besides, you know what Mr. Hague?"

"What?"

"You have a nice smile. Try and keep it."

This time, Murphy's tut was not silent.

Chapter Four

RICHARD HAGUE THOUGHT the grumpy bloke and the dizzy-sounding blonde would never leave. They asked question after question, about Katie, about her friends, about Brian. *Brian.* The lad who'd been keeping Katie out 'til all hours, sometimes all night—a pipsqueak, not now, not ever good enough for his little girl. And they asked about his own whereabouts and habits, and what he was doing to stay positive. He lied effectively enough about that last thing.

He was impressed by the man—Murphy's—professional manner and words when they met yesterday, and although initially he was less than impressed by the sergeant with the pretty name, she'd shown a rare intelligence that gave him more hope than the bloke did.

Plus, she was really cute. Not something he noticed too often; each woman he met he compared them to Gillian and found they simply did not match up. Alicia hadn't matched Gillian for raw passion, not that he could tell so far, but she more than competed in the intelligence department and ... what was that thing he could never pin down? That *don't-give-a-shit-*

ness Gillian put out there. Looks-wise, Sergeant Friend was a different animal, like comparing wolves and tigers. Both prized trophies but with very different rewards.

Sexist bastard, Katie would say. If she could read his thoughts. Measuring women like property, as if you can tick boxes on a comparison site and decide which is the most worthy of attention.

He decided to stop thinking about this.

With Katie missing he should be concentrating on her, not his confused feelings for women who were not his dead wife. He made it through lunch without eating, and the rest of the afternoon, snacking, drinking coffee, checking his phone for missed calls from the police. He even considered taking them up on the offer of a FLO—a family liaison officer—if only to know for sure he'd hear of new developments as soon as they were confirmed.

He paced a lot.

He tried to watch TV, but drama, documentaries, some dark movie ... all drifted before him without sinking in.

The only phone calls he received were from family members and friends he'd contacted the previous day, all asking politely if Katie had shown, with Richard only able to reply with lies.

She'll be okay.

I'm sure she's fine.

Just blowing off steam somewhere.

By the time the sun disappeared behind the neighbours' houses, Richard's need to do something—anything—made his hands clench and unclench over and over. And he paced some more.

A drive.

Yes, probably a good idea, to clear his head, occupy his thoughts.

He put on a jacket and went through his kitchen and into his two-car garage. His silver Merc stood next to Katie's blue Corsa, not quite touching, but close.

Katie couldn't park properly for toffee.

He changed his mind about the drive.

Instead, he popped the boot and lifted the spare tyre and took out a small pouch manufactured in smooth black leather, about A4-sized with a zip down one side, like you might use to carry an iPad or compact laptop. He slipped it under his arm, replaced the tyre, and closed the boot.

Outside, walking in the chill evening, he considered his situation: a father and husband, his wife dead of cancer, an unstoppable killer if ever there was one, and his daughter, his only child, snatched off the street and held by a man with some sort of control issue. Doing things Richard could barely think about.

No sexual assault.

That's what Alicia said, what *Sergeant Friend* told him before she left. But he couldn't be sure that was true.

He walked Main Street with safe, warm houses either side of the busy road, thinking way too much, thinking things he never should, things no father should even consider. But there he was, imagining blood and flesh and naked violations. Until he came to the Red Lion pub.

He brought a younger Katie here for the Rugby World cup final, the year England won it Down Under, and the landlord hadn't cared. What age was she? Ten? Eleven? Her mom was still alive, but tired, too tired for a trip to the pub. But Richard wanted Katie to experience a big-game atmosphere outside of their living room, and he still pictured her goofy smile, eyes wide, as Johnny Wilkinson kicked the winning drop-goal and her screams at the final whistle, bouncing on the seats along with the drunks and her sober father. A sober father who wanted to drink so much back then; a celebration, a quick lager, nothing much ... but he resisted.

It was his toughest one-day-at-a-time since his first one.

Now, entering the bar of the Red Lion, he felt that urge again. Football streamed on the big screen, a game in which this lower-league supporting pub held no real interest, except one group of young lads who thought following a team meant picking the most successful one. So the regulars, those round-of-belly / thin-of-hair blokes drinking Black Sheep bitter, analysed the racing pages and avoided eye contact with Richard—a stranger who entered their domain.

"Glenmorangie," Richard said to the barman. "And a diet Coke on the side, please."

The barman delivered and Richard sat at the end of the bar. He sipped his Coke. The barman watched the match. And Richard wondered what he would do if one of the men here slapped a hand on his shoulder and told him he'd release Katie for a small fortune. Or in exchange for Richard's own life. He'd thought many times over the past hours that he would gladly swap places with her—what father wouldn't?—but it was never going to be an option. All he could do was sit and wait, and maybe...

He lifted the single malt to his lips and sniffed. The ten-year-old whiskey burned gently in his nose and the back of his throat, mere vapours reawakening memories of America, of his time on the road, of loneliness and drinking himself to sleep so many nights. And he remembered the one thing more pleasurable than drinking.

He put the glass back on the bar, the single malt untouched, then downed his Coke and left the pub. He was lucky with the number 46 bus and it dropped him half a mile away from his destination—the less-than-affluent suburb of Chapeltown.

The cold bit deep, chafing his face, his cheeks in particular. He pulled his cap down low as he passed the groups of young black men and spotty white youths huddled on the corner of the chip shop, avoided their curious stares, and pulled his coat tighter as a police car glided by. The loud *crack* he heard moments later, he told himself, was a car backfiring, not a gunshot. He wondered what Gillian would make of his behaviour, whether one destructive act was worse than another, and if such things can be quantified.

Like most nights in this neighbourhood there lurked a road lined with horrible women in short skirts and way too much makeup, most smoking and shivering and trying to catch his eye. A street with so many displaying their goods, though, was likely to be run by a pimp or gang, and such men repulsed Richard to a degree that he would not dare give his trade to one of them. Instead, he made his way to the adjacent road, where a gaggle of skinnier women loitered; pale, gaunt, skin hanging off them through rapid weight-loss; dregs for whom the only trade was the poorest of clients.

The first woman Richard stopped next to could have been mid-thirties or she could have been late-forties but when he studied her a moment longer he realised she was probably under thirty. Yes, this one needed him.

"Fifty for full sex," she said.

Richard said, "Thirty."

She took a deep, deep drag on her cigarette, her fingers trembling, eyes up and down over Richard. "Forty."

"Thirty's enough for a hit around here."

She shrugged, nodded, and tossed her fag into the gutter. "Where you wanna go?"

"This way. I have a place."

Richard held out his free arm and she took it, and they walked like any couple, except for her staggering gait and that she had to keep pulling her skirt down. The woman attempted small talk but Richard deflected her questions. He tried to imagine they were strolling the banks of the Seine, but the woman's perfume was so pungent the image faded to black. At least the scent drowned out any lingering memory of whiskey.

What made him do this? Why seek out *this* woman, rather than, say, pick up a normal person? He was handsome enough, he knew that. Heck, Alicia's body language suggested he could attract a woman some fifteen.

And yet he resorted to this.

Yes, he expected the therapist-speak was "self-destructive", a synonym for "committing acts he knows to be wrong to deflect his own attention from more hurtful aspects of life." If Katie had not been kidnapped, he would not be here tonight. He was certain of this because it was only the second time he'd indulged since leaving the States.

The other was in the weeks after Gillian died and he thought his body would eat itself if he continued to resist.

"Here we are." Richard presented a small complex of lock-ups, deserted at this time of night. Many of the iron doors were warped and rusted but Richard's was still in fine nick, only damage being graffiti and a few dents. Of course, the lock had been destroyed and the handle ripped off by would-be thieves, but that was Richard's own doing, illusions that served as better security than any real lock. Plus, there was a remote system that alerted Richard to any break-ins here, so he knew it had not been breached in the year since he last checked up on the place.

In the wooden frame he found the recessed flap, enabling him to get his fingers into the real lock mechanism and swing the door. It opened the same way as a domestic garage but the hinges were to the side, swinging it out then in, revealing a tidy workspace and a 1995 Ford Escort van.

"Wow," the woman said. "That is going to be *cold*."

"I have blankets," Richard said, and ushered her inside the lock-up and shut them in.

He flicked on the light and led her to the back of the van and opened the doors. It was dark inside the van but easy to make out a mattress, two pillows, and a duvet that Richard bought from Marks and Spencer after the last time. He glanced at the woman and she seemed impressed—a hint of life in her sunken, dark-ringed eyes.

"By the way, I'm Mia," she said.

I doubt that, Richard thought, but said, "Pleased to meet you. I'm Brian," and took off his coat.

"Mia" crawled into the van on her hands and knees, a rustling noise all around her, then turned to face him, leaning on her elbows, knees in the air. "So how you wanna do this?"

"Slowly," he said, and climbed in beside her. He laid out the pouch he'd taken from under his spare tyre.

"What's that?" Mia asked.

"Something I used to rely on a bit too much."

"Yeah, I can empathise with that."

Richard raised an eyebrow at the three-syllable word.

She said, "Oh, yeah, I went to school. Quite clever, me. But I doubt you'd guess, cos of, y'know..." She mimed injecting her arm then stuck her tongue out and pretended to be high.

"Indeed."

"People think I'm just some skank junkie, and hey they're right about that, but—"

"Why don't you quit?" Richard asked. "If you're so clever?"

When she laughed, her head rocked too far back, revealing her answer to be practiced and well-worn. "I never got round to it. Maybe I will next week or something. Right now we got business. You gonna shag me or what?"

Richard sat up and placed the pouch on the wheel arch. He

gripped the zipper in his thumb and forefinger, and pulled. The teeth clacked open one by one.

The black pouch opened on a hinge like a book.

Inside were strapped six clean, bladed instruments. Richard selected a slender knife with an ivory handle and a jewel in the hilt.

"This," he said, holding it in front of Mia's face, "is a stiletto. The shoes that slags and hookers wear are named after it due to the thin blade and sharp point."

Mia's wide eyes followed it. "It's beautiful."

"It is." Richard slid it back into place and removed a military knife with a thick handle and serrated edge and held it firm in his hand, again close to her face. "This is a titanium MPK as used in the US by their navy SEALs. MPK stands for Multi-Purpose Knife and is utilised during active missions because of its durability in seawater and other harsh conditions."

Mia didn't seem to like that one as much. "Why exactly are you showing me these?"

"Well, it's like this," he said, and slammed the blade hard into Mia's chest.

In these situations, Richard liked to think he felt the heart beating around the metal of the blade. He imagined it labouring to carry on its function, but withering, flapping uselessly, then giving up and sagging like a deflated balloon.

Mia's blood was surprisingly warm on his hand, and he almost regretted killing her. She had a little potential. That one word "empathise" had piqued a moment of regret but ultimately it was her own life, and she had chosen drugs over a decent future. That was the reason she was on the streets of Chapeltown selling her scrawny body for thirty quid a ride. If she'd chosen more wisely she would not be dead right now.

It didn't take long for Richard to clean up. He folded in the plastic that had rustled so loudly when Mia climbed in, taped up the sides, rolled her up like a carpet, and sealed the ends with cable ties and packing tape. He took his MPK to the sink in the corner and opened a pre-prepared bottle containing diluted sulphuric acid, poured a good depth, and dropped in the knife. It hissed briefly and once it was clean of blood and other evidence he took it out using tongs. He emptied the sink and filled it with water and added a lot of salt, then submerged the knife again, swilling it clean of any trace of the dead prostitute. Finally, he rolled up his sleeves and cleaned himself.

Back in America he would have been far more careful than this. He used to wear two pairs of surgical vets' gloves—the sort that go right up the arm—and over them a pair of leathers, then he'd burn everything he was wearing along with—usually—the instrument he used. As far as he was aware no one ever suspected him or found any of his clothing or weapons.

And now, a victim of kidnapping and near-grieving, who would even suspect him of this? One final risk to take, though.

He opened the lock-up door, fired up the van and drove out into the night with the plastic-wrapped corpse in the back.

It was the most dangerous part of this, he thought, the idea that he might be caught by a curious copper or by a drunk driver shunting him, or simply falling asleep at the wheel. But with the pouch beside him, all the knives now back where they belonged, he felt safe. In fact, he felt like he could go out there and find Katie himself.

Actually...

Richard should *understand* her captor, be able to all but *see* him. Who better than someone who had avoided detection for so long? Not that dizzy copper, no matter how cute she was or how much she made Richard smile. Or her sad lanky partner. Richard should *know* this man, how his mind worked.

How to find him.

And that was Richard's new target, his latest aim in life: to find his little girl before she died, no matter what stood in his way.

So, sticking to the speed limit, with one eye out for drunks and coppers, Richard Hague drove out of Leeds to the place he last disposed of someone whom he encountered during a weak moment. To where, he knew, that body had never been found.

Chapter Five

MURPHY'S INCIDENT room was basically a vacant office in Glenpark Police Station, a building that had stood for decades but was in the process of being dismantled, its services to be absorbed by Sheerton and Chapel Allerton. Although the new police commissioner would not allow redundancies halfway through his tenure, he had initiated a region-wide freeze on recruitment, and mentioned—in passing—that "natural wastage" was unlikely to be back-filled. For now, though, the room was sufficient: four desks, two computers, a large whiteboard, and one phone. No windows, though.

He and Alicia returned from re-interviewing witnesses—at Alicia's behest—at nine p.m., and hammered out a timeline on the whiteboard. If nothing else, the girl had energy. And, once Murphy persuaded her that love hearts over the "i"s were not appropriate, he was able to concentrate, eventually agreeing with her that Katie had to be found within the next three days, or else Wednesday would see them inform a third father that his daughter would never come home again.

At ten p.m., the extent of Murphy's night shift team—Ball and Cleaver—hustled in and Ball asked, "Who's the bird?"

Murphy knew what was coming but was a too tired to stop it.

Alicia held her hand up and said, "Oh, that's me. Me! I'm the bird!"

Ball said, "Hi."

Cleaver looked at Murphy. Murphy nodded. Cleaver said, "Hi."

"Alicia Friend, this is Sergeants Ball and Cleaver." Murphy indicated each of them, and explained Alicia's status on the case.

Ball was verging on nominative determinism, that is to say his name being "Ball" increases the chances of him becoming a ball in later life; to Murphy's recollection, Ball's double-breasted suit jacket had not been buttoned for a good two years. His usually-unkempt beard made him ideal for undercover vice work—the dirty old man incarnate—but whilst working with him Murphy had insisted on smarter, trimmed face fur. He was assigned to the case because Pippa, the first victim, was assumed to be a prostitute, and they called in Ball to help identify her. He was twenty-four hours in by the time they discovered she was not a sex-worker, and Murphy came along to relieve him. The ground Ball made by going through witnesses and other detritus meant he was already full of knowledge, so in the end he just stuck around; Murphy suspected his DCI was happy to loan him out. When the second girl went missing, they suspected a connection, and Ball recommended his colleague.

From what Murphy recalled, Cleaver had always been skinny. Now in his late forties, though, middle-age spread ate into the ample cloth of his suits, and his years were beginning to show. But he was an analyst, and a decent one at that. It was why he and Ball were paired so often; Ball's people skills—at least reading people—set off against Cleaver's ability to spot a financial or chronological inconsistency from thirty yards.

In another time, Murphy might have liked these guys. But they were both supposedly mature men who too often acted like juveniles, and sometimes were downright rude. Now, despite their skills on the job, Murphy could barely stand the sight of them.

"Alicia," he said, "Ball and Cleaver have been working nights on this—it's where the majority of witnesses seem to live—but I've put them on your theory as of today. Came in a little early to set up the civilian researcher team."

"Yeah," Ball said. "Five *hours* ago. We're back in his life and now we're in yours."

Cleaver formed a gun with his finger and fired it at Alicia. "Lucky you."

Neither had taken their eyes off her since they came in. She leaned over one of the tables and pouted like Marilyn Monroe, then spoke breathily like her too, "Well, boys, we have a lot of work to do." She snapped into business mode, running down everything she told Murphy—the sinking mud, the local angle, the sketchy psyche profile of Katie Hague and her "nice dad." All the while, Ball and Cleaver sat with their arms folded—schoolboys, with a crush on the teacher. Murphy didn't see the attraction. Alicia was cute, sure, but like a kitten or a puppy; nothing sexual about her at all. Yet, guys like Ball and Cleaver don't always think the same way as guys like Murphy.

"Any questions?" Alicia asked.

Ball raised his hand. "What time you get off?"

Cleaver added, "New members of the team get the first round in."

Alicia smiled patiently. Again, the teacher analogy occurred to Murphy, as if Alicia were mulling over how to deal with the class clown or aggressive *I-know-my-rights-you-can't-do-nuthin'-to-me* kid. She held their eyes and went over to the board, took one photo of each girl, and stood over the pair of sergeants.

She slapped a photo of Hayley Davenport's corpse on the table in front of them.

"Dead."

She slapped down a photo of Pippa Bradshaw, the one of her grinning, holding the koala, helping its paw wave for the last photo of her young life.

"Pippa Bradshaw. *Dead*."

She held up one of Katie Hague's photos, another grinner, this time in an England rugby shirt. She waved it in front of their faces.

"And this is Katie Hague. *Missing*. Probably being held by the same gentleman who killed the other two. We have about fifty hours before he kills her, possibly less if his mental state is deteriorating."

She turned away whilst tossing the photo. It span in the air and came to rest on Ball's lap. He wasn't smiling any more.

He said, "I was trying to lighten the mood."

"And I appreciate that, Sergeant Ball, really I do. I wish more coppers were a bit more cheery." She glanced at Murphy. "But for now, let's focus. It's late, and I need my beauty sleep."

Murphy reluctantly entered the conversation. "Sergeants, I'm assuming you would have called me if anything turned up regarding parolees?"

Cleaver nodded. "No bites so far. I've only examined that pattern you specified, though. Tomorrow I'm going through all violent parolees released in the past year. Civvies're combing through the records tonight, should have a full list soon. We'll get some kip for now, then start checking alibis as they come in."

"Good," Alicia said at Cleaver accepting Murphy's order. "Ball?"

Ball nodded. "I'll have a crack at the ones that don't check out on paper."

"And the Hayley Davenport forensics should be here first thing too. So we're all agreed? Nothing more to be done tonight except wait?"

"Agreed," Cleaver said. "Unless the civvies turn up something big. But I've given them the boss's number, so they'll wake him up if we need to move."

"Thanks," Murphy said.

Ball stood and turned to the door, but couldn't resist a final dig. "I guess our new assistant didn't like your other theory, then?"

Alicia lasered in on Murphy. "There's another theory?"

Murphy closed his eyes. Not only was he physically tired after a fifteen-hour day, he was pretty sick of getting the piss taken out of his "alternative" theory on the case.

"Oh yeah." Cleaver already had his coat on. "Hasn't he shown you the forbidden file?"

Alicia practically bounced. "Ooh, ooh, a forbidden file? I love forbidden files. Who forbidden-ed it? Is that the word? No, can't be. *Forbade*. Who forbade it?"

"The big man," Ball said, zipping his coat, the only garment that fit him properly. "Chief Super Rhapshaw."

"It's nothing," Murphy said. "Let's get our beauty sleep."

"No way I'll be able to sleep now," Alicia said. "Talk. What's the forbidden file?"

Murphy intentionally took a long time digging the file out of his personal briefcase. Not the official casebook, naturally. He set it on the table at the head of the room, standing hunched over it before explaining.

The "forbidden file" was a missing persons case. Tanya Windsor. "No relation to the queen," Murphy said, "but by all accounts her family rarely correct people who assume they are."

Alicia grinned at that. "The little Windsors pretending to be the big Windsors."

The little Windsors lived in a house that wasn't quite a

mansion and wasn't quite a house in the traditional sense. Eight bedrooms, a study, two living rooms, a dining room, a huge kitchen, a staff of three—cook, cleaner, and live-in butler—and ten acres of land stretching like a finger into National Trust moorland. Their money came from the nineteenth century and it fluctuated along with world economies: tough in the 30s, booming in the 50s, stuttering in the 70s, peaking in the Thatcher-driven 80s. The crashes in the 90s barely touched them, and the recession of the late 2000s was of less concern still, largely thanks to heavy investment in one of the few industries unaffected by any economic downturn.

"Weapons," Murphy said. "They invested in every weapons manufacturer they could. Plus middle-eastern construction, which has boomed in Dubai and Qatar and other areas. But the point is—"

"That they're rich beyond most people's wildest dreams," Alicia finished.

"Right. Anyway, Henry's wife, Paula, died of a stroke in the nineties; his brother and sister-in-law died in a vehicle collision in 2009; the only survivor of the crash was his niece, Tanya. She moved in with Henry and Henry's son, James, and they all lived together happily until James's twenty-first birthday party." Murphy paused to allow chuckles from Ball and Cleaver to peter out. "Eighteen months ago, in the middle of the party held on the grounds of York racecourse ... she was surrounded by society folk ... star of the show ... and she disappears. No witnesses saw her leave. No blood, clothing, no sign of a struggle. Nothing."

Alicia was deep in thought, and when she spoke it was as if she'd forgotten about that perky nonsense she seemed to enjoy so much. "When did they find her body?"

Ball said, "They didn't."

A second of thought later, Alicia's blue eyes twinkled wide

and bright. "Details, please." Her internal mini-computer appeared to be whirring.

Murphy said, "Thirty-eight members of the well-to-do community attended a sit-down dinner after a private race-meet, which Tanya had organised for her cousin, to be followed by dancing and variety acts. At approximately six p.m., after the dinner, Tanya took herself away from the marquee 'for some air.' She never returned, and hasn't been heard from again."

Alicia stared at the file.

Cleaver said, "There are a number of background statements that suggest she was a runaway, but the main suspect was her boyfriend."

"But maybe not," Ball said.

"They're not sure he existed," Murphy said. "Some of her friends thought she was in love with some guy and planned on running away with him. Others—including her uncle—said she'd been getting help from someone to get into the university she wanted."

Alicia stared some more. No indication she heard anything.

Ball said, "We had a CID civvie follow it up this month with the key witnesses—her guardian, best mate Hillary, her drinking pals, cousin James."

"Did they get hold of James?" Cleaver asked.

"No," Murphy said. "He wasn't available and DCI Streeter didn't want us spending resources on tracking him down. Not without more evidence."

Ball continued, "Tanya's parents died just as she was entering her teens, got her mitts on her parents' cash aged eighteen and went off the rails. Never really got back on. Tattoos, drunken holidays, more men than the posh-nobs considered 'proper', that sort of thing."

"So," Murphy said, "she was written off as a runaway. A few things didn't add up though. One, her bank account hasn't been touched since she paid for the party. Two, all her friends were at the party, barring the elusive boyfriend who, like Ball said, may or may not exist. Three, according to her cousin, James Windsor, she was starting to calm down a little, and this party was her way of saying sorry to Uncle Henry, proving she could be a society lady like her mum."

Cleaver tapped the file. "Trouble is, the investigating officer ignored or missed that the party might have been the last purchase chronologically, but sixteen days earlier she paid deposits for two tickets to Goa in India."

Alicia looked up. "No body?"

"No body," Murphy said.

"Disappeared in a public place?"

"Very public."

"And she was popular, wild ... beautiful?"

Murphy paused, showed Alicia a head-and-shoulders of Tanya Windsor.

Alicia said, "This girl is fairly plain."

Which was true: Tanya was far from what Ball and Cleaver might term "pig-ugly", but did not come close, in material terms, to the beauty of Pippa, Hayley or Katie.

Murphy said, "That's the main reason we discounted her. She isn't special. Not as pretty, not a particularly nice girl, and the real clincher—that absent body. It's only the circumstances of her disappearance that rang a bell, and so long ago ... it's hard to justify a comparison." He gave her a beat to speak but she was still processing. "What does your computer say?"

Alicia stood up straight, craned her neck to meet Murphy's gaze, and broke into a smile. She picked up the file and held it up like a trophy. "Gentlemen, I do believe we have our killer."

. . .

Alicia stood with the file aloft for far too long. Murphy could tell Ball and Cleaver were trying to come up with something to undermine her but she caught them unawares. They expected her to agree with them, to mock Murphy as they had. The girl, Tanya Windsor, did not fit the profile of the missing girls.

"It's perfect," Alicia said, finally lowering the file. "Perfect fit. My god, if I'd known about this earlier we'd be focussing on it now. Coats off. Your naps can wait."

With a grumble or two, Ball and Cleaver did not put their coats back on the stand but leaned on a table, arms folded again, eyes glazed.

"It's perfect," Alicia said.

Ball sniffed. "You said that already."

"Right."

Murphy said, "Perhaps we should start this in the morning."

"No," Alicia said. "Listen to this. It's what we call a 'trigger'. An event that sets off his psychosis. Our guy gets fixated by this Tanya girl. He loves her, loves her so completely he thinks it's destiny."

Cleaver interrupted, "You can't tell that from a file."

She rapped him on the head with said file and told him, "I'm formulating a hypothesis based on events. My conclusion will make sense. God, when you two get the hump you make Murphy look like a ray of sunniest sunshine." Back to business: "Okay, so he's fixated with her. Loves her. But she doesn't want *him*. So he lures her outside—"

"Or waits for her," Murphy said.

"Probably lures. It's a skill of his. He *lures* her outside, and takes her. Holds her, explains they'll be together. This boyfriend chap—we'll get into him tomorrow—maybe they can't be together because of her uncle ... whatever, this obsessed someone kidnaps her, realises they will never be true lovers—"

"This 'trigger' you mentioned. Rejection."

"Right. He was always psychotic, probably hurt people before, animals, that sort of thing, but the rejection spurs him on to new heights ... kills Tanya rather than lose her."

The men watched her, waiting; Murphy for validation of his own theory, Ball and Cleaver so they could go home at long last. When she started up again she was more fluid.

"He kills her, hides the body and no one finds it. For eighteen months, he's wracked with guilt, misses his fantasy lover, misses the woman he believed her to be. And he looks for a replacement. Maybe it's not eighteen months. What if these are the only ones we've detected? Whatever. It's a long time. He sees people who look like Tanya, the slim frame, the dark hair, the fiery personality—because she might not have been acceptable to the crowd she belongs to, but she's a forceful woman, which appeals to a particular type of man. So he watches. He finds someone who has the hair, the body, an upgrade in the looks department. He gets to know her—her habits, her personality. Donny, you said these girls are special in more than looks, right?"

Ball and Cleaver smirked at the "Donny" crack, but Murphy just said, "Right."

"Nice girls, who know their own minds. Tanya doesn't only *fit* the profile, she *is* the profile. A *template*. Don't you see? He's stealing women who look like an idealised version of Tanya. And he won't stop until he finds the perfect replacement. And what, gentlemen, is the perfect replacement?"

Ball and Cleaver shrugged, and Ball said, "Why don't you tell us so we can get to the pub before last orders?"

"Nuh-uh. No one goes home until someone answers my question."

Murphy said, "The perfect replacement is one he can subdue, and who will love him back."

"Correctamundo! And you know what else?"

"What?"

"If I'm correct, not only is there a body out there to find, but the killer's name..." She tapped the file once each on Ball's and Cleaver's heads. "Is in these pages. He knew her *personally*."

Ball and Cleaver perked up for the first time in ten minutes. Together they said, "Shit," in a good way.

"Damn right, shit," Alicia said. "We need to speak to the senior officer on this case, get as much out of him as we can. Think we can dig him up?"

Cleaver nodded. "I'll pull some of the civvies off the parolees. We'll be on it first thing tomorrow."

Finally, Alicia released the sergeants from her thrall, insisting they head out for a pint. Once the pair left, she said to Murphy, "Not a bad day's work after all."

"No," he said. "Go on home. I'll shut the computers down here."

"Ooh, green as well as grumpy."

With that last dig of the night, Alicia left Murphy alone in the incident room, with nothing but the whir of the motherboards' fans for company. He was spot-on after all. He didn't relish telling Rhapshaw that the case would need to be reopened, that the dirty laundry of his pal Henry Windsor was about to be rummaged through before airing it throughout the station.

This time it wouldn't be suppressed.

He was going to dig out the things the Windsors didn't want the police to see, and he would use those things to find Katie Hague. And, damn it, whilst turning off the last of the computers, Murphy couldn't help but smile. He checked his watch. Eleven-thirty. Damn.

He was twenty quid down.

Chapter Six

IT WAS DARK. Always dark. Pitch black, except when the man came to feed her or allow her to relieve herself. Katie Hague had hours ago stopped trying to communicate with the other girl. "Please talk to me," she said, over and over. "He's not around, he can't hear you." But of course there was no way to be sure. He could be listening through the wall, watching on some monitor, masturbating himself raw or whatever perversion brought Katie to this place.

The man kept her like a pet, not responding to questions or showing any sort of emotion, whilst looking at the other girl with his eyes soft, his tongue touching his lips, as if constantly restraining himself from ripping off her clothes; it was as if she was his lover, and Katie was his dog.

Sat in the same chair, she had been fed pasta and fruit for several days, and she drank flavoured water. The stranger helped her urinate and defecate in the sort of bedpan you see in museums. All with her hands tied behind her back. It was either constantly dark, like now, or the man turned on the spotlight. Sometimes he turned on the other girl's too, but the other girl never spoke or even tried to. She just stared at Katie.

The scariest place she visited before this place was Tanzania in Africa, when she was only ten. It was the summer holidays in England and her mum was volunteering at a school project after completing a TEFL course—Teaching English as a Foreign Language—whilst Katie's dad mostly looked after her. He took her on safari so often it got a bit boring. Things picked up, though, when they trekked to the lowest camp on Kilimanjaro. Another young kid and his parents stayed overnight too, listening to the monkeys whose screeches and hoots sounded so close she was glad her dad was nearby.

But on the way back down, in the Land Rover driven by a local guide, they stopped at a checkpoint; an unofficial one run out of a lonely roadside house by three male villagers. The guide yelled at them and they yelled back and arms were waved along with the rubbing of thumbs and fingers, the universal indicator for "money". When someone produced a machete, Katie's dad disembarked the vehicle, Katie clawing at him to come back, come back, don't get hurt ... but the other parents simply held their boy, as if cuddles would protect him.

Katie's dad persuaded the guides to translate and they all moved around the back of the Land Rover, opened the boot, and took out all the rucksacks. Katie's dad, the guide, and the makeshift guards carried their bags inside the house. Nothing happened for five or six minutes. Then Katie's dad emerged with the rucksacks and the guide in tow. No guards accompanied them.

The rucksacks went back in the Land Rover and Katie's dad returned to his seat and was nearly crushed by Katie's hugs. The other father asked what happened. "Nothing much," said Katie's dad as the driver got back in. "Talked him out of it, right Ndeme?"

The driver turned, his face still a mask of shock, probably

from the confrontation. "That's right, sir," he said, "talked 'em outta it."

The driver fired up the engine and gunned it back toward Moshi Town, not speaking another word. All the way back, Katie thought of nothing except how great her dad was, how he was so brave, and that he could do practically anything. He even tipped the driver a wad of dollars at the end, shooting him a wink as they departed. Whatever he said to the guards to let them have their luggage back must have been pretty special.

Now, an opening door clanged through the ... what was this? Dungeon? Cellar? Prison? Whatever it was, the door sounded, and the familiar footsteps fell on what were almost certainly stone stairs. They padded closer and the man's hand caressed Katie's shoulder. She instinctively pulled away, her shoulder filling with pain.

Two—or was it three?—days in the same position will do that to a limb.

The man in the dark said, "Katie, I want you to trust me a moment."

Through her gag, she replied, "Uh-huh."

"Relax. I won't hurt you. Just do as you're told."

She nodded, realised it was pitch black, and said, "Uh-huh," again.

She felt his hands on her wrists, heard the key click in the cuffs. He released her hands. Her shoulders sighed with relief, although her legs were still bound by rope. Then he untied the gag.

"Please let me go," she said, strangely embarrassed by her words.

He did not reply.

"I won't tell, I promise I won't."

All she heard was metal clattering on stone, clanking back on itself. A chain.

"What are you doing?"

"Close your eyes please, Katie," the man said.

"Why?"

The spotlight crashed to life. Katie cried out, but the illusion of pain cleared as the dancing colourful spots dissipated to nothing. She saw that the other light was also on. The girl was still tied up.

The chain grew louder, closer. Katie's throat was hot and tight. She felt for her inhaler. Still in her lap, where the man left it. Her shoulders ached, locked up, so she lifted the inhaler to her mouth, arm bending only at the elbow, and breathed it in. Her throat opened and her lungs filled with air.

Then the man stepped into the light, striking her again how he was less ugly than she originally imagined: clean-shaven, a pleasant smile. But something in his eyes—or something missing from them—took away anything gentle about him.

But he'd *shown his face*. More than once. She could never forget it.

"I like your spirit," he said. "You haven't freaked out. A little pleading which disappointed me, but other than that I'm impressed."

Katie bowed her head and said, "Thank you."

"Don't patronise me, Katie, it's rude. The last girl to do that ended up in a lake. Well, one of them did. The other is sitting right over there." He pointed to the girl, the dark-haired captive. "You..." He raised his face to the spotlight, eyes closed. "You will please me tomorrow."

Katie knew what this meant, or thought she did: the "R" word. *She'd seen his face.* She was going to die unless she did something about it. One chance.

She glanced at the other captive.

Can't save her, Katie thought, *only myself. Come back for her later.*

With all her strength, biting through the ache in her shoulder, she swung an elbow aimed squarely at the man's groin.

Pain flared. The blow faltered in mid-arc, never met its target. She could stand but not pull away from the chair. With a simple shove, the man made Katie sit down. She whimpered as her bum hit the chair.

"Your joints are locked up from being in the same position so long," he said. "But stretch, move around. You should be okay by daybreak."

"What are you going to do?"

"That, Katie, is entirely up to you." He bent down in front of her, eye to eye, his breath sweet and warm. "You do as instructed, and you might—emphasis on *might*—get out alive."

What if she hit him over the head? Knocked him out? Maybe, ordinarily.

"How?" she said. "How can I get out alive? Tell me what I have to do."

She found herself sobbing. That pissed her off. She shouldn't cry in front of him. She *wouldn't* cry in front him.

Although it hurt like hell, she wiped the tears. She pushed it all down, the fear, the confusion, and let it boil, deep inside her. And as this man pulled the chain across the floor in a hail of noise, as he knelt before her and took one foot and attached it to the chain via a medieval-looking manacle, as he smiled up at her and said, "That'll do it," she processed her fear, her loathing, and let it bake into hot, writhing anger.

The man then freed her legs so she could stand, walk as far as the chain would allow. He sauntered over to the other girl, practically gliding, his casual gait somehow grotesque. He freed her hands and feet, removed the gag.

For the first time, Katie noticed a tattoo on the other girl's arm: a tiger, so full of colour, so bright, prowling from her shoulder to her bicep. She was free now, with no restrictions, able to stand if she chose, to roam uninhibited. The man stroked her hair, though the girl remained expressionless.

"This, Katie, will be a demonstration in obedience. Her name is Rachel. She patronised me some time ago, pretended she loved me the way I love her. But now she no longer pretends." He returned to Katie, touched her face. "You are both so beautiful. I know Rachel loves me, and I know you hate me."

"That's not true," Katie said. "I *can* love you, and I'm *not* patronising you..."

The man swung a fist at her head, but pulled up short of actually hitting her.

"Don't do that." He seemed angry at first, but this melted as he lowered his arm. "Don't ever do that again." He backed away and continued. "Rachel is free to wander but not speak. She may not approach you, touch you, or communicate with you in any way. Does Rachel understand?"

Rachel nodded without looking up.

"Good. Katie, you may explore as far as your chain will allow. I would ask you not to speak to Rachel, but I know you will, as I know Rachel will not respond."

"Please tell me what you're doing," Katie said.

"In time. But for now, get your shoulders working again. Move your legs. You have a few hours yet." He walked to the edge of the spotlight. From out of the darkness came his final words of the evening: "Get some rest."

And now Katie wondered if her dad could talk his way out of this. Maybe not, but he would certainly *try*. She decided she should follow his example. She wouldn't give up. She would stay alive, she told herself.

She would stay alive, and make her dad proud.

. . .

Alicia closed her apartment door, took off her coat, kicked off her shoes, and replaced them with fluffy black and white slippers with a blue foam police light on each. She worried her weary sigh would wake Roberta, but she needn't have. In the living room, Roberta was wide awake, watching a DVD of Lethal Weapon; the first one, the best—if you ignored the now-awkward homophobic exclamations that peppered the script; a film of its time, most definitely. Half a bottle of Cabernet Sauvignon sat open, waiting on the coffee table alongside two full glasses—the vino equivalent of a go-go girl flashing her garter.

Roberta beamed at Alicia. "Hey." Her dark brown skin reflected nothing, her eyes standing out like happy seashells. "Get over here and knock this down your skinny throat."

"Oh, Robbie, you are an angel." Alicia snatched up a glass and gulped. She sat on the deep couch next to Roberta, its softness snuggling all around her.

Roberta Munroe was once a schoolteacher on the island of Montserrat, though she was working her father's bar through the holidays when Alicia met her. Alicia's boyfriend had treated Roberta like some skivvy, and the relationship ended there and then, Alicia moving out of the five-star hotel and into a room above the bar, quaintly called The Spunki Munki. She and Roberta—*Robbie*—spent the rest of the holiday hanging out with the locals, eating seafood, drinking and dancing. They wrote to one another for three years, until the island's volcano spewed to life yet again, and scattered the inhabitants into the sea and mostly to America. Alicia insisted Roberta come live with her. It was supposed to be for a couple of months, which became a couple of years, and would probably now last a whole lot longer.

"Tough day?" Robbie said.

"There's a nasty man out there kidnapping girls and I'm

partnered with a bog-standard detective. Dull suit, miserable, even has a moustache."

"Not one of your usual British CIA cases?"

"FBI is closer. But no. I have to work with this Murphy chappy and he's just so ... so ... I don't know. He's *boring*. But he has potential."

Robbie laughed with her mouth wider than most humans can actually manage. "You think everyone is boring."

"You aren't." Alicia scrunched her fluffy-wrapped feet under her and leaned on the sofa's arm. The furniture was so soft, so deep, so warm, that Alicia didn't want to ever move again. She dribbled a little wine and laughed at herself, not really caring that the blouse would stain. "Thanks, Robbie."

Roberta curled her arm around Alicia, and she cuddled in close. "No probs. Didn't want to start without you. Anyway, what else you gotta tell me? Don't pretend there's nothing."

Alicia told her friend about her encounter with Richard Hague, how it was only as she shot past her exit on the M1 that she realised he'd been occupying so many of her thoughts. Katie held captive. The longest a victim lasted was seven days. Tomorrow was Katie's third. And yet Alicia was more concerned with the father.

Robbie smiled. "He's vulnerable and you wanna take good care of him. Am I right?"

"I don't hold much faith in Freud, you know that." She closed her eyes and saw Richard's face. "But yes. I sensed something ... different about him. Something... good."

"You sensed that about the last guy. And the one before him. Oh, *and* the one before—"

"So I don't always pick a winner." Alicia considered her most recent boyfriends, unable to hate any of them, even the ones who treated her like crap. "That's why I'm being so careful lately."

"*Barren* is more than careful.

She thought about it. Six months since Mr. Sexy Pants moved to Scotland.

"Go to bed," Robbie said, taking the glass from her. "I'm just gonna finish up with Mel and Danny and I'll be shutting down myself."

Alicia rose and padded across the floor to her room. "Thanks again, Robbie."

Then she went inside, closed the door, and did something she hadn't done since a long night of good wine and better food in Italy: she fell asleep in her clothes.

Donald Murphy had a cat. Her name was Tinker. She was ginger. And when he got in, she purred at first, then curled around his leg, tail winding up his shin. When he didn't go instantly to the cupboard to serve her tea (which was four hours late already) the cat mewled and reached up Murphy's trousers, clawing the material. He shook his leg and Tinker disengaged, watching him leave the kitchen with a surprised expression. She soon realised he was not coming back and followed him into the living room.

Murphy opened a bottle of scotch which he selected from the bar he built six months after Susan left. Tinker leapt onto the drinks cabinet and he nearly dropped the bottle. He tried to ignore her, but the mewling grated down his spine. She pushed against his hand as he poured a drink into a crystal tumbler, and splashed half the measure on the counter. Bloody thing.

He acquired a cat partly for the company, sad as it sounds. A companion until Susan returned, although that possibility was now pretty much sucked out of existence. But he kept the cat anyway. Tinker also forced him home on nights like tonight, to feed the little madam, otherwise he'd work until the unexpected brightening of the day, grab a cat-nap in an unoccupied cell, and start all over again. Not long ago, he was making himself ill. More-so after Susan left. The thought of a hungry cat helped. He'd considered a dog, but it'd need walking and he could never guarantee he'd be home in time to prevent dog shit cascading over his carpet. Cat flaps were a great invention.

He surrendered, hands in the air, and led Tinker back into the kitchen. As he emptied the packet of fishy meat into the cat's bowl, she stood on her hind legs, pawing at him, jumping backwards when he lifted the bowl from the counter. He set it down and she dug in. He stroked her and she shot him a look that said, "Yes. Thank you. That will be all."

On his sofa, he allowed the scotch to comfort him while fish-breathed Tinker finished up. The drink warmed his throat, settling in a pleasant pool in his stomach. He thought about cheese on toast or something simple to eat. When he realised he'd have to move again, he vetoed the idea. Once finished, Murphy refilled his glass.

Tinker mooched along eventually, sat on his lap, clawed herself comfortable, and curled up while Murphy stroked her. She purred until she was asleep.

Murphy's last coherent thoughts before sleep took him too were of Detective Sergeant Friend. She was clever. She was annoying. But looking on the bright side, she had given Murphy hope. He felt it, warm as the scotch in his belly, rising in him. They would get this guy, free Katie, alive and as unharmed.

And with the right amount of luck, they were going to do it tomorrow.

There are many ways in which a man can act when he experiences a full-on midlife crisis. Some will buy a sports car in which he looks utterly ridiculous, but he knows all his mates will envy him; others will take up squash or some activity to stem the tide of flesh pouring over his belt; but others, like Wilcox, might already be active down the gym, and might already own the sports car, and have always driven sports cars from back in the 80s when he made his first million. So he might not have anywhere else to turn but the arms of a sweet-seeming gym bunny that genuinely likes him for who he is and not, repeat *not*, the oodles of cash at his disposal. So it's bye-bye wifey of thirty-five years and hello loft conversion in the city, wall-to-wall sex, and a subscription to Little-Blue-Pill Weekly.

But when Freddie's bubble of newfound happiness burst upon the discovery of his gym bunny naked on the sofa with a gym bear, in a position Freddie couldn't hope to get into without an overdose of cod liver oil and yoga, he faced reality and returned to the woman who stuck by him from long before he even thought about a Porsche. Only now she didn't want him, and he was all alone, as he now believed he deserved.

There are many ways to react when your wife doesn't want you and your mistress replaces you and your friends think you're a total bastard and have sided with your wife. Some would throw themselves into work and booze; some might forgive the gym bunny and bribe her to be faithful; but others, again like Freddie, might choose simply to isolate himself as much as physically possible.

So leaving his wife-cum-ex-wife half his liquid assets and the whole house in Surrey, Freddie returned via train to his native north with a holdall full of cash, a pinstripe suit, and his child-hood dream of living off the land, like Tom and Barbara in *The Good Life*. He put his money into a Post Office account, got himself a plot of dirt which even boasted a well upon it, and turned his hand to carpentry, knocking together a nice little hut in which to live while he constructed his simple, self-sufficient house. The land, in addition to the well, bore the husk of an old farmhouse, which Freddie intended to tear down and rebuild and live in until he died.

Yet, when he spoke to the builders, to the architect, to the planners, all he could do was mumble. He had plans, but these plans were too abstract, too undefined to verbalise. For each person he met, he rearranged four meetings, and every plan he made he put on hold. Until, now, five years later, his hut was a damp pile of wood, and he was living in a makeshift shelter in the husk of the old farmhouse.

One of the shelter's walls was solid brick. Several planks of wood created a kind of triangle with the floor, and he'd water-proofed it with the sealant people use for sheds and garages. He slept on a mattress with a winter sleeping bag and wore striped pyjamas as he had all his life. When there was a breeze he pulled a plastic tarpaulin over his shelter, but tonight was breeze-free, albeit bitterly cold. The beard he'd grown helped, as did the thermal underwear, but mostly it was the sleeping bag, which encased him completely, allowing only a small hole for him to breathe through. Despite all his plans going awry, he was actually pretty happy, snug, under his little shelter.

Until, that is, a car engine awoke him.

Reluctant to de-cocoon himself into the cold winter night, he shifted his body to where the headlights were pointing. He should be angry, yelling "Get off my land" at this intruder, but the fact he'd not had a single visitor since he chased that smart-arsed architect away four years ago made him pause. The head-lights pointed directly at his well. A round wall four feet high protected people from falling in, and although there was no picturesque roof with a bucket hanging from it, it was still the prettiest little object on Freddie's land.

Freddie's well descended thirty feet to an underground stream, and had existed for a good hundred-and-fifty years or more. How they discovered water all the way down there, he'd never know. It flowed down from the Pennines, through Ribblehead and under Skipton, to here, in the hills between Leeds and Harrogate, providing Freddie with constant fresh water. He was enormously proud of his well; it set him apart from most of humanity. How many people these days had wells, after all?

But in the white beams of the headlights, the well seemed anything but inviting. And when the footsteps crunched, Freddie confirmed he was right to stay hidden. He soon saw a man. He was carrying something. Something long and heavy. The man grunted as he hefted the object onto the wall of the well. He was well-built, Freddie thought, like himself when he was a gym regular, but it required visible effort to tip the plastic bundle through the well's mouth.

A *litterbug*, Freddie thought. *Fly-tipping bastard.*

He was so angry he had no choice but to give this prick a piece of his mind. So with a huge effort, Freddie manoeuvred his arm out of its snug position, up through the sleeping bag to the zip. By God, he was gonna unleash some hell on this guy. It's one thing people wanting to look at his pretty well, but dumping crap in it, that was another matter entirely.

He gripped the zip and pulled it down, struggled out of it, arms and legs flying. In a burst of anger, he threw the roof off his shelter and strode out of the wreckage of the farmhouse, and—

Bollocks.

Freddie scanned the empty land. Moonlight was sparse. Taillights receded into the distance. He was too late. The litterbug had fled. Shame he didn't even get the guy's licence.

Probably not worth reporting to the police, Freddie thought. But then, what if they could get fingerprints off the bag of rubbish? Perhaps it was possible. But would they? For such a small crime? If they showed him a list of known fly-tippers and/or their accomplices Freddie could pick him out of a line-up or something.

He had, after all, got a good, clean look at the man's face.

Chapter Seven

AT 7.30 A.M. ALICIA ENTERED THE new operations room that Graham Rapshaw arranged early that morning, along with the transfer of all files pertaining to the case. No windows. A sense of darkness, even with the strip lights burning. It reminded her of a hospital ward whose patients had all died.

"Oh, this will never do."

She moved eight files from their positions strewn across the larger of six desks to a neat pile on one of the others. She did this with all the paperwork she could find. Two computer terminals using software from 2010 looked indiscriminately dumped in the middle of a desk each. She was about to move them when the uneven desk legs wobbled, and for a moment she thought the desks themselves might collapse in a cloud of wood and gigabytes.

She transferred biros to plastic boxes, and left the boxes open at jaunty angles. She stood markers on end next to the whiteboard so their colourful lids acted like hats. One lid was missing, and she felt sorry for that one pen, all alone, hatless.

"There," she said. "Much better."

"If you've touched my stuff, I'm going to hurl you round the room by that cute little ponytail."

Okay, so Murphy had entered.

"Hi, Donny. I've put it all in a neat and tidy pile."

He wore a dark blue suit, smarter, snappier than the grey one, which looked like he hadn't worn it for some time; too tight at the shoulders. And his hair was tidier than yesterday. He flicked through the neat pile of manila files, frowning.

Alicia held out her hand. "You owe me something."

Murphy looked at her a moment, taking time to glance at the stationery in its new home, and when he met her eyes a brief smile flashed under his moustache.

"Okay, you got me." He slapped a twenty into her hand.

"So we're friends now?" Alicia said.

"Wouldn't go that far." He sat down. "But I appreciate your insight last night."

Alicia didn't know what to say. She wanted to clap, but settled for a professionally sombre nod of the head. "Ready?"

"For what?"

"Well we can't sit around here all day waiting for a clue to leap up and say 'look at me, I'm a clue'." She put on her jacket with a flourish, flashing a handwritten note at Murphy. "Ball did his job well last night. We're off to see John Wellington."

John Wellington—detective chief inspector, *retired*—shook hands with Alicia and Murphy in turn. He was tanned a deep brown, wore a bright red tracksuit top and shorts while his face sported a neatly trimmed goatee beard; white, almost silver. The older man looked in better shape than Murphy, especially when he first appeared to them: a head and shoulders poking out from high on a rocky outcrop, wind blowing the stray hair from under his helmet. He abseiled down smoothly, disengaged the ropes, and jogged away from the throng of sixty-plus-year-olds that greeted him at the bottom.

"Last year," he said when Murphy asked about his retirement. "Best thing I ever did. The group's a bit fuddy-duddy but I get to do things I haven't done before. Like this."

He sucked in air rather ostentatiously, then out louder than necessary. His gaze hardly settled on anything but the view. Alicia understood why.

She used to come up here, to the Cow and Calf rocks, when she was a teenager. Sometimes it was for rude reasons, but mostly to read or work. The two rocks—a large one that John Wellington whooshed down, and a smaller one—protruded from the top of a steep hill half a mile outside Ilkley, overlooking fields and farmland and houses for miles around. There was a nice pub here too, also called the Cow and Calf, which unless you knew specifically, you wouldn't guess was a part of a chain. Hard to believe they were less than an hour's drive from Leeds.

"Mr. Wellington, we need to ask about an investigation you headed up," Alicia said.

"Yes, Sergeant Ball said so on the phone. The Tanya one. Unfortunate business that. I never closed it."

Murphy said, "It may be connected to my current case."

My current case, Alicia noted.

"A second kidnapping?" Wellington said.

"Second, third and fourth."

"Oh."

"If you could help with any information ..."

Alicia fiddled with one of Wellington's buckles, tugging it hard. "I used to do a bit of this."

Wellington smiled, looking down at her. "You want to try?"

"Sure!"

Murphy said, "I don't think we have time."

"Oh, we can talk and climb," she said. "Can someone get me some shorts?"

Alicia donned the shorts under her skirt, removed the skirt, and tramped up the slope to behind the "Cow" rock. Wellington was grinning, and Alicia figured her being in a smart blouse and a spare pair of old lady's shorts made comical viewing, but hey, she wasn't about to let an opportunity like this pass by.

"So this Tanya went missing around May time last year?" Alicia said as she stepped into a set of straps that would secure her either side of her hips and thighs.

"Twenty-somethingth of May, yes." Wellington already had his straps on and now attached a pulley to the buckle on the front of his belt. "The party was at a barbeque, a *big* one. Had a shark on the go."

"Like a society event?"

"Private invite, hired a marquee. Her cousin James's birthday."

A burly instructor with a full wiry black beard helped Alicia into a second harness, this one full of buckles and clips. He ignored the shop-talk. Another ex-copper, she guessed.

Wellington went on. "She was last seen talking to her uncle —posh name ... Henry, I think."

"Henry Windsor," Alicia said. "Tanya's guardian."

Wellington tugged at his harness, threaded ropes while the instructor saw to Alicia's. They postponed police matters while the instructor drilled them. Then both Alicia and Wellington hung their backsides over the lip of the rock, feet placed square and firm on the face. Alicia convinced herself the quiver in her stomach was excitement, not nerves. She turned her head and a few wisps of hair caught the wind as she stretched her eyes to take in the landscape.

Although a cloud's shadow fell on the gathering here, the

sun shone over hills and fields in the near-distance, a straight line cutting off light from dark.

Wellington said, "DS Friend, may I ask how old you are? You seem awfully involved for someone so young."

She smiled. "I'm older than my teeth and the same age as my tongue."

"That's an old person's answer."

"Talk to me about Tanya. Then I'll tell you my age."

Alicia pushed away from the rock, and loosened her grip on the rope beneath her which momentarily disengaged the pulley on her belt. As she dropped four feet, her stomach swam upwards, a tingle jolting up her spine. She cried, "Wheeee!" and then made contact with the rock face, reapplying pressure to her safety rope.

Wellington joined her. "Tanya was nineteen when she was taken. She wasn't particularly close to her adopted family, but her uncle was protective of her. He was her father's brother."

"And Tanya threw the party?"

"Yes." Wellington leapt out further than last time, descending at least six feet.

We'll see about that, Alicia said to herself, and dropped, whooping, to where John Wellington waited.

"Nice," he said.

"Okay then, a taster: I'm in my thirties. Now get on with it."

Wellington smiled. Despite his white beard, he didn't seem old enough to be retired.

He said, "It was Tanya's money. The Windsors used to be one of the wealthiest families in the country, but some investments on Henry's side of the family went belly-up."

That was contrary to what Murphy's report said, but Alicia didn't interrupt.

"They maintained their standing and lifestyle by selling properties and artwork. Most people were aware of the situation, but pretended they weren't. No point getting on their bad side. Not sure what the thinking is. Etiquette or something."

"Basic survival," Alicia said. "A once-powerful family might become powerful again one day."

Wellington shrugged. "Some of Tanya's friends said old Henry only took her in for the cash."

"You believe that?"

They pushed off together and dropped five more feet. Wellington spoke before they halted again.

"Henry Windsor took her on aged fourteen before he even knew about the inheritance. Plus, I've told too many fathers their daughters are dead not to recognise genuine grief. The money was irrelevant."

Another drop. Now they were only ten feet from the ground.

"So a girl with money is adopted into a family with none. I take it she saved the property?"

"Yes, but after an extensive renovation her uncle wouldn't accept any further financial support."

"And five years later she's kidnapped during a party she paid for."

"James was the only remaining relative she was close to, according to her best friend—Hillary, I seem to remember. He was fun, he listened to her, couldn't do enough for her."

"We should talk to him," Alicia said.

"Last I heard he was heading for India, planning on spending the year out there. Maybe Thailand."

"My ex works for Interpol. I'll see if he can track him down via his passport. Meantime, his dad'll have to do."

They completed the final leg of their descent in one huge whoosh and Alicia hit the ground softly, heart beating, face cold, her hands sore.

Bracing.

She changed back into her skirt and relayed the conversation to Murphy, who took notes.

"You should try it," she said to Murphy.

"So what do you think?" Wellington asked. "You have everything you need?"

Alicia was cautious about what she said next. She worried about offending Wellington, especially as he'd been so pleasant to her. "Mr. Wellington, on the surface, this looks like she ran away. Was this the original theory?"

Wellington removed his harnesses. He didn't speak until he began helping Alicia out of hers. "Tanya disliked her home life. Her wealth was a burden. Her friends, they said her uncle was using her for the money, always nagging her to leave the Windsor house and come live with them. But at the same time, *they* wanted her money. Yes. It's a classic case of no proper friends and an unsatisfying life."

At least she had *some* friends as a kid. There are those out there who never made any, who didn't twig on until they got to university that you need to project an image of yourself that others will like.

Alicia said, "She probably knew, deep down. People sense when others are more interested in what you can give them. So if her uncle showed real affection toward her, why would she leave?"

Wellington disengaged the straps from Alicia's waist and tugged them down. "I figured maybe she'd been hoarding cash and did a runner. The fact there was no note wasn't a problem. It happens quite often."

"But?" Alicia said.

He glared at Murphy, then softened when he went back to Alicia. "But James insisted he'd have known. She'd have told him about it, about her plans to run. There was no chance she'd leave without saying goodbye first. Then there's the final angle. This didn't come out until a week after the disappearance." He took in the view once more. The cloud above blew to one side and allowed the sun through. "It was only then that we took it seriously."

The three of them stood in the sun, the cold air belying its brightness. Murphy shielded his eyes but Alicia absorbed it, glad of the rays on her face, about to smile until she remembered where she was, what she was supposed to be doing.

No. Actually, if I want to smile I will.

And she did.

"Something funny?" Wellington said.

"Sun in my eyes," Alicia replied. "Please. Go on."

Wellington heaved his equipment onto his shoulder and returned Alicia's borrowed items. He said he was calling it a day, and Alicia and Murphy walked him to his car, a new Volvo estate, parked next to Alicia's Focus.

"We got a warrant to monitor her bank accounts, the house phones. All her so-called friends gave permission to tap their phones too. Her bank didn't get touched for another week, she didn't phone or write. Her uncle got in touch with various MPs and pressure mounted. Soon it was a definite kidnapping."

"But it looked like she ran," Murphy said.

"At first, yes."

"And you feel bad about it," Alicia said.

He threw his stuff into the boot. "Wouldn't you?"

"I'd have made the same call."

He closed the boot. "It's all in the file. You could see how I screwed up from my notes. Why do you need to talk to me?"

Murphy and Alicia exchanged a glance. They'd already agreed Murphy would field this one.

He said, "There are things we come across that we can't put in official files. I know it, you know it. DS Friend knows it. And you were one of the best coppers I worked with. We all get feelings, John ... hunches."

"Yes or no, Mr. Wellington," Alicia said. "Do you know who did it?"

The wind tossed their hair about, their clothes batting against them. Distant rock formations produced faint howls that tumbled across the dale.

"No," Wellington finally answered.

"No hunches?" Murphy said. "No inklings, no one we could apply pressure to?"

He sighed and looked back at the "Cow" rock. "I used to think about James. But he's accounted for, right from when Tanya was last seen up to the end of the party. Six hours after the last witness spoke to her. The uncle, we wondered perhaps he wanted to be 'closer' than he should have been, but again he's covered. One of her friends? Sure, maybe they had a falling out, a fight that went too far. But sniffer dogs scoured the grounds surrounding the party. Fifteen square miles. No. There was only one theory left. One so thin it isn't even in the file." A thicker cloud flew across the sun and the air cooled further. "A secret lover."

Alicia noticed Murphy roll his eyes, but thankfully Wellington did not.

"Tanya snuck off to see this guy, something bad happened, he buried her. Her pals couldn't say for sure whether she had a man or not. When I put it to them they said it would explain a lot."

"How so?" Alicia asked.

"She'd been so much happier lately. She still bitched about her uncle and the pressure of being wealthy but she seemed happier in herself."

Ah, the pressure of being wealthy. Easily as distressing as the pressure of having nothing left, of a volcano sweeping away your home and business, the places you played as a child. No, being a millionaire at eighteen is far tougher.

She said, "It's a credible theory."

"Right," Murphy said. "Adds to the notion of needing a trigger to set off the chain of events."

Wellington perked up momentarily, then pointed out, "But there was nothing in her room, her diary, no word to anyone. If there was a lover, he was probably married. Her dirty secret."

"This was your final case?" Alicia said.

He nodded. "Chief Rhapshaw took me off it after three months. Even Henry Windsor resigned himself to never finding her alive. He stopped dogging us so the family could grieve." Wellington set his jaw again, his eyes sadder than before.

Alicia squeezed his arm. "Sometimes you get to know someone even though you've never met."

Wellington pressed his key fob and the alarm on his Volvo beeped once. He opened the door. "I think we've covered everything."

"Sir." Alicia rested on the door frame. "This man, he kills within days. Murphy's been on it for some time and three more girls have been taken. Two dead. If you treated it like a kidnapping from the start, if you were certain she hadn't run away, she would still in all likelihood be dead."

Wellington tried to smile as he lowered himself into the driver's seat. He shut the door, started the engine, and wound down the window. "Promise me one thing?"

"If I can."

"When you find him, if it's the same guy, let me see him?"

"Sir, I'm not sure if..."

"Not to be let in a room with him or hurt him, nothing like that. Just to see him. Look at him in the flesh instead of a photograph on the television."

Murphy leaned in near the window. "No problems, I promise. When we catch him, you'll get a good long look in his eyes."

The wind rumbled around them and a cry of joy shot across from the Cow and Calf. The latest oldie had made it to terra firma without breaking her hip.

Finally, Alicia said, "Thirty-two."

Wellington blinked back at her. "Pardon?"

"I'm thirty-two."

"Oh."

And with Murphy's promise hanging, and with a confident, fixed jaw, John Wellington put the Volvo in gear, and drove down the steep hill towards Ilkley.

Before setting off, Alicia placed the request with her ex at Interpol. Tony Proctor and she dated for six months after meeting on a cross-over case, split up due to their vastly differing professional lives, but remained friends to the extent that they sent one another cards at appropriate times of the year. He was eager to help and told her to drop him the request via email and he'd shunt it up the queue.

Once Alicia steered them back onto the road to Leeds, Alicia asked, "You two know each other well?"

"John mentored me when I first joined CID."

They passed the ruins of some old cathedral, Alicia wondering about the people who lived there back when it was shiny and new. Then it was behind them and out of sight.

"Thought that was Rhapshaw."

"No. He got lumbered with me when I was a probie. Wellington mentored about fifty coppers in CID. We were never mates, just colleagues. But still, I don't think he liked me not saying anything while you accused him of incompetence."

"One bad call is not incompetence."

"Switch places with him. How's it feel?"

He was right.

Murphy said, "But I didn't stop you. You know why?"

"Yes. I do."

"There's no place here for egos. If finding Katie Hague means upsetting a retired CID officer, so be it."

"I said I know, Don. You don't have to justify it to me."

"Not to you, no."

He activated Alicia's Bluetooth hands-free kit and paired his mobile to it, then called into Glendale control room and asked if anything new had turned up.

The controller didn't answer him at first. The line was open. She wasn't speaking.

Murphy closed his eyes. Alicia pictured a middle-aged woman, mouth open and moving only slightly, trying to phrase it right.

Please not that, Alicia thought. *Don't be what we both think it is.*

Murphy rested his head back, eyes still closed. "Are you sure it's her?"

Alicia swallowed hard, as upset for Murphy as for the man waiting for news of his daughter. The news, although obvious now, was something Alicia could do without hearing. She could jam her fingers in her ears—

"It is confirmed," the operator replied in a clipped, Eastern European accent. "It matches the description you gave." The patched-through radio signal clicked off at the other end, then crackled back on again. "I am sorry, Murphy."

Murphy fumbled for the button to hang up. He couldn't find it. Alicia pressed it for him and pulled to the side of the road, where they sat in silence, trying to digest the news that the man who took Katie Hague had killed her two days earlier than anyone expected.

Chapter Eight

FREDDIE WILCOX WONDERED if he'd done the right thing. He watched from afar, across the road and up a tree, his knapsack hidden in a shrub at its base, using binoculars purchased from the same shop where he made the phone call. As far as his eyes could tell, no one had located his home. He'd cleaned it out pretty well.

Men, or possibly women, in white suits with funny hoods had descended into the well (actually his toilet, oh yuck!) harnessed to a cable fed by a truck. It seemed someone had already explored the well before Freddie got back from the shops. They'd utilised a long cable, like a giant version of the camera a doctor once slid up his bum-hole to check his prostate, so it was probably that. Now the scientist-type people were here.

What if they found his stuff?

Sure, he had all his money safely tucked away, all his personal items too, but there were still his pans, his plates, his latest Stephen King. He'd protected them by placing them all in a carrier bag, and buried it close to his shack.

But what if they brought dogs, dug it up, thought bad thoughts?

When Freddie's wife suspected he was cheating on her, she cut up all his trousers. And that was back in the nineties before he actually *was* cheating on her. If the police thought he'd *murdered* someone...

He tried to calculate the scale of punishment. Cheating equals trousers cut up. So an offence like drink-driving must mean jail. Therefore, murder had to be even worse.

What could be worse than jail?

Maybe they had different levels of jail these days. Freddie hadn't seen a television or read a newspaper for three years and his memories of the "real" world were hazy at best. He preferred Freddie-World, where you could make your life whatever you wanted. Fiction was far more satisfying than reality.

Case in point—"reality" was happening here and now. Silent men and women, black uniforms, stab vests and white space-suits, vehicles to-ing and fro-ing, coming and going, more visitors in one day than in all his time here before today. And they were unwelcome guests, worse than in-laws or cousins who tried to force their holiday photos on you.

Couldn't they just take the body away so its spirit wouldn't haunt him? Do some fingerprints or DNAing?

Can "DNA" be a verb?

Freddie lowered the binoculars. He thought about what would happen if they did not leave. They were erecting a tent of sorts. Were they going to camp out, hope the criminal returns to the scene? Dumbos. That only happens in stupid films. He knew *that* much about real life.

No. He had to do something before they wrecked Freddie-World forever.

He climbed down the tree, far harder than climbing up, his feet not as sure. He had the vague memory of doing this as a kid, frustrated at not finding his footholds on the descent. In that distant youth of his, he would simply have jumped.

He imagined that tent going up, a little impenetrable wigwam, Freddie ruing his time battling this stupid tree. The police and those scientist types would quote squatters' rights and he'd be stuck with them as neighbours forever. And here he was dangling from a branch like Garfield the cat.

So he let go.

The ground came up fast. He intended to land softly, possibly tuck his right arm under himself, roll, and end up back on his feet, dusting himself off and looking up proudly at the branch from where he'd dropped. But that was in Freddie-World. Right now, the laws of Freddie-World were absent, the rules of reality prevalent, and it was one of these rules that somehow prevented Freddie from rolling and landing unharmed.

Instead, a bolt of pain shot from his left ankle straight up his leg. He fell, crashed sideways into the mulch and leaves, and didn't get up for several minutes. He held the injured ankle in the air, could feel it swelling, pushing against the Hush Puppies he bought last month.

And it wasn't getting better lying there.

Using the tree to lean on, he stood, and tried his ankle; it would not support his weight. He eventually found a branch sturdy enough to act as a walking stick. Then he set off to explain that he no longer required police assistance, but thanks a bunch anyway.

PC Wayne Dobson was cold. The sun shone high and bright, but the wind dropped the temperature by a good few degrees. It didn't help that he happened to be tramping up an incline to guard the highest point of the crime scene, unable to hear even mutters of what was going on.

Probies always get the crap jobs.

He was partnered with the constable who found the body, or rather the constable who responded to the call, smelled the vague hint of rotting flesh emanating from that old well (all Dobson could detect was excrement—human or animal, he wasn't sure), then called in the experts.

Gary Webster would still get the credit though.

And because of this, Gary was allowed on-scene. *In* the scene. While Wayne Dobson guarded a dirt road.

Four SOCOs staffed the scene, under the command of DCI Chambers, who Wayne's colleagues called "a wet dream for teenage boys", like the gift of a slender teacher or best friend with a young mother. He heard regular use of the term MILF, but only one officer had survived Chambers hearing it; the others were ground up and fed to her pigs, or so the rumours went. Besides, Dobson hated the way his colleagues referred to her like that, as if her physical mien were of any relevance to her work. No, Dobson had sat in on briefings she led, talks she gave on modern investigative techniques, and lessons in crime-scene protocol. And each time, because she was so damn *good* at this, he paid complete attention, even shushing Rick Davies one time when he whispered that he could see Chambers' bra through a gap in her blouse. Now he was missing out on watching her in action first hand.

Webster now conversed with the chap from the council, a planner, someone on the team which analysed this land, passed the structure as safe. Chambers spoke on her mobile, meaning little filtered through Dobson's radio. All he knew was what he'd heard in the initial build up, before Chambers arrived. Two women, dead. One recent, the other reduced to bones and gnawed flesh. Lovely image.

One of the SOCOs emerged from the well, pulled up via the winch they'd brought with them. He'd left another scene of crime office down below, and to another colleague he handed a plastic bag containing what looked like—from Dobson's distance—a human hand. What remained of it, anyway. Webster bent over to have a look before they tagged it and sealed it into the forensics container. From Dobson's days at the academy, not more than a month ago, he could not remember them removing body parts so quickly in any given scenario.

When Wayne Dobson faced the way he was supposed to be, a man approached, halfway between him and the gate covered in police "Do Not Enter" signage. He was dressed in a suit and a shirt and tie, and aside from a few smears of dirt, it appeared to be a nice wool blend. Not inexpensive either. The man, however, bore a shock of wild hair, as if he had recently been electrocuted. He limped forward, his grey beard a lop-sided triangle pointing down. He used a long stick like a crutch and flailed his free arm toward the crime scene.

"Sir," Dobson said in the firm voice his training demanded. "Sir, you can't come in here. Didn't you see the signs?"

"Now you listen up one minute," the man said, closer now, not stopping. "This has been my home for the last two years. I only called you in to get rid of the body. Don't want it haunting up my place."

Dobson held a hand out. "Body? What do you know about a body?"

"The body! The body in the waste pipe of course!" He stopped six feet from Dobson. "I called you—on the phone—but I didn't think you'd disrupt everything like this. How long are you going to be here?"

"Sir, you need to give a statement."

"Will that make you go away?"

"I can't say." Dobson looked around, at the well, the activity from which he was excluded, back to the wild-looking oddball. "Sir, if you'll come with me, I'll see someone takes your statement."

The man rolled his eyes, and tutted. "Young man, my statement is this: a woman got herself killed, and the killer dumped her in my toilet. End of story."

"A woman?" *How did he know for sure?*

"Yes indeed. A *dead* woman. In the pipe. Now get rid of her and go. Arrest whoever did this to me."

Dobson thought about this man, what he said. *His home.* He knew it was a woman. Knew she was dead.

Dobson felt for his truncheon, checked his pepper spray and unhooked the clip. "Sir, you have to come with me."

"I ain't going anywhere, not until you people get that body out and bugger off."

Dobson was close now, close enough to touch. "Sir…"

"Ah!" The man hefted his stick-cum-crutch, narrowly missing Dobson's hand, and pointed it. "Don't touch me."

This man was a suspect. Aggressive. Ordering a police officer to desist in his duty. No choice.

Dobson whipped out his truncheon—a standard issue black Monadnock—and with a flick extended it to its full twenty-four inches. He knocked the branch to the side. The man dropped it and staggered, landed on his bad foot and fell. Dobson dropped the baton and slapped handcuffs on his first ever prisoner.

For a moment, he forgot how to read people their rights. Then it all came flooding back, as he'd practiced on his girlfriend, and arrested the man for trespassing on a crime scene, hopeful he could soon trump it up to murder.

Meanwhile, close to the well/pipe, with Webster and the council guy out of the way, senior Scene of Crime Officer, and crime scene manager, William Hopper was able to finish his over-long report relating to the initial crime scene. He logged the few surviving body parts, completed his initial findings, and he had bagged and removed the evidence to preserve it. Rats swarmed all over the place down there. That there was this much left showed there may be a God after all. Human waste also pervaded, which was a job for the junior officers—"good for their development," he told them. The more intact body would be removed for closer examination. ETA at the Sheerton morgue was two p.m., three hours from now. He also added the suspected cause of death:

Body 1: unknown. Body 2: single stab wound to the chest.

After proofreading it twice, he rephrased the gruesome bits with less panache—a bad habit he'd developed since becoming addicted to Patricia Cornwell novels—and pressed "send". He smiled, knowing the 4G satellite-capable laptop in front of him represented a mere fraction of the advancements made in this job over the years, that paperwork should soon be even easier.

He even knew how it worked: the information he compiled was disassembled by the newest software available, encoded by a chip far more expensive and well-tested than you get in civilian computers, and shot up into the atmosphere, through the ozone layer and into the cold clutches of space. The time it took to reach the satellite from the time he hit the "send" key was less than 0.5 seconds. From here, a satellite relayed the encoded data to a similar computer in the morgue, and also one at Sheerton police station, where DCI Chambers was based. Here, the computer decoded the data with similar speed, and presented it to anyone with high enough clearance.

William Hopper knew all this because he'd been on a course.

What Sergeant Hopper didn't know, however, was that this same satellite interpreted several words, including "homicide" as in "two likely *homicide* victims", and a clause in its programming came into effect, forwarding a second copy to a Home Office computer. This computer, thanks to Britain's special relationship with the United States, shared the data with an even more powerful computer based at 935 Pennsylvania Avenue, in Washington, D.C. This machine then fed the information into a vast database known as ViCAP—the Violent Criminal Apprehension Program, housed in the famed FBI stronghold at Quantico.

ViCAP logs every murder in the United States—its circumstances, its victims, and even, in some cases, motive. Where possible, murders are shared from other countries too. After all, people who live for murder need not hunt exclusively on their home turf.

But monitoring this database would be more than a full-time job for one person. So it is only when you input relevant data that matches are spat back out. It is a secure system. Only law enforcement agencies—with permission from the guardians of this program, the FBI—are granted access. Some agents—senior agents—are allowed to view it from home, for those nights where they wake in a cold sweat, their subconscious disturbing something missed during the hours of daylight. And when they leave the agency, this access is taken away.

Unless, like Alfie Rhee, you hide a code in the remote networking software, a code that provides access even after you've been forced out of your job. Even six years after he cleared his desk for the final time, meaning it this time, really quitting, even now he'd be disturbed by some traffic noise, grow restless, and wander from his bed, power-up his laptop on the antique desk overlooking Manhattan, and surf through ViCAP as a teenager might shop for music.

Tonight, after twenty years of searching, he found what he needed.

Chapter Nine

ALICIA HAD SEEN men's faces turn grey before, but Murphy's was a new shade. "Ashen" would have been healthy. And as they drove in silence through a wide, leafy street with wheelie bins awaiting collection and nice cars and well-kept hedges, Alicia wondered about the people living here, if one of them might be next, joining Katie in wherever murdered girls end up.

The wide street gave way to a main road, and the road led to an industrial estate called Evergreen. They followed the waving constable's directions to the far end where two squad cars and a SOCO team were already on scene. The old railway tracks criss-crossing waste ground at the back of the estate used to serve the canal, transporting goods from the rag trade to the narrowboats that would then head to Bradford and Lancashire.

The SOCOs had enclosed Katie's body in a white tent erected over the tracks, and now dozens of drafted-in officers sucked up overtime as they conducted a fingertip search of the surrounding area. Aside, two female police community support officers—PCSOs—shared coffees with a man and woman in office attire. Alicia and Murphy showed their IDs to the officers and received an abbreviated overview of what happened. Then they pressed the man and woman—Terry and Jean—to tell it again.

The two worked in an office overlooking the waste ground spanning beyond the railway tracks. They popped out on the roof for a smoke when they spotted a man—hard to discern his height—carrying a bulky package over one shoulder. Joking that it *must* be a body, they watched, though Terry thought it was probably building waste or something the council tip wouldn't accept. The guy was dressed in a long coat and had a baseball cap pulled down over his face, and they seemed to think he was white but, when pushed, neither could say for sure they saw skin.

Alicia filed the image in a part of her brain that had many like it; the Hollywood vision of a serial killer—trench-coat, baseball cap, all dark colours.

Was this guy a fan of other murderers? Did he watch the movie version of John Wayne Gacy's life or some made-up psychopath and try to emulate them this way?

When the two plucked up the courage to investigate, Terry maturely "dared" Jean to take a peek at the "body." They were perhaps expecting a gardener's leftovers.

"The face." Jean dabbed her eyes. "That poor girl's face."

Terry curled an arm around her. Alicia wondered if this was an illicit office romance—he wore a wedding ring; she did not.

"Thank you," Murphy said, already on his way to the SOCOs' white tent.

Alicia caught up with him as he spoke to one of two white-clad women at the entrance flap.

"We're a little short today, Inspector," the SOCO said. "Got a double find over in Eccup."

"Okay," Murphy said. "Can I see her?"

"Not much to see. Nothing helpful at this point anyway."

"Can I *see* her?"

The woman pulled the tent open enough for Murphy to stick his head inside. He wasn't supposed to do that without a protective hood, but they allowed him a peek. He withdrew slowly.

"Not nice, is it," the SOCO said.

Alicia was beginning to feel left out. "May I?" She poked her head into the tent and the SOCO peeling evidence off the corpse moved to one side.

Katie's jaw was smashed into a right angle and her teeth had caved in, many of them missing. Her nose and eyes were swollen beneath the dried blood. One ear was missing. Unlike the other victims to date, she was naked. Through the filth, Alicia discerned massive bruises and scratches to her forearms—defensive blows—and tell-tale binding welts around her ankles and wrists.

It wasn't the worst thing Alicia had seen, but it didn't mean she'd look at it longer than necessary.

She joined Murphy who sat cross-legged on the dusty gravel. He picked up a stone and lobbed it into the wasteland.

"Careful," Alicia said. "Might be evidence."

"What's happening?" he asked.

"You're throwing stones and a man is planning to kidnap another girl. Probably tonight, if he hasn't taken her already."

"And we can't wait because it means we have another crack at him. Another three or four days for a body, maybe two since it looks like he's speeding up. Interviewing useless bloody witnesses, and we still haven't even spoken to Henry bloody Windsor, because this new clue has shown up. *Katie.* Katie is *dead.*"

Alicia sat next to Murphy and followed his eyes over the rocky black field, the route the man walked, to stand right here, where Murphy threw another stone.

"Not even making a tiny bit of effort to conceal her this time."

"No." Alicia recalled the maybe-lovers' statements. "Almost the opposite. Like she's on display."

"But in black bags. Discarded rubbish. Could it be they're losing their appeal?"

"Dehumanising her. It's the natural progression."

Murphy threw another stone.

Alicia found a bigger stone, half a house brick in fact, and hurled it after Murphy's pebble.

She said, "Stuff like this comes up more often than you think. We estimate there are at least ten serial killers in Britain at this moment. People who kill maybe every two or three years. Start as rapists mostly, but women these days are more willing to go to court, look them in the eye and say 'Yep, he did it, m'lud'."

"What's your point?"

"My point is that serial killers do not do this. They don't kill every seven days then five days, then three. Except right at the end. In the spree phase."

"Like Bundy."

"Yes. Like Bundy. But we usually catch them before then." Alicia found another rock to throw and aimed it at her first one. She missed.

Murphy rose with a creak to his knees and Alicia walked with him in silence to her car. His face remained set. As Wellington had grown affectionate toward Tanya Windsor without having met her, Murphy clearly liked Katie, missed her as if it had been his duty to protect her. And he failed.

The worst part was yet to come. Alicia had vowed to fight for Katie Hague. She promised Katie's father so much, given him such hope, hope she'd seen in him last night. Alicia's next job was to rip that hope away, and inform Richard his daughter would never come home again.

. . .

Richard Hague was not numb. At first, when DS Friend delivered the news, yes, he felt nothing but a heavy lilt to his limbs. Only a *moment* of numbness. The sensation morphed into one of falling, falling a long way, through cold air, ice flakes stinging his body. Then the tingling behind his nose expanded, releasing tears. Soon, he was in the back of their car, the man—Murphy—driving. What was DS Friend's first name? Alicia. That was it. The pretty name. She sat alongside him, holding his hand again.

Last night my hand was covered in blood. Soon, it will be again.

"Katie has been taken to Sheerton Station," Alicia told him. "I have to tell you that she isn't ... she isn't how you remember her. I'm afraid her face is quite..."

"I don't care," Richard said. "I need this."

He squeezed her hand, knowing it hurt her, that she pretended it didn't. She would keep up the pretence until serious damage threatened. Damage he could so easily inflict.

He added, "You said I don't have to look, but I do. I really do."

Richard stayed with Gillian for two hours after she died, holding her, kissing her, unable to believe the cold mass of flesh before him was the woman who bore him a beautiful baby girl. He staved off the urge for as long as he could before killing the hooker and dumping her in that well. He didn't exactly do a lot of research, but he knew about the structure from a school trip years earlier, and when he recced the place he heard the faint trickle of water down below. The body could turn up somewhere, but in all likelihood it had been swept away for the animals to munch on, or to take up space in an unexplored cave system.

But now he had a specific target in mind. He would find the man who robbed him of Katie, use the skills honed during his time in the States, and visit upon him ten times Katie's pain. He didn't *want* to hurt Alicia to attain the information he'd need. But he would.

If he had to.

The station was yellow brick and modern. Reporters staked out the lobby, but Murphy drove around the back. They all got out. Alicia—still holding his hand—led Richard through a door that required a card swipe. The corridors echoed with every step. It seemed vulgar somehow, the noise, the clattering.

Murphy swiped his card at another set of doors with the word "Morgue" printed on them. These swooshed open and the floors here were tile rather than stone, muffling their footfalls.

Richard pictured the killer: for some reason this was a man in leather pants, naked from the waist up, holding a knife before him. A strange image, and he couldn't understand how he'd constructed it. The man was also muscular, grinning, offering to put down the knife, to fight Richard fairly, himself in a smart suit—the one he would wear to Katie's funeral—and he'd take up the offer of a fair fight, allow the leather-pants man to land a punch in his midsection, before using a K-bar hunting knife to gut the miserable bastard inside out, then—

"Donald will see if she's ready," Alicia said softly.

"Thank you," Richard said.

When Murphy reappeared, he nodded, and the three of them went inside.

Richard expected a morgue like in US telly programs, all chrome doors and gurneys. This was mostly blue with hints of grey. Yet it was the grey that stood out, less of it, but like the two colours had fought over who would dominate the room and the grey won. There was only one door, where he imagined all the bodies went. One lay outside, in a black bag on a table next to the wall.

Katie.

Alicia asked once more if he was ready. He said yes. She took the zip in one hand, the bag in her other, and pulled. Now he'd see what the damage. Feel it, the pain.

Katie's pain.

The zip clacked open, a smell, kind-of perfumed, leaching from within. They warned him so many times about the state of her that no further concern was necessary. A tech cleaned her, they said earlier, collected what Murphy called "evidence" but Richard knew was the blood and other matter that would have coated his daughter.

Alicia Friend then fixed him with a stare that said "last chance" and Richard nodded.

She parted the bag.

Katie was visible from head to collarbone. Beaten, cleansed of blood, but mangled, destroyed. This wasn't the person he raised, who started reading sooner than any kid at her school, the ten-year-old in the middle of a pub screaming for Johnny Wilkinson to kick that ball ... the girl who, years later, drank pints to save queuing.

He ran his finger over his daughter's neck.

So pale.

And her collarbone, intact. Which struck Richard as odd.

What had the man seen in her that he felt compelled to destroy her face so comprehensively?

Richard himself killed, yes. But he wasn't a *sadist*.

He opened the zip wider, not embarrassed by the corpse's nakedness. Katie would be mortified if she knew, but he needed the clues, to understand how this man thought.

His finger moved the edge of the bag and something suddenly wasn't right.

God. He had been so gullible.

"There's something on her shoulder," Richard said.

Alicia moved the bag for a clearer angle. One of the girl's breasts popped out, grazing the zip, but Alicia didn't draw attention to it. She was looking at the thing on the corpse's shoulder. "It goes all the way down her arm." She opened the bag further to gain a wider view. "It's a tiger."

Murphy examined it too. "Couldn't see it for the blood earlier." He caught himself, apologised to Richard.

"That's okay," Richard said, smiling. "Katie doesn't have a tattoo. This isn't my daughter."

Chapter Ten

ALFIE RHEE WAS DONE PACKING. He turned off the water, donned a pair of comfy pants and ensured he packed a change of socks in his hand luggage along with a book on Hillary Clinton, his iPod, passport, and an empty and activated credit card in his wallet. The credit card was a work of art. Saving his cash, he made semi-regular large purchases on it, paying it off in instalments that attracted a little—but not too much—interest, until he worked the credit limit all the way up to $25,000. If he maxed it out, no problem. Once it served its purpose, it was unlikely Alfie could ever return to the United States.

He looked around one final time, and ran an electromagnet over each side of his computer, erasing the disk. He was set.

A knock at the door.

Alfie's place was a good size. Not too big, but open-plan, kind of like the apartments in that old sitcom, *Friends*. He'd bought it with a payoff from his former employer, the result of suing for racist discrimination having cited several white Americans who breached similar procedures and did not suffer the mental anguish he was forced to endure.

Alfie opened the door to Special Agent Turner.

"Hey," she said, presenting her FBI creds, as if Alfie wouldn't know who she was.

"What?" Alfie said.

"Going on a trip?"

"What gives you that idea?" He let the holdall drop from his shoulder onto the floor and placed his small case on the kitchen table.

"Inviting us in?"

"Depends who 'us' is."

A man stepped into the doorway, his creds also on display. "Agent Morris." Perfect suit, set hair, broad shoulders. White. Well-spoken, no accent, and Alfie pictured him wearing real expensive shades outdoors. Like a model hired to pose for an FBI recruitment poster.

"You look okay I suppose." Alfie stood aside. "And you're with Gail Turner, so I guess I can trust you around my expensive china."

They gathered in the kitchen area. Alfie offered coffee. The two agents declined. He was glad. He'd have had to turn the water back on.

"You mind telling me where you're going?" Turner said.

"Visiting friends."

"Going far?"

Alfie shrugged.

"You haven't booked a flight yet," Morris said.

"You tapping my phone?"

"Your financial records, actually. It's routine when we trace someone hacking into our systems."

"I'll be sure to let you know if I hear anything about that." He shook his head. "Nasty business. Goddamn hackers. Makes me glad the Patriot Act exists."

Morris sat at the table, pulled Alfie's hand luggage towards him.

"If you don't have a warrant, leave that the hell alone," Alfie said.

"Oh right," Turner said. "Nearly forgot."

She handed Alfie a signed search warrant.

He read it. "Says here you can seize all computer equipment and official documents," Alfie said, snatching his bag. "Seize away. I got a plane to catch."

"Sir, you don't have a plane to catch at all," Morris said. "We already established you haven't booked one."

"I know. I was hoping to get a cheap last minute deal to Aruba." A glance at Morris. "It's where my friends live."

"Okay, enough bullshit," Turner said. "Sit down and listen."

The three now sat around the table.

Classic Bureau tactics. The old *put-the-suspect-at-ease* play, then hit 'em. It wasn't standard practice to do it in a suspect's kitchen, though. If they were here to take him down for hacking into ViCAP they wouldn't even have knocked. He'd be hand-cuffed, face down, with Morris looking even smugger than he did right now. Which was pretty damn smug.

"You're heading to England," Turner said. "The warrant is down to the hack, but it isn't why we're here. We have an IP address but no solid evidence. Just enough for a warrant. But I've personally known about the code you planted for years now. I knew why you did it and I persuaded our tech guys not to send it up the pipe. You're looking for something that isn't there, but I figured if we took that away, you'd do something far more stupid."

"For something that isn't there, it looked real solid to me. Still does."

"You weren't objective enough to make that decision. Hell, you weren't even a profiler."

"And profilers are never wrong?"

"Not with something that big, no. Your wife was killed by a

burglar, Alfie. Not some boogie man. I mean, Jesus, Alfie. They even have a guy in custody for the thing in England. I checked."

Alfie stood quickly, clattering the chair into his stove. He caught himself, didn't shout, didn't swear. Just pointed. "I know what you think. But now I have proof. He's surfaced."

Turner wasn't fazed by the outburst. She watched him carefully. "In *England*? You really believe that?"

Alfie leaned on the counter top, head down. All the years he'd known Turner, before and after he left the Bureau, never once had she believed him, believed what he knew. It was simple, too simple for her.

"He's surfaced," he said again.

Turner stood up slowly. "Alfie, we can't let an ex-FBI agent race around England chasing an imaginary killer."

"You can't stop me."

Morris said, "The code implanted in our system is enough to hold you."

"When the evidence is declared unusable I'll be free—free to go to England and free to sue you assholes for harassment, false imprisonment and whatever else my lawyer'll throw at you."

Turner and Morris noticed the magnet simultaneously. Turner said, "Fine. But hear me out one last time?"

Alfie checked his watch.

Why did I do that?

He was going to jump on the next plane that came up. Figured it might avoid a scene like this one if he didn't book it in advance. He guessed Gail watched him, bugged him, made sure he wasn't using the information for nefarious means. His crime was relatively minor, so unworthy of FBI man hours.

"You knew," Alfie said, moving toward Turner. "You were watching, flagging the same things I was."

"I was worried," she said.

"You were worried? Worried what? Worried I might catch this guy?"

"No..."

He was close to her now. Morris rose and edged forwards.

"You know I'm right. You know he's real, that he killed Stacy, that he killed the others."

"Alfie, I was *worried* about *you*. I still am." So this was not just an official visit.

"You know I'm right." Alfie put his face up to hers. "Say it. *Say I'm right.*"

"That's enough, buddy." Morris was on him, his thick arm about Alfie's neck, a frowned-upon "sleeper" hold in effect, pulling him off Turner. He gripped Morris's elbow in one hand, wrist in the other, and pushed the elbow toward his eye. Morris let out a yelp and Alfie was free. He pressured the arm further and held the agent on the floor with one hand.

"Stop struggling," Alfie said. "It'll hurt more."

"Let him go," Turner said, without concern for her colleague. "And get this through your head. There is no killer. Hundreds of people all across America are murdered by a single stab wound every day."

"Not to the heart. Not to the *heart*."

"Yes to the heart! Stacy was not the victim of some mass murderer. She was killed during a break-in."

Alfie released the agent. Morris stood up, rubbing his shoulder.

"I've worked on this for years," Alfie said. "I don't need some profiler telling me that a serial killer doesn't change his weapon or his methods or his victim profile. Single stab to the heart, let them die. That's his trick."

"And one report of a stab wound to the heart and you jet off across the Atlantic."

"Plus an older corpse found next to it. It's his dumping ground. Who knows how many more they'll find."

"You think you can track down one man in an unfamiliar country?"

Alfie picked up his bags again. "I got a contact over there to act as tour-guide. Besides, a country the size of my butthole, how hard can it be to find one guy?"

"You're pushing fifty, Alfie. Think you're up to this?"

"I run ten miles a day. I bench-press one-twenty. And your pal here knows I can handle myself."

Turner exchanged glances with Morris. She hugged Alfie once and he wanted to hug her back, but his hands were full.

"Be careful," she said. "I doubt you'll find what you need, but be careful. If you get in trouble, we can't help you. Here, you got friends. Over there…"

Alfie nodded and led them out into the hall. Locked up.

"Be careful," Turner said again.

"I will." This time, Alfie initiated the hug. "One thing," he said to Morris, breaking away. "You might have had a warrant, but this wasn't official business. I don't know you from Adam, so what brought you along?"

"I owe Agent Turner a favour."

"She save your life or something?"

"Nah," he said, rubbing his arm. "Nothing that lame."

Turner smiled, kissed Alfie on the forehead, and winked. "He knocked up my sister."

Alfie guessed he was free to go, and walked away toward the stairs. In the street, he hailed a cab, and settled in to plan what he'd do when he located the man who murdered his wife.

Chapter Eleven

ALICIA AND MURPHY checked in with the operations room, which was now thick with the strange odour of middle-aged men hard at work on not that much, Ball and Cleaver having arrived three hours early for their night-shift at Murphy's request. They were updating what they already knew, had brought in a new whiteboard and placed Tanya Windsor's name on it as Alicia had the others.

It had to be her.

Odd, though, that the file mentioned no *specific* tattoo, but they'd been told she had them. The detail would be somewhere, maybe one of the hundreds of boxes of statements and other evidence accumulated during Wellington's investigation. According to the abridged version Murphy carried, she was also exhibiting "wild" behaviour, and "dressing differently."

How dare a young woman not behave in the way men of a particular class expected her to? What a disgusting Jezebel.

No. Concentrate on the case. On the facts.

The description of her clothes on the day she disappeared would have hidden the ink. Maybe it was new. Maybe she hadn't told anyone about it. Or maybe the man who kidnapped her painted it like some sort of brand.

They'd need to confirm with Tanya's friends.

Alicia allowed Murphy the honour of outlining how they now believed Tanya Windsor to be both the latest *and* earliest victim of the man holding Katie Hague.

"So Brunette Bertie did a blonde," Cleaver said, chuckling along with Ball. "He swings both ways, then."

"Brunette Bertie?" Alicia said. "Really?"

"I told you I don't want you using that name," Murphy said. "Not here, and definitely not in the pub with journos hanging round."

Alicia located a *Yellow Pages* and flicked through it. Yep, a phone book. Made of paper.

"What's up, love?" Ball said, standing over her. "Do we offend you?"

Alicia chose to smile at the man she was reluctantly beginning to think of as a dickhead. "Nobody offends me."

Hygiene only just about bearable. Married, hasn't had sex with his wife for at least a year. Probably uses prostitutes, which is why he prefers vice to murders.

She'd save that for later if she needed it; now it would only push him further from her. "I'm looking for something."

"You know," Cleaver said. "That humming box is connected to a thing called the internet."

Dickhead number two.

Ball asked, "What do you need? Hairdresser?" He and Cleaver sniggered, not even qualifying as a chuckle.

"Bikini wax?" Cleaver offered.

"Thank you, no," Alicia said. "But you're in the right area. Bodily improvements."

Murphy slapped Cleaver and Ball on their backs, buddy-style. "There's a cell free now, so catch a little shut-eye if you can.

You're spending the rest of the evening checking out tattoo parlours."

"Ah, come on, boss," Ball said. "Some constable can do that."

"Yeah, boss," Cleaver said, "We need to chase down this posh bird's mates and make sure it's her. If it isn't the Hague girl then—"

"Hey." Alicia ducked under Murphy's arm, still attached to DS Ball's back, and popped up so they huddled like a basketball team. "Here's an idea. Katie should be dead by now, but isn't. That's great news, donchya think?"

Ball and Cleaver nodded, Murphy looking at each in turn.

"But Tanya, who we already thought deceased more than a year ago, was killed instead. Which is sad, right?"

Again, the nods.

"Which means what, gentlemen?"

Nothing. They weren't enjoying this and, despite the grin, neither was Alicia.

"It means he is not going to give her up," Murphy said.

"Correctamundo!" Alicia said.

With a backslap of her own, the huddle disbanded and Ball and Cleaver sat on a desk facing her and Murphy.

She paced between them all in turn as she spoke. "This person took Tanya eighteen months before Pippa Bradshaw. We are reasonably certain he took no one else in the meantime. So why now? He's held Tanya for so long, keeping her alive, doing whatever he does to them—"

"Which is nothing," Cleaver said.

"Nothing *physical*," Murphy corrected.

Alicia thought for a moment. This was tough. At least Murphy *listened*.

She said, "Do either of you know how much sheer willpower it would take to do what he did to Tanya?"

Ball shrugged, glanced at Cleaver. Cleaver shrugged.

"Two years ago, a gang of British and Italians got together and they swiped a young man off the streets of Rome where he was holidaying. The young man—can't tell you his name; it's confidential—was the son of an oil baron. The *policia* called in Interpol, who called us because the oil baron was British."

"Which oil baron?" Ball said.

"Still as confidential as it was four seconds ago. But he owns a portion of Russia the size of Yorkshire. Anyway, he pays the twenty million euros with help from ourselves and Interpol."

"No Eyeties?"

"No. We're racists, Sergeant Ball, and believe Italians are all corrupt." She winked. "They played a monitoring role, but with the threat of the oil baron suing their cute arses, they weren't keen on handling it alone. The *commandatore* was a jolly nice man by the way. I still get birthday cards from him."

Murphy coughed.

Oh, right.

She continued. "But the gang got greedy. They decided to go for more cash. While the Italians bargained with them, we ran the investigation. But we suspected they were holed up somewhere in the hills. For a month, Interpol and ourselves negotiated with the gang. In the end, they simply left the lad where he was being held, buggered off with the cash, and we got a phone call telling us where to pick him up."

"Where was he?"

"A penthouse apartment in the centre of Rome. Had a lovely view of the Colosseum and everything. In the debriefing, he said the kidnappers didn't harm him. They fed him well, they'd even go out drinking while one stayed guard, took it in turns. Having a great time, they were. When we asked why they gave up, I was expecting him to say the pressure got too much. But no."

"It wasn't the pressure?" Ball said.

"You weren't getting too close?" Cleaver said.

"No." Alicia placed a hand on each of their shoulders. "Forty-nine days after kidnapping the son of a billionaire—who would probably have shelled out a further twenty million—with all that cash at stake, they gave up because they were *bored*."

"Bored?" Cleaver screwed up his face.

She stood shoulder to elbow with Murphy. "After a month and a half."

Ball gave an admiring whistle. "And our lad holds 'em eighteen months at a time. That's staying power for you."

Alicia let the dust settle, knowing that despite Ball's quip he and Cleaver were contemplating the man they sought.

"We all need to do our bit, gents," Alicia said.

Murphy said, "One of us will visit Tanya's circle of friends, and ascertain whether or not the tattoo was Tanya's. Fingerprint analysis will be twelve hours due to the double murder up at Eccup getting top billing."

"Aw, come on, this is way more urgent," Ball said. "We've got a live one out there."

Alicia smiled at the newfound urgency in Ball. "They landed with their body first. It's like a polite queue."

"You've something of a night ahead," Murphy said. "And I know I cut your sleep short for this, so hit the sack for a couple of hours if you need it. Then hit the Yellow Pages. Or the humming box. Your choice."

Ball turned to Cleaver. "I can cope without a nap. You?"

"Sure," Cleaver replied with a shrug.

"Let your fingers do the walking," Alicia said, then turned smartly on one foot so her ponytail swung out, and she and Murphy left the room. Although happy with the change in attitude, she wished *she* was canvassing the streets instead. What was to occur next, she was not looking forward to at all.

. . .

Alicia had never properly faced the press before, mainly because she couldn't be herself in front of the cameras. The bubbly personality for which everyone commended her would sit behind the façade of a ball-breaking woman officer who'd do-anything-to-get-the-job-done. But she wasn't Tennison or that one played by Gillian Anderson who she liked. Alicia Friend was Alicia Friend. And if she couldn't be Alicia Friend, then she'd be the quiet one at the end of the desk. It was her one concession to politics—shutting up for the good of a case.

The only reason they were going public was the similarities between Pippa's death and Tanya's, and the fear someone might connect them before the police announced it. But not Hayley's yet; the details of her death were still under lock and key, and nobody wanted the killer knowing they had connected Hayley too. That would endanger Katie further.

But a local hack would pick up on a high-profile murder like Tanya Windsor. Tanya was a story and a half. Or would be once identity was confirmed. Society girl goes missing so long ago, is now dead. Alicia could only picture the scene when a pair of specially-trained officers gave Tanya's uncle the news. Grief first. Then would come anger. Anger at the police for assuming she was already dead. If a man with Henry Windsor's connections wanted blood, blood is what he would receive.

The table was laid out like on Crimewatch. Microphones for each of the six chairs, and a tiny room full of reporters from each field of the media. Four of those six seats were filled: Detective Chief Inspector Streeter—Murphy's direct superior—in full dress uniform, his hair grey and probably styled for the occasion; Anne Leader, head of public relations for West Yorkshire Police; Daphne Wilson, press officer for CID, retiring shortly; and, the one person Alicia knew—Chief Superintendent Graham Rhapshaw, also in uniform. Alicia's boss, as well as her friend. He was also the senior officer in charge of DCI Wellington's original investigation, so it would be his blood to be spilled should Henry Windsor choose.

The middle two seats, the main focus of the room, were vacant, gaping and ready for Murphy and Alicia.

Oh. Dear.

Murphy pulled the seat for her. It scraped on the floor.

A vague whisper travelled the room. A couple of coughs. So many eyes upon her.

She lowered herself to the seat, a dark plastic one, instantly too hot for her bum, and too hard.

Murphy sat beside her and undid his jacket to prevent bunching.

DCI Streeter coughed loudly, took a final sip of water, and addressed the ladies and gentlemen of the press. "Okay, we all know why we're here. This is Detective Inspector Donald Murphy and Detective Sergeant Alicia Friend—"

The first interruption, a newspaper man: "Did you say 'Friend'? As in F-R-I-E-N-D?"

Alicia met the journalist's eye and was about to say something when—

"That's correct," Streeter said, irritated. "May I proceed?"

"Sorry."

"Thank you. DI Murphy will read a statement and there will be a short time for questions. DI Murphy?"

Murphy raised the specially-prepared report, a Daphne Wilson and Anne Leader collaboration, and scanned it through. "Right," he said, still reading. He wasted ten precious seconds courtesy of a sip of water. "At approximately two p.m. today, a man was reported carrying a large package across wasteland adjacent to Evergreen Industrial Estate. He dropped the package on a disused railway line and retreated back across the waste ground where he fled out of sight. A witness investigated, and found the body of a young woman wrapped in black bin liners."

Hands went up, but Streeter stared them down.

"The police were called and we are currently investigating a possible..." He squinted here, shot a harsh look at Streeter, who nodded for him to continue. "We are investigating a link between this murder and that of Pippa Bradshaw. Both murders were violent and non-sexual. The second victim has not yet been officially identified so we cannot release further details at this time."

Bulbs flashed throughout, pens scribbled, recording devices were mumbled into. Alicia's eyes swam with shapes and colours, like airborne fish and worms. She'd have enjoyed the experience under different circumstances.

The first question: "Helen Johnson, Yorkshire Evening Post. Do you believe this to be the work of one man?"

"As opposed to a gang?" Murphy said.

He's good at this, Alicia thought. *He's done it before.*

"Yes," Murphy continued. "A very strong man has taken at least two young women from public places, and murdered them for reasons unknown."

The first journo again: "*At least* two? So it's possible there's a serial killer loose in Yorkshire?"

Murmurs again, louder this time. Excited. At least four journalists began texting. Alicia imagined a small Victorian boy in flat cap and britches receiving a message in a loud print room, the latest iPhone vibrating against his leg, the boy reading the message, eyes agog, and then—for some reason he had a high-pitched cockney accent—yelling to the supervisor, "Guv'nor! Guv'nor! Stop the presses. *Stop the presses!*"

Something jabbed her arm. Murphy. Nudging her.

Rhapshaw said, "Alicia? The gentleman asked a question."

"Hmm?" She scanned the room and noticed a man standing.

"Robert Clancy," he said. "The Sentinel."

Uh-oh. *The Sentinel* was the latest red-top tabloid to enter the fray of sensationalist journalism; like *The Sun* but with even more salacious lies about celebrities, angrier vitriol against immigrants and the poor.

He said, "Are you okay, Sergeant Friend? Can you answer my question?"

"Easy, Robert," Streeter warned.

"Thank you, Robert," Alicia said, her mini-computer working up a sweat. "I apologise. I was in my own little world for a second."

No, she thought. Ball-breaker. *Ass-kicker*.

"And what little world might that be, Ms. Friend?"

The words were out of her mouth before she could stop them. "Victorian London."

The reporter began to jot this down then stopped as mild laughter rolled through the crowd. "I'm sorry?"

"Detective Sergeant Friend," Rhapshaw said pleasantly. "Robert was asking how likely it is that this man is a serial killer in the vein of the Yorkshire Ripper, and the possibility that he is perhaps imitating Peter Sutcliffe's crimes."

"Oh. Right. Well, the possibility is there, of course, but it's too early to tell his motive. I've only dealt with serial crimes three or four times before—"

"Which is it?"

"Sorry?" She did that daft leaning forward thing, presenting her ear more prominently.

"Is it three times," Robert Clancy asked, "or four? You must know."

"Four," she said confidently. "Three murders and a rapist."

"Funny. I don't remember three serial killers over, what, the last four years. You can't have been in the job that long. What are you? Twenty-five?"

It was Rhapshaw's turn to engage with Robert Clancy. "Careful, Robert. Alicia's a proven officer. Show her some respect."

"Sir, I'm only concerned that this girl is not in tune enough for a case of this magnitude."

Girl...?

"Our readers want to know—and I'm sure the tragic victims' parents want to know—that the officers running the case are competent. If Sergeant Friend cannot even recall her most important cases—"

"Robert," Alicia said. "May I call you Robert? I joined the Force eleven years ago. I'm thirty-two. My birthday is the fifteenth of July. If you'd like to remember it, all presents are gratefully received."

Another ripple of smirks, this time on Alicia's side rather than at her expense.

"I completed a psychology degree with first class honours when I was twenty and went on to do a masters. But then, rather than do a PhD, I did another masters, this time in criminology. I specialised in serial crimes. Within two years of joining the Force, I was transferred to the Serious Crime Agency, where I have an excellent pass rate."

She cringed at the term "pass rate". Why couldn't she have said "track record?" *Damn.*

"The four crimes you're asking about are as follows: in Lincoln, two women were found dead in a house that was abandoned six months earlier. The former resident, Mr. Gunther Ramelow, used the house when here on business. He was living it up back in Germany when the *polizei* broke down his door following my analysis of sixteen crimes in cities across Europe where Mr. Ramelow had business dealings."

Robert smiled. "So the European Union's open borders allowed a serial killer to operate freely?"

Nice angle, Alicia thought. *For a newspaper that trades on fear and loathing.* She was shaking, blushing, but under the lights she hoped it blanched out. She heard Roberta's voice in her head: *Calm down, girl.*

"Second was a gun for hire. 'Bad' Johnny Makepeace liked to torture his targets—"

"Alicia," Murphy said, a hand on her arm. "I think the gentleman has enough to be going on with for now."

Robert Clancy saluted facetiously. "Thank you. But the original question stands."

Alicia took a steady sip of water. No shaking. "Two murders of similar M.O. are not enough to say this man is another Yorkshire Ripper."

"I think someone else deserves a question now," Rhapshaw said. "I see a few hands."

"Just one more," Robert said. "Then I'll leave you alone."

"Okay," Alicia said. "Shoot."

"You say 'him' all the time. How do you know it's not a woman?"

"In the last decade I can count on one hand the number of female serial killers identified. Plus it's easier to talk in terms of men. I say 'he' because 'he-slash-she' is an awful mouthful, and 'they' is grammatically incorrect."

"Do you hate men, DS Friend?"

"*That's enough!*" Rhapshaw bellowed.

Robert Clancy sat down, grinning.

The rest of the questions were mundane, mostly how long until they'd know the victim's identity, had the family been informed, what was next. No one mentioned Hayley Davenport or Katie Hague, but it was only a matter of time. Alicia dearly hoped they'd focus on the body in the pipe, at least until they *needed* public support. There was no way she was doing another one of these.

The trouble was, the next task on her to-do list was even less pleasant.

Chapter Twelve

KATIE HAGUE WAS NAKED. Warm, in a ceramic bath full of soapy water. The spotlight was on and she washed herself with what would have been, under different circumstances, jolly nice cosmetic soaps. The water was now blood as much as suds. Her inhaler worked not long ago, but it was running low. When she asked the man about it, he ignored her.

If he wanted her to remain alive, he needed to help her soon.

For now, her tears all cried out, Katie chose instead to plan. That girl, the one he called Rachel, she had him believing she loved him, truly loved him, right up until the final moments when she was about to die, when she cursed him with language more ferocious than Katie had heard before.

Now Rachel's blood floated, diluted in the bathtub.

Katie scrubbed more shampoo into her hair, all too aware of the streaks that had splattered her as that final barrage broke through Rachel's skull. She'd read somewhere, or maybe her father told her, that there were thousands of veins in the head which cool the brain, our most energy-hungry organ. That's why it bleeds so much when you hit it. And Rachel had bled. All over the floor and over Katie and over the cackling freak who, when it was all over, hosed the place down as casually as washing a car. Then he ran a bath from the same hose, added a dollop of Stress-Relief Radox. "To help you relax," he said. He told her how he was proud of her, how Rachel wasn't worthy any more.

Katie tried to lose herself in the water, but the soap and the scrubbing brush would not cleanse the blood from under her nails. They would not wipe the sticky sensation from her skin even though it appeared clean under the light.

"I think you are done," the man said. "Stand up. Get out of the tub."

Katie cared nothing about her nakedness. She deserved this. She stood, dripping beside the bath, while the man put the hose on a warm, gentle jet, rinsing her of suds and the final red smears. She remained there, hands by her side, not bothering to cover herself.

Once the hose stopped, she sensed him there, looking at her. Then a large soft towel landed in her arms.

"Please dry yourself and get dressed."

Her clothes lay on the chair, laundered, fresh-smelling. She patted herself dry over the cuts, and rubbed herself where it didn't hurt. She tried to push it all down, the memories of what happened, save it as anger and fury to be unleashed upon her captor—her *jailer*—at the right time.

Once dry, she dressed slowly, carefully, for the floor was still wet.

She could never forget today, certainly not while Rachel's blood clogged her fingernails, the coppery tang of it in her nostrils. No, she could never forget, not while the horrible thrill of killing a fellow human being still coursed like electricity through her bones.

The man stepped into the spotlight behind her, placed his

hands lovingly on her shoulders, his lips brushing the nape of her neck. He breathed words at her. "Oh, Rachel. *Rachel.* My dearest girl. You are my First now. I shall bring another Second."

Chapter Thirteen

DOYLE'S ART Emporium was a dump. Even Doyle knew it. And Sergeants Cleaver and Ball definitely knew it. But shit, Doyle didn't care what they thought. He wanted them out of there. The only reason he remained open was a client booking in half an hour, a first-timer who wanted a tattoo to impress his new girlfriend. First timers were great. They had no idea what went on in here, and Doyle could charge pretty much what he liked.

"Nice place," the one with the beard said. Sergeant *Ball*. He carried a manila file and a handheld radio.

"No it isn't," Doyle said. "But it's clean. It's hygienic. It meets minimum standard, and then some."

The Emporium was a room and a bathroom above a comic book shop, and faced a street full of mostly Asian-owned businesses; grocery, newsagents, clothing. Doyle himself didn't like Asians particularly, always jabbering about God-knows-what, but since no one wanted to live near them their proximity kept the rent cheap. He was always outwardly friendly, though, especially with Mr. Shah from whom he negotiated a discount due to the amount of Rizlas he bought in the man's shop. And he didn't *hate* them (he never considered himself an active racist), but he was uncomfortable around them.

As Ball chatted, Cleaver inspected the framed hygiene certificate awarded a little under a year ago. He perused the wall covered in designs for tattoos, photos of Doyle's work, of other people's work Doyle claimed as his own, of geeky Star Trek-style designs (the Borg symbol was one of the most popular amongst the patrons of the store below). Doyle's own body art was mostly dragons and skulls and other fantasy shit, much of it covering names of exes and rock bands that no longer appealed. Ten years ago, he swore never to do anything like that again. He now boasted two snakes with huge fangs and red eyes, one down each arm, intertwining across his spine, though in his denim waistcoat you couldn't see this right now. He'd nurtured his professional image carefully, moulded it into how he thought a tough-guy tattoo artist should look. He even grew a thick, unkempt biker-goatee.

At the sink, Cleaver fingertip-searched the freshly-cleaned needles and paint tins.

Recycling. I'm such a good boy.

Then Cleaver tried the cupboard. Locked.

"What's in here?" he asked.

"Chemicals," Doyle said. "Law says I gotta keep 'em locked up."

"An upstanding citizen. We need more like you."

"Thank you."

"Do you know a Tanya Windsor?" Ball asked.

"Nope."

Cleaver went back to the artwork wall. He pointed at a tiger picture. "You did this design for her in maybe April of last year."

Doyle burst out laughing. "April? Last *year*? You have any clue how many bints come through here in a month? Jeez, guys. Besides, how're you so sure it was me?"

"You specialise, so we hear. Mythology. This particular tiger apparently counts. You and a couple of others advertise them, but yours is the closest match online."

"You remember every person you arrested in April last year? Bet I do ten times more tattoos than you do arrests."

Ball said, "Do you keep records?"

"Nah. And even if I did you'd need a warrant to get hold of 'em. Confidential you see."

"Would it help if I told you someone's life may depend on letting us see those records?"

"It might. If I kept 'em."

Cleaver sighed and returned to inspecting the odds and ends. Doyle sat on his stool and offered Ball the reclining chair, like a dentist's, where the tattooist plied his trade. The bearded copper declined.

"So no records of any client," Ball said.

"Not that far back. Would either of you like a tattoo? Might distract from your bellies."

"You're not exactly Twiggy yourself," Cleaver said, self-consciously sucking in his gut.

"Mine's good and paid for through Tetley's. What's your excuse? I reckon you've seen your fair share of fry-ups."

Ball showed Doyle a glossy studio photo. "This is her. Does it jog any memories?"

Oh yeah, Doyle remembered this one alright. He grinned, so they'd be sure he knew her. "Sorry. Can't help."

Ball held the photo in front of him, closer. "Try harder."

"You know, the longer I stare at that picture, the more blurred it gets."

The snapshot went back in the manila file. "Sir, I don't believe you're cooperating with us. In fact, I think you're hiding something. Probably what's in that cupboard."

"Gents." Doyle stood and opened his arms like the most

innocent man alive. "I've nothing to hide. Not one thing. But my clients often want a confidential service. For what reason, I can't possibly say. But me, personally, I'm peachy. I'm pure as the driven snow. Prick me, I bleed. Insult me, I hurt. If you don't believe me, get a warrant, and I'll open my very heart if necessary."

"I think I smell marijuana," Cleaver said.

"What comes in on my clients' clothing is nothing to do with me."

"No," Ball said. "But it's enough for a warrant and then we'll see what's in that cupboard of yours."

Richard Hague arrived at Doyle's Art Emporium for his eight o'clock appointment. He sat in his car with his window down, watching the two policemen leave, listening to them discuss the uncooperative prick as they passed his car, then debate whether it was too late to pay a visit to someone called Hillary Carmichael. The large, bearded one suggested it wasn't but the less-fat one said it was. They discussed it for all of ten seconds, decided it wasn't too late, and drove away.

It had been easy to track the design once he'd located a directory on the internet. Two hours of surfing narrowed Richard's hunting ground to five possibles, but this guy's art was the closest match to what he saw in the morgue. The detectives' presence told him he was on the right lines, and their conversation about lack of cooperation suggested Richard would be ahead of them before the night was out.

Now he was full of something positive, and had been since DS Friend dropped him back home.

Glee.

That was the word. Not happiness or wonderment or relief. But *glee.* Someone else's little girl was dead, not Katie. Someone else would experience what he went through on the way to the morgue. He should feel bad, but most people felt guilt like that out of obligation. If he didn't feel that way—*gleeful*—then something would be seriously wrong.

But now wasn't the time for glee. Now was a time for business.

Once the police were gone, Richard ensured he made it quickly inside the comic book shop's side-door. He wore a cagoule and didn't want to be seen on the street with it, not on a dry evening.

Inside the studio, the man he presumed was Doyle perched on a stool, prepping a rack of needles and inks. The guy said, "Hi. Place looks like a dump, but it's clean and I'm damn good at this. Hundred quid for the design you wanted. Up front if you don't mind."

He was painted on every bit of exposed skin, keeping it from the outside world, as if it had wronged Doyle in the past and was now paying for it. Lowlife. And his customer service skills left much to be desired.

"Well?" he said. "You gonna take that thing off and let me see some skin or what?"

"You want my money first?"

"Y' got it."

"What if I don't like your work?"

"Dude, everyone likes my work. That's why I stay in business. Look at this shit." He swept his arm toward a wall of pictures. "This is what I *do*. Now I've stayed open an hour longer than normal cos you phoned so late, and as a consequence I hadda put up with a visit from the pigs. I did that for *you* cos you sounded like you *really* wanted this tattoo. Must be a special lady. So I figure, hey, why not. But you're still a first-timer, mate, and first-timers often get one touch of the needle and they're up and out the door. When they bolt, I don't see one penny."

Richard assessed the man in silence. What Richard saw behind the tattooist's eyes, aside from the prospect of ripping off a genuine customer, was bravado. It would be no problem.

"I'll have to take this off to get my wallet," Richard said, removing the cag. Beneath he was wearing a black wool mix sweater and jeans. He also wore a tool belt. "Just a moment," he said, and moved behind Doyle to hang his waterproof on a chair.

Doyle followed Richard's movements, his buttocks lifting only slightly, too lazy to shift his whole body.

From the tool belt, Richard removed an ice pick and jammed it into Doyle's right-side deltoid muscle, cutting through the flesh two inches back from the collarbone. At first, Doyle tried to scream, but the pain would have been too much to vocalise.

This area is a pressure point. If you sneak up behind someone and knobble your knuckle hard into that area, your victim will fall to his knees no matter how big and strong he is, so an ice pick slicing into it is too much for most.

It was too much for Doyle. He fainted.

Because it's mostly muscle, there is a minimum of blood-letting, so Richard could patch it up after donning surgical gloves and locating a towel and some packing tape. It would still be agony once Doyle awoke.

After locking the door and closing the blind, Richard stripped the man to his boxer shorts by slicing his clothes with a straight razor, laid him on his chair, secured his hands to the chair arms with plastic cable ties, and bound his feet together with packing tape.

Then Richard shoved a balled up rag in Doyle's mouth and administered smelling salts.

Muffled, Doyle screamed himself awake. His head lolled to one side, toward the wound, his wrists pulling at the plastic ties, his left hand naturally stronger than the damaged right side.

Soon, Doyle worked out that pulling with his right hand extenuated the pain, so he ceased, transferring his efforts to his left. The secure-a-tie bit into his wrist and blood seeped around it.

Richard watched all this from Doyle's own stool, wondering how much longer it would be until this man would be able to help him.

A kettle beckoned. A cup of tea would hit the spot right about now. But would that be too depraved?

Richard had wondered throughout his life what really counted as depravity, how far you had to go to become a total monster. He didn't categorise himself into groups like Peter Sutcliffe, the Yorkshire Ripper; *he* wasn't insane.

Doyle fell motionless. His muffled cries were replaced by heavy breathing. As he stopped panicking, he eased the gag out of his mouth using his tongue. His voice had taken on a higher pitch.

"What do you want?" he said. "The shit's under the sink. Key's taped under the stool. There. Where you're sat."

Richard said nothing. Let the man talk.

"I'm sorry if I'm on someone's patch, but I been doing this for years. No one's bothered me before. I stick to my regulars. If it's a cut you want, fine, but it ain't much, I can tell you."

"What do you think I want?" Richard asked.

"The weed. Don't you?"

Richard smiled sadly. "Sorry. Not quite." He showed a set of wire cutters, each blade an inch long. He clicked them together like scissors.

"Wait. *Wait!* What you gonna do? *Ack—*" His pulse must have quickened, meaning more blood flow, meaning the wound hurt even more.

Richard lifted Doyle's bound legs and positioned the cutters behind his left knee.

"Please. What are you doing? What do you *want*?"

"I'm going to hamstring you," Richard said. "Watch."

He gouged the points in the skin either side of Doyle's hamstring, that ropy bit that runs behind the knee. Although Doyle's first reaction was to struggle, he soon froze. The blades pressed, fine points of blood spotting the tool, Richard ready to snip away Doyle's ability to walk.

"I'll do *anything*," Doyle said. "Anything at all."

Richard pretended to think. "Okay." Allowing the legs to fall, he stood over Doyle. "Remember the last time you stood up? Tell me about it."

"What kind of question is that? I went to the cupboard to get the inks."

"See? This is upright." He waved the clippers in Doyle's face. "If for one second I think you are screwing with me, walking back and forth from the cupboard will be your last memory of moving like a normal human being. Do you want that?"

"No, man, no. I'll do it. Whatever you want."

"Where are your teabags?"

"My what? What sort of crazy wanker *are* you? You want *tea*?"

Richard slammed a fist into Doyle's groin. The bound man tried to double over, but could not. With the effort his shoulder wound tore and he screamed again, forcing Richard to reapply the gag. His legs drew up to comfort the dull burning in his balls.

While Doyle calmed down, Richard made a cuppa.

Back to square one, and Richard took away the gag. Doyle's feet returned to their position though his thighs were closer together. Richard sipped his tea, *snip-snipp*ed the pincers together and said, "Okay. Now let's talk about what those policemen wanted."

Doyle stared at the pincers. "They wanted a girl."

"With a tattoo. The tiger. Royal Bengal, I believe."

"Yeah. That's right. From her shoulder down her upper arm. Some symbolic shit, I dunno."

"The tiger is subject to many myths. According to the link on your website, this particular design is usually accompanied by a counterpart, a mate. To me, that implies she was not alone. Am I correct?"

Doyle nodded. "Paki. Posh bird had a Paki boyfriend."

Richard abhorred racism. He knew Doyle was not going to live past the next half-hour, but things like this drew the matter out. "Tell me everything."

And Doyle spoke. He blathered. He used the word "Paki" too often, but eventually directed Richard to his records, under the sink near his chemicals and massive marijuana stash. The handwritten ledgers and receipts stretched all the way back six years, though it was clear he was using the tattoo business to cover his drug dealing. Richard found the name he was looking for and noted it. Also, the credit card number the guy had paid with.

"Okay," Richard said. "Now, you haven't missed anything, have you? No memory lapses, no lying by omission?"

"No." He shook his head as far as it would go without pain jolting through him.

Richard stuffed the rag back in Doyle's mouth and gouged the pincers back in the crook of his knee. He pushed harder this time, blades caressing the hamstring, scraping; Doyle's legs frozen in place, his eyes bulging, pleading with Richard, *no, no, don't do it.*

Richard set down the man's legs and placed the tool back in his belt. This torture business was giving him no real pleasure, and it was no longer necessary to achieving his target.

He washed up the cup and put his cagoule back on. Then he removed Doyle's rag, ignored the thanking and the *you-won't-regret-this*-ing, and reached into the back of his belt. He swished out the Navy SEAL blade, and sliced through Doyle's windpipe and flesh with little resistance. The helpful blood groove in the blade filtered off the majority of mess, although some of it squirted through the air, as usual.

Richard took one of the bags of marijuana and stuffed it in Doyle's throat, gaping like some comedy second mouth.

He pocketed the other three bags, all about the size of a packet of crisps, and headed for the door. He turned one last time to survey the scene. He left the ledger in the cupboard for the police to find. No sense in hanging a lantern on it through its absence.

Overall, it worked out better than Richard hoped. Mr. Doyle had now been caught up in a drugs war.

Chapter Fourteen

WHITELOCKS IS the oldest pub in Leeds. It is located up a small alleyway you might miss unless you were looking for it, a narrow establishment with a high bar and earthy traditional ales in thick-handled glasses. Bustling when Alicia arrived, it was loud with men's voices, not one under fifty, few without a cigarette, albeit unlit. The craze for e-cigs had not yet penetrated the masculine veneer of this particular establishment.

Alicia and Murphy chose not to face the police bar, not after the way the press conference played out. They were on their way here when Cleaver and Ball filled them in on the emporium, so they postponed the drinks and worked quickly on a warrant—a slam-dunk now a society girl was dead. With the paper in her pocket, Alicia was now on her second scotch and Murphy sipped what Alicia bought him when he said he didn't care what he got, as long as it was wet and alcoholic: *Murphy's*. Alicia thought it would lighten her mood.

Murphy drinking Murphy's.

Ball and Cleaver bustled in, loosening their ties simultaneously. Cleaver sat while Ball ordered two pints of Theakston's Best.

Cleaver didn't wait for Ball to join them. "Hillary Carmichael. Twenty-three. Married to Henry Carmichael for a year. They live at—"

"Come on, Sergeant," Alicia said. "Get to the juicy stuff. The tattoo. The mystery man." It would have been more useful for Alicia to conduct the chat with Hillary herself. She hated third-hand information. But the warrant took priority.

Cleaver sighed and flicked a couple of pages. "Hillary had seen the tattoo. She omitted it from her initial statement because it might have gotten Tanya in trouble with her uncle."

"Makes sense," Murphy said, sipping his Murphy's.

"She claims to have confided this in DCI Wellington, once the disappearance was considered suspicious."

"Any mention of a lover?"

"Yes."

This was it. This was what they needed. Sudden momentum. By way of a toast, Alicia necked the last of her scotch.

Ball placed the drinks on the table, spilling a little, and sat heavily on the leather couch.

Cleaver took a long drag on his pint, put a cigarette in his mouth, and continued. "Hillary confronted Tanya on the day of the barbecue and Tanya confirmed she *was* seeing someone. Also hinted her family would never accept the bloke."

"Who?" Murphy asked. "Any idea why?"

"Only that Tanya liked to slum it. She was applying to university, to go into halls of residence rather than buying a flat. Somethin' else her uncle didn't approve of."

Ball picked up the, um … *ball*. "When Tanya holidayed she didn't go for the five-star deals—preferred to strap on a back-pack and head off somewhere a bit different. Hillary couldn't understand her. Then the tattoo business." Ball caught himself in mouthful of beer.

Cleaver took over again. "There was a story behind it. An old

Indian myth. Something to do with a Royal tiger, a Bengal, falling in love with a white tiger. Not a good thing for tigers."

"So we're looking for an Asian man with a white tiger tattooed on his arm," Alicia said.

Cleaver said, "She didn't mention the man having one."

Alicia's mind, her mini-computer, ticked over, generated a whole host of theories. The simplest were always worth exploring first.

She said, "But something happens. Either Tanya changes her mind or he does. It gets unpleasant and..." Her computer crashed. This made no sense. If university was her plan, why change it to run? "Did she mention running away to Hillary?"

"She told Hillary she'd soon be free of her uncle," Ball said. "She'd miss her cousin though."

"That could have referred to her university plan. Of course she'd miss little Jimmy."

"Wonder why Wellington never got this far," Murphy said.

"He did," Cleaver said. "Hillary went to him one night, but made him promise not to put it in the file unless it became relevant. She told him everything she'd missed out from when she thought Tanya was still alive."

Wellington knew. Wow.

Alicia asked, "How did she react when you told her Tanya was only killed today?"

"We didn't," Cleaver said. "I thought we were waiting for confirmation."

Good. Alicia wanted to make time to see Hillary's reaction herself. As well as Henry Windsor, she planned on volunteering to break the news to Hillary too. As soon as the positive ID came in.

Murphy told Ball and Cleaver their leads were solid, gave them the pats on their backs they apparently needed, and Alicia passed them the warrant and said they should take a locksmith to the emporium in case they couldn't get hold of Doyle himself. When they were gone, Murphy finished his Murphy's but Alicia left her drink. The drive back home to Wakefield beckoned. Before that, though, she had one stop to make, the one she had been dreading since before the press conference.

The lights were still on in Richard Hague's house. Alicia could see him moving around inside. She was aware of the alcohol in her system. Also that she shouldn't really be driving. Only a smidge over the limit, but still. Without the family liaison officer present, she felt compelled to keep him up to date, to do so herself.

In person.

Just as she felt compelled to inform Tanya's next of kin once forensics gave her the go-ahead.

In the street, she hugged her suit jacket around her. She should dig her coat out of the boot, but it was bulky and made her look even younger, like a girl trying on mummy's clothes. She rang the bell.

Mr. Hague's silhouette bloomed in the frosted glass before the door opened. He wore a fresh-smelling t-shirt and corduroy beige trousers, Snoopy slippers and a wedding ring that Alicia was sure wasn't there last night.

"What is it?" he said. "What's happened?"

"Nothing," Alicia replied quickly. "We've heard nothing more. May I come in?"

He nervously led the way to his living room, sat her on the couch and muted the telly. Adverts were playing but he'd been watching the National Geographic channel.

"Tea?" he said.

"Please."

He went to the kitchen and Alicia heard the tap run and the

kettle begin to boil. On the coffee table, a framed photo of Katie faced the most recently-vacated chair.

She should have known better than to assume a body's ID. Especially one as badly treated as this one. If he hadn't been so brave, so desperate to see the body, Mr. Hague would have been grieving for twelve hours instead of the thirty minutes to the morgue.

"Here you go."

The tea steamed in a Tom and Jerry mug, Tom being smacked in the face with a teapot strapped to a mallet. Mr. Hague sat beside her, stress wrinkling his face, expectant.

"I meant it, Mr. Hague, it isn't bad news. There's no news."

He relaxed slightly. "Okay. Then ... don't get me wrong, but why are you here?"

Alicia was glad for the mug in her hands. She was as nervous as at the press conference. "I wanted to apologise again, Mr. Hague—"

"Okay, before we go on, I need you to stop apologising. I'm not going to sue, and I don't hold you responsible. I'm her *father*, and even *I* didn't recognise her."

Alicia sipped her tea. It tasted funny. Probably the two whiskeys. "Mr. Hague—"

"And call me Richard. After what we've both been through today I think we're on first name terms."

"Both? You thought your *daughter* was *dead*."

"And you got screwed on national telly."

Her cheeks warmed. "I wanted to curl into a ball and bounce right on out of there."

"Off that guy's face, you mean. He made you out to be a right numpty." He placed his hand on Alicia's shoulder, held her eye, deadpan serious. "If you want me to, I'll kill him for you."

She gave a little laugh, unsure how much mirth was polite. She must've looked like a beetroot with blonde hair.

"Don't worry about it," Richard said. "They're trying to label you a bimbo or something. But I know you aren't."

"Thanks." Alicia removed Richard's hand from her shoulder, holding it a moment, his skin somehow tough and soft at the same time.

They both sat back, allowed the soft couch to plump up around them. It was nice, nicer than Alicia's. They weren't physically tiring, days like these, but it had started at seven this morning and finished after eight p.m. Although it was never really finished. At any minute, she could be on her way to examine another dead girl with dark hair.

Alicia said, "There should be more people on this."

"The press release didn't mention Katie."

"We decided going public would endanger her. We can't hide the killings, not when they're so similar, but we can postpone the full announcement. Which presents a vicious circle; unless we go public we can't increase the payroll."

"Politics."

"And money."

Richard shook his head, lips tight, about to speak, but thought better of it. "Can you talk to me about leads, how you're going about it?"

She shouldn't, but after what she'd put Richard through she figured it'd be okay. "The girl is Tanya Windsor. Not confirmed, meaning we haven't told her guardian yet, so keep it under your hat."

He lifted an imaginary hat and replaced it.

It made Alicia smile. "She's been missing for over eighteen months."

Richard frowned. "He's held her all that time?"

"Sure. Which bodes well for Katie." She felt cheap saying this, pouncing on the spindly thread of hope that was only just repairing itself. "She was blonde when she was taken, during a society event, but she'd been gone so long she was back to brown." She revealed sparse details about the tiger tattoo, emphasising the idea that there may be a break tonight.

"Doyle's?" Richard said. "Sounds awful."

He carried his and Alicia's empty mugs through to the kitchen, ran a tap, and returned with two glasses of water.

"How'd you know I needed water?" Alicia asked.

"Salesman's hunch," he said. "Is there anything else you can tell me?"

"We have to go see Tanya's uncle, give him the bad news."

"He's a suspect?"

"No. His alibi's airtight. Locked up, key thrown. Son too. In fact, all her acquaintances are in the clear." She decided to omit the prospect of the lover. "I still think the killer knew Tanya personally. Not necessarily the other girls, but definitely Tanya."

"And if it does come out, the full story?"

"Unless we control the flow, it'll skip and jump and be all-singing, all-dancing circus. Motivate the guy to show off, make mistakes, take more girls, or..."

"It's okay, you can say it: or he'll panic, kill Katie, and disappear."

"Yes. If he's angry, playing out a fantasy, he'll panic, kill, then hide until he can't control himself. If he's a control freak, he'll carry on. I think he's the latter."

Alicia watched the framed picture. From where Richard sat now, its back was to him. She moved it so it faced the couch.

"Sorry," he said. "I don't know why I keep that there. Looking at me while I watch telly."

"What were you watching?"

"You won't believe this, but something about tigers."

"Really?"

"I noticed it was on as I was hopping about."

Alicia giggled. She had an image of him bouncing on one foot, remote control flailing.

"The *telly*." He prodded her, playfully. "It reminded me, that's all."

"Well it's our best lead so far."

They watched the silent TV. Monkeys yelled nothing at each other, swung from branch to branch, taunting a bigger ape, the ape ignoring them as they buzzed about him. Eventually, the big one's patience wore thin and he swatted a smaller one, and the pack legged it back into the trees.

"So how are you?" Alicia asked. "Really, Richard, how are you? Most folk have a friend or something around at times like this. Family."

"I have no family," Richard said, "and all Katie's friends are together. They call me, but they don't want to be here. As far as they're concerned, she vanished and they don't know where she is. I told them she'd probably run away with some guy, that clothes and condoms were missing."

Alicia's turn to prod back. "You know they'll report back to whatshisname. Katie's boyfriend."

"Brian," Richard said. "I know. I'm evil."

She liked that he had a sense of humour even now. A gallows humour admittedly, but it meant he was not cracking under the strain. Not yet.

"But I'm okay," he said. "Really. I even spoke to Brian. Briefly. Figured I could be civil to him, at least for a while."

"When he and Katie are sat around the table, in full meeting-the-parents mode?"

"I'll be extremely evil to him." He made a "snip-snip" gesture with his fingers. "You went through all that I take it?"

"It's easier for boys. Bring a pretty girl home and *bam*, your dad's the proudest alive."

"Bet you made a few fathers proud of their sons in your time."

Alicia couldn't remember not smiling since she arrived here tonight. Now it seemed to widen. "You smoothie."

"Nah. Just honest. You've got what my mother would have called a button nose."

"I always wondered about that phrase."

"As in 'cute as a button.' It brings out the eyes somehow, makes them seem wider without making you look like a frog. And blue eyes and blonde hair ... it's a winner."

"Oh, stop it, you."

Oh, stop it, you.

She may as well have slapped his hand and giggled. Things were verging on inappropriate. Well, "verging" might be the wrong word; "plummeting toward" inappropriate was more like it.

She said, "You'll have me believing you soon, and we can't have that."

"I don't see why not."

He shaved this morning, she noted, but the shadow was bristling through. When he smiled it was more obvious, fine lines moving the angles of tiny black hairs. She was closer to him than before. Did his position change without her realising? Or was it when he came back with the water? "I should go."

He said, "You don't have to."

Alicia couldn't read this any other way. When they first met, those initial blushes, the daft *what-a-pretty-name* non-chat-up line, the information and his body language all processed quickly, spontaneously. The computer was tired now, running low on batteries. Here was a full-blown come-on and she wasn't sure she'd hold out much longer.

She wasn't sure she wanted to.

Her phone rang.

Both sat up stiff and straight, and Alicia answered, "Yes. I mean, hello. DS Friend."

She listened weightlessly to Sergeant Ball describe the scene at Doyle's Art Emporium. In the background, Cleaver spoke to Murphy on the corresponding call, and she tried to grasp exactly what was happening to this case. It was too much of a coincidence—a dead link in the chain when they were so close to a new avenue.

"Is there anything I can do?"

"You deserve some kip now, love. We'll wake you if we need to move quickly."

Alicia thanked him and hung up. Still a tad dazed, she told Richard what had happened. With a final platonic pat of his arm, Alicia exited the property—"exited"; very professional—and made her way to the car, bipped the alarm off, and turned to watch Richard close the door to his empty home. The lights in the house turned off. The windows blackened. Then the garden lights also fell dark.

Alicia returned behind the wheel and drove the hour back into Wakefield, fidgeting her legs to get comfortable all the way, hoping desperately that Robbie was still awake.

Chapter Fifteen

--WHAT YOU DOING HERE?

--Why shouldn't I be here? It's my wife.

--Alfie, you're on leave. Let us investigate.

--I've found something. On ViCAP. Might be worth getting Behavioural involved.

--Okay, quick. If Turner catches you in work, you're deader than mullets.

--Stacy was killed with a goddamn knitting needle, right? Through the heart?

--Single entry. By the looks of it, she disturbs a burglar and he takes the first thing to hand. NYPD are all over their snitches. Some street punk'll blab. Plus our forensics. We'll get him.

--That's just it. You won't. See?

--A list of unsolveds, Alfie. What are you seeing that I'm not?

--It's a pattern. Look. Portland, Pocatello, Jamestown, Minneapolis, Chicago, Springfield. He's moving west to east. There's more...

--Who? Who's moving west to east?

--Him! The guy who killed Stacy. He's a drifter or something.

He's killed people, more than one, in each state west of New York.

--*There are fifty fatal stabbings every day in L.A. Hell, there were probably ten in New York this afternoon.*

--But the *way* he does it. Perfect, direct, in and out. Dead.

--*Buddy, I honestly don't see it. I'm sorry, you know I am. I liked Stacy, liked her a lot, and I want to catch this piece of crap so bad it hurts. But you gotta calm down. Stay at home. Say goodbye properly. We'll find him. I promise.*

"Sir?"

--There's more to this. And I'll prove it. This isn't some kid jacked up on meth.

"Sir?"

--*Go home, Alfie. We'll talk later...*

"*Sir!*"

Alfie woke with a limey stewardess shaking him.

"Sir, we're landing in a few minutes. You have to put on your seatbelt."

Alfie grumbled something even he didn't catch, fastened the seatbelt, and tried to go back to sleep, but the pressure in his ears kicked in. It hurt, really hurt. Time spent in the air, chasing leads, chasing ghosts, landing in one state to liaise with an agent in charge about a specific case, changing it to something else, always the same thing. Sixteen years of the same thing: too much travel, too much flying, too much pressure.

He shoved his thumbs in his ears, forcing the pressure out. Equalising by holding his nose and blowing only made it worse. It hurt like holy hell and he couldn't wait to be down.

--She lay there for two hours. Two hours!

--*I know.*

--He probably watched her. Saw the life pouring out of her eyes.

--*I doubt it, Alfie, he more than likely ran...*

--No. No, he didn't run. He's still out there. I *will* find him. And when I do—

The plane touched down. Alfie's ears felt full of slime and everything sounded tinny and distant. It would last around three hours.

The airport was the size of Alfie's bathroom and at this time in the morning it was close to empty. He collected his bag and headed for the Starbucks near the exit where he ordered a mocha and a muffin, and paid with dollars, much to the barista's annoyance.

Alfie missed the States already. The portions on the plane were for shit, and the shops in the airport lounge were closed. Thank God for Starbucks. They littered England as they did America, and although he never drank in them back home, here they served as a security blanket—a taste of America in a pissy little country full of assholes.

"Alfie Rhee?"

Alfie turned to find a ginger-haired man of about fifty. Leather jacket, blue jeans. "Red McCall?"

"The one and only."

They shook hands and Alfie gathered his things, leaving the overpriced mocha half-drunk.

"And the van?" Alfie asked.

"A' course. Fitted out like you asked. Did a ton of improv work in the Royal Marines. One time in Bosnia, we needed a bar setting up pronto, so I stepped up. Had the best damn bar in that shitty place. Another time..."

"What does this have to do with the van?"

"Nothing."

They crossed the parking lot, wind like icy sandpaper in his eyes. At least it wasn't raining. Alfie heard it rained a lot here.

In McCall's transit van, the Brit cranked the heat up full and Alfie asked if he could turn it down.

"Sorry," McCall said. "I've got poor circulation. My toes drop off if I get too cold."

"Pardon?" Alfie's ears were still dull and echoing. "What?"

"I said my toes might fall off."

"Thought you was in the army."

"Marines. Why do you think I got booted out?"

Alfie wound down the window a crack. Now his head froze while his body sweated. Plus he could hear even less. He decided it'd be better to sweat all over, and closed the window.

"So you read about our little double murder," McCall said. "You think it's the guy you've been chasing?"

"I can't say too much at this stage." Alfie sounded like an FBI agent again.

He found Red McCall through a simple web search, and told him that he'd worked with the FBI before and was consulting on this case. Red thought he was some sort of crime guru. Alfie hadn't lied exactly, but the truth was that even his P.I. license formally expired earlier this year.

He said, "Get me the information you said you can and I'll share everything with you."

"You have what I told you to bring?"

"This van is kitted out *exactly* like I said, right? And you got the other item too?"

"Yes, and yes. And I'm out of pocket at the minute. You bring what I want?"

"Soon as you show me the other item."

"Glove box."

Alfie opened the glove box and removed the rag-wrapped bundle, weighed it in his hand. "Heavy."

"Yeah, it's an old one, but it'll fire okay, if ya need it to. Now, one more time. You got what I asked for?"

Alfie replaced the bundle without checking it. "I had five thousand, two hundred and nineteen dollars in savings. I pulled it out and changed it to sterling. After the handling fee, that's about three and a half grand."

"We said four."

"I can pull the rest on my Visa. Chill out, man. It's covered."

"I negotiated her down from five-K. Plus my commission, of course."

"Sure. Visa'll cover that too."

Man, when did the Brits get so greedy?

Red asked, "You wanna go straight to the hotel? I know a strip club open all night. Great girls. None of them grannies all trussed up like past-sell-by-date turkeys. Well, maybe a one or two."

Alfie caught the words, "hotel", "strip club", "grannies", and "turkey".

He said, "The hotel's fine."

"You know what I never could get about the Yanks?"

Alfie didn't care. He just wanted sleep.

"The way you all talk funny. I mean what happened there?"

"We kicked your asses out and started the greatest democracy on Earth. Land of the free, home of the brave. Britannia might rule the waves, but in our own land, we're the friggin' daddy."

For some reason, McCall laughed. "Typical bloody Yank."

Alfie didn't bother to argue. If a man who loved his own country could be considered "typical", then he was more than happy to be "a typical Yank." Roll on the hotel, roll on morning, and roll on skint cop who needs the money for who cares what.

Chapter Sixteen

THE MORNING BROUGHT FABULOUS SUNSHINE, the sort a person might associate with childhood, school holidays and more romantic times. But few saw the sun in its full glory this morning due to the thick mist that enveloped Yorkshire; from the Vale of York down to West Bretton, right out to the Owlcotes Shopping Centre, then as far north as Mother Shipton's Cave in Knaresborough. But a short distance from the cave where the benevolent witch known as Mother Shipton used to reside, where people still hang ornaments and cuddly toys in the hope they'll turn to stone, the mist was thinner.

A sprawling house was only just visible from high up on a ridge; no fog up here. It merely swirled about the lower ground. The whole house was not visible, although its shape was hinted at through the trees. Bushes and hedgerow lined the side of the property, so the average person driving by would barely notice it.

But if you were sitting in a Ford Focus, and if you were looking for Henry Windsor's residence, then it would be perfectly natural to park up and watch the great house for a few minutes. You'd be forgiven if you felt a touch uneasy, as Alicia

Friend did. And you could even be forgiven if you mentioned to your partner that it looked, maybe, a little haunted.

Your partner would definitely be forgiven for rolling his eyes.

Likewise, it would also be understandable to not notice the phone ringing at first.

Murphy was behind the wheel so Alicia answered.

"Looks like he was hiding more than a couple of grams," Ball said, his voice breaking up due to the poor cellphone coverage here. In the valley it would likely die entirely. "A kilo of Mary Jane stuffed in his throat wound. Reckon we can safely say he was a dealer."

So it *sounded* drugs-related. It was the most logical thing. But the timing of it...

Alicia said, "Do you think your presence could've tipped off Doyle's supplier?"

"That's what I thought. Cleaver's finished looking through the man's books. Seems he did some bloody expensive artwork. Strangely, each session cost about the same as a gram of weed."

"Weird."

Murphy said, "What's weird?"

Ball went on. "Anyway, the books are pretty complete. If it came to court, he'd ace the taxman. Every transaction for the last six years."

She said, "Never thought I'd be thanking heaven for VAT."

Murphy frowned. He mouthed, "What's happening?"

"I have to go," Alicia said. "Keep us up to date. Won't you, love?"

He said he would and hung up. Alicia paraphrased the other half of the conversation.

"It's no coincidence," Murphy agreed. "Tanya turns up dead, and our one link to the elusive boyfriend is killed. Someone's covering his tracks."

He started the engine and pulled out into the road, tyres crunching over frozen grass.

They turned into the Windsors' grounds and passed through a corridor of pine trees and other winter greenery, parking at the top of the gravel driveway. The weeds were obvious; breeding, hidden, but living beneath the façade of a well-maintained road. Being winter, they were dying, but in summer it'd be a green adventure.

When they stepped out, Alicia checked her phone: yup, no service. Alicia wore her coat this time. Murphy buttoned his jacket, the dark blue one again.

The house itself looked Tudor but with a grander feel, the corners shaped almost like turrets, the stone grey. The newest-looking addition was the door, a thick wooden double structure with iron rivets that Alicia assumed were purely decorative. She'd phoned ahead from the top of the hill, so the man answering the door wasn't overly shocked to be presented with police identification.

Operating a manual wheelchair with ease and dexterity, he was a wide chap with a weathered face. *Lived-in*, her mother would've said. He was dressed in a black three-piece suit with the shiniest of shiny shoes.

"Mr. Windsor is expecting you," he said in a spooky Adams Family tone.

Alicia's haunted feeling returned.

The greeter expertly spun one wheel and Alicia and Murphy followed him into a cavern of an anteroom, doors left and right and a staircase ahead with a long corridor alongside. A twelve-foot Christmas tree towered, clinically decorated by some service or another, and dozens of greetings cards claimed pride-of-place on the wall leading upstairs.

The man gestured to a door on the left. "He is waiting for you."

"In there?" Alicia said. "That's not going to be a lab or something is it? With test tubes and lightning and stuff?"

"I don't believe so, ma'am." The doorman or butler or whatever he was appeared fat through lack of activity, but seemed able enough. He held his arm in place, eyes stern and deeply unhumorous.

The detectives entered the room, a study as it turned out—disappointingly absent of test tubes and lightning or, indeed, any hint of Christmas—and were greeted by a man who couldn't be more friendly.

"Henry Windsor," he said, shaking their hands.

He exuded the image of a pure country-set gent, right down to the flowing handlebar moustache and tweed jacket, yet sounded too posh to be genuinely posh.

"Can we sit down, Mr. Windsor?" Murphy asked.

"Of course. We shan't be disturbed. James is away on holiday and Lawrence has his duties."

"Lawrence? He's your...?"

"Butler. It's a bit old-fashioned, but Lawrence likes the title, he likes the work. Not many jobs for cripples, not that get you room and board in quite such luxury anyway. No below-stairs accommodation here, thank you. Lawrence gets a main bedroom—en-suite of course—a physio visit twice a week, and since my needs are few these days he gets plenty of spare time."

Alicia detected a faint whiff of class-embarrassment. Not uncommon with people like this, eager to justify their existence to the lower rungs of humanity; their charity work, job creation, or treating their minions fairly, as if those things were extraordinary instead of basically decent.

Henry Windsor directed them to a leather sofa against the wall. An open fireplace gaped, spacious enough for Alicia to walk inside, turn around, and do some star jumps without getting a speck of soot on her; a great desk—probably antique—faced the window, and a dark wood-and-glass coffee table served the sofa itself. Windsor opted for a large leather chair, darker than the sofa, highlighting himself against the floor-to-ceiling window, a tall yucca plant to his right.

Alicia found it hard not to smile at psychological tricks the yuppies ceased using in the 80s. She really hoped he wasn't trying to intimidate a pair of police officers, no matter how bad their tidings may be.

"Mr. Windsor," Murphy said, "I'll come right out with it. I'm sorry to tell you, but Tanya's body was discovered yesterday."

Windsor nodded, stroking his 'tache down, allowing it to spring back up. He crossed his legs. "I see."

"Yes. I am sorry, sir."

"Well, it's a crumb of comfort I suppose. We all assumed she was dead soon after she disappeared. At least now we'll be able to bury her properly."

"Sir." Murphy stood taller. Coughed once. "Sir, I need to explain something. And we understand this will be extremely difficult to hear, especially after the investigation wound up some time ago." A breath for courage. "Tanya was only killed yesterday."

Mr. Windsor fixed Murphy with a stare. Alicia and Murphy already agreed he should do the talking, that Henry Windsor would respond better to Murphy. Alicia would only step in if they were wrong. Now wasn't the time.

See how he acts, observe.

Henry Windsor teetered, anger in his face. Then, simply, he collapsed. Doubled over, head in his hands, cheeks flushing red, his whole head glowing beneath thinning hair. He shook once, before sitting upright.

He wiped a tear. "All this time..."

"We don't know for sure exactly what happened," Murphy said.

"Where was she living? I know she had the old class-tourism bug, but surely she could not have hidden for so long."

"We don't believe so, Mr. Windsor." Murphy inhaled, puffing out his chest, his next words slow and deliberate. "We believe she has been held captive for most of that period. She was killed only recently."

"How can that *be*?" Henry Windsor's mouth hung open, fleshy jowls shaking. Either he was the world's best actor or this was news to him.

"I mean what sort of person...?"

"The sort of person who has killed two others that we know of," Murphy said. "He is holding a third."

Mr. Windsor stood and posed regally next to the fireplace. Coughed once. "If there's anything I can do—anything at all—you name it."

"Well, sir," Alicia said, also standing. "You can be one hundred percent honest about everything we ask."

The three of them gathered in the cold outside. The ground mist held firm and beaded the foliage with moisture. Cold soaked into Alicia's face, although her body was toasty warm in her thick coat. The monument to Tanya Windsor was a small but beautiful white headstone, as high as Alicia's hip, bearing the inscription: *Tanya, beloved daughter, niece, and cousin. Wherever you are, rest in peace.* It stood in a clearing beside Paula Windsor's grave—Henry's wife—as well as three generations of Windsors.

"Your setup, sir," Murphy said. "Can you tell me about it? Here. This house."

"There's only myself and Lawrence in residence permanent-ly," Windsor replied. "He cooks well enough, although I used to have a live-in chef too. No need anymore, although I hire him back for special occasions, entertaining, that sort of thing. An accountant of course, plus a regular gardener. I'll forward you their details as soon as I can."

"How many rooms?"

"Eight bedrooms, two studies, a large kitchen, a second one —we use the smaller one unless I'm entertaining, which is rare —two dining rooms, a drawing room, and my library."

"No cellar?"

"No. Well, yes, but it's now a garage. My hobby. Classic cars. Access is from the rear. Would you like to see?"

"I don't think that's necessary."

Alicia said, "Are the cars all, like, *really* old?"

"Some are, yes. I have an E-type. An original."

"Excellent. Come on Murphy, let's look at the cars."

With a subdued "harrumph" from Murphy they walked around the house. It was bigger than anyone needed, would probably cater for ten poor families. Most of the trees had shed their leaves, but evergreen bushes filled out the land. Beyond them, pines lined up symmetrically, a man-made woodland that sparkled with frost and shimmered in the foggy sunlight.

"Sir," Murphy said as they walked. "Tanya disappeared during James's birthday?"

"Yes."

"That must have been hard on him."

"He took it badly, yes. He was sad that Tanya planned to go on tour with the lower classes, but he understood why. He worried terribly about her when she went on those jaunts. 'Backpacking', I think they call it. She had more money than most of the countries she visited but preferred to camp down on the floors of rug merchants."

"The 'class tourism' you mentioned earlier."

"Yes. Something of a fad. A lot of well-off youngsters do it.

You saw young Harry not long ago rounding up kangaroos in Australia. It's common these days."

"*Prince* Harry?" Alicia said. "You know him?"

"I met him once, yes. When he was a toddler, mind. Mother was a charming woman. A little flaky, though, not really queen material. Sad end."

"Sir," Murphy said. "Your son, he's not here? You mentioned a holiday."

"Ah, no." Windsor practically chuckled, as if the question were absurd. "When it was clear Tanya wasn't coming back, James took off. He's out on his mission: giving away Tanya's money. He visits all the places she did, you see, hands out money to the people who were kind to her."

"James has Tanya's money?" Alicia said.

"Of course. After so long missing, Tanya was declared officially dead. You didn't think she'd leave it to evil Uncle Henry did you?"

They stopped beside a steel door, two of them, actually, the size of garage doors on an average house. Windsor lifted a plastic flap built into the brickwork and inserted a key, turned it, and the door rose into a thick metal roll. A huge elevator gradually revealed itself.

Over the noise of the mechanism, Henry said, "The last I heard, he was in Bangalore, looking for a man who let Tanya sleep on his settee for two nights in return for her babysitting his kids. He was a local politician or some such thing. Whatever they have out there instead of normal government."

This man is getting more ridiculous with each and every sentence.

Alicia had seen it throughout university, throughout her life, people with an image of themselves, desperate to impose that image upon everyone. Including themselves. She said, "I think they have politicians, sir."

"Well, I suppose they have to have something. But yes, he

wants to buy the family a nice home. Two or three thousand should suffice he thinks."

"How come?" Murphy said.

"How come what?"

"How come James got the money?"

"Oh, that. He was the heir. She hated me for some reason, but James she treated like a younger brother. Made a will aged eighteen, as soon as her trust fund matured."

The lift was surprisingly quiet as it descended. Clean, solid. They emerged into what looked like a swish car showroom. Alicia whistled her appreciation. It stretched into a dimness that brightened as strip lights flickered on one by one. There were at least a dozen vehicles.

"Financially, the cold war was good for my family," Windsor said. "We had a little warren built down here in 1962 as the Cuban crisis loomed. I was young then, but it had everything— servants' quarters, kitchen, bathrooms, even a room for radios and TVs, for news of how any war was going. Naturally, as things eased in the eighties, the place wasn't really maintained."

Alicia ran her hand across the side of an old, long Ford.

"Please don't do that," Windsor said. "Lawrence will have to clean it again otherwise."

"Lawrence?" Alicia said. "He cleans all these?"

"Yes. Don't let the wheelchair fool you—he's an extremely dedicated butler."

"I didn't think butlers existed anymore. Figured they only worked for the queen herself and even then it looks like a tourist thing."

"They are not dinosaurs, my dear. As I said, Lawrence is the only permanent staff I have. He is paid partly out of Tanya's estate, as is his physiotherapy. To remain employed here as long as he chooses." Windsor appeared to have finished, but Murphy and Alicia said nothing, compelling him to expand. "He was with Tanya's father—my brother—in the first Iraq war. My brother was an officer, and Lawrence was a cook, took a hit when the Yanks bombed them by accident. Peter got away with a spot of shrapnel, but Lawrence was crippled. Tanya brought him with her after her parents' accident. She was like that, you see. Kind. Loyal." He faltered a moment, steadied himself. "I think that was partly what made Tanya and James so close—his fascination with her butler. Jim had been interested in all that army stuff, ever since he was a boy. Considered joining up until ... well, until what happened with Tanya. My brother refused to indulge his questions about the war. Found it ... distasteful."

"Sir," Murphy said, "Tanya was snatched from the barbeque which she paid for, is that right?"

"Correct."

"Meaning she must have either known or trusted her abductor."

"Yes. The last officer, what was his name..? He said that too."

"Wellington."

"Yes, Wellington. Good chap him. At least I thought he was." Henry's eyes narrowed and then closed. "It was his fault wasn't it?"

"Sir?"

"His fault that Tanya was held captive for all this time. He said she was dead or hiding intentionally." The man's face flushed. "He convinced me to stop trying!"

"Sir," Alicia said. "The original investigation was flawed, no arguments from me, and I have no doubt that the powers that be are facing a huge lawsuit—"

"Lawsuit? *Lawsuit!*" He stepped closer to Alicia so quickly that Murphy moved toward Windsor, who did not back down. "A lawsuit is the least of your worries. I'm going to destroy each and every last person involved with that clusterf—"

"Yes. Absolutely," she said. "The police screwed it up worse than we can ever apologise for, but there is still a girl missing. We need to find her."

"Then why are you here? You must have a file with all our statements."

Murphy placed his hand on Henry Windsor's shoulder, outwardly friendly but really ushering him out of Alicia's personal space. He was a head taller than Windsor, so looking down at him had a calming effect.

Murphy said, "The file was put together by the same people who left Tanya in the hands of this killer."

Mr. Windsor breathed slowly, shook off Murphy's arm, and leaned on a sleek-looking purple sports car. "Wellington. Yes, he was Mr. Friendly when we were accommodating him. Liked a cigar. Appreciated good brandy. Knew his cars."

A lull in the anger. Perfect.

Alicia said, "I like that purple one." She was about to touch a sports car but remembered the previous admonishment. "Which is the E-type?"

"This one," he said, indicating an animalistic racing-green machine. His face slowly drained of the fierce red as he led them to the Jaguar.

Alicia took it in from all angles, seeing why some girls were shallow enough to grade men according to material possessions. Even Murphy would jump three or four sex-points if he pulled up in this.

Murphy said, "Tanya had a tattoo at her time of death. Would you know anything about it?"

"A tattoo? No, I'm afraid not. Do you mean the man who ... who *did* this to her ... he *branded* her as well?"

"She did it herself a week or so before she disappeared."

Alicia guessed Windsor was about to deny this, then, "I suppose she could have. She was acting strange before she disappeared. Different. More..." He nodded at Alicia. "More like *her.*"

"Like moi?" Alicia said, feigning shock.

"What?" Murphy said. "You mean flaky?"

"Yes. Flaky."

Alicia now feigned insulted, her bottom lip sticking out.

"But also," Henry continued, "she was determined to renounce her heritage, at least temporarily. The only reason she didn't give all her money away was because it was everything her parents left her, all she had to remember them by. You know about them, I assume?"

"Yes."

"Terrible. Terrible." He shuddered. "And now this." He guided Alicia away from the Jag and ushered her and Murphy toward a staircase that ran alongside the lift. "Would you be interested in the aviary?"

Up in the open air, Alicia was colder even than before. The wind had gotten up and the mist danced icily upon her face as she tried to look happy and enthusiastic at the prospect of seeing caged birds. Henry feigned being unaffected by the cold, and Murphy also pretended badly too. They walked along a narrow path through a glade of trees, Alicia having transformed into the Michelin Man, waddling along with her freezing face poking out the top of her coat.

"Tanya paid for the garage, by the way," Windsor said. "She loved my cars but they were suffering in the old barn that I used. The aviary you're about to see, she had this built too. It used to be a ... play area for James. He hadn't used it for a while and Tanya asked if she could do something ... pretty with it. James said of course." He paused, staring at the house, then resumed. "She didn't like me much, didn't care for the traditions of our people. But she was grateful. Knew we didn't *have* to take her in."

"You cared a great deal for her," Alicia said.

"For the first two years of her being here I didn't even know there *was* a fortune. Nor did she. I thought my brother's businesses had gone the same way as mine, but I suppose that was only for tax purposes." He gave a proud little chuckle. "A solicitor turned up on her sixteenth birthday with a cheque and an invoice for his services. Another two years before she could touch it. Turned her into a frightful little madam."

The trees gave way to a chicken wire cage the size of Alicia's flat. It was full of not-so exotic birds—not native to Britain, but no parrots or parakeets: a few brown things with colourful tummies, twittering blue and white ones, like large swallows, and two fluffy, ground-based birds with bright yellow Mohawks.

Such beautiful creatures, caged, for the amusement of one man.

"Sir," Murphy said. "Hillary Carmichael—"

"Gold digger," Windsor said dismissively. "No cash of her own. No title. Needed to marry into money. Had the lifestyle, the friends, but no genuine class. For all her elocution lessons, her mother was still a civil servant, and her father was basically a factory worker."

"I read that Hillary's father owned a chain of factories making plastic moulds for the mobile phone industry."

"Yes. A millionaire. But he had to *work* for his money. They *bought* their way into the social scene. Hillary's family were middle-class at best. I didn't like her hanging around with Tanya."

Alicia felt the cold more intensely; wet and deep and all around her. The birds seemed to be looking at her, twittering, clattering their hard feet against the wire. One more shriek, and Alicia said, "Oh, come on, stop fannying around." She rubbed her icicle of a nose, trying to thaw it. "Tanya was shagging someone you wouldn't approve of. Do you have any idea who he might be?"

"I *beg* your pardon?"

"Sir," Murphy said. "Hillary knows Tanya was seeing someone. She also wanted to go to university, live with other students, *like* students."

"Like 'common' people."

"Yes. Like the song," Alicia said. "She was either going to the same uni as this guy you wouldn't approve of—which, by the way, sounds like everyone but the *royal* Windsors—or she was running away for good. Like the tigers."

Windsor's breath misted and billowed from his nose. Alicia's was daintier, wisps floating from her mouth like angel-steam ... whatever that was. Murphy coughed a giant cloud.

"I expect," Henry Windsor said, "it's time you were leaving. I doubt I can help any further. I'll be in touch about claiming Tanya's body. And my lawyers will be in touch about the gargantuan balls-up you people made."

Murphy said, "We'll be sending you a FLO—a family liaison officer—to keep you in touch with the investigation and offer any help or advice." He handed the pompous twit a card. "Can we contact you again if we need to ask anything else?"

"Of course. *Anything* to help." He turned to the cage, the card clasped in both hands. "I think I'll stay here with the birds a while. Feed them myself this morning."

"Thank you for your time," Murphy said.

They started back for the car, through the trees and around the corner of the house. Upstairs, a curtain twitched and then closed. Both officers clocked it.

"Lawrence?" Murphy said.

"Don't know, don't care," Alicia said. "It's too cold. Let's go. You drive."

In the car, Murphy started her up and turned on the heaters and set off down the drive. "So what am I missing?"

"Aside from Mrs. Rochester in the window up there?"

"Who?"

"Mrs. Roch— You never read Jayne Eyre? *Mrs. Rochester*—never mind. Let me think. My brain doesn't like the cold."

"Guess that makes me the brainy one for a change. *I* know what we achieved there."

"Go on then." She prepared a prod.

"He didn't ask about the tigers," Murphy said proudly.

The prod would wait. "What do you mean? What tigers?"

"Exactly. You blurted out the comparison between Tanya's plan and the tiger story. He didn't look surprised. *My* first question would have been 'what tigers?' *He* carried on as normal and chucked us out."

Alicia replayed the conversation in her head as it defrosted. She imaged microchips coated in ice, dripping slowly, lights flashing and information stuttering back to life.

She said, "We need to stop in the next village."

"Why?"

"I need to buy a hat."

Chapter Seventeen

CLEAVER WAS nervous about asking DCI Streeter for help. Perhaps it was his disrupted sleep patterns; partial night shifts, swinging back to evening, and now it was morning after three hours kip in a vacant cell. But Ball seemed less hesitant, perhaps for the same reason. He bulldozed in and came right out with it.

"We're stuck, sir. Alicia and Murphy are incommunicado, and there's movement on the case." He ran down the happenings at Doyle's Emporium, giving Cleaver credit for the receipt, which Ball presented to Streeter in an evidence bag. Streeter asked for more details and Ball explained the ledger.

"Paavan Prakash," Cleaver said, once Ball finished. "That's the name we're interested in. We ran it through the usual databases and there are a few of them, but we can't get hold of Murphy and Friend. We need a senior officer's sign-off to go deep on this credit card."

"Fraud squad," Streeter said. "Go see Darla Murphy over at Sheerton. I'll make a call."

"Murphy?" Ball said. "Any relation to the boss-man?"

"None I know of."

Streeter held the phone in one hand, his other poised over

the buttons. He glanced at the clock, 9:32 a.m., and stared the two officers down, indicating that they were already wasting time.

Richard Hague sat in a ten-year-old Volvo outside a branch of the IBA Bank in Chapel Allerton, an area of Leeds that had, over the last decade or so, become a miniature Greenwich of the North. Bohemian types earning more money than Bohemians really should resided alongside residents who'd lived here decades prior to the 90's housing boom. He was waiting for someone he'd gambled on actually existing. Earlier that morning, the gamble had paid off.

She was four or five years older than Katie, far thicker around the hips, fleshy face, most likely couldn't sprint up the stairs let alone complete the Great North Run. That was no sin, though. Single mother, working, doing what's right. The bank would be a great job for her. Drop little Charlene off at the school down the road, then straight behind that little window, earning whatever tellers earn.

Yes, Richard Hague knew the name of this woman's six-year-old daughter.

It was part of his gamble. Hanging around the school, mingling with the mums and dads, a peaked Disney hat with floppy ears to indicate what a fun father he was, seeing his pride and joy off into the care of strangers.

It was surely only moments ago that he did the same with Katie.

This part of the gamble—identifying a target—was more an educated guess. Little risk. And when he saw a bank uniform poking out from under the coat of the woman who called her daughter Charlene, his chips were getting cashed.

Now he wore a large coat with a furry hood, and running

shoes, just in case. The Volvo was his, stored in another lockup under yet another assumed name. He called himself paranoid for procuring the lockups, all the trouble of faking an ID, opening credit cards, obtaining bills, basically creating a new person out of thin air. But you never knew. Perhaps he left a fingerprint in the States. Plus, DNA technology had come a long way since his extra-curricular adventure over there.

Richard entered the bank with his hood up. There were three tellers, although only one was serving. Luckily it was the one he wanted. *Un*luckily she was currently occupied, the other two busying themselves with something not related to customer service. Richard read leaflets, his hood still up, until the customer left. He waited thirty more seconds, then approached the glass, and removed his hood to reveal the floppy "good-dad" hat.

To put her at ease *and* obscure his face from the cameras.

"Morning," the single mum said. Her name badge indicated she was called Donna. "How can I help you today?"

"I'd like to request my credit card statement, please," Richard said.

"You have your card?"

"No, Donna, I'm afraid I don't. Here's the number." He presented the piece of paper on which he scribbled the number from Doyle's ledger.

She smiled awkwardly. "Are you not registered for internet banking, sir?"

"I don't trust it. I just need a statement, if it isn't too much trouble."

"What name is it?"

"My name is Paavan Prakash."

Her face visually tied itself in knots over the disconnect between Richard's skin tone and the name offered.

She said, "Do you have any other ID, Mr, er, Prakash?"

"Of course." Richard took a square of glossy paper from his pocket and slipped it under the glass.

She read it. *My name is Paavan Prakash—honest!*

"I'm sorry, is this some sort of joke?"

Richard smiled affably. "There's a photo on the other side."

She turned it over and the fake smile dropped. She brought it closer to her face.

"No crying," Richard said. "Don't want your colleagues thinking there's anything wrong now, do we?"

Donna shook her head, eyes fixed on the Polaroid of little Charlene, bound with leather straps and gagged, squatting in the back of Richard's Volvo. *Polaroids.* Yes, another old-school resource he favoured over the new.

"Now. My name is Paavan Prakash, and I'd like a printout of my statement please."

She sniffed. "Six months? Sir?"

"Eighteen would be better. Also, I could do with being reminded of my address. I've been a little absent-minded of late."

She stared at the photo some more. "Please. I don't know why you're doing this—"

"Donna." Richard held out his hand for the photo. He took it and placed it back in his pocket. "She'll be fine. I need you to breach that pesky data protection act for me. For Charlene. She's a brave little girl. Hasn't cried once. Not yet."

"I can't simply hand it over the counter."

"Yes you can." He thought about his actions here. Threatening a little girl to save his own. It was justifiable, but not by much. He wasn't like that man, had no intention of killing Charlene. But putting Donna through this, did it make him a monster all the same? "You want to see your girl first, yes?"

She stared, blankly.

"That's okay. When's your break, Donna?"

"Ten."

"Thirty minutes then. Come alone, bring the statement. The bowling green up the park."

She nodded.

"And, Donna? Don't worry. I'm not a monster. All I want is that statement."

Upon arrival at Sheerton, the first thing to hit Cleaver was a sense of jealousy. Why did he have to work in the most dilapidated building in the whole of the West Yorkshire Police Force? In their reception, you walked on floor tiles, linoleum ones; in Sheerton, it was polished wood. The desk itself was like something from a corporate headquarters rather than a butcher's counter.

He and Ball signed in and the kid on duty made a call. Ten minutes passed, during which Cleaver commented on several fittings, the nice rug, and the air conditioning. Ball eyed up the noticeboard, grunting agreement with everything Cleaver said.

Ball said to the kid on reception, "Had your own murder up here yesterday, right?"

"Yeah," the constable replied. "Looks a few years apart, but we're pretty sure they're linked. Press conference this afternoon."

"You arrested someone?"

He grinned. "Probie got him. Dobson. His first arrest. Some tramp lived up there. Been telling everyone his theory on the subject—bloke's gone back to nature, he reckons. Feral."

Ball smiled through his beard.

Probies. They're loads of fun.

A woman showed up from somewhere nobody noticed. "You the two from Millgarth?"

Darla was a skinny runt, Ball thought, a plain girl with

mousy hair and glasses. Classy specs, though; designer frames—
didn't suit her one bit.

"I haven't much time," she said without introductions. "But
DCI Streeter said it was urgent. Follow me."

They did. Ball slouched, hands in pockets.

"So you worked here long?" Cleaver said.

"Yes," Darla replied.

"How do you like it?"

"Fine. When I can *do* my job. I was watching a series of transactions on a Debenhams credit card stolen from an eighty-three-
year-old woman. Beaten into a coma a fortnight ago."

"Is someone watching it now?"

"What do you think, we drop everything when Serious
Crimes comes a-calling?"

"No, but..."

"Here." She opened the door to an office, sat behind the desk
where a computer hummed quietly. "This is the best we have.
It's a system that talks to all the major credit card retailers. We
do have a live action one, but like I said, that's in use. This one,
you have to hit the refresh button every few minutes to update.
It's a little slow, but it'll give you what you need."

Cleaver was impressed. The last two years of transactions on
Paavan Prakash's Barclaycard scrolled up and down the screen.

"Here," Darla said, moving the mouse around, "is where you
print it. This is where you click if you need details of the place
where the transaction went down, and this is how you turn it off
on your way out."

She stood to leave.

"Wait," Cleaver said. "You can't go yet."

"You computer illiterate or something? I'm trying to coordi-
nate an arrest in there."

"Okay." Defeated. He accepted that. "Thanks."

She left them alone, both pretty sure she'd have slammed the door if it wasn't on an automatic closing mechanism.

Ball said, "If there's one woman I've met this week who needs a good shag..."

Cleaver tried to laugh, but he was on the computer, scrolling, hoping for more good news.

"Wow," he said.

"What?"

"He is making this too easy."

"He used it recently?"

Cleaver had to get himself one of these. "This morning. A Priceway supermarket. Bridlington."

"Our boy's gone to the beach for the day."

"Lots of historical transactions. Looks like he lives there. Yep, there's his registered address. Must work. He spends a lot, pays it off in full each month." Cleaver pressed "print" then "OK", realised he'd set it as landscape as one hundred and thirty-two pages spat out of the printer. "Oops."

He and Ball exchanged naughty-boy looks, knowing the bean-counters running the police would collapse, foaming at the mouth if they saw this. Cleaver accessed the details of that Priceway branch, and printed them too. He also pulled up Prakash's most regular transactions, the petrol station, a pizza shop.

Ball unlocked his phone. "Wonder if DS Friend is back on the air yet."

"Bridlington," Alicia said, hanging up her phone. "Ball and Cleaver are contacting the Humber-guys and they're on their way to an address."

"We going?" Murphy said.

"And don't worry about speed limits. I'll let Barry know we're on our way."

"Barry?"

"Ex-boyfriend. He moved to the east coast when we split up. Now he's with Humberside, which covers Brid."

"*Another* ex-boyfriend? First the guy at Interpol, now Humberside? Know anyone in MI5, MI6, the SAS?"

"I once dated someone I *thought* might be MI5. Does that count?"

"You break Barry's heart then?"

"I always do."

Murphy turned at a roundabout and aimed at the A58. "Don't want to talk about it?"

"I loved him. He loved me. But he got all serious. It would never have worked."

"Oh, you're one of them."

"One of what?"

"Just out for a good time. Should've known."

"No, I mean he got *serious*-serious. Boring-serious. I'm happy to make a commitment, Uncle Donald, but too many guys associate 'commitment' with 'serious'. They get confused. I'd have married Barry the next day if he'd asked me at the right time."

"He asked you to marry him?"

"On the day I planned on ending it with him, yeah."

"So what did you do?"

"I ended it with him."

"Cold-hearted cow," Murphy said with an unfamiliar smile. "He'll be pleased to see you?"

"Doubt I *will* see him. He's ARV. But it's polite to say I'm in town." She got his answering machine, left a quick message and hung up, hoping he'd chilled out a bit since they last met. "So what do you think about our splendid classless society?"

Murphy negotiated his way onto the dual carriageway that

would shoot them all the way to the east coast, careful on the next roundabout.

"Classless?" he said. "You want to know my theory on class?"

Alicia got the impression he was winding himself up, like a toy. She could not resist an insight into this nice but grumpy man's psyche.

"Leave nothing out," she said.

"Okay, but don't forget, you asked for the full version."

"The suspense is killing me."

They passed an abandoned double-decker bus on the left, converted into a café. Murphy glanced at it, but started his story.

"The way I see it, around twenty percent of us are working class, proper jobs, you know, plumbers, bus drivers, that sort. People who keep the place going."

Alicia nodded.

"Then there's around sixty percent, what I'd call the middle class. Not the cheese and wine party snobs, but they're included. It goes from the office bods through to chairmen of companies, politicians, chefs, coppers. Normal folk, up to the verging-on rich. No better or worse than the working class, just a different mind-set."

Murphy slowed behind a mini, one of the old ones, spotted a gap in the oncoming traffic, and sped around it to a clear road.

"Then there's the ten percent like Henry back there. Do nothing, but think they're entitled to wealth and status. Look down on us like we exist to pay them tax so we can breathe the same air."

Alicia made a show of counting on her fingers. "That's ninety percent. Where's the other ten?"

They passed a sign for Scarborough, forty-eight miles. Around sixty to Brid.

He said, "That's what I call the sub-class. Shoplifting, alcoholism, drug addiction. The people who *could* recover but don't.

Or won't. And I'm not talking unemployed either—I know plenty who are trying their best to work, take anything they can get. But there are people who don't even try. Kid trips in the playground, they sue the school. Funds come from policing or hospitals, then they blow it all on booze or drugs."

The clues to Murphy's grumpiness grew clearer to Alicia. "So what do you reckon we should do, oh wise one?"

He thought about it. "You know, back in the eighties, I used to feel sorry for them. The idea that 'greed is good' was all over the place. Rich and poor got further apart and folk like me, we were stuck in the middle. Then in the nineties, the promotion of wealth made it to the mainstream, like it was the new normal. Your Sex and the City, programs like that. Ally Mc-bloody-Beal. Friends."

"Wow," Alicia said, "that's some dated pop-culture references you have there."

"Well, I don't watch much TV anymore. Point is, they all promote a lifestyle your average person can't afford, and since all these mingers do is—"

"Sorry, Donald, 'mingers'?"

"The sub-classes."

"Oh, we're back on them. Go on."

"These minging people watching telly all day and night, and getting it in their heads they're *entitled* to that kind of money."

"Like Henry. Ooh, we've gone full-circle."

"After the millennium, it got worse. I started to get scared."

"So Sex and the City and Ally McBeal are responsible for the collapse of British society," Alicia said. "But what about a solution?"

"Well, I thought about that. I first came up with it when I got stabbed in the arm with a heroin needle. My house was burgled twice. I got scared. My wife got scared. And because I was so driven to put this scum in prison ... Susan left me."

Alicia suspected there was more to it than that, but it was a conversation for another time.

"After Susan went, I stopped being scared. I still put them away. I live down there, I see them all the time, and you know what?"

"No. What?"

"I'm not scared of them anymore. I'm just so bloody *bored*. Bored of those idiots on Jeremy Kyle yelling at each other and screwing and making babies that'll all end up like themselves or using abortion like normal folk use condoms—"

"I had an abortion," Alicia said. She swallowed, unsure why she blurted that out.

Murphy kept his eyes on the road. "Yeah? How old?"

"Nineteen. It was the end of my decadent party lifestyle. My mum and dad insisted it would ruin my life, so ... poof! Gone."

"Nothing 'poof' about that, Alicia." He held the wheel with his right hand, moved his left toward Alicia, but something— maybe the tension in her shoulders—caused him to take it back. "You regret it?"

"Some days. When I think about how many single mums make a career and a life for themselves. Other days I know I wouldn't be me without everything that came before. Then I'll see some twelve-year-old kid and wonder, what if? Schoolyards, missing kids, I start thinking about it. Things like that."

Like days out at the seaside, she thought.

After a long silence, Murphy said, "Those Jeremy Kyle types, they're breeding faster than you and me, Alicia."

Alicia forced a smile, fluttered her eyelids in a "thank you" and said, "Scary stuff."

He breathed through his nose as the dual carriageway merged into a single-track road, coming up behind a caravan. They slowed from eighty to fifty.

Murphy said, "We should scoop them all up and give them

their own estate on an island out in the North Sea. A weekly drop of special brew, pizza and oven chips should see 'em right. Once a month, some fresh needles and a barrel of smack. Possibly the latest Spice Girls CD they can play as loud as they like."

"The Spice Girls split up about a million years ago."

"Glad you get my point." He leaned to the side, trying to see around the caravan.

"I do get your point," Alicia said. "People who contribute nothing to society should not be *part* of that society."

Murphy didn't seem convinced. "It's not that they *add* nothing. It's what they take *away*. You've never had something wrenched out of your life—" He stopped abruptly, like a criminal trapped in a lie.

"You can tell me if you want."

He sighed. "Why do I feel like I'm in a shrink's office?"

Alicia smoothed Murphy's hair back, tidied it up. He frowned but didn't stop her. She took out a hankie, spat on it, and wiped his cheek.

"Hey!" He pulled away, steadied the car.

"You had ketchup on your cheek from that sandwich."

"Oh."

The engine rumbled in the silence, the outside noises now distinct.

Alicia patted Murphy's thigh and said, "Now. Tell me all about your mother."

Murphy cracked a smile. Yep, another one. The noise of the engine faded to the background again. The first sign for Bridlington crawled past: fifty-three miles. Murphy pressed the button for the siren and the light flashed on the dashboard. The caravan slowed and pulled as far over as possible.

"The housing estate," Alicia said. "We could call it 'Mingland'."

Murphy nodded agreement, dropped to third and accelerated past the caravan, up to seventy before skipping fourth and settling into fifth. They'd be in Brid before lunchtime.

Richard sat on a bench with Charlene, watching old people in thick pullovers roll balls around a green.

Crown green bowling. Is that an Olympic sport?

He'd given Charlene his spare coat from the boot and she sat like a good little girl, watching the game like father and daughter.

Richard wondered if he could be a father again, if it was worth it when people could snatch your children so easily from you. It didn't surprise him how simple it was for a strong man to take a woman like Katie, like the others. All he needed to entice Charlene was the lie that he was a new teacher, the promise her mother had bought her a mobile phone, and the notion that she had to sign some paperwork in the car. She was only six, bless her.

Donna showed at the opposite end of the green. Charlene leaned forward, but Richard placed a fatherly hand on her and said, "Remember what we discussed."

She sat back, watching her mummy approach.

Donna scurried, her feet close together. Richard stood between her and Charlene and adopted the cold stare he reserved for people whom he was about to fire or those pleading for their lives. She ignored the look, knelt straight down beside Charlene, hands trembling, kissing, kissing her daughter.

"Okay, that's enough." In the hand not holding Charlene, Richard flashed a compact blade. It was a throwing knife, an implement that required a skill he spent many years trying to master, but had never successfully used it against another human—not lethal enough, not guaranteed. "You have something for me?"

Donna fumbled in her handbag, a brown envelope rustling out. Richard opened it with the tip of the knife, blew to widen the hole, and fished out the papers. Screen prints of Paavan Prakash's card history. Plus his stated address.

Bridlington.

Just over an hour's drive. No probs.

"Good." He let go of Charlene's arm. "I need my coat back."

Donna stripped her girl of the coat and threw it at Richard. She backed quickly away, fear now replaced with disgust. She was still looking around, into bushes, back at Richard, as if expecting an ambush.

"I won't bother you again," Richard called after her. "I promise."

Holding Charlene's hand, Donna all but dragged the girl away, hurting her more than Richard had done in tying her up for the photo.

Richard's stomach squirmed.

Odd. He didn't know what it was.

Watching this woman walk away with her daughter, a daughter recently abducted by what she probably thought of as a madman (how wrong could she be!), yet knowing she would never feel truly safe again. He didn't like the word "jealousy", but that's how he felt.

He was *jealous.*

Donna had her girl back, alive and well. While Richard was one step closer.

He hadn't been to Brid in a while. Better pack some sandwiches. And a flask of tea. Or maybe he'd have fish 'n' chips. Yes, he thought. Nothing quite like fish 'n' chips beside the seaside.

Chapter Eighteen

AT ELEVEN A.M., Alfie Rhee was listening to Celine Dion. Again. Outside Red McCall's van, the city of Leeds zoomed by, the tiny buildings grotty and short. Even the Christmas lights seemed like they couldn't be bothered, despite it being daytime and all they had to do was hang around. Occasionally, though, a shining tower of apartments or a brand new office block reared out of the ground, but that was all that indicated proof of what he read; he understood Leeds to be a big city. He asked McCall how come people think this is "big."

"It's got a big heart," McCall said.

"Seriously."

"Seriously? Oh. It's big financially. More millionaires per square mile than London. Businesses move here all the time. Loads of 'em. KPMG, HSBC, that sort of thing. It's a good night out an' all."

Through sheer volume of use, Alfie already deduced the phrase Red used—"an' all"—was a contraction of "and all", which was in turn a northern England term which meant "in addition to the thing just mentioned". So Leeds, as well as being a sizable financial centre, was also an excellent place to get drunk. Good to know.

A small park rolled by on the left, then they stopped at a busy intersection, signs to places like Scot Hall and Chapeltown, Harrogate and Harehills. The English had weird names for places. Alfie let McCall get on with the driving, didn't ask questions, just held onto the envelope full of English money. Four grand.

It had better be worth it.

They passed under a green overhead sign indicating they were on their way to Meanwood.

Sounds great, Alfie thought.

"So what's Alfie short for?" McCall asked.

"Nothing. It's my name."

"No, come on. Alfred, Alfonse, what?"

"It says Alfie on my birth certificate."

"Like the Michael Caine film?"

"I don't know. Never asked. It's my name. That's all."

McCall wound down the window and spat out of it. "I know, get this. What's E.T. short for?"

"What?"

"E.T. In the film. What's E.T. short for?"

"Extra Terrestrial."

"Nah. It's cos he's got little legs." McCall cracked up laughing, slapping his thigh to boot.

Celine Dion was singing something Alfie hadn't heard before. "You got anything else we can listen to?"

Red shook his head. "Not really. She relaxes me. Last night was okay. There was no traffic. But I need to relax. My doctor says I should take more baths." He slammed on the brakes, leaned out the window and yelled some British insult—*tosser* or something—and pulled back inside. "Anyway, ordinarily, I'd've been out the door, chasing that prick up the road. Celine keeps me, I dunno, centred."

"Praise God for Celine," Alfie said.

"My sentiments exactly."

They turned left at some lights, now firmly in suburbia. Hundreds of young people wandered the many shops and cafes either side of the road, their fashion sense ranging from the bizarre to the ridiculous to the downright mundane.

"This is your Mean Wood?" Alfie said.

"Nah, we passed through Meanwood a way back. This is Headingly. Student central."

Traffic crawled. Celine sang. McCall gripped the wheel. Each time the car in front moved even six inches, he'd accelerate into the tiny gap. Eventually, he manoeuvred into a parking space near a quaint war monument opposite a bar called The Sky Rack and a charity shop for animals. They hit the street where students hurried up and down, Alfie getting pissed at dodging weirdoes and grannies on the narrow sidewalk.

"In the summer, this place is chock-full of totty," McCall said. "Sometimes I think I can do without my Viagra."

Alfie raised an eyebrow. You can part with too much information sometimes. Besides, McCall wasn't *that* old.

"Yeah, yeah, most guys're ashamed of it," McCall went on. "But I don't care. It's a stress thing."

"Hence Ms. Dion."

"*Exactly*. When I'm with a lady, I still worry about stuff, you know? I stick Celine on the stereo, pop a little blue pill, and it's how's yer father time."

Alfie was either still jetlagged or McCall was speaking something that only *sounded* like English. He understood less than half of that. "What if the lady don't like Celine Dion?"

"She soon perks up when she sees what 'Little' Red can do. *Bam!*" He thrust his hips forwards, scattering three girls of about eighteen into the road. "Viagra. Best invention since Velcro. What you think I need my commission for? It ain't buying flowers, mate. It ain't flowers."

They crossed the road and proceeded into Starbucks. McCall bought the drinks while Alfie went ahead to secure seats upstairs. He found two sofas, both facing a low table with dirty cups and plates, so he sat facing the door. All the less-comfy chairs were taken, text books open, students scribbling while nursing a coffee and a hangover. A boy and girl, maybe sixteen, maybe nineteen, ate each other's faces on another couch, mouths wide, tongues thrashing like eels.

McCall brought Alfie the desired mocha with an extra shot and a swirl of cream; McCall opted for a venti-sized iced coffee. To Alfie's enormous discomfort, McCall sat on the same couch as him. Their knees touched.

"Your contact's late," Alfie said.

"Woman's prerogative."

"Woman?"

"Yep. Oh, and wait till you see her. What Little Red could do with her..."

"I'm not late." A female voice, from the side.

Alfie looked her up and down, not concealing his interest. She was as tall as him, wearing a figure-hugging trouser suit, low blouse. She held a soft leather case. Oh yeah, Alfie was glad he waited for this one.

"DCI Chambers, meet Alfie Rhee," McCall said. "A colleague of mine from the States."

She sat opposite. "I'm not happy about this, McCall. It's an ongoing investigation."

"Thought you had someone in custody."

"He's a nutcase. He might have done it but I doubt it. Frigging probie overreacted."

"Probie?" Alfie said.

"Probationary constable. Looks like our nutter was living up there, using the well's pipe as a toilet. Probie freaked out, decked him."

"And you're sure he didn't do the two women?"

"No, not sure. But there's no weapon. We found his other things, pans and cutlery, but nothing that would penetrate. Besides, he's the one who dialled nine-nine-nine, and only claims to know about *one* body. There were two."

"How'd the other die?" McCall said.

"Why don't we talk about something else for a moment?"

"Of course." Alfie handed Chambers the envelope as overtly as he could. Doing it shiftily would draw far more attention. "You can trust it's there. Red checked it for you."

"If it's wrong, I'll do something to you Viagra won't fix," Chambers said to McCall.

McCall sipped his coffee. Grinned hornily.

Chambers took a file from her case and laid it on the table. "You can read it here, Mr. Rhee, but I'm not risking you taking it away. Not for a measly four thousand."

Alfie opened it on his lap. Photocopies of photos, copies of reports, no originals. He pointed this out.

"I don't mind you eyeballing it," Chambers said. "But if the tabloids get hold of it someone'll be for the chop. Probably me."

Alfie shrugged. He began to read. Examined the crime scene photos. The excrement in little bags at the bottom of the well.

How neat.

Chambers told McCall to go get her another coffee. When he was gone, she asked Alfie, "So why do you want this?"

"I'm writing a book," Alfie said.

He carried on reading. The arrest of Freddie Wilcox, some detail on him. Preliminary autopsy of the intact body.

Single blow, straight to the heart. A sharp, strong blade.

"You used to be FBI?" Chambers said.

"Yep. Started in BAU—that's behavioural science ... serial killer. Then robbery detail."

No forensic evidence on the body.

"So why'd you leave?"

"Personal issues."

Last seen on her usual street talking to a man in a hat or baseball cap. Descriptions all from long range, some saying well-built and handsome, some claiming he was fat and ugly, one saying skinny and plain. A hooker? Yeah, she was seen with a lot of men.

"What sort of personal issues?"

Alfie closed the file. "I wanted to catch a killer. They didn't believe there *was* a killer."

"Ah." Chambers reached out for the file. "And you think this might be related."

Alfie snatched the file back. "Yes. And I'm gonna hang on to this for a while."

"That wasn't the deal."

McCall returned with Chambers' coffee, plus a cookie. She waved the cookie away. McCall's face dropped into sadness.

Alfie stood with the file. "I'm changing the deal."

Chambers reached for it. "You give me that back right now."

Alfie moved for the exit.

"McCall, stop him," Chambers ordered.

People were looking now, glancing up from their books, from each other. The couple making out on the one chair ignored it all.

"Er, I'm not sure if..." McCall started.

Alfie pushed his face up close to Red's. "You're working for *me* at the minute. Not her. I'm *pay*ing you."

"Red, if you stop him walking out of here with my file," Chambers said, "I will screw your brains out five ways from Sunday."

McCall dropped the cookie, reached for the file, and fell to the floor. Alfie's counter-strike shot pain through his shoulder, ribs and left knee all at once.

Alfie stared at Chambers, daring her.

Go on, he thought. *Try me.*

"Please," she said. "If it gets into the wrong hands..."

Alfie waved the file. "This man killed my wife. And you people have arrested some bum cos you have even less of a clue than the damn Feds. You wanted five-K, but I'm sorry. Four grand sterling is plenty for what you've given me. I need time to look through this. And I ain't doing it in some coffee shop."

"Mr. Rhee, try and understand—"

Alfie grabbed McCall by his ear and pulled him up. "Limp it off. You're still working for me." He paused by the door to the stairs. To Chambers, he said, "When I'm done with it I'll make sure Red brings it back to you."

"Hey," McCall said. "You only said I got to get it back, right? No time limit on that shag is there?"

Before Chambers could respond, Alfie yanked McCall out the door.

Chapter Nineteen

THE SUPERMARKET CLEAVER identified as being the most recent place anyone used the credit card was located five hundred yards from Paavan Prakash's house, making the car park an excellent staging area where backup would await instructions. The Bridlington Police allowed a black-and-white to idle with two bored uniforms in the front while the suits spent close to two hours working out the logistics and jurisdictional elements. Alicia's Serious Crime Agency status trumped everything, so it was she who now chatted to Humberside's public relations officer while Murphy briefed Cleaver and Ball.

"We go in, me and DS Friend," Murphy said, having now lost track of their shift patterns. The "inspector" side of his job title wondered about what overtime charges would hit this month, but for now he didn't question it.

"Come on, boss," Ball said. "*We* found him."

"He isn't a suspect yet. Just a potential witness."

"He's the only bugger without an alibi. And your new DS seems to think being dumped is a good whatsitcalled ... *trigger*."

"He hasn't had opportunity to *provide* an alibi, and if he's living and eating here, it's a long bloody way to go to drop a body." Murphy struggled to keep his voice even. "For now, he's a witness, Sergeant Ball. Am I clear?"

Ball turned away, hoiked up his trousers and blew into his hands.

Although they lingered in bright sunshine, frost glistened in the shade. Years ago, Murphy and Susan loved coastal days like this: bitterly cold, a cutting wind, a salty tang in the air.

He tried to imagine what Alicia would say to Ball and Cleaver about their egos, but he was too distracted by the Technicolor dream-hat she purchased from the old dear in a village they passed through as they neared Brid. It was a snug fit and had earflaps that she tied over her head for the time being. She'd tell them to stop being such silly little boys and do as they're told. If they're good, she might buy them fish and chips.

"Sergeant Ball," Murphy said. "Cleaver." He passed Ball a twenty-pound note. "While we're away why don't you grab us all some fish and chips or something."

Ball took the money sullenly. "Sure, boss. No probs."

"Salt and vinegar and a can of dandelion and burdock." He gave them directions to a chippy he frequented when Susan and he were together.

The two skulked back to their car and took coats from the boot, and started the walk past the Priceway's glass entrance, ignoring the three teenagers smoking and drinking glass bottles of Coke (Murphy thought they didn't do those any more), and through an alley, where they would descend a steep trail of stairs to the sea front.

A sharp jolt pricked Murphy's right buttock. He jumped, turned. Alicia had pinched him.

She said, "Let's go visit Mr. Prakash."

. . .

Parked a hundred yards away, opposite the Priceway's, Richard Hague used a high-powered camera to watch Alicia talking to some guy in a suit. If challenged by anyone but Alicia or Murphy he could say he was a journalist—freelance, of course.

God, Alicia looked so cute in that hat. If only they'd met under different circumstances. He'd underestimated the police's speed of response and, more specifically, the effectiveness of the fatsoes he'd seen at Doyle's. All you hear about these days is police brutality, incompetence, and red tape. But, Richard now realised, the huge number of crimes that actually get solved didn't sell newspapers. When this was over, Richard would again consider his offer to kill the reporter.

He hoped Alicia hadn't yet seen today's edition.

Having planned to get to Paavan before the police he now wished he hadn't staged the tattooist so much like a drugs slaying. He should have chanced taking the ledger. It was inevitable they'd find Paavan Prakash eventually, but this fast?

Was Alicia that good? Was Murphy? Surely not the fat coppers at the tattoo parlour.

It was his first mistake in years. He had to own that and move on.

Researching the original kidnapping on the Internet, it was hard to find anything specific, just that she'd disappeared, presumed murdered. Perhaps a runaway. There was far more about Henry Windsor. Quite a man about town, Tanya's uncle, or rather he *was*, before she disappeared; a key figure in the upper class social scene.

DI Murphy appeared to brief the fatsoes, handed them money, and sent them on an errand. Dinner?

Richard planned to eat his own sandwiches once the matter of extracting information from Paavan was over with, perhaps during, but he was hungry now. Sod it; you only live once. He unwrapped the foil, waiting for movement in the Priceway car park.

Richard had taken one bite of his ham and pickle sandwich when Alicia and Murphy set off and disappeared from view. He turned up his police scanner, and waited.

Murphy and Alicia rounded the corner to Belle Vue Drive into a harsh headwind. Alicia untied the flaps and retied them under her chin.

"What's the press boy have to say?" Murphy asked.

"Wants us to acknowledge the Humberside contribution."

"Sitting in a car park?"

"Well that's hard work at the best of times."

He smiled.

"Getting easier, though," she said.

Damn, he thought. Why'd he smile at that?

Number thirty-two was a small semi; two and a half bedrooms, nicely kept, stone slabs in the front but with rose stems poking from the soil, now brown and hard until the spring. It sloped upwards from the road, a dozen stairs leading to the door.

Murphy rang the bell.

An Asian man in his early twenties opened the door, his skin dark, approaching black. He was mostly lean, a slight paunch, wearing slobbing sweat pants, a Game of Thrones t-shirt, and Spider-Man slippers.

"Paavan Prakash?" Murphy said.

"Yes?"

They produced their IDs and introduced themselves.

"What is it?" Paavan said.

Alicia said, "It's very cold, listen." She exaggeratedly chattered her teeth, lifted the flaps on her hat. "Look. My ears are going blue. Feel my hands."

She pressed one hand on Paavan's. He pulled away.

"Fine," he said. "Come on in."

The place was immaculate. Clean-smelling, fresh, the windows open, gas fire burning. The living/dining room was compact, a three-piece suite facing a flat-screen telly, and what should have been the dining area sat a sturdy desk on which lay an Apple Mac and the best-looking peripherals Murphy had seen. Lever-arch files bulging with paper filled shelves beside the work area. Murphy touched a radiator, roasting his hand, and looked inquisitively at the open patio windows.

"I like fresh air," Paavan said, reading the question. "But I also like to be warm."

"Expensive habit," Murphy said.

"And not friendly to Mr. Environment," Alicia added.

Paavan shrugged. "What do you want?"

"What do you do for a living, Mr. Prakash?"

"I'm a writer."

"What do you write?"

"I'm trying to write a novel. A literary horror."

"Publish much?"

"A few short stories here and there. An agent's been sniffing around my book. Nothing solid."

"Can I see?" Alicia asked, removing her hat and unzipping her coat.

"No. You can't see. What do you *want*?"

Murphy took out his notebook, flipped it open showily. He had no need to look at his notes, but wanted a prop, a gesture that usually worked well on folk who weren't hardened criminals.

"Do you have a tattoo?" Murphy asked.

"No."

"Mind lifting the arms on your t-shirt?"

"Got a warrant?"

"Come on," Alicia said. "We just want to see."

Paavan waited for Alicia's sweet-as-candyfloss smile to melt. It didn't. So he rolled up the right sleeve past his shoulder, revealing a darker stretch of skin at the top of his arm, about the size of Tanya's tattoo. "I had it removed six months ago."

Murphy did the maths. "When Tanya was officially declared dead."

Paavan sat heavily on the chair beside his computer. "Why do you want to know about Tanya? Who sent you?"

"Please answer the question, sir."

The young man breathed through his nose. His eyes didn't focus on either officer. He simply said, "Yes."

"It was a tiger?"

"Yes."

"Sir, you need to tell us everything about your relationship with Tanya Windsor."

"Will you go away if I do?"

"Probably," Alicia said with a smile.

"Fine."

Paavan said he met Tanya in India. He was over there visiting family, meeting a girl they were trying to pin him down to marry. If he didn't like her, he could say no, but an arranged marriage was still traditional for the Prakashes.

Tanya was travelling with an Irish girl called Mary who used the word "feck" like punctuation. They were staying at a hotel in Agra. Tanya had actually tried to learn some Urdu and stopped Paavan, now dressed traditionally, to ask directions. He under-stood "temple" and "Shiva" but nothing else.

"Hang on a minute, love," he said. "*Where* you wanting to go again?"

Rather than forcing them to negotiate the streets alone, Paavan escorted them to the temple and bade them farewell, told them he was headed to his grandparents' village.

Tanya asked, "Is there any way to get in touch with you again?"

"Sure," Paavan said, and gave her his mobile number.

She called him ten minutes later. He turned the car around and picked them up.

"Okay," Tanya said. "We've seen the temple."

And Paavan agreed to show them the village Khandaui.

Mid-afternoon, and Tanya and Paavan drank tea and ate hard cakes at *The Great Tree Café* which was basically a trestle table, an urn, and a Tupperware box of cakes, located in the shade of a large tree. Paavan told her he'd be turning the fiancé down, no matter what.

"How do you know?" she asked.

"Because if I didn't take the chance and ask you to dinner, I'd be thinking of you for the rest of my life."

And that was that. Paavan had already finished university with first class honours in English literature, so he currently had no commitments. A little family money. Tanya, recently turned eighteen, claimed she was travelling for a year before deciding what course she'd do. Mary went north, while Tanya and Paavan headed for the airport. It wasn't for another month, when the pair of them hit Oz and were lying on the beach on Christmas day, that Tanya revealed how wealthy she was.

At Tanya's request, he never told his family about her money. She wanted them to love her for who she was, not what she could bring them. So when, in a swanky restaurant in Agra the following February, Paavan announced their engagement, even the promise of a traditional wedding, right here in India, changed nothing. Tanya wasn't of their caste, of their religion, and any children would be half-breeds. Paavan's father cut off his funding, ordered him to fend for himself.

It was that night, when everyone was asleep, that Paavan's grandmother, Pria, woke him. She told him to be quiet, and let him out into the rose garden. It was deathly quiet. The only sounds were chirruping insects and his grandmother's sandals on the sandstone path. No electric lights at this time, so the stars were bright, each one visible, innumerable.

And Pria regaled him with the story of the Bengal tiger and his girlfriend. Of the royal Bengal falling in love with a rare but lowly white tiger. The Bengal's father declared he would be exiled from the tiger palace and be forbidden to return. So the Bengal and his love fled, and lived in the wild, without royal trappings, without luxurious food, but happy, until the end of their years.

It is not a tale many people tell their young, for it gives them ideas like the one already embedded in Paavan.

When they returned home to England, Paavan felt like half a man, living off Tanya's trust, but as she pointed out, *she* hadn't earned that money either. And besides, it was there to make her happy. She could attend university, attain a degree in social studies and ancient culture, while Paavan worked on his writing, followed his dream. So he started a novel based on their romance. He called it Two Tigers; it would sell millions.

But after meeting Tanya's guardian, it was clear he was not welcome in the house—

"Wait," Alicia said. "You *met* Henry Windsor?"

"Of course. Seemed like an odd relationship. Tanya didn't get on that well with him, but she loved him. Guess she felt, I don't know, obligated or something. She even built him a frigging parking lot under the house for his car collection. They weren't exactly in the best of shape in the barn."

"And what happened?" Murphy asked. "You announced you were engaged?"

"We stressed we were waiting a while, until Tanya finished uni at least, and told them our plan, that Tanya would live in halls for the first year and then I'd move down to Exeter to be with her. I'd spend that first year writing a draft of my book."

"What happened to the book?" Alicia said.

"I burned it."

Murphy's pen scribbled away, the notebook no longer a prop. His stomach was empty, though, could virtually taste his seaside fish 'n' chips. He thought of them going cold, of Ball and Cleaver debating whether they should eat it themselves.

He asked, "When did you last see Tanya?"

"The day before the party. After, when she disappeared, Henry said she probably came to her senses and took a holiday. That police officer, Wellington, he put pressure on me. Came to Tanya's flat, found me holed up there."

Interesting.

Murphy saw Alicia also perk up at the mention of DCI Wellington.

"He hit me. Here." Paavan pointed to his left kidney. "Then in the face. I was on the floor and he took one of those truncheon things, the long black one—"

"A police baton," Murphy said.

"He pressed it against my throat and told me to confess. He said I killed her because she wanted to dump me. According to him, I flipped, went berserk, then hid the body."

Murphy remembered Wellington as a solid guy, secure, serious, wanted results, but always by the proverbial book. He'd share that with Alicia later.

Paavan continued. "I refused. I blacked out, and when I woke up I was sick. The place was done over. I knew the police would be back, that they'd pin it on me. So I took my novel, my files, and I ran. I went to James for help."

"James?" Alicia said. "Henry's son?"

"He was the only one who approved. He wanted Tanya to be happy. I knew he'd help me."

"And did he?"

"He got his dad on side, even though his dad hated me. He trusted James, though, wanted me out of sight, away from the cops for some reason. I stayed in the granny flat—"

"Sorry," Murphy said. "But 'granny flat'?"

"Yeah, you know, a property on your land where you stick an elderly relative? Someone too frail to live alone but doesn't want to go in a home? Anyway, I stayed there. A week later, James comes to me with a credit card, an address, and a map of Brid. He told me to come out here, stay in this house, the card will be taken care of. I should live off it until things blow over. Had no problems with it since."

"Why did they help you?"

Paavan looked at each officer in turn. "James is Henry's only son. He has sway, and don't forget they still only had Tanya listed as missing. It wasn't until much later they told me the house was mine to keep."

"They bought you a *house*?" Alicia said. "How cool is *that*?"

"I'd rather live on the streets if it'd bring Tanya back to me."

Murphy's radio crackled. He decreased the volume so it was only just audible. "Do you have anything of hers left?"

"I have some old letters upstairs. Travel journals, that sort of thing. I'll show you."

As the trio traipsed upstairs, the radio crackled again. This time Murphy turned it up slightly, adjusted the squelch, heard Ball: "...DI Murphy, come in."

"I'm here," Murphy said.

"Your chips are getting cold. You going to be long bringing the boy out?"

"Not long." He turned the radio down.

They all stopped dead.

"What do you mean?" Paavan said. "Why would you be bringing me out?"

"We'll need you to sign a statement," Murphy said.

"Just routine," Alicia added.

Paavan carried on upward. "This should answer a lot of questions."

The tiny room contained about twenty boxes of papers and files, a small sofa bed, black bags of what looked like clothing. Through the window, a grey sliver of North Sea gleamed.

"You owe me a penny," Alicia said.

Murphy frowned. "Why?"

"I saw the sea first. You owe me a penny."

It hadn't even occurred to Murphy, but they'd been in Bridlington an hour and not cast eyes on the ocean. He'd have a proper look before leaving.

"Been meaning to go down the charity shop," Paavan said, kicking a bag to one side.

He moved four boxes, leaned on the windowsill to reach a pile he said was probably the one with the letters. Then he stopped. Focused out of the window.

"You bastards," he said.

"What's wrong?" Alicia looked where he was looking.

"Bastards!"

Before either could react, Paavan flung open the window and jumped through. He landed on the porch roof and hung from there before dropping to the ground.

"He saw the panda car," Alicia said.

Murphy checked the view: the Priceway was also visible from up here.

Into the radio, he shouted, "Get over here. He's bolting. *Get over here!*"

Chapter Twenty

PAAVAN FLED AHEAD OF ALICIA, not quite touching distance. *"You're not a suspect,"* she cried.

No response. He vaulted another fence. She thanked her decision to wear trousers today, but he put more distance between them. It was harder going for Alicia, being so short, even though she was fit, athletic.

But if she caught up with him, what then? She was no match for him, and the few pointers she received in judo at the academy were as real to her as last Thursday's scary dream. She hadn't been in a physical fight since high school, and that was only to hit a boy in the balls with her clarinet case because he was picking on her brother.

One final garden, and Paavan hit the main road. Alicia reached the tarmac three seconds behind, causing Ball to veer his car around her. Paavan made it over the road, heading for the Priceway, for the alley down which Ball and Cleaver headed to pick up lunch.

No cars could follow him. It would be him and Alicia. Alone.

She couldn't let that happen.

She found a further reserve of energy, like a turbo-boost, and pumped her legs higher and harder. Gaining on him.

Oh please let him give up easily.

The three teenagers still loitered in the supermarket entrance, laughing and pointing, drinking Coke.

When Alicia shoulder-barged Paavan, she hit him with what she thought was the force of a rabid bull. He lost balance, flew lengthways into the little gang. Bottles dropped, one smashing. They all fell in a heap, swearing, not laughing any more.

Alicia knelt next to the panting Paavan, who lay there as the teenager demanded compensation for police brutality and lost Coca Cola. Footsteps behind announced the arrival of Ball, Cleaver, and the unis.

"Okay?" Ball said. "This him?"

Alicia nodded.

With difficulty, Paavan sat up. "Bitch. You tricked me."

"If you've nothing to hide, son," Ball said, "why run?"

Paavan glared at the officers. Then, fast as a snake, grabbed the remains of the Coke bottle, swung his arm around Alicia's neck, and held the broken glass at her throat.

"I'm not going to jail!" he said. "I've done nothing wrong!"

Alicia yelped as he hefted her up off the ground. Ball backed away. Cleaver too.

Where are they going? No! Help me.

She pulled at Paavan's arm, but it was too strong. The glass poked into skin at the side of her neck. She froze.

Murphy arrived in a fog of puffing breaths. The panda car pulled up too. Everyone was out. The teens had scattered. A perimeter established automatically, a crescent of men holding out placating arms, saying, "Take it easy, take it easy."

"I want a car, right now!" Paavan yelled. "That one. I'll take that one," nodding at the black and white.

"All police cars have trackers," Murphy said. "You won't get away."

"Get me one without a tracker."

Ball turned down his radio to prevent feedback and Murphy spoke into his own, asking, Alicia knew, not for a car but a hostage negotiator. In the meantime, it was Murphy's job to do the best he could.

Ball turned his radio back up. A voice familiar to Alicia squawked out.

"Alicia Friend? Confirm, please. Alicia *Friend* is a hostage?"

"Confirmed," came the reply. A controller. "But ARV is not required. Repeat, ARV is not required."

"Sorry," came Barry Staples voice, loud and clear over the radio. "You're breaking up. I'm going off air until I can get this fixed."

"Unit 376, you are not to attend. Respond, unit 376. ARV is *not* required."

"What does that mean?" Paavan said. "What's ARV?"

Alicia closed her eyes, dreading the next sentence, wanting it to be unreal, that the last five seconds never occurred. She'd be okay as a hostage with Paavan. He wasn't a killer and, besides, she was sure Murphy would talk him down.

"*What is ARV?*" Paavan said again.

"Armed Response Vehicle," Alicia said. "My ex-boyfriend wants to help."

Richard listened on his police scanner with a certain amusement. He saw the situation clearly: the Asian lad waved his broken bottle about, shouting demands, although Richard was too far away to hear them.

Paavan Prakash backed into the store, dragging Alicia, her

feet struggling to keep up. She lost a shoe. Richard lost sight of her entirely. With guns on the way, headed by what sounded like a rather enthusiastic policeman, the situation was not looking particularly positive.

Richard climbed out of his car, leaving behind his bulky jacket and donning a long-peaked cap. Under his black pullover, he secured a hunting knife in a scabbard, the size of the one Paul Hogan used in the Crocodile Dundee movies—messy, but efficient. He also carried the throwing knife and SEAL weapon. He didn't want to use this one, though. Couldn't keep using the same knives, didn't want these deaths linked to the "same" man, especially now his dumping ground had been discovered up in Eccup. Switching weapons after each kill, varying the ethnicity of his victims, and using different methods of choosing them, all kept him off the ViCap radar while he was active in the States. In this, the smaller country, and in a compact time-frame with a clear connection to one another, he would not be able to hide for long.

Sneaking around the back, Richard found the staff entrance, which was locked via a digital combination, flush smooth metal that worked through light touches to each relevant number. He breathed on the handset. Thanks to a mix of the cold air and staff using sweaty fingers fresh out of toasty-warm gloves, the most often-used keys misted over. Four digits. He guessed the combination on the third go.

Inside, pulling on black driving gloves, he had no idea where he was going, so kept his head down, the cap low. Sometimes they kitted out these stores with more cameras than the Big Brother house.

The corridor split in two. One way smelled like a canteen, so he plumped for the other.

Success.

He poked his head out of the door to the sight of Paavan between aisles, yelling at shoppers and staff, ordering them outside. He could see Paavan's head over the bathroom supplies shelves. He couldn't see Alicia.

He slipped out, closed the door quietly behind him, and kept low. He unhooked the clip of his hunting knife and crouch-walked to the next aisle.

Alicia talked quickly. "Paavan, you are not a suspect. You're a witness. Please believe me."

"Shut up," Paavan said. "If you only wanted a statement you'd have said. You're just like the other guy, Wellington."

Wellington.

A name Richard had not heard so far. He made a mental note and unsheathed the knife, shining silver under the fluorescent lighting strips.

"Tanya's uncle has been lying to us all along," Alicia said. "Him and James, they bought you off because Henry knows more than he's saying."

"Keep talking."

"He either knows why Tanya was kidnapped, or he paid someone to do it. For her money. And I think it might be the latter."

The stress in Paavan's voice eased. "You don't think I did it?" A pause, then the stress returned. "Of course you're going to say that."

Richard crouched at the end of the aisle. He peeked around. The two of them were right there, amidst bubble baths and toothpaste. Paavan could see the doorway from where he stood and constantly glanced towards it.

Richard put the knife away. The distance was too great to risk rushing Paavan. He selected the throwing knife, and sat himself out of sight. If he got this right, it would be beautiful.

Once, he thought he had mastered it. He drugged a college girl in a bar in Texas and took her, sleeping, to an area of national park which he knew guaranteed privacy. When she awoke and was alert, aware of the situation, he released her, hunting her through the woodland like a ... well, a hunter. He tracked her, found her hiding in a small clearing, got the throw just right. The blade landed in the centre of her back with a good healthy *chug*. But it didn't kill her. Reluctantly, he slit her throat and buried the body.

He did not count it as a success.

Here, in the Priceway's, mastery was not required; adequate would suffice. He practised with an air-shot, using a bag of dog food as an imaginary target—bring the elbow down, and at the last millisecond, snap the wrist and release.

Okay, he was ready. Land it right between the shoulder blades. Not enough to kill the guy. Just free Alicia without burying Paavan along with any info he may have. It was possible he talked some at the house—they were in there for a while—but Richard couldn't run the risk of a bullet to the lad's head. This way was much better.

He positioned himself. Held the blade between his thumb and first two fingers, retracted behind his head.

Make the target. Pull down hard, then snap. Chug.

It'll be gorgeous.

A click from somewhere. A mechanical noise he recognised.

He lowered the knife, palmed it, and ducked back down. The staff door through which Richard entered was open a crack. A man in a peaked cap with the black and white checks of police branding leaned into the store, looking right at Paavan Prakash. Paavan hadn't seen anything. Richard and the policeman locked eyes. He was rough-looking, unshaven, wearing body armour.

The door opened fully and the policeman snuck through,

followed by another. Both were armed, automatic pistols pointed at the floor.

"Sir," said the first. "You get out of here. This way."

Richard nodded, the throwing knife still hidden in his gloved hand. The second officer held the door and, once Richard crawled in the back area, closed it silently. He was alone in the staff-only section.

This was all going wrong. He couldn't allow it.

Then he heard the order: "Let her go, now!"

Richard opened the door and snuck back into the store.

The officers aimed at Paavan.

"I'll kill her!" Paavan yelled back. "Get me a car. No. A helicopter."

"Ain't gonna happen, boy," the lead officer said. "Let her go or I *will* put a bullet in your head."

"I'll count to five, mister." Pavaan's orders rose an octave. "You back off or I cut her."

"No. *I'm* gonna count to five, boy. Then *I'm* going to shoot you through the face."

Alicia said, "Barry, stop this. I can talk him down."

Barry?

Richard had never killed a policeman before. That was wrong. Even if one caught him one day, he would not harbour any ill will towards them. They were doing a tough job after all. Still, this was more important than principle. He needed Paavan alive in order to locate Katie.

He pulled back his arm. Ready to duck back inside the staff door should he need to *chug* this blade in the officer's neck.

"One!" Paavan said.

"Two!" the officer said.

"Man, stop that!"

Alicia said, "Yes, Barry. Stop it. Your macho nonsense isn't helping. What happened to you? Did your penis fall off, because this is some serious over-compensation."

Paavan actually giggled, but caught himself. "Don't mess with my head. Making me laugh so they can shoot me."

"I'm not. Really. It's a penis issue."

Barry said, "Come on, put it down!"

"Three," Paavan whimpered.

"Four!" the officer called.

Richard tightened his grip on the knife. He would not allow Paavan Prakash to die. The moment either one of them said "five", his elbow would come down, knife cutting the air, embedding in the policeman's jugular. His partner would either turn and kill Richard, or Richard would duck inside and slice up the partner when he came a-searching.

Either way, Paavan lived.

"Okay, don't shoot!" Paavan yelled, his hands raised and visible above the shelves.

Richard backed inside the rear door, observing the scene.

Footsteps, fast, panicked.

Alicia bursting into the arms of the lead ARV officer.

A quick hug, then, "Barry, you idiot. If you killed him I'd have doubled your penis problems."

"I do not have penis problems," he said.

"Keep telling yourself that."

"Whatever you did to me, if it saved your life, it'd be worth it."

"You still shouldn't have come."

"I'd do anything for you, baby, you know that."

And as the second officer completed the arrest, disarming Paavan and snapping the cuffs on, Richard stared through what was now only a crack between the door and its frame, watching the officer touching Alicia in a familiar way, calling her "baby", Alicia thanking him, calling him Barry again, calling him a big daft lump, shaking, the big daft lump taking advantage of her, of her state of mind.

Richard wished he'd killed the man anyway. Still might. Could he? Without Alicia spotting him?

From the front door, the store flooded with officers, Murphy and the two fatties included, and Richard decided to let the man live. For now.

Chapter Twenty-One

SIOBHAN. That was her name. Nothing else. Like Madonna. Only, according to Julian Watson, the head of her record label, she was going to be bigger. No, Siobhan was not another flash in the pan, another kid who'd won a TV talent show.

She was *The Next Big Thing*.

Okay, yeah, she *did* win a TV talent show, but this was more credible than Britain's got Talent or X-Factor. She *wrote* her songs. She collaborated on the *music*. She was a *musician*. And last month, she outsold the previous year's X-Factor winner by a margin of five-to-one. This year's winning single was released this week, and Siobhan ranked neck-and-neck with him for the Christmas number one slot.

And now, aged a mere twenty-one, six months since eighty-four percent of the nation voted for her to win Talent Trek, she was signing copies of her autobiography in a music shop chain store, flanked by the best guarding company in the biz. It was mostly young, spunky ex-military and failed policeman types, but a few older people too.

At last, the lunchtime crush was easing, and after scribbling her name five hundred times, maybe a thousand, her wrist needed a break. She held out her pen to the guard called Ronnie, who took it and placed it in his pocket. Not bad, efficient. Especially considering he'd only joined the Siobhan entourage this morning. She extended an empty hand toward the manager of the shop, who filled it with a glass of iced water. She sipped it, then held the cool surface against her aching wrist.

"This is too cold." She returned it to the man. "Thank you."

Ha! Get that "thank you?" Who said she was getting too big for her boots? She could have, if she'd wanted, dropped the full glass. Let it smash. Or even chucked it in the man's face. Wouldn't that have been something? They'd have cleaned it all up without comment. But she didn't. She wasn't some *diva*.

"Take the ice out," she suggested helpfully, "and then bring it back."

"Of course." He waved a minion over and relayed the instruction.

Siobhan rubbed her wrist again. She'd have to hire someone to teach her how to be ambidextrous. Surprised she knew such a fine word? So were many chat show hosts and newspaper people. She was intent on ensuring she didn't get a reputation as a dumb blonde, so much so that she read a thesaurus as often as she played X-Box, and although early on in this experiment she was ridiculed for occasionally using an ever-so slightly incorrect word or phrase, she was soon able to deflect this when she learned about malapropisms, claiming she was being ironic all those other times. In fact, such was her desire to drop the dumb blonde tag that she stopped dyeing her hair and reverted to her original brown.

Treated and styled very well, though, naturally.

"Hello."

The man held out an unauthorised biography, as well as her entire back catalogue of CD singles and both albums.

Oh great. Who bought *physical* music these days? Obviously a weirdo.

He was her age, maybe older, well-built but geeky-looking. She extended another empty hand Ronnie's way and received the pen.

"So who do I make this out to?" Siobhan asked.

"Oh, er, Simon. Your biggest fan."

Siobhan heard the smirk from Ronnie. She saw the effect wash over Simon, the poor lad.

She said, "Well it's always great to meet my biggest fan. Especially when he's so cute."

Simon beamed, wrinkled his nose at Ronnie, collected his newly-signed merchandise. He leaned toward Siobhan. "Any chance of a kiss?"

Siobhan's initial reaction was revulsion, and she pulled back. Ronnie's shovel-like hand gently eased Simon away.

"That's close enough, mate," Ronnie told him.

Siobhan's biggest fan seemed crestfallen once more. It was another fear she had—losing her fans. All it would take was this guy falling out with her and telling the papers some sob-story about how she had him booted out by her pet gorillas...

"Oh, a little one won't hurt," she said.

She reached over and pulled him closer, landing a soft peck on his cheek. When she saw his face, she found herself a little scared. He bit his bottom lip and, bent slightly at the waist, thighs not moving far, he backed away, trying to say thank you, but the words didn't make it. She half-expected him to explode.

"Urgh." Siobhan collected her clutch bag from the second bodyguard. "I need to clean my face."

"Sure," Ronnie said, following.

She used the goods lift to ascend one floor where Ronnie ensured the ladies toilets were clear of members of the public.

"Go grab a coffee, Ronnie," she said, patting his muscular chest. "I'll be a little while."

"It's okay, ma'am," he said. "I'll wait."

"No." Siobhan opened her bag and slipped out a packaged tampon. "I have to do more than wash my face."

"Ah." He looked embarrassed, but he obeyed. "I'll keep an eye on the door," he said, and headed for the coffee bar at the opposite end of the floor.

Inside, at the counter of three sinks, looking in the mirror, Siobhan smiled at her thoughts of the big lump. The way Ronnie gazed at her, too, she knew she could have him at any time, but it was better she carried on dating the rap star she'd been photographed with on holiday in the Seychelles. She had a book to promote and a second album coming out early next year. Maybe after that they could hook up—

"Hello, Siobhan." A man's voice, the door closing.

Simon, her biggest fan.

"You can't be in here." Her hand found a metal nail file in her bag.

Simon gradually approached, reached the counter. He smiled, breathing in a half-laugh, half-whimper. Hands trembling. He placed the signed CDs and book on the side.

"I always knew we were meant for each other," he said. "I voted for you eight thousand six hundred and forty-two times. My dad wanted to throttle me. He doesn't have much money, you see."

"Well ... thank you." She hid the nail file behind her back.

"But that kiss..." He held his cheek where she'd touched him. "You felt it too, didn't you, Siobhan?" He reached for her cheek, brushed it lovingly with the back of his hand. "You and I will be a wonderful couple."

She swung the nail file at his eye. "*Eat shit and die, psycho!*"

He caught her wrist easily. Squeezed. So much stronger than she expected, forcing her to release the makeshift weapon.

"You might not feel like it right now, Siobhan. But in time ... In time I think you can love me the way I love you."

The door burst open and Ronnie came charging through. "Get away from her *now*!"

Simon released Siobhan. She fell back onto the clean tiles. Ronnie slammed a fist into Simon's face. A sickening crunch echoed through the bathroom. Simon actually lifted off with the force of the blow, hitting the counter and bouncing off, landing hard on the floor. Blood covered Simon's face and Ronnie's fist. Ronnie lifted the fan by his neck and pushed him against the wall, allowing him to stand, dazed, nose oozing.

"Ronnie, it's okay," Siobhan said. "Don't hit him again, I think he's out."

"No," Ronnie said. "It's not okay at all."

And the hulking bodyguard kicked Simon in the throat. Blood erupted from his mouth. He gurgled, drowning in his own fluid as he slid to the floor.

Siobhan was too shocked to scream. Despite Ronnie's size and muscular body, he'd been so sweet, so gentle, all day long. This wasn't like him. When he came to comfort her, to hold her hand, she pulled away, more disgusted even than when her biggest fan tried to kiss her.

"But Siobhan," Ronnie said softly. "You have to come with me. I want you to meet my first. You shall be my second."

Chapter Twenty-Two

AT NINETY MILES per hour westbound on the A58, the winter sun rested low in the sky, and Murphy took one hand from the wheel to don sunglasses. Alicia squinted to see as orange spikes of light bounced off the police van in front; the vehicle containing Paavan Prakash.

Arriving at the outer suburbs of Leeds, the pace slowed and they listened to the press conference held at Sheerton station, DCI Chambers speaking to press, TV and radio. There was a nervousness to her voice that Alicia found hard to articulate. It was as if her mind was elsewhere.

The most recent body was identified as Melanie Sykes, survived by three children of various fathers. Chambers said she was "a woman who sometimes worked in the sex industry." Alicia heard men around the Force scoff at terms like this, calling it "political correctness." Often, they added "gone mad" of course. But Alicia understood the modification to the language. Identifying her simply as "a prostitute" can give the impression that, somehow, what happened to her was her own fault. It also boils her down to a noun. Yes, if she'd been a binman they might reference her job a "refuse collector" rather than "a woman who works in the refuse-collection industry" but she would not be defined by her profession. They—the press, the public, the police—would refer to her as a person first. But because she was "a prostitute" she'd be referred to as "dead prostitute Melanie Sykes" or "murdered prostitute Melanie Sykes" or even "Melanie Sykes, *the prostitute* known as Mia on the street." Melanie herself probably thought of herself as a mother first and foremost. Yes, "murdered mother-of-three Melanie Sykes" is far more palatable.

And accurate.

The other body was yet to be identified, although it was thought to be that of Sally Shaw, who was known also to vice. DNA evidence was currently under examination. Cause of death in Ms. Sykes was a single knife wound to the heart, inflicted by someone of high skill, such was the precision of the blow.

Someone of high skill.

Alicia wondered what profession would prepare you for that. Butcher? Military? The people surrounding the Windsors were either in the military or huge fans of it. Tanya's dad, her cousin, her uncle ... there couldn't be a connection could there? No, Alicia gave herself a mental slap. Don't be silly. Katie was taken for a reason. Melanie Sykes was a thrill-kill. A power-seeker.

On the radio, they said Ms. Sykes was seen talking to a man on the street shortly before she departed with him, and the police are interested in speaking with this man. No charges relating to the sex-trade will be brought; they want to interview him as a witness, nothing more.

Like Alicia and Murphy had with Paavan Prakash.

The person of interest was of average height, indeterminate build, fair to dark hair, aged between thirty five and fifty. "Probably" white.

Alicia picked up on Chambers' pessimistic tone. Murphy's "Hmm" showed he did too.

Chambers went on to detail the location of the bodies, the fact that the man in custody was no longer a suspect, but would be helping the police further. She ended by asking if anyone at all saw something suspicious to call this number. She repeated it three times. Then the questions.

"So the police have absolutely nothing?"

They had a witness, someone who could identify the man if he saw him again.

"Is this the witness currently being interviewed by mental health experts with a view to sectioning?"

He was in the company of a social worker and a lawyer, his state of mind being rather erratic, possibly due to witnessing the disposal of a dead body.

It went on like this. Police incompetence was currently selling newspapers, like rabid dogs, paedophiles and Muslims-are-gonna-get-ya have done, this current rash featuring mistake after mistake. It was why Alicia got harangued so badly by the journalist from the Sentinel. Robert Clancy. She hoped to meet him later, when she brought Katie Hague out from whatever dark place she currently resided.

They passed the West Yorkshire Playhouse, a big theatre, currently showing a ballet version of *Wind in the Willows*. How odd, Alicia thought. But she might have to go, if only to see Toad of Toad Hall in a tutu.

"What's so funny?" Murphy said.

"Was I smiling? I smile a lot, often for no reason. Thought you realised that by now."

They pulled around the City Market, approaching the final road to Glenpark Police Station, the soon-to-be-mothballed base for the West Yorkshire constabulary close to the city centre.

"Not the last day and a half," Murphy said. "You've not been the bouncy, perky thing I met with Rhapshaw."

Was she being dragged down, into the shadows where no one is happy? Where work, this job, *everything*, takes place on a lower tier of existence? She couldn't be. She thought about herself over the last few days, almost panicked when she realised the last fun thing she tried was abseiling with what was now a potential suspect. If not a suspect in the murders, then she foresaw a case file heading to Professional Standards Department; PSD were tasked to investigate corruption in *former* officers as well as serving ones.

She was strangely glad to see a swarm of photographers attacking the van containing Paavan.

Cameras flashed in the dusk light, men and women leaping, snapping futile shots of dark windows and the side of the van. Murphy slowed the Ford Focus.

Robert Clancy morphed out of the crowd. He was there suddenly, stepping out from behind a cameraman, *his* cameraman as it turned out. She forgot *the Sentinel* had a digital video edition. He was the calm in the storm, unreal, central to the melee of newsmen, as if frozen, while all around him the world ran amok. He tapped the youngster on the shoulder and pointed straight at Alicia.

The first flash smacked Alicia in the eyes with red and brown dots, floating, blinking in and out of existence. Robert Clancy approached the car, making a windie-down-the-window gesture, but, predictably, they ignored him.

Flash.

The photographer's lens kissed the passenger window.

Clancy called, "Any comment on the latest kidnapping?"

So it was out in the open. Katie was now fully exposed. More than that: *Richard* was exposed. Raw, laid out for the nation to focus upon. Their next sound bite to twist into more police incompetence.

Flash flash.

"Any comment, DI Murphy? DS Friend? Any leads?"

More press spotted them. Photographers and reporters left the Humberside police van and blocked Alicia and Murphy.

Flash flash.

...

Flash.

"The public are scared. Are you any closer to catching this person?"

The van disappeared into the underground parking garage, the gate swinging shut behind. Murphy made a beeline for this gate, trying hard—though not too hard, Alicia suspected—not to hit any journalists. But now, without the van to chase, the swarm had found a new target.

They inched along, the car like an obstruction in an artery, dislodging gradually. Alicia glanced at Murphy. He was set, serious, no expression. Alicia realised now that hers was not an icy exterior, that she'd been horrified since she spotted Clancy.

She expected to look bad in print tomorrow.

The gate opened as they neared. The pack of newsmen stopped as if by an invisible barrier and, once the Ford was inside, the gate closed creating a real one. They wouldn't violate this area. They'd be arrested, their privileges crushed.

Alicia and Murphy parked up in time to see two constables ushering Paavan into the elevator, taking him to be booked in, having been arrested for assault, taking a hostage, criminal damage, and generally being a silly little boy. It was a real shame. If he'd not panicked like that they could all have eaten fish and chips on the beach, taken his statement, and come home far sooner. His witness statement would have been enough to walk the search warrant application that Ball and Cleaver were currently processing.

Alicia and Murphy took the stairs. Murphy had said nothing since parking the car. He still said nothing on the stairs. Her voice a little loud, with a tinny echo, Alicia broached the subject of Wellington's possible involvement.

Murphy's answer also echoed. "No. He was straight. Wouldn't be bought. No matter what. He had his faults, but being dirty wasn't one of them."

"How do you know?"

"Back then, a lot of coppers were on the take. Small stuff. A cut of a dealer's stash or something. Nothing major. But you always knew who they were. They did it too much and one of their mates would take them aside and give them a bit of advice. Namely that we all knew, and it was making us nervous. They'd stop, or put the extras on hold, and no one said any more. A moment of weakness is forgivable. Covering up a murder isn't. Wellington just wouldn't."

"Enough money can make a nun pole dance," Alicia said, the words resonating up the stairwell and, possibly, all the way to Heaven.

Murphy sniffed, buttoned his jacket, and said, "Depends on the nun."

Detective Chief Inspector Streeter's dress uniform hung in the corner of his office cocooned in polythene ready for his next TV appearance. He wore his usual suit, a tired-looking grey number like the one Murphy wore the day Alicia met him. His hands busied themselves with little nothings as he signalled them to sit.

Alicia sensed the kind of nervousness that came with political fallout. She guessed there had been a leak somewhere; that

Katie being given up to the press had hit him hard and he was now feeling pressure from above. For once, though, she was wrong.

"You know the pop star, Siobhan?" Streeter asked once they were all settled. He didn't need to enquire about Paavan Prakash; Murphy had already reported in.

"Better than the usual pop-kids," Alicia said. "Writes her own stuff."

"I hadn't heard of her. Until today."

He flopped an A4 glossy photo on the desk. The colour drained from Murphy's face. Alicia's legs went numb, a sickness grabbing inside her. She actually wanted to cry.

"She's a match," Murphy said. "Perfect."

The most beautiful so far. Although Alicia wondered how much was airbrushed in this publicity shot.

"And that's why they're outside," she said.

Streeter nodded. "Her agent stirred the shit right up. Some folk figured it for a publicity stunt, but that's gone now."

Murphy crossed his legs and scratched his nose, then his ear. He looked at the photo for a while longer. "It's so frigging cold, I can't believe they don't have something better to do."

"Well, something good's come out of it," Streeter said. "The chief super's given you the extra men you wanted—Serious Crimes have made their interest official. Superintendent Rhapshaw has allocated a full squad to be based in Sheerton station. First thing in the morning. As of right now your budget is unlimited."

Alicia first felt relief at the reinforcements; they could canvass five times as fast, search property, financial records, question suspects, all far quicker than alone. But then she had a thought that lowered her opinion of Chief Superintendent Rhapshaw more than any time she'd known him.

She said, "So now someone famous is missing, we get the bodies?"

"It's not like that, Detective Friend," Streeter said. "It's just..."

"It's just that Siobhan is so much more important," Murphy said. "That's right, isn't it, sir?"

"No. And don't take that tone with me, Detective *Inspector*. Friend gets a little slack because she's protected from on high. You watch your mouth."

"Fine," Alicia said, standing. "If I've got protection, then listen up: of course I want the bodies, but it's disgusting, vile and putrid. It *stinks*. Poor Katie's been in the hands of some maniac for nearly a week, and only now someone who can sing a bit has joined her do you authorise the budget increase." She willed back tears.

"You never even asked for it before."

She couldn't stomach this. It churned inside her, that one human life was worth so much more than another. The furore outside had nothing to do with a lovely young woman and her fraught father; such aggressive press coverage was reserved for celebs and rock stars. It was as if Jesus had returned to Earth, but a bus hit him before he managed to say anything important.

"No, I didn't ask for extra help," she said. "Because I knew what the answer would be. Murphy had already tried." She was too angry to talk straight, the words flying out as soon as they formed. It was wrong. It wasn't Alicia. Too much anger, too much hate. She needed to do something about it. So she thought of camping on a beach, of the surf hissing at the shore, of moonlight... "And another thing. You better protect Richard on this ... Mr. Hague. You'd better not be exposing him—"

"Detective Friend, you may have some leeway, but do not threaten me. Especially when the threats are pointless."

Hmm. That was an odd thing for him to say. She allowed him to elaborate.

"Richard Hague has already agreed to make an appeal to the kidnapper. Live. Sky News, the Beeb, ITV ... they're all in the press room. Channel 4 is on the way."

Alicia didn't believe him. That Richard would volunteer ... it didn't seem right. He'd been pressured, had to be.

"And they're waiting for *you*," Streeter said.

Alicia stopped talking, thinking, breathing. She felt Murphy stand beside her, take her arm.

"Don't worry," Streeter said. "It's just TV. No gutter press. And the talking's already been sorted. Mr. Hague is being briefed right now. You have ten minutes."

"Ten minutes for what?" Murphy said.

"To read this." He tossed a sheaf of paper to each of them, a dozen sheets in each stapled bundle. "The preliminary report on Siobhan's kidnapping. Witness statements. Details of one Simon Pitt's death. Read it, consume it, figure something out. But go. Now."

Outside, Alicia was too nervous to read. She let Murphy. She concentrated on rehearsing some clever put-downs, something comprehensive, yet authoritative and professional. Halfway to the press room, Murphy finished reading.

"Simon Pitt. Nice chap. Had restraining orders out relating to Kylie Minogue, Pixie Lott and Kelly Brook. At first looked like he was trying to protect Siobhan, but now seems he was hitting on her. Anyway, he died from drowning in his own blood. Ruptured trachea, massive internal trauma. Broken nose for definite."

"Professional stalker," Alicia said, keeping her mind off the impending conference.

"Siobhan was abducted by her bodyguard, a chap known as Ronnie. He showed up at the hotel claiming to be someone called Carl's replacement. Carl was found dead at his apartment half an hour ago. Ronnie presented authentic-looking paperwork from the agency that supplies personnel to SecureBiz, so no one batted an eyelid."

"SecureBiz?"

"Security for showbiz personalities."

"Oh."

"He had photo ID, references, everything. All disappeared since Siobhan was taken."

They passed through double doors that led them into a cold, echoing corridor, a service area that many officers used as a shortcut. Alicia wished they weren't cutting through like this.

Murphy outlined how it went down—the coffee, the loo, the amorous Mr. Pitt. "This 'Ronnie' emerged with her hand in hand, practically dragging her. Used a fire exit—pre-planned escape route for real emergencies—and into a car that we think was a good-sized executive class vehicle."

"Nothing specific?"

"No. Ronnie might've been thirty, might've been twenty-five, maybe forty. Car could've been a Lexus, possibly a Merc. Only one witness, and he was on his arse, shooting up at the time."

They reached the press room, noises emanating from within. The vibration of a mike test.

"So what do we know?" she said.

"That the record shop has decent CCTV, but it was ordered turned off for the visit, advice by Mr. Ronnie the bodyguard. He said he used to work in retail, and when a star as gorgeous as Siobhan comes in, they use the cameras to close in on breasts and legs. Digital images end up on the Net. Apparently she ordered these instructions to go out to all her next appointments."

"Nice girl." Alicia reached for the doorknob. "So no image?"

"None. He thought of pretty much everything."

"Except?"

"No. There's no 'except'."

"So there's no 'pretty much' either, is there. He's thought of everything."

"Well ex-*cuse* me." Murphy adjusted his tie. "We know his build matches the description of the guy from the wasteland, and we know he's strong enough to beat a fellow human being to death. Man *or* woman. And he won't go down if me and you turn up with a pair of handcuffs and a sniffer dog."

Alicia thought for a moment, again about herself. That sort of reaction wasn't *her*. She was about to apologise when the door swung open. Daphne Wilson, PR officer for Glenpark Station, stood there, hands on hips.

"About time," she said. "We're waiting."

Alicia took one last reassuring look at Murphy, and amid a shower of lights and calls from the TV people, they all stepped inside. Richard Hague sat behind the table, his fingers thatched, eyes upon his knuckles.

It had been a long day for him.

When Alfie Rhee turned away from the television in the hotel bar, he necked a bourbon and started on what McCall claimed was the best beer in Europe: Stella Artois. It was okay, but he'd finish this one and then buy a Bud. The press conference with that piece of ass Chambers was over and he was still none the wiser. Alfie signalled to the barman he could turn the volume back down. He'd spent five thousand dollars on nothing. He could have watched YouTube. The details Chambers released were hazy, though more scientific in print, in the file. But big fat hairy deal. The only thing this damn file did was confirm what he already knew—it was definitely the same guy who murdered his wife.

"Take it easy, man," McCall said. "It's only four in the afternoon."

"I'll do what I like. I just wasted five Gs. Thanks a bunch."

"What about my money? You promised to pay me."

"You were supposed to help me find a killer. You done nothing but spend my money on a bent cop who I'd rather screw than do a deal with. What you think, I can't read a paper, watch TV? I coulda found this out from Manhattan."

"Oh, come on, mate, I need this."

"Well until you point *me* in the direction of something concrete, your *dick* sure ain't touchin' solid. Now either make some calls or get a round in. J.D. Straight."

The afternoon had been okay, sat in an English pub, kinda quaint in a theme park sort of way. And the food wasn't even that bad, though they only offered three types of cheese, and the bread only came in two varieties: white or brown.

McCall returned with two Jack Daniels. "I guess this won't do me any harm being as I'm gonna have to call my lady friend and cancel."

"You do that," Alfie said.

"Don't suppose you fancy tackling another murder do you?"

"What? Another stabbing?"

"Nah. Ent this UnSub guy. It's a kidnapper. Sick bastard. Pretty girls. Nabbed a pop star. It's on telly now."

Alfie glanced up. Another press conference. Leeds, West Yorkshire. He'd write a letter to the mayor of Detroit on his return to the States, recommending a twinning ceremony. Hah! The Brits were always so superior about crime in the U.S. They reckon they don't get as much murder and shit here, but look at that. Two murders from a serial killer, now a kidnap-murder all over the BBC.

Alfie finished the rest of his Stella. "I'm taking a piss then I'm getting a Bud." He stood and walked toward the bathroom.

McCall turned the television back up, bored so easily after

Alfie moved. Alfie pitied the guy. Not that that would make him like the asshole any better. He kept on walking.

"I am appealing to the man holding my daughter, Katie," the voice from the TV said. "I'm sure you have your reasons for doing this, but please, take a look at her, take a look at Katie."

Alfie paused at bathroom door, unable to move. Thinking. Like walking into a room and completely forgetting why he was there. Something subconscious, something there but not, floating like mist through his mind.

"You *are* human, I know you are," the man's voice continued. "And I know you don't want to hurt Katie like you did the other girls."

Turning from the bathroom, Alfie found himself drawn slowly closer to the TV. It was high up next to the bar itself. He stood beneath it, looking up, up, falling through nothing, dropping through time itself...

He was looking up at someone he recognised.

Someone he ate dinner with once upon a time. A man Stacy had worked with, whom she had liked a great deal. His kindness, his help in getting her a promotion out of the typing pool and into his office, though he was away for long stretches at a time.

Stacy's boss.

She brought him round once, and Alfie cooked steak on the deck. This was back when he was still an FBI agent, of course. There was no sexual spark between Stacy and the guy, no hint of an affair, just mutual respect. Friendship. Alfie never suspected anything at all. He liked the guy. Trusted him with his wife.

Hague, that was his name.

Richard Hague shook Alfie's hand at the funeral. Richard Hague hugged him in that manly bear-hug way and said, "If there's anything I can do ... anything at all."

Him. Here. Now.

Two people dead in this town. A town in which a man lived, a man who knew Alfie's wife—his *dead, murdered* wife—a lifetime ago. A man who travelled all over the United States, who was always welcome in the Rhee household.

Who would have had no trouble gaining access to the house.

"What you doing boss?" McCall said. "You get lost? It's just over there."

"You know," Alfie said, his eyes still on the screen, eyes on the man who killed Stacy Rhee. "I'm glad I came now."

Chapter Twenty-Three

AT FOUR P.M., half an hour after Paavan was booked in and shown to his cell, a lawyer presented herself at the front desk. Gretan Fortune was about forty, tanned, expensively-dressed, and in a foul mood for some reason. She claimed Paavan was a victim of racial profiling, that if he'd been a white man there's no way the ARV would have been called out and there's no way he'd have been bound inhumanely and hurled down the motorway at a hundred miles an hour. Murphy was the lucky one to greet her and pointed out that no one called ARV. He also mentioned that the responding officer was now suspended on disciplinary grounds and that the motorway was in fact an A-road, and finally the reason for the haste was a) because of the urgency of getting him back to Leeds, perhaps to identify a suspect, and b) to ensure his safety; Paavan was obviously frightened of something. He also held a police officer hostage and threatened to cut her throat with broken glass. Ms. Fortune was quietened but not satisfied. Now it was time for her to confer privately with her client.

While she did that, Murphy sipped a fresh coffee in the operations room, awaiting the all-clear to commence the interview.

Alicia sat with her feet up, reading the report on Siobhan's abduction yet again. Alicia's mobile chirped and she answered. She said a few negative things, swore, and hung up.

"That was Ball," she said. "They didn't get the warrant."

"So we can only go into the Windsor estate with the owner's permission?"

"Yup. If you're a society type or a celeb we might as well have two police forces."

It was so weird to Murphy, having only known her a few days. Which of her "five stages" had he entered? What were they again?

Disbelief, irritation, acceptance, reliance, collaboration.

Acceptance, or so it felt. Maybe reliance. Collaboration may have been approaching. Whichever stage, he hated hearing her talk like that.

He said, "Ball and Cleaver on the way back here?"

"Nope. Cleaver has a lead to chase, doesn't want me getting too excited. And Ball is knackered. He's going home for some tea. His wife's giving him ear ache apparently."

"So why didn't we get the warrant?" Murphy asked.

"Brass said it was ludicrous. Circumstantial. Let the man mourn in peace, apparently." Alicia rolled her eyes. "Word from on high. What can you do?"

"We can get Paavan to talk. Then we take it to Wellington."

Alicia checked her watch. "Lawyer'll be a while. I'll see if Richard's finished with the press office, offer him a lift."

When she was gone, Murphy stood in front of the white-boards bearing the names of dead or missing girls. He added Siobhan's name and bullet-pointed her abduction. Then he added some issues to the section with Tanya's name at the head. The final thing he wrote before standing back and reading it all again was: *John Wellington, Detective Chief Inspector, retired.*

.   .   .

Alicia had not been herself. The decline in Alicia-ness was a by-product of allowing things to squirm inside her and nestle within. It happened from time to time. The bounce was back now, though. She just hoped it hadn't made its welcome return through the prospect of seeing Richard again. When she entered the family room in which Richard had been placed after the press conference, she saw him smile, and she knew that, unfortunately, it was definitely bounce-related.

The meeting was over and the press officer was gone. A little coaching session for Richard on how to treat the press who would almost certainly be at his home. An officer was stationed there, to keep them off his property, out of his bins, leave his flowerbeds untrampled.

Richard said, "Hi, what are you doing here?"

"Personal service." Alicia smiled back at him. Casual. Y'know, a mate popping by. "Seeing if you needed a lift anywhere. Heard you got driven in from your house."

"That's right. But they've put me up in a hotel not far from here. I was going to catch a cab. Less conspicuous."

"Don't be daft. I'll drive you. Besides, I could do with a chat. I'll let you know where we are after today's shenanigans."

Shenanigans? Really?

Alicia signed out a maroon Vauxhall, disengaged the airbag as usual, and drove them out of the underground garage. They passed the photographers, who didn't see inside and therefore were slow off the mark to realise maybe they'd missed something. It was cold and night was descending, streetlamps now lit.

They had a clear road out to the Travel Inn.

Sergeant Cleaver felt like an ass. The reception to Sheerton was lit only by a few fluorescent strips, as if the building itself was growing tired. A man on a ladder changed bulbs, a whole section cordoned off. Cleaver hated winter. Dark at five p.m. and so cold that brass monkeys were breaking out the thermal undies.

Cleaver felt like even more of an ass when he asked the kid, same one as this morning, if Darla Murphy was still in the building. The kid dialled her extension and confirmed that she was, asked what it was regarding, and Cleaver said it was confidential. The kid relayed this, held the phone away from his ear as a barrage of abuse spat back at him, and softly replaced the receiver.

"She'll be right down," he said.

Cleaver smiled awkwardly. Then he stood, also awkwardly, rocking back and forth on his heels. There was no easy way, he decided, to wait for a fellow police officer, in a police station, holding a bunch of flowers that, in all likelihood, stank of petrol. The kid behind the desk looked at them as if they were porn.

Darla's voice: "What is it?"

There she was, stood in the double doorway like a bad-tempered siren in need of a daytime TV makeover.

"Er, these are for you," Cleaver said.

She glanced at the flowers without expression. "And what do I do with them?"

Cleaver shrugged. "Look at them? Put them in a vase or something."

"This is a police station, Sergeant Ball, not a garden warehouse."

"It's Cleaver." He stepped forward before speaking again. "Anyway, I wanted to say thank you. We have a decent lead now."

"It was my pleasure," she said flatly. She took the flowers in one hand and held them upside down by her leg. "Anything else?"

"No. Just ... thanks." Cleaver turned to go, this time the defeat final, never to return.

"Sergeant Cleaver," Darla called.

He stopped.

"There *was* something else. Wasn't there?"

He took a breath, trying to build up his courage. Well, "build up" might have been exaggerating. *Create* some courage might be more accurate.

He said, "Two things. The first one I think you'll definitely say no to, so I'll ask you the second reason I came here."

She nodded at him to get on with it.

Voice low so the probie on reception didn't hear, he said, "I was wondering if—and you can say no if you want, I'll understand—I was wondering if you'd be willing to help me break the law for an hour or so."

"No. Absolutely not." Her gaze wandered to the floor, crept toward the probie who was watching them. She ushered Cleaver further out of earshot. "How much law-breaking are we talking about?"

"I'll say I tricked you. If I'm caught, I'll say you set me up on the computer and left me to it. But I really need to look into someone's financial records. I don't have a warrant."

"This is to do with the missing girls? That Siobhan woman too?"

Cleaver nodded once.

"It'll be inadmissible," Darla said.

"I know. But we have a theory and I need to know how close we are."

Darla wanted to say yes, Cleaver could feel it. This morning she was so spot-on balls-adamant she had to get back to tracing the old lady's credit card, pissed that she'd been dragged off to help someone else's case. This wasn't a woman who cared nothing for her job. She wanted to catch them all. She reminded Cleaver of himself a decade ago.

"My daughter likes Siobhan," she said. "Personally I think she'll be in the bargain bin by Easter."

"There's more than one girl you know."

"Yes, but it's Siobhan the public will focus on. And that's what'll make them feel unsafe. That a well-protected star like Siobhan can be taken."

Cleaver understood. "How old's your daughter?"

"Nine. Why? What does that have to do with anything?"

"Can we go inside?"

Darla held the door for him and they headed for the same room as before.

"I have two myself," Cleaver said. "Fourteen and sixteen. Boys. They live with their mother."

"Really?" Darla said. "And what makes you think I'm interested?"

They spent the rest of the short walk in silence. In the office, she booted up the computer and logged on with a *lot* of asterisks. The flowers lay on the side of the desk.

"Okay," she said. "What do you need?"

He produced a scribbled page from his notebook, told her the names and addresses of the two people he was interested in.

"Shouldn't be too hard." Darla's fingers set off, tap dancing over the keyboard, only pausing occasionally to use the mouse.

Cleaver watched her, watched her face when he could. Her angular lines made her swish glasses look abnormal, her untreated hair pulled back in a long, straw-like ponytail. She dressed frumpily, but it failed to hide from Cleaver what he was sure were superb breasts.

Ah the mind of a gentleman.

"Stop it," she said without pausing.

"Stop what?"

"Stop looking at me like that."

"Sorry."

She ceased working. The light from the screen reflected in her glasses, hiding her eyes. "If you want to ask me out, you don't have to buy me flowers or make up illegal hacks. You have to prove you aren't like Chrissie's father."

Cleaver felt his cheeks burn. "It's not made up. I really need this."

"Okay." She started again.

"So will you?"

"Will I what?"

"Go out with me. You know, when I get done with this."

She stopped typing again. Examined the screen. Took one glance at the flowers.

"No," she said, and resumed working.

The Travel Inn was only a matter of minutes away by car, and Alicia could not remember entering the hotel arranged by the Family Liaison team. She was sure she flashed her ID to the manager who greeted them and allowed them in the back door, but she did not remember being invited up to Richard's room. She automatically followed him. No words, nothing, and now they were alone together. Richard looked out of the window, squinting toward the canal where it wound its way invisibly through the night.

Alicia sat on one of the chairs beside the writing table, comfy-looking but too hard for her. She figured it was safer than the bed.

"We have a suspect," she said. "But it's going to be tough getting a warrant. We're putting pressure on the guy we brought in today, but he's scared. Not sure if it's jail he's scared of or the guy who paid him to disappear."

"What's his name?" Richard said.

"I'd rather not say at this point. You understand."

He nodded reluctantly. Then he perked up as he spotted the complimentary drinks beside the kettle. "Tea?"

Alicia checked her watch. No probs. Ms. Fortune would still be with her client, and Murphy would phone when it was time. She was only five minutes away at the most, and that included getting to the car.

"Yes, please. Milk, no sugar."

"Sweet enough, I suppose," Richard said with a sly smile.

She had no reply, holding inside her the worst case of unreasonable hormone activity since she fell for Bradley Donovan, a drummer at her high school who thought it was cool to keep rats as pets. His long hair and lack of any sort of direction in life was Alicia's first rebellion against her parents' ordered, perfect lifestyle. He was an idiot, but she loved him, was going to marry him, have his six kids and live life the way *she* chose, not become a lawyer like her dad.

And now she wasn't living how she chose. She was living by the will of those who do harm, who take from society and give nothing back, who take and take until there's nothing left.

She definitely was not herself. "Don't think I'm sweet enough tonight."

Richard said, "Sugar it is." Then, "So who's this Wellington guy I've been hearing about? Some ex-CID officer I gather."

"Where did you hear that name?" Alicia asked.

"The other officers talking at the press conference before you arrived. The chubby fellows."

Cleaver and Ball. Oh well.

She said, "He's not the prime suspect, but we think he knows more than he's letting on. I don't know how we'll prove it without a warrant and full investigation into his finances. But that will implicate someone else, and the political fallout if we make a boo-boo of it ... it's tough getting what we need, but we'll do it. I know we will."

Richard poured water into two cups with a teabag in each. He plunged them and added milk. One sugar sachet for Alicia. He held the cup out and she took it, her fingers brushing his. He sat opposite in the twin of the chair she'd taken. She drank, the milk tasting sour, as per usual in hotel rooms.

Over his cup, Richard's eyes met hers. There was little more to discuss. No more ground on Katie, and nothing more to say about Wellington. Unable to mention the little Windsors. Alicia, wondering how rough Richard's stubble was right now, figured the time had come to politely leave.

She placed the cup on the bedside table, her arm making contact with Richard as she leaned past him. He stood and gently took her hand.

And that was it.

The hormonal surges that plagued her throughout her teenage years were on the march again. They found their way to her fingers, knees, toes, as well as the usual places. Before she could think of one more reason not to—and there were many— Alicia was on her tippy-toes, hand clasped around the back of Richard's head, pulling him towards her. His lips smooshed into hers, soft, moving just right, every rule under the sun broken by that one act. Tongues tested one another, then explored fully, Richard's hands circling her back, strong and powerful, and he lifted her slightly so the pressure was off her toes. Her arms slid around his neck, hands running through his hair, his lips firm on hers, moisture down below growing more severe, uncomfortable even, but a good uncomfortable, one she hadn't experienced for a long time. Richard smoothed his hands down her back, finding her rear, holding her there, pushing himself against her, and she could feel him, make out his shape. She unbuckled his belt in a furious fumble, and—

Alicia's mobile rang. It was loud, sounding louder than it really was, making them both jump.

They disengaged the kiss, grinning, forehead to forehead. Alicia bit her bottom lip.

"Go on," Richard said. "It might be important."

She flipped it open, sat on the bed whilst adjusting her hair. "Alicia Friend speaking, how may I direct your call?"

"Alicia, get back here," Murphy said. "The lawyer's ready for questioning. How long you going to be?"

Alicia continued to straighten herself—her hair, her blouse. "I'm not sure, I..." She looked at Richard, hands in pockets, trying to look nonchalant. Failing. "Can you do it alone? Something's come up. I think Richard needs me."

He nodded at that.

"No, Alicia," Murphy said. "I need you here."

If this wasn't concluded one way or another, here, now in this room, it was over forever for them. She and Richard would be embarrassed each time they met. And Murphy was more than capable. The kid wasn't a suspect; he was a witness. There were no new insights, nothing Alicia could exclusively help with. It was more important she stay here. Richard needed to remain strong, and she needed to see to it that he did.

"Donald, take Ball or Cleaver in with you," she said. "Sounds like Ball would like to get away from his wife anyway."

"Yes, but—"

"No buts, mister, just do it. I'm the psychologist, remember? Katie's father needs me here more than you need me there. Ring me in a couple of hours."

She hung up without a reply. Then she reached for Richard's belt, pulled it out of its hoops, and eased him onto her so she lay on the bed beneath his body. His lips found her neck and her hands untucked the man's shirt.

And she wondered exactly how much trouble this was going to land her in.

Cleaver couldn't be raised, and Sergeant Ball made the appropriate harangued noises for the benefit of his wife, but when he arrived at the station the only indication that he'd been put out was the absence of a tie. He and DI Murphy entered the interview room and announced their names for the tape. Murphy read Paavan Prakash his rights once more, and Paavan confirmed he understood.

"Interview commences six-fifteen p.m.," Murphy said. "Right. Mr. Prakash, I'd like you to explain how someone who isn't working and isn't claiming benefits can afford to live in a three bedroom semi-detached house."

"Don't answer that," Fortune said.

"He can answer what he likes."

"He answers what I tell him to answer."

Paavan's hard stare confirmed this.

"Fine," Murphy said. "Then how about you go over your relationship with the late Tanya Windsor?"

"No," Fortune said. "Not that. It has no relevance to his arrest."

"It has every relevance."

"It does not. He has been arrested for the situation arising at the Scarborough Road branch of Priceway's in Bridlington. You may ask about that."

"The relationship was what we were investigating when your client decided to bolt. Mr. Prakash's motivation for running is perfectly relevant."

"Mr. Prakash's motivation for running is that he was scared of two police officers crowding him into a small room. He felt threatened. We all know how the police behave toward ethnic minorities, don't we detective."

Murphy wished for the olden days, when this type of interview was a straightforward session of threats and counter-threats and finally compromise with a ton of information and a nod and a wink to say they'd release the prisoner without charge *if* the statement checked out. Now it was burgeoning your way through a wall of ego-driven lawyers trying to get one over on the police.

"DS Friend and I were not *crowding* him. He was looking for property belonging—"

"That *you* requested. You told him it was standard enquiries, and yet you'd thought to bring along not only a local black and white, but two more CID officers from this station as well." She nodded at Ball. "A little heavy-handed for one man about whom you claimed to be 'enquiring'. Don't you think?"

Murphy thought for a moment. This woman was a ball-breaking bitch with a point to prove. A real ego problem. She was also a private practitioner.

"Who's paying for your time, Ms. Fortune?" Murphy asked.

"That's irrelevant. My client is the one under arrest, not me."

"Not yet," Murphy mumbled.

"Don't even try to imply a threat, Detective Inspector."

"Paavan. Tell me about your relationship with Tanya."

"He's told you everything already."

"For the tape. Tell it again."

She tapped his arm. "Do not say anything. They can't make you."

Paavan laid his chin on hands, folded on the table. Murphy met his gaze, the lad's mouth quivering slightly. Scared. Of whom though? The lawyer? Or of jail? Neither. He was scared of something else. Murphy needed a plan of attack, one he could use to circumvent Gretan Fortune.

But he'd taken too long to think

"Paavan," Ball said in the softest voice Murphy had ever heard him use. "If you won't talk about Tanya, she's going to rot. She's going to be put in the grounds on the Windsor estate and the worms will eat her—"

"That's enough," Fortune said.

Ball's tone dropped an octave. Sterner. "The man who killed her is still free and he's holding two more girls, innocent girls like Tanya."

"Was she innocent?" Murphy said.

Paavan sat up, looking at Fortune.

The lawyer said, "Stop this right now. My client is not under arrest for murder, he is under arrest for taking a hostage. This line of questioning is over. If you have nothing else, I am taking my client out of here."

"And then what?" Murphy said. "The last guy with any connection with this case, fella called Doyle, he died pretty horribly. You want a dead client on your hands?"

"We won't catch him," Ball said. "Not without your help. What would Tanya do if this was reversed? If it was you in a fridge waiting to be cut open, already having tests carried out on your corpse? What would Tanya do?"

A flicker in his eyes.

Murphy caught it.

The lawyer said something else, threats of legal action, accusations of harassment and racism, but Paavan ignored her.

Murphy said, "If you'd been killed by your uncle Bengal tiger because you wanted to marry a white tiger, what would she do? Would she hide behind a lawyer? Like a cub?"

"No," Paavan said.

"Do not say one more word," Fortune warned. "Not one more."

Paavan's eyes were full of tears. "Please leave."

"I'm not going anywhere." She crossed her arms.

Oh yeah, that'll work, Murphy thought.

"I waive my right to legal counsel," Paavan said.

Paavan's words hung all around, especially around Fortune. Finally, she stood, composed herself and, at the door, pausing before she left, she told Paavan, "Remember what I said."

The door closed and Paavan leaned forwards, eyes darting side to side as if expecting assassins to break through the walls.

He said, "I'll talk to you, but you have to protect me."

And Paavan told his story.

At the exact moment that Paavan Prakash burst into tears and began wailing for Tanya to forgive him, which was close to the end of his statement, Detective Sergeant Alicia Friend was across town in a hotel room, experiencing an orgasm of such magnitude that her fingernails gouged a series of small canyons down Richard Hague's back.

And, in the afterglow of it all, Alicia still didn't regret it. Morning could be another matter. Richard was kind, a good man, though sad, hiding something of his true self. Alicia didn't mind so much. If she could free Katie for him she would have plenty of time to unravel what secrets lay behind the façade.

Lying with her head on his chest, listening to his heartbeat winding down to its regular rhythm, she told him of her fears, of becoming someone she wasn't. That she was losing something of herself, allowing the darkness in, pushing her personality out. She was about to confess to the abortion of her teen years, how it had been playing on her more than usual since the trip to Brid, but then Richard suggested they shower, and the darkness was banished once again.

He soaped her all over—every part of her body lathered—tenderly moving his hands over her smooth skin. He took time to wash her intimately, then rinsed her with the skill of a beauty therapist. She returned the favour and they kissed some more, held one another.

Richard said, "Perhaps you'd make more ground if you were … 'you' again."

She saw in his eyes that he felt the same way as her, that this was *right*, that it was *meant* to happen. Whatever happens.

"Alicia, you're right. From the woman I met two days ago, you have changed some. Not as happy, not as hopeful."

He kissed her neck, water spraying off his head.

"You're also right about the darkness. If it gets inside you it's hard to get rid of. And you are too beautiful a creature to lose to it."

His mouth moved to her breasts, not hard, not suckling like a starved baby goat like her previous boyfriend; Richard was teasing, considerate.

"Trust me, Alicia. I know about that sort of thing."

His tongue on her belly, circling her navel, then down.

"Alicia, you are truly a special woman. You can't be wasted on the evil that is eating away at you. Come back to me. Be yourself again."

His words made it to Alicia's ears, but as he raised her thigh onto his shoulder and buried his mouth inside her, the words ran away, stored in the back of her mind for another time, as all guilt about leaving Murphy alone with Paavan Prakash faded away in the shower, beside the man with whom she was fairly certain she was falling in love.

Chapter Twenty-Four

THE GIRL SEEMED familiar to Katie. She was strapped to the chair opposite, gagged, struggling with her bindings. The man who visited them that evening had freed Katie briefly, then manacled the chain to her leg once more, and he left without a word to either of them. Katie had approached the girl in the chair, a mess, her eyes pleading, but the chain stopped her a good six feet short. She wanted to help, but knew the time would soon come that her captor would give the order to commence.

And Katie would have to try and kill this girl, to remain this man's First, whatever the hell that meant.

It was self-defence, she kept telling herself. And it would be self-defence again.

She'd been ordered not to speak to the new girl, another spitting image of Katie, like the one who died, who the man called "Rachel", but who was not Rachel, not at all. For now he referred to Katie as Rachel, which was as frightening as anything that had happened so far.

The new girl tried to speak through the gag, but Katie refused to respond, as per the instructions. She hated obeying, but it was how to survive. Obedience.

It was *him* who put the crowbar in the girl called Rachel's hand. It was *him* who ordered the Rachel-girl to attack. It was *him* who told the girl to prove her love for him by extinguishing his Second.

Soon, the man would give Katie a weapon and tell her when he wanted this new Second wiping from his life.

Katie wondered how hard it would be. Could she? Could she be the aggressor here if it meant surviving?

He said he'd kill Katie in this girl's place if she didn't obey. Last time, the girl attacked first, without question, and it was thanks only to her dad's insistence on teaching her how to destroy an attacker much larger than herself—"attacker" meaning "man" or "rapist"—that she beat the girl away.

Yet it was rage, the anger she'd been saving for the man keeping them here, a will to live that had enabled Katie to slam the girl's head on the floor until her blood sprayed everywhere, until the moment the ear tore from the girl's head. Katie remembered looking at it in her hand, curious at first as to what it was. Then when she realised what she'd done, how much damage she inflicted, she simply stood up and backed away, handed the ear to the shocked-looking man, and sat in the chair.

Now she knew.

There was no way either of them, here in this room, was leaving alive. It had taken too much to push her to that point. She remembered little of the actual fight; only the aftermath remained vivid. The girl in the chair wouldn't fight either. She'd seen nothing of this guy. Whatever happened to the first Rachel must have been unthinkable, something able to spring her into action on a whim. And whatever it was, Katie vowed it would not happen to her.

It was self-defence.

It *was* self-defence.

Next time it wouldn't be.

"I'm Katie," she said to the girl.

The girl's eyes softened. The tears that had been welling spilled in a stream of gratitude and hope. What Katie had been unable to glean from the last girl, this one had achieved from Katie. Things were going to be different this time.

"I'm going to tell you what this guy has planned," Katie said. "I'm going to try and stop him. But I need your help."

Chapter Twenty-Five

THE GUILT ALICIA predicted would descend circled high overhead, not bothering her one little bit. Her early morning rush from the hotel to her apartment, and subsequent interrogation by Roberta, another quick shower and change, all added to the feeling of running, of movement, of not standing still long enough for the cloud to catch her. Whilst showering, Robbie stood in the bathroom and Alicia regaled her with last night's perfection. She questioned the ethical side of things but Alicia reminded her that the ethics of the police and her own morality were two different entities. After all, she didn't stick around for a morning repeat, dashing out at 5 a.m. It would be vulgar while Katie was still missing.

"And besides," she added, stepping from the shower and into a fluffy bathrobe, "I've not been myself lately. I've been blindsided by a few things and it's all down to me letting them get to me. From now on, it's one-hundred percent Alicia."

"Glad to hear it," Robbie said, running a tap for her toothbrush. "Now get to work, you dirty whore."

It was at work where she felt least like herself. Since

Monday, anyway. It was now Thursday and it was a clean slate, a new day, the day she would take back control.

At seven a.m. she signed in at Glenpark, and the constable said, "You do something different with your hair today?"

"Sure did," Alicia replied.

"What? I'm not sure."

"You'll never make CID at this rate."

She flashed a smile and skipped on over to the door. It buzzed and she entered, tugging on both pigtails, making a *parp-parp* noise as she went.

They were Robbie's idea. She said they made her look younger, made the suggestion as a joke, but Alicia needed them today. She needed to replace the business-like ponytail with the schoolgirl hairstyle. And she absolutely adored them. She even tied a little pink scrunchy round each.

"What the hell do you look like," Murphy said in the operations room.

He was wearing the same suit as last night, hadn't shaved, and smelled a bit funny. The guilt cloud hovering around Alicia then swooped like a vulture and seized her with its claws.

"You stayed all night?" she said.

"It was two a.m. when I finished the report. Here." He passed her Paavan's statement. "I need a coffee. Then I need to pop home and feed my cat. Maybe grab an hour."

He left the room and Alicia read the statement.

Yes, Tanya disappeared on the twenty-third of May last year, and yes, Paavan maintained his story about Wellington beating him and adding the warning that he needed to leave town.

How very cowboy.

He also claimed that James Windsor—although nice to him initially—threatened him, told him to disappear. He'd gotten the credit card, the house, all of it through Tanya's estate—

—how was that possible? Oh, Murphy asked that.

James told Paavan that Tanya came to her senses and left Paavan, buying him off with these offerings, which meant Paavan knew something was up. He made enquiries of those investigating her disappearance. It was *then* that Wellington came to him. Not before, as Alicia had assumed. So Paavan accepted the bribe, knowing they could monitor his spend, and he vowed to make enough cash of his own—cash "they" could not trace—to hire an investigator, someone to locate Tanya, so he could understand, so he could *know*. That was why he switched from his "great" novel to commercial horror fiction; the money he arrogantly assumed he would make, but failed to materialise.

No, he didn't think she was dead. She was alive somewhere, maybe living abroad; he was sure of it. She had to be. No way James would harm her.

It was here that Murphy informed him of the recent discovery on the old railway tracks behind Evergreen Industrial Estate. Paavan didn't watch television and avoided the news. He was too busy with his writing to be distracted by such things. His cries were illegible on the page, just a note of when he started sobbing and when he stopped.

"I'm guessing James hurt her," Murphy said, returning with coffee. "Loved her too much, made his move at the race course party, and she rejected him. His dad helped cover it up. Kept her somewhere so she couldn't press charges."

"Where?"

"I dunno. Probably subcontracted that. Some gang. Or professionals. They'll have known private security firms through the arms industry, so it wouldn't have been too hard to find someone willing to hold her. Sent James abroad in case we put the pieces together."

"But she's dead."

"Ball has a crazy theory."

"Yeah? I love crazy theories. Hit me."

"Pippa, Hayley, Katie. All taken by a maniac. Tanya ... killed by the people holding her and made to look like the others. Could be Tanya isn't connected to Katie."

Alicia asked, "Have we confirmed James is abroad?"

"We confirmed he left the country, yes. Interpol are tracing his movements."

Alicia read the whiteboards again, several things bothering her, unsure which things, unsure why they bothered her, positive they didn't tally with what she and Murphy were working on. Ball's theory was neat, but a bit "out there."

"It's too..." She couldn't think of the word. Actually, the word was "scootchy" but she made that one up. "Too many threads, too much falling neatly. Could be the mercs or whatever decided to kill Tanya, but took the other girls first to obscure Tanya's death. That would signal planning of great magnitude. True obsession, but incredibly high organisational skills too. Someone like—"

Sergeant Cleaver entered, looking as bad as Murphy, also in the same suit as yesterday, also unshaven. He also looked rather pleased with himself.

He said, "You are going to love me, babe."

"I love everyone this morning," Alicia said. "Well, except one guy, but hey."

"Get a load of this." He carried a sheaf of paper, some colour prints, a lot of numbers. "I was up all night, but it'll never see a courtroom."

Was I the only one who had any sleep? Alicia thought. *Then again, there wasn't much of that...*

She read through the sheet he handed her. Then he handed another, pink highlighter daubing certain lines.

"You stayed up doing this?" Alicia said.

"Me and Darla Murphy over at Sheerton."

"And how is my brother's little girl?" Murphy asked from the doorway.

"She's your niece?"

"Hope you didn't keep her out past bedtime."

Cleaver started again, explaining about the account numbers, the transfers of money through fictitious companies. One of these companies paid Paavan Prakash's credit card each month. Another three paid share dividends to one John Michael Wellington.

"It's seven-thirty," Cleaver said. "Can I bring Wellington in?"

An hour later, Murphy and Alicia watched through a two-way mirror as John Wellington was lead into the interview room and politely asked to sit. Murphy still couldn't believe that this man might be integral to a murder investigation.

Through the speakers mounted above this side of the mirror, Wellington reminded Ball and Cleaver that he was here voluntarily, and added he had a ten o'clock tennis session. It was already eight-thirty.

Alicia watched him closely, concentrating as the door closed and he was left alone in the room. His head dropped.

"It's all fake," Alicia said. "The friendliness, the bravado, the beard."

"His beard's fake?" Murphy said.

"Gotcha!"

Either Alicia was now more annoying since Monday or lack of sleep was making him grumpy. He had managed to feed his rather annoyed cat, wash, and dig out a fresh shirt, but didn't catch any kip. Alicia didn't seem to care.

"Come on," she whispered. "Make me right."

As if he heard her subconsciously and was following these instructions, Wellington stood angrily and stomped over to the mirror, head up against it. Were this a normal window, he would have been eye to eye with Murphy.

"Look, you know I know these tricks," Wellington said. "I'm not some animal. You want to ask me questions, then ask. I cooperated out of respect for the police, for what *was* my family. Respect goes both ways."

Alicia reached up to the glass with a red dry-wipe marker and scribbled a pair of glasses on Wellington's eyes. Murphy snatched the pen from her and shot her what he hoped was a disapproving fatherly look. Alicia ruefully wiped the pen off with a tissue.

Outside, Murphy asked if she was going to put her hair "back to normal."

"This is normal for me," she said.

They entered the interview room, Murphy dour and deliberate, Alicia as joyful as springtime. Something wasn't right about her today.

Wellington disengaged from the mirror.

"Hi, John," Alicia said. "Thanks for coming. It's great to see you again. Want a coffee?"

"Thank you, no."

They all sat at the fixed table, Alicia and Murphy this side, Wellington the other. They swept through the formalities for the benefit of the tape, emphasising Mr. Wellington was not under arrest and was here voluntarily. Wellington confirmed this.

Alicia said, "Okay, some easy questions to start with."

"Shoot away."

She smiled, hung her head to one side. "Was your nickname 'Welly' when you were on the Force?"

"No."

"Can *I* call you Welly?"

Murphy nudged her. She was going off on one. He wondered briefly if she was on drugs.

"You, my dear," Wellington said with a toothy smile, "can call me anything you like."

"Thank you. 'Mr. Wellington' is such a mouthful."

"John," Murphy said firmly. "We need to ask you about the Tanya Windsor case."

"I didn't think it was for my culinary skills, Detective Inspector Murphy."

"Tell us about the first moments, what you did when Henry Windsor first reported Tanya missing."

"It wasn't Henry," Wellington said. "And you know it. It's there in the file."

"That's right. Sorry. When her friend *Hillary* reported her missing, what was the first thing you did?"

"We asked everyone at the party when they last saw Tanya, to work out the latest she could possibly have left the scene. It was Hillary who we established was last to speak to her. She didn't recall about what."

"She's since had a brain-flash, Welly," Alicia said. "She remembers. Isn't that cool?"

Wellington fidgeted in his seat.

Murphy said, "It has emerged that Tanya had a boyfriend. Someone she met in India and kept a secret."

"An *Indian* man," Alicia said. "It's *so* romantic."

Wellington leaned forward, his grey beard ruffling as his mouth twisted. "And?"

"And Hillary claims she came to you with this information."

"She's lying."

"Is she?" Murphy said. "Okay then. Let's talk about the fact that this man is sat in a cell in this station right now."

"He's here?" Wellington said.

"He's here," Alicia said. "And he's very upset that Tanya's dead. For some reason he thought she was abroad."

"And why would he think that?"

Murphy gambled on a lie, one that might trip them up later in court or with the CPS, but they had higher priorities than convictions right now. "Because that's what he claims *you* told him."

"I told him no such thing!"

"So what *did* you tell him?" Alicia said.

"Nothing. I told him nothing."

"I thought you didn't know him at all," Murphy said.

"I—"

"I don't believe you, Welly," Alicia said. "Much as I don't like Freud, you made a Freudian slip."

"It's nothing. Try using it against me."

"Oh, Welly, do you really think I'd do that?"

"Stop calling me that."

Alicia shrugged.

Murphy took over. "*Mister* Wellington, the last time you made an entry to the case file you ascertained that Tanya had met with foul play of some kind, probably with a stranger, since everyone at the party was accounted for."

Wellington looked pointedly at his watch. "Get on with it."

Murphy checked the time. Eight forty-five.

"Welly," Alicia said. "When did you first realise that Tanya had met with foul play?"

Wellington now bristled at the name *Welly*. "After interviewing James Windsor. I grilled him thoroughly along with one of my Inspectors, Derek Doherty—ask him, he transferred to Doncaster last year."

"We will," Murphy said. "But for now, answer the question. What did James say that made you suspect foul play?"

"It's in the file, Donald. Read the damn file."

"I want to hear you say it."

Wellington gave an exasperated sigh. "James said that there was no way Tanya would have run away without telling him.

They were like brother and sister, not cousins. He loved her more than anyone, and she loved him. If she was running away, he'd have known."

"Then why didn't you follow up on the mystery man angle?" Alicia asked. "Wasn't it obvious she was seeing someone? With the tiger tattoo and everything?"

"The tattoo meant nothing. A lot of rich kids get tattoos."

"Is that why it isn't mentioned in the file?"

Wellington stopped. Frozen in time.

Gotcha, Murphy thought.

Wellington stood slowly, shakily. "I'd like to go now."

"What a shame," Alicia said. "We'd like you to stay. Please?"

"No. I have to go and play tennis. I'm expected."

"Sit down, Welly. We have a couple more questions. Then it's all over."

"I'm leaving."

"No," Murphy said. "You're not."

He was gradually regaining his composure and bluster. "Then arrest me for something and get me a brief."

"Gretan Fortune do?" Murphy said.

Alicia frowned. She wouldn't know who that was. She was off comforting some guy in a hotel room, a detective sergeant doing the job of a FLO.

Wellington frowned too. He clearly hadn't heard of Ms. Fortune. "Am I under arrest?"

"Interview terminated at oh-eight fifty-two." Murphy clicked off the tape and immediately presented the bank and money transfer records. "Whether you're under arrest depends on how you answer this."

Wellington read it. "My private share dividends. So what?"

"In companies that don't exist ... except on paper," Alicia said. "And if you go right the way back, you know, untangle all the tape and unblock the drains and ignore all the smokescreen 'winding up' orders, guess where they lead?"

Wellington's expression was stone.

"They lead to our good friend Henry Windsor."

Go on, Murphy thought. *Deny it, you smug arsehole.*

Wellington smiled now, sat down. Faking relaxed. "This is totally inadmissible. You have less than nothing. That's why you turned off the tape—"

Murphy slammed his fist on the table. "I'm not talking about what's *admissible*. I'm talking about what's *right*!"

"A girl's life," Alicia said. "Two girls' lives."

Murphy grabbed Wellington by the throat and pushed his chair back, using his own knee to steady the chair as it wavered mid-tip. "Tell me now! Tell me where he's hiding them."

Wellington gagged, croaked the words out. "I don't know. I swear I don't know anything."

"You were being paid off to cover up Tanya's kidnapping. But now it's murder. It's more than one murder. You're responsible, John. And you can end it right now. You could have ended it *days* ago."

"We'll recommend to PSD that you aren't charged in connection with any of the current murders," Alicia said. "We'll try and play down Tanya's kidnapping, but can't promise how Professional Standards will see it. Just say it. Say where they're being held."

"Okay, put me down," Wellington said, face now red, fit to burst.

Murphy lowered the ex-policeman to the ground and let go. "Talk."

Wellington composed himself, hands flat. He opened his mouth, defeated eyes focused on his hands, lip quivering. Tears welled and one spilled.

He said, "She's..."

Then the door opened and in strode Gretan Fortune, brief-case swinging, eyes revved up and firing. She stood, hands on hips, glaring at Murphy and Alicia like bad dogs. "How *dare* you interview my client without me being present? Get out, both of you. I need to consult with Mr. Wellington in private."

Seventeen minutes later, from the comfort of DCI Streeter's office, Murphy and Alicia watched through the window as John Wellington walked out of the station alongside Gretan Fortune, and drove away alone, off to play a much-anticipated game of tennis.

Alicia refused to let the defeat dampen her spirit. When Streeter finished bawling them out, steam practically venting from the top of his head, he explained that the task force that arrived half an hour ago were relocating the operation to Sheerton where they were better equipped. Where, if Murphy and Alicia hadn't tried to bluff a former senior police officer with illegally-obtained evidence, they may have been able to gather *real* evidence. The "time is a factor" excuse fell on deaf political ears. Murphy and Alicia were still running things ... *for the time being.*

"When a celebrity is hurt by some random maniac," Streeter said as Alicia opened the door to leave, "it makes the public even more scared than regular folk going missing. It's a good opportunity to restore some faith in the police. Go get her."

"Them," Alicia corrected.

"Of course. Get *them.*"

Alicia told Murphy of her misgivings, how something wasn't right about the theory they were working to.

She couldn't say what.

Murphy said he understood.

"Hey, Alicia," a uniformed sergeant said as they passed him

in the corridor.

"Hey, Nick, how's it hanging?"

"Free and easy. You?"

"Been better, been worse."

"You okay, though? I heard about Brid."

"Yeah, he's a pussycat really."

"Pussycats can hurt you."

Alicia smiled. "An old friend came to help out."

"Heard that too. What's happening to him?"

"Disciplinary."

"Bastards. They'll say it's nothing personal, but, you know."

"I know."

They stayed for a moment before nodding goodbye, saying good-to-see-ya, and went their separate ways.

"He knows Barry?" Murphy said.

"Me and Barry used to double date with Nick and his wife. But you know how it is when you break up with someone—your friends get shared out like a CD collection."

"Unless she ups and leaves."

Alicia wondered if this was a good time to ask, but he seemed to speak to himself as much as her. She also hoped her ex would not be in too much trouble.

They say it's not personal, but...

Why did that strike true?

"You okay?" Murphy asked.

"Quiet. There's something happening in my head."

A tinkling, like a percussion instrument nearby, rose in volume. An orchestra. Information in, out, loudly clanging about her skull. Bells tolled, waves crashed, a body surfaced in a lake, rolled down a muddy embankment, slapped hard on the rust of a disused railway line.

...not personal...

"It *is* bloody personal!" she said aloud, and she was off.

Chapter Twenty-Six

SO THAT'S JOHN WELLINGTON, Richard thought.

The ex-DCI emerged from the station shortly after nine, arguing with a severe-looking woman, probably a lawyer. The pressmen still hanging around, those not invited inside or recalled for whatever reason, ignored the event. Richard tried to imagine what sort of pain he would have to inflict upon this man to extract all the information he needed.

Wellington climbed into a new Volvo estate and drove away. In his own anonymous Volvo, Richard followed.

His night with Alicia still fuzzed his mind. The woman was an absolute wonder. She'd made him feel in two days what it took over a month to feel with Gillian. At first he was grooming Gillian to be his latest beautiful kill, but she was so giddy, so alive, that it struck him a waste of time and energy. And, indeed, a waste of something *truly* beautiful.

A month of wining and dining and rutting like animals, and Richard decided to give up his hobby. He needed to be with her, to start a family without baggage, without the dissatisfaction that always came with missing a goal. *She* was his new perfection.

So he stopped by a male college, watched a frat-house party from the bushes, waited for it to wind down and for the paralytic lads to turn out the lights. Then he stabbed seven drunk, virtually comatose young men in the heart with a WWII bayonet he purchased the previous week at a military fair and, after scattering enough gang paraphernalia to indicate a robbery, his quota was filled.

He dedicated his new life to raising a family, a perfect family in a perfect house. But he could not do so in a country that allowed people to go around stabbing folk in the heart willy-nilly. He asked Gillian to marry him, and they moved back to England where Richard became a consultant and Gillian soon fell pregnant.

Katie was born healthy and loud, and Richard's target was now an ongoing one, a rolling ambition that would move with the conditions. But this was the last good thing that happened for many years.

When Gillian finally died, his need to replace one perfection with another resurfaced. The drug-addict / prostitute, whose name he never learned, was the right person at the right time. But he risked exposing Katie to his dark side, his deepest desires that he swore to keep in check. So he stopped again to raise his daughter, mould her into a woman, protect her, *prepare* her for whatever may come her way. He manipulated her into becoming a fitness freak (*no, jogging's not for little girls; only daddies can jog*) and into learning to defend herself, teaching her the dirtiest self-defence techniques.

And now she was gone.

During those four days—or was it five now?—Richard added two more deaths to his growing list. In a way, he hoped he wouldn't need to kill John Wellington. He didn't want Katie close to more violence. They'd probably move out of Leeds anyway when he got her back. Take her abroad, with fake IDs—he had plenty in his lockup for them both—maybe Australia, Mexico, Brazil. Somewhere hot and sunny, somewhere they liked sport. South Africa! That's where they'd live. Rugby freaks, adventure sports. Plus Katie had always wanted to learn to surf.

Yes.

When this was all over, he would move with his perfect daughter, and start a new, perfect life in South Africa. He wondered how Alicia would feel about that.

He wondered, in fact, what last night meant to her. Was it as special as it had been for him? Or was she so wound up by the case that she needed the release?

John Wellington pulled into a driveway in front of a huge house, detached, at least five bedrooms, with a front garden that would justify a sit-on lawnmower and a fair amount of land around the back too. This was not the house of a retired police officer.

As Richard swung by, Wellington used a key in the lock, then peered inside, perhaps expecting burglars, perhaps the police.

Or, maybe, to see if Katie had escaped her prison.

No. It wouldn't be that easy.

He parked around the corner and walked down the street, casually swinging his innocent-looking knife case. Each house was huge and clean, with thick walls and wide driveways. The sun shone, but clouds bloomed in the distance. The cold was more severe than he expected, but that was okay since he would not look out of place wearing gloves. He examined the CD player instructions he carried from the car, pretending to follow directions, counting off numbers, even straining to see across the street to numbers mostly written as words rather than digits. Standing before the one Wellington entered, Richard made an "ah-ha!" gesture, and walked up to the door. He was about to press the bell when he heard voices inside. A woman's first.

"I told you never to come here again!"

"But you went and blabbed," the man said. "We agreed—"

"Tanya is *dead*, John. She's *dead*. How can you let that guy get away with it?"

"What guy?"

"The one she was seeing. It's him, isn't it? It's him who killed her cos she wouldn't leave with him. Wasn't it?"

Richard rang the doorbell. The voices cut off immediately.

John Wellington opened the door. "Yes?"

"Hi," Richard said. "I'd like to talk to you about God."

"Not interested."

He swung the door to close it. Richard's foot jammed it open. He smiled toothily. "I'd *really* like to talk to you about God."

Wellington narrowed his eyes. "Get out."

Richard stepped inside. He wasn't as tall as Wellington, but had him on age and muscle. He easily shoved the ex-policeman inside and unzipped the case. Wellington held himself so he looked fitter, bigger. Richard kicked him in the balls. He doubled over and Richard rough-housed him into the living room, their feet sinking into a thick shag carpet.

The bath-robed woman was far younger than Wellington, around twenty-five, pretty, with a large bosom and fleshy hips. Her hair was freshly washed.

"Who the hell are you?" she demanded.

"Quiet," Richard said, flipping open his knife collection. He selected the bayonet, since he was just thinking about that one.

"What do you want?" Wellington demanded.

Richard showed him the bayonet and punched him in the nose. He fell to the floor, bleeding, hands cupping his face.

"That's a *new* carpet!" the woman shouted.

"Stay where you are," Richard said. "Or I'll cut your throat in under a second."

The fear in her eyes tried to hide within a frosty, indignant face, but she remained silent.

Wellington's beard was streaked red and Richard threw a foot into his soft belly. He knelt over the ex-cop with the blade.

"Please don't hurt him," the woman said.

"Hillary, shut up," Wellington said. "This doesn't concern you."

"Hillary?" Richard said. "Where have I heard that name before? Recently, I mean. What possible connection could you have to my missing daughter?"

She shook her head stiffly. "I don't know. I don't know. Just … please don't hurt him. He can't help you."

"That's not necessarily true, is it, Mr. Wellington?"

"You can do whatever you want," Wellington said. "But I won't talk to you."

Richard pricked the point of the bayonet into Wellington's neck, enough to hurt without drawing blood. Wellington set his eyes on Richard, nose bubbling. Richard's knee on his chest held him in place.

"You kill me and everything I know dies with me."

Richard pressed harder and a tiny ball of blood leaked down his neck. Wellington swallowed hard, closed his eyes.

"Fine." Richard stood up. "Let's try a different tactic."

He ripped the flex from an expensive-looking lamp and roughly shoved Wellington onto his front. First he tied the man's hands, then brought the cord down to his feet, binding them too, and pulled the cord tight so Wellington's arms reached back toward his legs. Hogtied.

Exactly how he pictured Katie right now.

Richard said, "Okay, now let's discuss this."

"It won't work, I tell you. I can't talk. Do what you want to me, but I won't tell you a thing."

"I know a lot about people, doing what I do. I can see when someone really means something. With you, it isn't that bravado crap I've seen in so many folk." He thought a moment. "You've experienced torture before, I take it."

"Iraq," Wellington said. "First Gulf War."

"Republican Guard. They're good at that." Richard weighed the bayonet in his hand. "But the Iraqis were lacking one thing. A trump card I wasn't expecting. I could inflict a massive amount of pain on you, or cut something off you really value. You'd break eventually. Everyone does. But it's messy, it takes time, and I really don't want to do that. It's ten o'clock already and I really hope to have my daughter home for tea."

Wellington stared hard at Richard.

"Watch this." Richard grasped Hillary by the arm and dragged her to the floor, kneeling so Wellington could see everything. "First, I'll cut off her nose."

Hillary screamed, "No!"

Richard pulled her head back by the hair. "I won't slit her pretty throat, oh no." He ran the blade along the woman's shoulders, over the curve of her chest.

Wellington closed his eyes calmly.

"I'll take an ear, maybe cut off a breast and wear it like a hat, one of those Jewish things but with a cute little nipple pointing at God."

Wellington glared, his attention fully on the intruder.

Richard grabbed Wellington by the jaw. "If you don't watch, I'll slice off your eyelids. I have a straight razor with me too. Want to see?"

In between panicked sobs Hillary managed a "Please, John..."

Wellington said, "Okay, don't hurt her."

Richard let her go. She fell to the floor, flat out, curled herself into a ball, and lay there.

"But you take her in another room," Wellington said. "There's no need for her to hear this."

A compromise. A man at the mercy of Richard Hague was asking for a compromise.

Cutting an ear off the woman may have changed Wellington's mind, but he was pushed for time, so Richard acquiesced and moved Hillary to the spacious, glaring white kitchen, where —with gaffer tape he located under the kitchen sink—he bound her to a chair beside the breakfast counter. When he returned to the living room, he sat in a deep, deep chair, and told Wellington he may proceed.

The ex-detective chief inspector took a deep breath and told Richard everything he needed to know to find Katie.

Freddie Wilcox was no longer under arrest. And about time, too. He was still, however, at Sheerton police station, which was insane. The woman, DCI Chambers, was a pretty girl, someone Freddie might have been interested in once upon a time, before women ruined his life. Living in a hovel without women suited him fine. DCI Chambers persuaded him to meet with the police artist here in the cosy family room. The artist was a young man with a wispy bum fluff beard and spiky hair.

"Dark hair," Freddie said. "Quite bulky."

"A little more specific, Freddie," Chambers said.

"Please be patient, Miss Chambers," said Joyce, the social worker who declared Freddie was not mentally ill, at least not enough to justify a section order.

"He was a big guy," Freddie said. He didn't like this. How do you *describe* someone? "Like me, but bigger. Without a beard, and he was wearing a cagoule. Can't you question everyone who bought a cagoule recently?"

Chambers rolled her eyes, ran her hand through her hair. "Jeez. Why do I have to be the one to do this?"

"You could wait outside," Joyce suggested. "We'll be done soon, I'm sure. Won't we, Freddie."

Freddie nodded, happy with Joyce, not happy with Chambers. "The sooner I'm back in my home the better."

Chambers collected her newspaper, tossed an unlit cigarette in her mouth, and left the little room.

Freddie tried to describe the man he saw, but the words he needed didn't exist. When he got home, he was going to invent some new words. "Hubadub" would describe the exact build of the man who deposited a body in Freddie's well.

The finished article looked nothing like him, but Freddie said it was exactly like him. They got the hair right, but not the *hubadub* build and certainly not the eyes. Of course, Freddie had been too far away to see eyes, but the jaw was clear and the nose too, and they were inaccurately drawn. He'd know the man if he saw him again. He'd pick him out of a line-up easily.

Chambers came back in without the cigarette, slapped the newspaper on the table and asked if they were done.

She snatched up the drawing and held it close to Freddie's face. "Is this him? You're sure? I'm not going to put this out there and get some priest in trouble am I?"

"It's him," Freddie said. "Can I go home now?"

"We have to find you somewhere first," Joyce said.

"But I want to go back to my land. I like it there."

"That is no place for someone to be living. Besides, it's not your land anymore, Freddie. It was repossessed a year ago and sold to the council. It's *their* property, and once this investigation is over—with your help, Freddie—the council are closing the site and will probably demolish it. Out of respect for the families of the ladies found up there."

They were tearing down his home!

"Freddie, the council are grateful to you for reporting this, and they'll do everything to make sure you are rehoused somewhere nice."

He wanted to break something. So he took the coffee cup Chambers had been drinking from and smashed it on the floor.

"You bastard," Chambers said. "I got that for Christmas."

Freddie threw Joyce's mug against the wall, the artist ducking as it smashed near his head. "I want to go home. *My* home. Not someone else's."

"Freddie, please..."

"Still think he doesn't need sectioning?" Chambers said. "I can make a call."

"No, he's just upset. *Freddie.*"

Freddie prepared to tear up Chambers' evening edition of a local newspaper. "Let me go home or I'll do it. I'll rip up your paper."

Chambers said, "I'll distribute this picture now."

Then Freddie saw it. Below the newspaper headline, *Two Siobhans Swiped by Devil.* Four people at a table, sat before an eight-foot wide police badge and a photo of a pretty dark-haired girl. The man in the middle...

"This is him!" Freddie said, waving the newspaper. "It's him, here, look."

Chambers sounded bored. "That is the father of a missing girl, you numpty. This," holding the drawing before Freddie, "is nothing like that," pointing at the newspaper.

"Yes, that's what I'm saying. The artist's wrong. This is him, I swear it."

Chambers rudely snatched the newspaper, examining the photo. "You're sure?"

"I'm sorry. I made up the drawing cos I couldn't describe him properly. I wanted to go home. But that photo—you should have shown me that sooner. We'd have saved a lot of time."

· · ·

It was too much for Richard. He hadn't moved from the chair throughout Wellington's tale. He listened, he planned, he calculated.

He had no chance of freeing Katie by himself.

Which left *what* as an option? Only one thing: he had to tell Alicia.

With police help he'd be able to do it, though his methods would come to light. He'd have failed his target of family perfection. He'd be caught, tried, and most likely jailed for life.

A great sadness washed over him. He was losing something of himself. Alicia would not understand his actions, not here. Perhaps she'd understand the ones from America, the perfect killings, the beauty of them, but she was the sort of person who would not forgive him. The prospect of losing Alicia, after being so close, was too much to bear.

"Hey, hard man," Wellington said. "What you crying for? Are you going to kill me or let me go?"

Richard wiped the tears from his face, thought about killing Wellington and the woman in the kitchen, but there'd been enough bloodshed. And Alicia would probably hate him even more if he did this.

He didn't untie either person. He simply packed his things away and headed to the door, running Wellington's speech through his head once again.

The task was impossible for him alone. And if he told Alicia, she'd never let him tag along. So what was he to do?

Alicia was clever enough. When she worked backwards, she'd find him out, track him down.

No. His fantasies of fighting the man by himself, gutting him from groin to throat and showing the man his own insides, all of that would never be realised. He'd confess all to Alicia, even the bits she'd hate him for, then she'd send him to jail.

But Katie would be safe. At least he would meet *that* goal.

Richard stepped into the driveway, light and breezy now he'd made the decision. He felt free.

Two men approached.

"Morning," Richard said, all sprightly and neighbourly.

The ginger-haired scruffy one chuckled mischievously. The Chinese-looking one pointed a small grey box at Richard, pressed a button on the top, and two wires shot out, embedding themselves in his chest.

"Hey," Richard said, "that hurt."

"Then get ready," the oriental guy said with an American accent. "Cos things are only gettin' worse for you."

The man pressed another button and every muscle in Richard's body contracted under the force of a massive electric shock. Fire coursed through him, filled him completely, the world turning sideways, growing darker and darker.

His last thoughts before losing consciousness were of his daughter, bleeding to death in Alicia's arms.

For the first time in his life, Richard had failed.

Chapter Twenty-Seven

MURPHY STRUGGLED to keep up with Alicia. He breathlessly followed her into the operations room where men in cheap suits and loose ties shifted boxes onto trolleys. All four whiteboards lay on the floor waiting to be packed. She told a man about to lift one of the boards to leave it right where it was. She even pointed a finger like a gun and ordered him to drop it. Confusion at first, then she presented her ID and said, "Go ahead, punk. Make my day."

Someone said, "Ah, so you're Alicia Friend."

"Excellent. I love it when my reputation precedes me." She lined the whiteboards up again, side by side, oblivious to all around her.

"Come on, Alicia," Murphy said. "Let me in. What's going on?"

"Barry. My ex. But not just Barry."

"You're blabbering."

Too much going on at one time, unable to see clearly. Everything was personal. Everything. Right back to Tanya. Tanya. That's where it starts, that's where everything points, and everything points at her leaving with someone she knew. Someone she *trusted*. But the deaths, all of them ... so different. So incapable of reason. All of them inflicted by someone whose mood changed, from the slick abductions, to the calculated but angry beating of Pippa, the dumping of her in sinking mud—

"He tried to *hide* her!" Alicia said. "It was right there. I saw it, then forgot about it. I said it that first morning, even before I got your smile to work properly. Donny 'the Don' Murphy, we are so wrong it's unreal."

"Talk," Murphy said.

"If Henry or whoever wanted to use these girls as smokescreen, in preparation for killing Tanya, why try to hide the first body?"

"Maybe you were wrong about the sinking mud."

She shook her head. "I'm never wrong." She winked. "But no. Seriously. I don't think I am. He tried to *hide* her. That means they weren't going to let Tanya be found either."

"Meaning?"

"Meaning..." The information reached no conclusion. Her system was close to crashing. "Meaning we're stuck again. These crimes are *personal*. Passionate. They mean something to someone."

Murphy rested against a desk that used to have a computer on it. He read the boards. "Don't suppose you have any more exboyfriends to call on? No psychics?"

"Tony!" she said suddenly.

"Tony? The Interpol guy. Wasn't he tracking James Windsor for us?"

"Yes, and he hasn't reported in yet." She had a terrible thought that maybe he'd been killed too. She unlocked her phone and dialled. He picked up straight away. "Thank God you're not dead."

"Good to hear from you too, Alicia," he said. "What can I do you for?"

"James Windsor. Did you find him?"

"Not yet. But I'm kind of busy with a Croatian gang smuggling teens—"

"Honey, you know I love you to bits, right?"

"I guess so."

"Then just bloody well tell me if you found him." She smiled into the phone.

Tony had a laugh in his voice. "Sure, honey. He left Manchester airport on his passport but it didn't check in at Delhi. I did check for other movements but so far, zilch."

"How's that work?"

"Either he went through the boarding gates at Manchester and did a runner across the airport, or he got off the plane in Delhi and did the same."

"What? Legged it across the runway? Why would he do that?"

"Don't know."

"So he might not have left the country after all."

"It's possible."

"Thank you. Keep looking." She blew some kisses and hung up, and pointed at the Tanya board. "This is where it started. With Tanya and Paavan. They were in love and nothing would stop them from living as a couple. Not even the love of her cousin."

"James. The guy who screwed up Wellington's story when he blabbed in an interview. All that about being close, how she wouldn't leave him."

"And Henry's class war. His need to be rich, respected. Probably rubbed off on his son."

"And if Tanya left, she'd take her cash, her butler, and all the privileges the family had enjoyed over the years."

"And even Henry told us how much James liked having that butler around."

"Who wouldn't?" Alicia said. "Do you know how much they cost? I could do with one."

Murphy made another of his "hmm" noises. "So why these others? Why the other girls?"

"Why do you think?"

"Your 'trigger'. The prospect of losing her set him off."

"Not quite. The difference is subtle." She asked one of the new guys, "Has the file on James Windsor gone yet?"

"Yeah," he replied. "That whole section on the rich girl's kidnap is on its way."

She clapped Murphy on the arm and rattled her keys. "Time to make loud noises and flash our lights at motorists."

Alicia pulled the Vauxhall out of the station and blasted the siren at everything that got in her way. The light on the dash revolved and Murphy held on to the door handle as well as checking his seatbelt every few minutes. Alicia sat close up to the wheel, her short legs working the pedals as skilfully as any advanced driver he'd met.

Out of the city centre, traffic was lighter, but coming up to Headingly, where students would be starting their lunchtime drinking sessions, it snarled up again. Alicia tore down the wrong side of the road, grinning, glancing at Murphy and quoting lines from films like *Mad Max* and *The Fast and the Furious*. Cars pulled over for her, and others swerved to avoid her coming at them head-on. A journey that would take most people forty-five minutes, Alicia slashed to ten.

When she cut the engine in Sheerton's car park, Murphy peeled his fingers from the door handle and pretended he wasn't even remotely fazed by the experience.

Just another day at the office.

Inside, Alicia followed directions to the new operations

room and Murphy tried his best to keep up. He decided he'd take up jogging once this was done with. Maybe even yoga.

When they arrived, PC Rebecca Ndlove, a new recruit they'd benefited from thanks to Siobhan's abduction, greeted him with a nod and moved away from Alicia, back to whatever she was doing before they arrived. The room was vast compared with the operations closet at Glenpark, and bright and air-conditioned.

It even boasted a view of the car park.

Alicia quickly located James Windsor's file.

"Derek Doherty," Alicia said, "the guy who worked with Welly on the case, he wrote up a profile on each suspect, but they were barely touched because Welly cleared them all. But listen to this.

"James Windsor was in trouble with the police aged eight. He and some friends, hanging around the streets, tying fireworks to cats, all standard thuggish behaviour. At the time, his father was looking bankruptcy right in the eye, so James was neglected, finding new friends, friends from school. They got in trouble some more—vandalism, verbal abuse of OAPs, more animal/firework experiments. But the money troubles eased with the sale of more land and when Henry was able to lavish James with toys and attention again, his troubles ceased. Or at least went off the books.

"In his teenage years, he grew interested in war. His passion was Vietnam, and—bloody hell!—he even built a scale POW camp in the grounds of the estate. Worked out, built up his body, obsessed with fitness. He trapped and imprisoned all sorts of animals. Badgers with foxes, chickens and ducks, dogs with other dogs, and wagered with his mates who would win.

"This all came out in the wake of Tanya's disappearance, from an old school friend who stopped playing with James the day he suggested attaching razorblades to a fox's paw and a badger's head—to make it more interesting. Someone buried this information."

"Wellington," Murphy said.

Alicia continued, "The RSPCA ripped down the structure following an 'anonymous' tip, and the prosecution went away after the charity received a sizable donation. But his fascination with war continued. First and Second World War recruitment posters filled his walls, some from Vietnam and Korea. Photos copied from the internet on his PC: napalmed children, blood and guts from all over the world, all of it one big amusement.

"We should have been onto this from the start," Alicia said. "The animals, the fascination with violence. It's first year psychology. He should have been suspect number one all along."

"Practice," Murphy said.

"It was only when Tanya lost her parents and moved in with them that he began to calm down. His excitement of having a butler who lived through a real live war was soon abated when Tanya had a word with him, explaining that Lawrence's experiences in Iraq were still a source of great anguish and pain for him. James understood. Or so he claimed."

"Where'd this background intel come from?"

"Doherty again. Before Wellington nixed him." She returned to the file. "Under Tanya's influence, he knuckled down at school, achieving five As, an A-star, and a B, a vast improvement from the straight Cs predicted in his mocks. She was good for him."

Murphy paced, putting it together. "All this was exactly why Doherty had been so hard on James in the interview. Wellington played good cop, but really he was protecting the lad. He reigned Doherty in when he got close to the bone. When James insisted Tanya loved him and that she'd never leave him, that's when Wellington aborted the session. Doherty was close, and

Wellington needed him gone." He stopped mid-pace and shook his head. "I remember the original file. No major detail, just the facts. He threw Doherty off the case. Doherty requested a transfer out of Glenpark a week later."

Alicia said, "Tanya was someone James had been lacking. Only a few years older, but Tanya was the mother figure he craved."

"And what happened to his real mother?" Murphy asked.

"She died soon after they sold the park to the council," Cleaver said, entering behind them. He was in possession of the file that contained the financial records of Wellington's share dividends.

Murphy and Alicia turned. "What park?" they said together.

Cleaver grinned at them. "A slice of land that got incorporated into Roundhay Park. Where they found the Davenport girl. And guess what else? The family used to own the land where Pippa Bradshaw was found too, but was sold to the council in the sixties, where they built a bunch of crappy houses."

"And the railway lines?" Murphy said.

Cleaver nodded, still grinning. He handed Murphy the documents. "They made a lot of money in the rag trade, at least Henry's father and grandfather did. Owned all that land, but sold it off after the war."

"People," Alicia said, waving James's file in the air until the men arranging the room were as attentive as Cleaver and Murphy. "This is why I said being dumped wasn't the trigger for all this. The trigger was something else. He held her for so long he wanted to please her. Bring her a friend. The trigger wasn't being rejected by Tanya. The trigger was the *girl*—Pippa— rejecting *Tanya*. He couldn't bear to think anyone didn't love her like he did."

"So why kill Tanya?" Cleaver asked.

"Any number of reasons. Probably she begged him not to kill Katie. Maybe Katie didn't reject Tanya, but Tanya rejected Katie."

"Doesn't matter," Murphy said. "The 'why' is irrelevant. The 'who' is what we needed."

"And," Alicia said, waving the file, "I think I can safely declare we have a prime suspect."

She wanted to jump up and down and squeal with delight. It was all to do with James, his sick obsession with animals merging with an obsession with his cousin. And the task force was motoring.

Warrants were needed and needed soon. Now it was too much for even the most connected brass to reject. A psych profile, a disappeared suspect, a sturdy-looking aviary where it was stated, on record, that the disappeared suspect used to torture animals.

Alicia didn't want to wait, but this needed doing right. They still didn't know for certain where he was holding the girls, and if they went in too soon he might never tell; he could kill them or leave them to starve to death and start again.

Cleaver searched for news on James's mother, for a photo, anything, but it was one thing Doherty hadn't been thorough about—dead people didn't need a profile. Murphy set Cleaver the task of researching those dead people.

"Where's Sergeant Ball?" Alicia asked.

"Here," Ball said, walking in eating a yoghurt. "What do you need?"

"Surveillance," Murphy said. "Right now. Get out to the Windsor estate and watch it. Radio in with anything. Use the binoculars from up high. There's no mobile reception in the valley, so stay in touch. You're looking for an IC-one male, big build, twenty-one years old but may appear a little older."

Ball mock-saluted and turned. He stopped. "Hey, boss-lady?"

Alicia said, "Yes, underling-man?"

"Isn't Richard Hague the name of Katie's dad?"

"Sure is." She felt a silly little flutter in her chest. "Why?"

"Because they just put out an arrest bulletin for him. He's wanted for the murders up at Eccup."

Murders? *Richard?* Nah, different Richard. Had to be. She almost giggled at the stupidity, her misinterpretation. But no. Ball said *Katie's dad.*

"If this is some sick joke," she said, "you better tell me."

"No joke, love." Ball licked his spoon. "They've got a witness, watched him dump the body."

"The nut? They're taking the word of a mentally ill *vagrant*?"

Murphy's hand on her shoulder. "Easy, now," he said softly. "If it's a mistake, it's a mistake. Right now, we have other priorities."

No. Alicia had no higher priorities. Her mind was crashing, shutting down. It needed to reboot. She fled the room, memories of last night playing out again, but blurred, like images on a wall speeding by.

Outside the station, the cold smacked her face like a dead hand, the sun now extinguished, huge white-grey clouds blanketing the sky. But Alicia ran, not knowing where to go, no plan, finally resting on the borrowed Vauxhall in the freezing midday air.

Her fake-self was fighting her true-self, and fighting hard. An appearance was imminent. She wouldn't cry, though, not in view of the station, many eyes most likely watching her.

She climbed in, started the engine. And she desperately tried to remember where Roberta Munroe worked.

. . .

While the vehicle revved, then set off out of the car park, high above all that was happening, plummeting temperatures and increasing pressure teamed up against the moisture of clouds, flinging particles one way, then the other, so they were forced to gather together as if to share warmth. And, when the many particles bonded, they were too heavy for the cloud to hold. In a pattern that would never again be replicated, the now-solid mass descended, buffeted by a mild wind, finally coming to rest upon the ground, pursued by hundreds of thousands of similar, but not identical, objects.

The first snowflakes of winter landed silently on the Earth.

Chapter Twenty-Eight

THROUGH THE CHIPBOARD PARTITION, Celine Dion warbled something indecipherable. Alfie couldn't decide if it was worse hearing the song properly or trying to work out which one it was. Nor was it easy to tell if the nausea he was feeling was down to the music or the movement of Red McCall's van.

The man stirred.

Richard Hague.

Alfie felt strangely depressed at finally having him here, defeated and helpless. In the years since Stacy died he'd thought about this moment so many times. Capturing Stacy's murderer, the man who killed at least forty others, who treated it like a hobby or mission; indiscriminate except for that one thing: the single, solitary wound through the heart.

Alfie had envisioned hours of unmitigated torture. Not asking questions, not demanding anything from him, just putting him through the worst experience imaginable. Hence his specifications regarding the vehicle.

A sturdy wooden board bolted to the floor with large metal loops screwed in; two at the top, two at the bottom. Through each of these McCall had cranked a set of handcuffs, solid ones that he assured Alfie were liberated from police storage by one of his many contacts. The wooden board raised slightly at the head end and sagged gently in the middle, creating a crude drainage system. In a toolbox the size of a trunk, McCall supplied a number of instruments: scalpels, razor, bone saw, and a shit-ton of black plastic bags. The bags were not yet necessary.

Alfie never intended to kill this man, despite his desire to do so. For twenty years, he searched. For twenty years, fifteen of them with the FBI, he searched for similar slayings, for that telltale wound, the randomness of the victim. He thought so much, for so long, his internal voice no longer his own. Each thought in his head was now spoken by Stacy. Whether a recipe for kung po chicken or a plan of vengeance, it was always her, always with him. And she didn't want Alfie to become a monster.

Justice.

This was what he sought, what he'd always sought. From his fledgling experiences with the Feds, his fast promotion from a field office in North Dakota to a robbery task force blanketing L.A., he always believed in the Right Thing. Stacy was so proud of him, too. She followed him, followed his career. She didn't want one herself, old-fashioned and proud of it, desiring only a family, babies, a house, the cheesy American dream made real. And then another promotion took them to New York, where property was so expensive, and Stacy took a part-time job at Wicker Securities, soon becoming personal assistant to one of their top salesmen. An easy job, since he was hardly ever there. Her boss headed sales teams all across the country, training people to get into houses and flog security systems, making them explain to the potential customers how easy it would be to break into their homes right now, how Wicker products would protect their families from anything up to, and possibly including, alien invasion.

When her boss was present, he was good to Stacy. He didn't

grumble about her tardiness, the odd mistake when filing, nor her habit of taking an extra five minutes at break time. She was the envy of the other secretaries whose bosses all but had them clocking in and out for bathroom breaks. At times, Alfie grew a little jealous when she'd say over dinner what a great guy Richard was, how she'd been terrified to tell him about another little mishap on the phone or with an invoice, but then he smiled and said, "Mistakes happen. Learn from them." Alfie didn't really believe there was anything going on, their sex-life better than it had ever been, and not only because they were trying for a baby—it was so rich, so hot. But the doubt is always there in men. To assuage this nagging fear, the stupid, irrational, totally unfounded fear, he suggested Stacy invite Richard for dinner one evening.

Steaks. On the deck.

She was so excited and nervous that any doubts Alfie had were scorched from his mind. Were she having an affair, no way would she be so cold as to eat dinner with both him and her husband.

Richard seemed like a nice enough guy. His handshake was firm and they all relaxed into easy conversation. Work, family, love lives. Of these three Richard only dealt with the first; the others could wait, he said. It was then he revealed the wine Alfie was drinking cost twelve hundred dollars a bottle. Alfie nearly put it back in the bottle and buried it.

That was the first time he met Richard Hague. The last had been Stacy's funeral. Until now. A twenty-five-year-old upstart with a great job, good looks, and a mediocre secretary. And now he was cuffed to the floor of a van, positioned like a letter X, travelling at non-suspicious speeds through a small "big" city in England.

Richard Hague's eyes opened into slits.

"Hello." Alfie sat cross-legged next to Richard's head. "You know who I am?"

Richard shook his head. He was weak, groggy. Then, suddenly, he spasmed, his hands yanking at the cuffs, feet likewise. They clanked and pulled, Richard furiously whipping his head around to see why the hell he couldn't move. Alfie didn't flinch.

"Stop it," Alfie said. "You'll hurt yourself."

Richard calmed down some, the cuffs still tight on his wrists. "Where am I?"

"In a van. Leeds. Is that what this shithole's called?"

"Sure is," McCall said from the driver's seat. He couldn't be seen behind the chipboard partition, but his voice was clear. "Though I think 'shithole' is a bit harsh."

"It's a shithole, pal. And I can't wait to get out of it." He turned his attention back to Richard. "I don't know what to do now."

"You could let me go," Richard said. "Please. I have to *be* somewhere."

"I'm sure." Alfie opened the trunk-like toolbox and tipped out the contents. He selected a scalpel, held it so Richard could see. "I'm conflicted now. I got a voice in my head telling me not to do this, that it'll make me like you. But I got another voice pleading with me to go right ahead. Jail ain't good enough for folk like you."

"I think you have the wrong person, sir. I don't know who you're looking for—"

"I'm looking for *you!*"

He raised the scalpel and Richard cringed, closed his eyes like a big ol' baby. Alfie lowered it slowly, placed it back with the others. Richard opened one eye, then the other. Alfie shook his head, unsure why he was smiling. It was as if he'd scored some victory with that action, not giving in to anger, allowing the man to live.

"You're the playground bully, Richard. Look at you. You're terrified. You're shaking like some kid being led to the principal's office the first time."

Enough with the similes, Alfie, get on with it.

"I don't know how I feel," Alfie said. "That's my problem. I kill you, I become you. I torture you, cripple you, whatever, I'm worse than you."

"That's right. That's right, sir. Don't be like me."

"But that leaves me with a problem. A question of justice. And something else, something I'm trying to ... I'm trying to ... what's the word?"

"Articulate?"

"That's the one. Thanks. I can't *articulate* it. I don't wanna kill you, but I do want something that I won't get if you're in jail."

Alfie stood. The swaying of the van didn't unbalance him much. He kept his centre of gravity low, the way he'd trained, although the purpose for which he trained was not to stand up in moving vans.

"That's what I need," he said. "I need to know *why*."

"W-why what?" Richard said.

"Why *her*."

"Who? I don't know what you're talking about."

Alfie steadied himself with a hand on the roof. "You killed my wife along with around forty to fifty others over a ten-year period. You used your job to travel to cities all over the States where you butchered innocent people, randomly as far as I can tell, but who knows. Your knowledge of security systems meant you could break into houses and apartments at will, but sometimes you snatched 'em right off the streets."

Richard's expression darkened and the cuffs rattled and bit into his wrists even deeper. Still no blood yet.

"Don't," Alfie said. "Those are police-issue. The wood's solid. You're going nowhere."

Richard relaxed his arms, lay his head back, and stared at the roof of the van.

Alfie picked up the surgical bone saw from the collection littering the van. It was wire-free, charged up earlier. "Okay. Now you are going to tell me what I want to know. Or I'm going to start cutting things off."

"Yeah, man!" came McCall's voice. "Gonna get medi*eval* on his ass."

That man has seen too many movies, Alfie thought. "Quiet, and drive."

"We're nearly there, mate."

Alfie didn't respond to that one. They'd scouted the site yesterday, an area of national park—a pissy little orchard really —close to where Richard dumped his two latest bodies. He couldn't see the well itself, but the proximity was enough irony for Alfie.

"Why my wife?" Alfie said. "Why my *wife*?"

Alfie turned on the bone saw, a device that reminded him of a large pizza slicer. The circular blade whined and spun, and Alfie truly hoped Richard would talk to him. He needed answers. He needed what all bereaved people need: why *my* child? Why *my* husband, *my* girlfriend? Why did my daughter walk into the road? Why did cancer take *my* mother?

Why *me*?

Over the saw, Alfie said, "Why did you murder my wife?"

He held the blade near Richard's mid-section, having decided to cut open the man's stomach. He wasn't a surgeon, hadn't studied anatomy, but he knew a bullet in the gut was the most painful place to be shot, apart from the kneecap, and he also knew it took a long time to die from it.

The blade connected with Richard's clothing, ripping wool blend and cotton as if it wasn't even there. Closer to the skin.

"Alright!" Richard yelled. "Alright, alright."

Alfie turned off the saw and dropped it on the floor. "Tell me. Why her? *Why*?"

"Who was she?"

"You don't even know her. You don't remember me."

"Sorry. I killed a lot of people."

"How many?"

Richard chuckled. "How many do you think?"

"You got to around forty, maybe fifty. Then you stopped. I'd like to know why you stopped as well. If it ain't too much trouble."

"My plan," Richard said, calm now, no fear in him at all, "was to achieve one hundred perfect kills. I made my quota. So I stopped."

One hundred.

Alfie let this process. The emotionless voice, the matter-of-fact tone. "And my wife?"

"How did you find me?"

"Saw you on television. Shame about your little girl, by the way. But I knew. Those murders in the well, plus my wife, plus your old job, it was too much of a coincidence. I followed you from the police station last night, to that hotel. Then I watched you follow that old guy to this house. I take it you killed whoever was inside."

"Actually, I didn't. I don't want to kill any more people. I never did. I met my wife, and I didn't need to do it anymore."

"What about *my* wife? What about *Stacy*?"

Richard observed Alfie for a long while. Then smiled. "I know you now. You're Stacy's husband!" He sounded so happy, so normal, like he'd recognised an old school pal at a party.

"Ten out of ten," Alfie said. "Now explain."

"Usually it was just whether the fancy took me, but occasionally there was a reason. I had a reason for Stacy. Is that what you want to hear? My reason?"

"You know it is."

The van bumped up and then crunched to a halt. They were here. From the front, McCall said, "Hey, man, you getting medieval on him yet? Are ya?"

"Not yet," Alfie called back.

The driver door opened and closed, and a moment later the back door opened, allowing natural light to flood in. It was snowing. Quite a lot.

"This country is seriously dumb," Alfie said. "It was *sunny* when I got in here."

"How about some pliers and a blow torch?" McCall said.

"No pliers, no blow torch."

"Oh, come on, mate. Let's get—"

Alfie sighed. "Okay, fine. Go get some."

"Can I have some money?"

"No. If you want them that badly, take the other car and go steal some."

He sulked as he closed the door. Alfie listened to his footsteps recede and then an engine fired up. The car they'd stashed here—in preparation for this event should they need to set fire to the van—drove away with the annoying ex-marine at the wheel. Finally, they were alone.

"Back to business," Alfie said. "You killed Stacy. Why?"

"She was a lovely lass, your wife." Richard said this with an air of nostalgia, as if happy to be discussing it. "She'd knit these cute little booties for the baby you guys wanted so badly. She'd do it on her breaks and sometimes at her desk. She was always late, presumably screwing you before work, which wasn't a problem when I was away. But I like people to be where they're supposed to be when they're supposed to be there. One day, when she mentioned you were away for the night, I broke into your apartment using a lock pick and a little black book of alarm codes. I believe I used one of her own knitting needles. I thought it was making a statement or something. I'm not sure exactly what I was saying, but hey."

The van rocked gently with the breeze, a flurry of snow pattering sounding off the side.

"Can you imagine," Richard said, "how hard it is to get a knitting needle into the heart? You have to hold it with your fingers close to the pointy end, puncture the skin, then break through the intercostal muscle—you know, the stringy bits that hold the ribs together—and go in at an angle."

Alfie took the scalpel and knelt beside Richard.

"I found my way up there, holding little Stacy quite easily around the neck. Her heart beat so fast. On each out-beat I let it touch the point of the needle without piercing it. When I thought she was going to pass out, I shoved it right in."

"You watched her," Alfie said.

"Oh yes. She was quite the death. I sat in the chair next to her makeup cabinet. It's the weirdest thing. You can virtually see the life draining. And it wasn't the blood. There wasn't that much, at least not externally. But the *life*, slowly slipping from her eyes. It was beautiful. It was perfect."

Alfie put the scalpel to Richard's throat. His wife's "beautiful death" now played out, vivid in his mind.

"You letting me go now, Alfie?" Richard said. "I have to speak to the police."

"No. I don't think so." Inside him, Stacy cried at him not to do it, not to kill this man. But it was too hard not to. He'd never taken a single life, not one criminal, not one innocent, but here, at his mercy was someone who'd murdered a hundred.

A hundred!

A century of kills. And what was he asking? To be let go?

Alfie said, "You have to die, man. You have to die like all those other people."

"Please ... one phone call..."

"You ain't under arrest here. You don't get a lawyer."

"I need to speak to the police. Please. Give me my phone..."

Now it made sense. Now Alfie realised what Richard was doing. And this made him so happy, he nearly forgot where he was.

"You know where your daughter is," Alfie said.

Richard nodded. "Please. She's not a part of this. She's nothing to you..."

"Like Stacy was nothing to you. Like all the others."

"Not only *my* daughter. Someone else's too."

"Oh, yes. The pop star."

Stacy's voice inside him, *don't do this, don't do it.*

He said, "Maybe letting you live is more cruel."

"I already lost my wife. Not my daughter too."

Alfie sat against the side of the van, his back cold on the metal. According to the morning papers, Richard Hague was a widower, lost his wife to cancer, not a psychopath. And as Richard lay there, pleading for the phone, Alfie smiled.

The empty feeling inside him was now filled. He was satisfied. Now he knew what he'd do, what his plan was.

"I think I'm going to take a walk when McCall gets back. Then, Richard, I'm going to turn on the radio. And when your little girl's body finally shows up, I'm going to let you make that call, and you can live with the grief *I've* had to live with, for the last twenty years."

Chapter Twenty-Nine

KATIE'S PLAN was not complicated. She told it to the girl and she agreed via a series of grunts and head-nods.

The man entered, pressed the buttons to lock the door, and came down the stairs. And as he had before, a day (or was it two or three days?) ago, he turned on all the lights, revealing the entire room, and revealed himself in full military camouflage dress, including a black beret sideways on his head, and a firearm holstered at his hip. The room was ten metres long and five wide, the floor tiled in white, the walls also tiled but only to shoulder height. It was plumbed and had drainage, and the bath in which Katie cleaned herself sat in one corner, awaiting the next victim. An old-fashioned thing, no taps plumbed in. Shadows would not stay still. They merged with other shadows, then disappeared completely, fading in and out of existence with each movement.

The man placed a metal toolbox in the centre of the room and walked around the girls, hands clasped behind him, appraising them as if they were privates on parade. He nodded approvingly. Then he strode to the corner opposite Katie, behind the other girl, and brought the chain forward. He secured the girl as he had Katie, a manacle about one ankle, and then freed her from the chair. This chain was longer than Katie's at the moment, enabling her to reach Katie if so desired. He then wound out the slack from Katie's too. Both now had the run of the room. But both understood they must remain seated until otherwise instructed.

"You may stand," the man said.

They did so.

"You may remove your gag, Siobhan," he said to the other girl.

And when she did, Katie recognised her fully. It wasn't only the hair and the face. She was sodding famous! This maniac had stolen a pop star. If he'd managed that, to take someone who would constantly be surrounded by minders and her "people" what hope did Katie have? Or the one he referred to first as Rachel? Were there more?

"Now." He held his arms out like Christ on a cross, brought them together respectfully, as if opening a ceremony. "Rachel, you are my First, so you will be given the weapon." From the tool box he brought out a mallet with a rubber-covered head, meaning it was light but would do some damage. "I'm sorry, Siobhan, but this is how it works. My First has the advantage. My Second must rise to the challenge, like Rachel did last time."

Katie had not told Siobhan everything that happened, thinking it may worry her to know her new fellow captive killed the previous fellow captive. She felt ashamed now, dirty. This man's pride was not something she wanted bestowed upon her. She gripped the mallet in both hands. He stood within striking distance.

"I felt the crowbar was a little ... *base* for something like this. And a rubber mallet may actually prolong the contest." He unhooked the clip securing his gun holster. "You two are truly beautiful. But you must join me, join me in every sense. Only one of you may live. If you do not obey, I shall choose who dies."

Siobhan was trembling. She should have done something by now. Katie urged her with her eyes each time the man glanced away.

Go on, do it.

Siobhan shook her head.

Go on. Now.

No. I can't.

The man gripped the gun in one hand and removed it from the holster. It was an automatic, with a large barrel. He pointed it in the air. "If either of you refuses to fight, the other will kill you. If you both refuse to fight, *I* will kill you." He pointed it at Siobhan. "Is that understood?"

Clever, thought Katie. If Siobhan doesn't fight, she dies anyway. If I don't fight, that's okay, because Siobhan dies.

It meant that Siobhan—the one without the weapon—*had* to fight. And if Katie already killed one person, then she wouldn't mind killing another. This is what made Katie realise that yes, there had been others. If there had not, the Rachel girl would not have attacked her with such enthusiasm, and without hesitation. But just because Siobhan was now in a position where she had to fight, it didn't mean she had to fight *Katie*.

Siobhan began to cry.

"Stop that," the man ordered. "Stop that at once. You are to be warriors. Not crybabies. *Stop it!*"

Siobhan sank to her knees and sobbed hard into her hands. The man pointed the gun at her head.

"Get up and fight. Now." He cocked the weapon.

"It's okay," Katie said, the chain clanking behind her as she stepped forward. "I'll finish her where she is."

The man smiled and stepped aside slightly. Within striking

distance again. But could Katie be fast enough? Would she make it?

Siobhan didn't move. She cried harder, while Katie stood over her with the mallet in her hands. How much easier it would be to land one solid blow on the top of her head, right in the soft spot, where the plates of the skull converge. It'd be painless. And less of a risk.

"Ready?" Katie said.

The man hung his head like a contrite child caught stealing the last chocolate from his mum's box. "I'm sorry, Rachel. I shall try to bring you more of a challenge next time."

Siobhan looked up through her fingers. Katie winked. Then she swung the hammer down towards Siobhan, narrowly missing her—so close that strands of her hair wafted by—and in a reverse arc, followed through and into the man's groin.

He yelled out. He was wearing a box, like cricketers, but the force of the mallet was sufficient to flare pain right through him. Katie then thumped the mallet down on his head. With a wet crack, he dropped to the floor. He was breathing, but not moving.

Siobhan darted forward, grabbed the gun from the man's hand, and backed off, holding it in both of hers, the weapon now huge rather than the toy-like object their captor brandished, so huge, and clearly so heavy. She clasped it around the handgrip, her fingers away from the trigger, pointed at the man on the floor.

"What now?" Her voice cracked, trembling; eyes darting back and forth.

"Back away," Katie said.

They retreated in opposite directions, well out of reach should he regain consciousness. Katie dragged the toolbox to her chair and opened it. She didn't want to search the man for keys.

She found the crowbar and jammed the end into the manacle around her ankle where the two ends met. She pushed. Metal creaked.

"Keep watching him," Katie said, weak but angry, determined not to die in this hole. "If he moves, make sure you shoot him."

"I will," Siobhan said.

Katie was not convinced. They had to get free and go, run, before he could stop them. Who knew what other weapons he carried? Who knew where the girls were even being held?

She pushed harder, the metal bending rather than snapping.

"Break, damn it." She breathed hard, sweating now. "Come *on*."

They could be in forest, or in a city, a sewer, perhaps under a lake. She remembered water. Why was she remembering water? What the hell did water have to do with anything?

A rasping sound emanated from somewhere, and the harder Katie levered the jimmy, the louder the rasping came. It was like sand in a tray, moving side to side.

There!

The hinge snapped open and the manacle dropped off. She was free. She was going to make it.

"Are you okay?" Siobhan asked.

"Fine," Katie said.

But she didn't say it. She *tried* to say it. The word was stuck in her throat, lodged like a marble. She tried again, but could not inhale. The rasping sound, the sand in the tray, it was *her*. Inside her, in her lungs. She couldn't breathe.

"My inhaler."

Yet again, the words would not come. She searched for the inhaler, that life-giving tube of plastic. She scrabbled about on the floor. There was nowhere for it to hide, the floor clear, no drawers, no hidey holes, nothing.

"What the hell is *wrong* with you?" Siobhan screamed.

Katie, on the floor still, had no reply. She pointed at her throat, swelling, closing, in need of that last shot, something to save her. *No!* She'd survived this monster, only to succumb to a death so damn infantile, the one she'd been cursed with from birth.

That bastard, lying there.

She wanted the defeated form to be the last thing she saw. The man she'd clobbered with the same hammer he wanted her to kill with. He breathed, but blood had gathered around his temple. He was going to die, and Katie thanked God that she'd beaten him. It wasn't him that took her, and it wasn't some poor girl like Siobhan. The asthma killed her. She could live with that.

The man's eyes snapped open.

Katie would have screamed were she able. Siobhan was behind him so didn't know he was awake. She held the gun loosely in both hands, trigger finger not employed, panic oozing from her in waves, asking over and over, "What's wrong, what's wrong?"

He moved his arm. Siobhan screamed, scurrying backwards, gun extended. He did not stand. Siobhan cried for him to stop, to let her go. His arm swung out along the floor. In his hand was Katie's inhaler. Siobhan saw it, understood. The man grinned, head lolling to one side. Katie tried to reach out, but she was too weak. Her lungs filled with lead. Her fingers found the floor and she tried to drag herself along. To no avail. Her life lay three feet away, in the hands of a madman.

Now no air was getting in, not one fine channel. The room dimmed. Her fingers could no longer walk. She accepted it. Graciously too, she thought, under the circumstances.

The loudest *bang* Katie had ever heard rang out. It filled the room, hit her like a physical force, like someone jabbing a pencil in her ear.

Siobhan stood over her. No chain on her foot. Just a scorch mark on her leg and the impression of where she had been bound to the chair. She knelt beside Katie and lifted her up in a sitting position. They were so close to the man who'd held them, threatened them, and Siobhan would not go closer.

"Come on," she said. "We can make it."

A cough from the man. He'd left the inhaler midway between them and retracted his arm. He still looked stunned, weak, but it could've been a ruse.

Katie didn't care.

"Should I?" Siobhan said.

Katie couldn't even blink. Everything was unclear, moving funny, pressure now off her lungs but increasing behind her eyes, in her head. This was her brain dying, starved of oxygen. In less than a minute she'd be a vegetable. In more than a minute, she'd be dead. But at least Siobhan would make it—

She breathed.

The inhaler sprayed her throat and almost immediately a fine channel of air broke through, like a jet of cold water on a burn. Another squirt and she lifted her arm and held the tube. She pointed to go back, watch their captor, but he was still on the floor. Conscious, watching.

Grinning.

Siobhan pointed the gun. "Should I kill him?"

Katie still couldn't speak. She shook her head. No. Not like this. Not in cold blood.

She needed one more dose. She was always told only take two doses at once. If it doesn't clear up with two, you should call an ambulance. Three can harm you. But she didn't even know if there was going to be a phone. This guy was a military nut, so maybe he lived alone in the hills with no communication.

Her lungs were free again, but still not right. Still a gravelly noise in her throat. She needed the extra hit. She placed it in her mouth, depressed the trigger.

Nothing.

"Empty," she croaked. She threw it to the ground and shakily got to her feet. "Let's go."

With Siobhan's help she walked. Siobhan still held the gun, and the man on the floor continued to watch them. Katie used the wall for support as they climbed the stone steps, her legs shaking with each movement, so tired, yearning for sleep. Siobhan pushed the door. It was stuck fast. She tried pushing harder. The handle was solid; no moving parts.

"No!" Siobhan cried. "No. Please, no!"

Katie saw it first. The keypad. The combination on the wall beside the doorframe. Then Siobhan twigged too.

"The first number is six."

They spun around to find the man standing in the spot where he fell, his beret on the ground at his feet. He held a hand to his head, clearly in pain. Siobhan raised the gun, although Katie was not confident of anything finding its target other than an exceptionally lucky shot.

He said, "But that's the only clue I'm giving you. It's a four-digit access code. There's only nine-hundred and ninety-nine other numbers you need to try."

He limped over to the hose, coiled along the same wall as the door. Siobhan followed him with the gun, hand shaking more than ever.

"Should I kill him now?" she said.

"You *could.*" He ran the hose a little, splashed it over his head, dousing the place Katie hit him. "But that combination resets itself after three wrong attempts, like an iPhone. You can't try again for twenty-four hours. There's no food down here, and the only water available is from here."

"Shoot him," Katie murmured. "I'd rather die than stay."

Siobhan trembled, barely able to hold the gun straight.

He continued, "Nobody knows about this place. I found it by accident once. Did it up a bit, made it special. I really did it for us, Rachel."

"I'm not Rachel," Katie said. It was supposed to be loud, confident, but it came out like an extension of her breath.

"Oh, but you *are* Rachel. In a way. Although no one could be as beautiful. Tanya was the closest I ever came to finding another Rachel, but you bested her, didn't you? You were magnificent. Even now I'm not angry at this ... rebellion. I'm just impressed. And incredibly proud. Again."

Siobhan looked angrily at Katie. She had every right to. Katie hoped Siobhan would shoot her right now, get it over with, so she could sleep. She slumped on the top step.

"That's right, Siobhan." The man turned off the tap and stood directly below them, staring right down the barrel of his own gun. "Your friend there killed my First. She relieved her of the weapon and hit her head thirteen times off the floor—I counted. Took an ear in the process. According to the rules, she has to be my First now. You are the Second."

Katie, so drowsy, tested her breathing again. It worked, but if her lungs were a car you wouldn't chance the motorway.

She said, "Shoot him. Then us. Don't let him win."

"The fight had technically begun," the man said. "If you shoot Katie right now, *you* become my First, Siobhan. *You* become my Rachel."

Katie tried to think what she'd do given the option. Last time, she'd fought to stay alive, let the pain and anger drive her to the kill. This wasn't the same. This choice was impossible.

"You kill me, we all die. You kill her, you get to live. Come on, Siobhan. Make the choice. A true warrior kills without question, but always for a cause. This is my cause, and you all fight for it.

Only a pure woman can replace Rachel. And if you do this right now, if you kill little Katie, sat helpless on those steps, I guarantee you only have to take one more life to prove your loyalty. One more, Siobhan, and then it's all over. I'll bring you a Second. You'll be my First. And your weapon will be a sword."

Siobhan glanced side to side, Katie to kidnapper, the gun loose in her hand. She cried, wailing, "Please, please let us go."

"A *sword*, Siobhan. You get to fight the next girl with a *sword*."

Katie wished she'd hurry up, becoming surreally impatient. "Him or me," she managed to say. "Just do it. Kill one of us. Please."

Siobhan dropped the gun.

It clattered to the tiles below. The man watched it fall, and when he looked back up, it wasn't a look of victory or success. He gave a deep sigh, a slow shake of the head. He closed the gap between them in five long strides, collected the weapon, and slid it back in his holster. He gestured for Siobhan to move, and she skittered down the stairs, pressed hard against the wall, cringing the closer she got to him. She ran to the other side of the room, screwed herself into a ball, and squatted in the corner, sobbing.

Then the man carried Katie down the steps, like a groom carrying his bride, and placed her gently in the dry bath.

"It's comfier than the floor," he said. "And you need to rest."

He put everything away, back in the toolbox, and even tidied up the chains and the hose. He climbed the stairs and input the code, shielding the keypad with his body. The door hissed open and he walked through, pausing halfway out.

"I'll be back tonight," he said. "And we shall do it properly this time."

The door closed. The lights went out. The only sounds were the tears of a pop princess, and the laboured breathing of Richard Hague's daughter.

Chapter Thirty

SHE NEEDED to talk to Robbie. From the Vauxhall, Alicia watched her friend, there, in the high school playground, her gorgeous dark skin gathering snowflakes. Schoolgirls played all around. They texted on mobiles, applied makeup, admired how they managed to adapt their uniforms to look so ridiculous whilst presumably staying within the school rules. They were roughly the age Alicia's child would have been, just a little older.

She didn't feel right unburdening herself on Robbie. Especially while she was working.

I should go.

Her phone rang. She ignored it.

Robbie, laughing with the girls, all fourteen, fifteen years of age. So different from Alicia's time at school. There were no mobiles, and your tie had to be knotted in a specific way. They skipped ropes and played netball during break times back then. Now they texted boys and each other, discussed sexual techniques and contraception.

Roberta once came home and opened a bottle of wine, her shoulders unusually low and refusing to chat. Eventually, after Alicia challenged her to an impromptu game of Twister and drinking half the wine, she talked. A thirteen-year-old girl had been found crying in the locker room. Roberta comforted her, said all the usual things, asked her what's wrong, got her to open up. Her boyfriend had dumped her by text. The reason? Because she gave rubbish blow jobs. The girl begged Roberta to teach her how to do them right, so she could win him back.

Fourteen.

Nothing in the world worked as it should.

Thirteen-year-olds were expected to give good blow jobs, pop stars' lives were worth more than everyday folk, and innocent men got accused of murder.

Would Alicia's daughter have fretted about blow job technique? Would her son have been the sort to pressure a girl into improving?

Her phone beeped to announce a message. This time she answered it, listened. It was Murphy. She needed to get back to Sheerton and fast. Fine. It might be good news for once.

She put the car in gear, and drove carefully through the thickening snow.

"My name is Hillary Carmichael. About an hour ago, I was assaulted, and mine and my friend's lives were threatened." The woman was in her twenties, but dressed elegantly, like a middle-aged rich woman.

"Hillary," Alicia said. "Why ask for me specifically?"

"That man you sent to ask me about Tanya—the sergeant—he gave me your card."

"And you can't speak to anyone else?"

"No."

In Sheerton's reception, a cleaner was already mopping up melted snow, bright yellow "Wet Floor" signs stationed on every corner. Alicia invited Hillary to follow her to a family room, with soft chairs and cuddly toys. She thought about taking her pigtails out, but she'd promised to leave them all day, to be *herself* again. All day. It was what she needed to stay ahead of everyone. To keep sharp.

Hillary looked at the sofa as if it were coated with snot. Alicia almost laughed at the image. *Almost.*

Murphy joined her as requested, Alicia explaining to Hillary that she wanted "her boss" in on this. In truth, Alicia didn't trust herself. She wouldn't be much use until this prank or mistake, or whatever it was, got cleared up.

"My friend, a male friend, came round to update me on a few things," Hillary said. "My husband was at work, but he knows of the friendship."

I'll bet, Alicia thought.

"The bell rang, and my friend answered the door for me. Then this man came in, assaulted John, and threatened me."

"Did you know this man?" Murphy said.

"No. And neither did John. But he knew who John was. He wanted information."

"What sort of information?"

Hillary adjusted herself on the couch, uncrossed and re-crossed her legs. "Should you be offering me tea or something? I mean isn't that procedure? I pay a lot of taxes. I don't think a cup of tea would be too much to ask."

Alicia stared, her mouth open slightly. Murphy followed her lead.

"Fine," Hillary said, standing stiffly. "You're obviously not interested. I'll be in the reception waiting for whoever runs this place."

Good, Alicia thought. *Time to get back to work.*

"The man was quite mad," she said as a parting shot. "Seemed to think John knew where his missing daughter was hiding. Crazy fellow. Him and his friends."

Alicia sprang to her feet, Murphy standing in her way. They called Hillary Carmichael back.

"What friends?" Murphy said.

"Milk, two sugars please."

Murphy reluctantly used the phone to call in the order, and Hillary refused to speak until they met her hospitality expectations.

This woman might have seen Richard.

Alicia hoped Hillary was wrong. She hoped what she heard so far was about someone else, some guy who thought his runaway girl was hiding with "John." Was that Wellington? Had to be. But Hillary was tight-lipped.

Alicia was bored of this. A first year psychology student would have pegged Hillary as an attention-seeker and power-monger. She needed control. Delaying the conversation was a common way of achieving this.

PC Ndlove delivered the drink in a polystyrene cup, which Hillary handled with revulsion. She drank from it. Her face said it wasn't particularly good.

"Mrs. Carmichael?" Murphy said. "Perhaps we can continue?"

She placed the cup on the coffee table. "John refused to talk. Until he took me hostage, and then he couldn't *stop* talking."

"This is John Wellington, yes?" Alicia said.

"Yes. How did you know?"

"Lucky guess."

"Well, John said he'd talk, but only out of earshot of me. So the man ties me up in the kitchen and goes back to see John."

"Did you hear what they talked about?"

"No. But it must have been satisfactory because the man left soon after."

Alicia dreaded asking the next question. But it needed asking. "Can you describe him for us?"

"Yes." And the man she relayed was Richard to a tee.

Alicia iced over. Doyle in the tattoo parlour was not a drugs slaying or a little-Windsor covering his tracks, the bodies in the well were the work of the man she slept with last night, and she was certain that Richard Hague was in possession of information they needed.

"Ms. Friend, are you alright?" Hillary said. "You're ever so grey."

"Alicia?" Murphy said.

"I'm fine," Alicia said. "Continue. You said this man had friends."

"They came to meet him. John got free straight away—he wasn't any good at knots, so you can cross 'sailor' and 'boy scout' off your list of suspects. John freed me and we both went to the window. They were all arm in arm, like best friends. The man who assaulted me got in the back with a Chinaman, and the other drove away."

Chinaman? Seriously?

"Can you describe the van?" Murphy asked.

"Hmm. A big one. Blue, I think. Or maybe grey."

Alicia stopped herself from rolling her eyes.

Then Hillary said, "Would the registration number help?"

Alicia held her sweary tongue as Hillary Carmichael fished about in her bag. They needed this, but Alicia needed none of it. The van, when they found it, may be burned to a crisp, with a dead kidnapper inside, Katie mysteriously released unharmed. The plates would be fake, but a panda car might spot it.

"Here it is." Hillary presented a folded Post-It note.

Alicia reached for it, but Hillary snatched it back.

"What do you say?" she said.

"Please, just give me the number," Alicia said.

"Not until you ask nicely. Manners never cost anything."

Alicia considered her next action. It went into the little

computer, ticked around, spat out the answer: *No, don't do it*, but she did it anyway. She took the edge of the coffee table and with one furious sweep, heaved it over, sending tea and magazines flying, clattering. Murphy leapt back, out of his seat, and Hillary cowered.

Alicia snatched the Post-it. "Mrs. Carmichael, thank you, you've been very helpful. Now get out."

Then Alicia raced from the room to find someone to do her a PNC check.

"Ronnie 'Red' McCall," Alicia announced to the dozen-or-so coppers in the operations room. "He knows the location of one Richard Hague. Hague, we believe, has important information pertaining to this case. Bulletins are out to everyone on the street. McCall is a known lowlife. A *dumb* lowlife, but still a lowlife. Seems he didn't see fit to change the number on his van before barging into our investigation. So if he's around, we should pick him up."

A private investigator and security expert, apparently. Had Richard hired a PI to supplement the police investigation?

Alicia said, "Sergeant Cleaver is picking up John Wellington again. I realise some of you may have known him as a police officer, but we have reason to believe he has been obstructing justice for some time, but that's not our concern here. This is bigger than old loyalties, folks. *He knows where Siobhan and Katie are.*"

The room buzzed, voices grew, some reluctant but all positive, all on board, every single comment regarding the case. Often, it was about drinks, clocking off. But not this time. The people recruited thanks to a famous girl losing her freedom all hit the streets.

And moments later, Alicia found herself alone in the clean,

white room. She was blocking and doing it well. She should be happy about the snow outside, falling much earlier than usual.

"You slept with him, didn't you," Murphy said from the door.

Until now, she'd tried to imagine another Richard, someone they'd mixed up with the one she'd spent last night with. Murphy's direct question shattered the wall she'd erected. She leaned forward on a desk, arms extended, head bowed. She nodded.

Murphy sat beside her. "We make mistakes, Alicia. We have to live with them. If it's true what he did, then you know this isn't everything."

"It's not true," she said.

A long silence. Alicia sat up on the desk next to Murphy, laid her head on his shoulder, her mouth glum as glum could be. She watched the snow settling thick on the ground. Murphy sat up straight, made his arm comfier, watching the Christmas card scene evolve outside.

"She was assaulted while I was working," he said. "Working hard on a graffiti artist of all things. Some obscene stuff had gone up near schools in the area and there was pressure from an MP whose kid had repeated some swearing. One night I decided I knew where the guy was going to strike next, one of my famous hunches, so Susan was home alone."

Alicia tried to make out shapes in the snow, like you can with clouds, but nothing stayed the same long enough for her to sculpt a definite form.

"A burglar broke in. She disturbed him. He beat her up. Not badly, but bad enough. After, she was too scared to go home. I promised to sell the house, but she wanted me to quit the force too. I said I'd think about it.

"Some of the guys, uniforms I worked with a few times, they found this smack-head with a bunch of my stuff, flogging it around bars—jewellery, a watch I got off my mum, that sort of thing. But they didn't bring him in. I went to them.

"While I was beating the shit out of him, he said how sorry he was. He didn't mean to hurt her. I told him that punching women in the face always hurts, and I was going to do a lot worse to him. He said that if Susan had done as he asked she wouldn't have been hurt, that it had been so long since he was with anyone. He got out of jail a week earlier. He was so sorry.

"I didn't want to believe it, that he'd done more than knock her around, but he said all this unprompted. He needed hospital treatment for weeks after, but it got him off the smack. I heard he eventually got a job with the council. But when I asked Susan if all he did was hit her, I saw something in her eyes. A complete violation. Like *I* was responsible. Like it was me who did that to her. That seeing me brought it all back. She cried a while, then the next day she headed to her mother's. Used to write to me but that's all stopped. Last I heard she was living in Worthing."

Alicia snuggled closer, her face nuzzling his soft muscle.

"So now we both know a dirty little secret about one another," he said. "I suppose we have to keep it that way."

He put an arm fully around her and she hugged him about his doughy middle. It felt good. It felt safe.

It was a lie.

Cleaver had been angry at Wellington's release, after all the hard work he put in. And he didn't even get a date with Murphy's niece. But this would make up for it. Not that it was over. He still had to thank Darla, and since she didn't appreciate flowers, maybe she'd prefer wine. Or some sort of gift experience.

Murphy had pulled him to one side when no one else was looking and told him that Darla was hurt pretty badly before.

Her kid's father, her fiancé at the time, ran off with a stripper he met on his stag night. So Cleaver better tread carefully.

Not a threat; *advice.*

He was a little overweight these days, but that hadn't seemed to be an issue for the woman. She hadn't even glanced that way at all. Perhaps she didn't need to.

"Nice house," PC Ndlove said as they pulled up outside.

A decent girl, Ndlove was. Cleaver and Ball had teased her a little, but then she *was* a junior member of the team. Not a probie anymore, but still fair game. And she reacted in the way you should act when your superiors are ribbing on you: you do a damn good job and make sure folk know it.

Cleaver got out, closed the door. The snow blew right at him. It wasn't quite a blizzard, but visibility was getting worse, and he'd left his coat back at the station.

Ndlove followed him up the short driveway to a neat, detached house with no garden at the front but a path leading around the back.

At the door, Cleaver said, "You want to put the cuffs on him?"

"Only if he knocks you out first," Ndlove replied.

Cleaver smiled. Rang the bell. No answer. He rang the bell again. For longer this time.

"Maybe you didn't press it hard enough," Ndlove said.

"Maybe you'd like to go across my knee."

"I'll settle for going around back."

She left Cleaver alone at the front and opened the back gate. Cleaver pressed the bell again, peeked through the letterbox. He called, "Hello? Mr. Wellington? Are you home?"

Ndlove made her way back to Cleaver. She was not grey, exactly, but she was a funny colour, whatever colour black people go when they lose blood from their face. She shook her head slightly, and Cleaver closed his eyes, a sense of anti-climax surging through him. He knew straight away what this meant.

He had to see it, though. She pointed into the garden, a good ten metres of snow-covered grass, to the far end next to the fence.

Swaying slowly and gathering snow on his shoulders and on his up-curled feet, John Wellington's body hung from a tree via a noose around his neck. A chair lay kicked aside. Flakes landed on his blueing face, not melting.

"You cowardly bastard," Cleaver said. He turned his back on the corpse, opened his phone, and prepared to deliver the bad news.

Chapter Thirty-One

ALICIA RELAYED Cleaver's report to Murphy and sent a text out to those task force members whose numbers she'd stored: *Welly dead. Hague + mccall now priority.*

Lazy but effective.

"What's the time?" Alicia asked.

"Three. Why?"

"Lunchtime. I need brain fuel."

On the way to the canteen, Alicia's phone went again. It was Ball.

"You still want me out here? It's snowing so bad I can't see a thing."

In all the rush she'd forgotten about him.

"I need *someone* there," Alicia said. "Keep an eye on the driveway. If anyone leaves, let me know."

She hung up, grabbed a sandwich and a fresh orange. Murphy took a muffin. Then the control room called her. "Two officers have detained a suspect they believe you may be interested in."

"Why do they think that?" Alicia asked.

"Their equipment flashed a number plate and it showed no

registered insurance. It's a car, not a van though. In the name of Tina McCall, but it's a guy driving."

McCall? Some luck at last? "And they've detained him?"

"No choice. They recognised the name McCall from the bulletin you issued, and followed at a distance. He went into a B&Q in Pudsey. Manager's annoyed at the police presence, but they're holding him until further instructions."

"Think the manager will mind hanging onto him a while?"

"Can't comment, but the guy *is* the one you're looking for. Ronald McCall, also known as 'Red'."

Alicia gripped the phone harder. She said thank you before hanging up.

Looks like the extra bodies paid off.

She told Murphy and they ate their lunches on the move.

The journey out to the Pudsey area of Leeds took an hour. Rather than waiting for the officers to bring him in, Alicia figured it would be better to interrogate him on-site; Pudsey might be where Richard was now hiding.

The roads were unprepared, traffic gearing up for the school run. The time she shaved off the Glenpark to Sheerton race was doubled, then tripled. The case was moving faster than them.

The Owlcotes Centre is an open mall with an Asda, Marks and Spencer, and a few smaller retailers. There is also a B & Q from which, it since emerged, Red McCall was banned for life. Here, the manager, Pete, greeted them and led them through the warehouse section. Pete wasn't aware of the ban, but he was new, and one of the longer-serving staff had raised the point.

Red McCall stood, remonstrating with two uniformed officers. "I got banned cos of my *wife*. She doesn't *work* here anymore. You can't arrest me."

"Sir, if you were under arrest I would have cuffed you," the taller of the two said.

"Red!" Alicia said. "How the hell are you?" She was forcing this self, her *true* self, out into the open, walking with a determined bounce that made her pigtails bob, pushing her cuteness factor to the max. If this associate, this *friend*, of Richard's knew where he was, and it was likely, then she'd need her wits about her. She needed to be Alicia, the best Alicia. Happy Alicia. "You are looking *good* today."

"Hey, thanks, darling," he said. "You in charge around here?"

She showed him her ID.

"Nuther copper, huh. You arresting me or letting me go?"

"Well, I've had a good think about that, Red, and I'm going for option..." She produced a drum roll with her tongue, hand actions going in time. "Option number ... *one!*"

"Ah, damn it." He punched the air and kicked the floor. "All I wanted was some pliers and a blowtorch."

Something in her brain clicked.

"It's tough to buy things without money," Murphy said.

"Oh, don't be such a grumpy-pants, Detective." Alicia was still trying to locate that click. "Mr. McCall probably forgot his wallet or something."

"That's right," McCall said. "That's right. It's in my car."

"Okey-dokey. Shall we go get it?"

"My other car. It's in my other car."

"Your van?"

"Yeah, that's it. My van."

"The blue transit that you and your Oriental friend were driving earlier today?"

"That's the one!" He was practically dancing he was so nervous. "Yeah, yeah, that one. I needed pliers and a blowtorch to fix it."

Pliers and a blowtorch...

Alicia located the click. "Pulp Fiction."

"Pardon?" Murphy said.

"It's a line from a movie. Pulp Fiction. Haven't you seen it?"

"Yeah, sure. A while ago."

"Marsellus Wallace says he's gonna go to town on someone's ass, with pliers and a blowtorch."

"Yeah," McCall said. "And it's great, cos you never actually see what happens, but you know that big nig-nog's going to torture the shit out a' the rapist guy."

"Cuff him," Alicia said.

"Hey!"

And the two uniforms grappled McCall to the floor, snapping cuffs on him while he swore and struggled.

"What's going on?" Murphy said. "We need him to cooperate."

"They're not Richard's friends," Alicia said. "They're assassins."

She dismissed the two uniforms and explained to Murphy the prospect of what was happening to Richard right now. That he had extracted information from John Wellington, but he wasn't sharing it with Red McCall and the other one. They were going to torture him, whether it was for information or something else. Henry Windsor, she theorised, had recruited thugs to clean up after him.

She dearly hoped these two killed Doyle, and the women. Sure, perhaps Richard had demanded information from Wellington, and perhaps he hadn't only been using her to keep tabs on the case. Perhaps her mentioning Wellington had spurred him into action. Perhaps it was the first time he'd done something like this.

Perhaps, perhaps, perhaps...

...it was a mistake after all.

On the floor of the warehouse, Alicia jammed her knee into the base of McCall's spine, and pulled his head up, hyperextending the muscles around his vertebrae.

"How much is he paying you?" Alicia said.

"Ow, that hurts!"

"Really? Then this must *really* hurt."

She pulled harder and he yelled out to stop, okay, he'd talk.

"A thousand."

She let him go. "A thousand? He was paying Wellington much more than that. He bought Paavan a house. Don't you think that's a little stingy?"

"Ah, that Yank knobhead. I knew he was holding out on me."

"Yank? Henry isn't American."

"I don't know no Henry. Alfie. Alfie Rhee, man. He wanted to catch the sick bastard who murdered his wife. Get medieval on his ass."

Alicia processed this. Too much. One minute Richard was innocent again, the next this whole new angle jilted her sideways.

Murphy said, "This isn't to do with Tanya Windsor?"

"I doubt it. Unless the psycho knob killed her too."

Alicia launched at him, her leg poised for a kick, but Murphy scooped her easily off the ground and set her down.

"Thank you," she said.

"And I thank you too," McCall said.

Murphy pointed. "Shut it."

"Shutting it right now."

Alicia tried to find herself again. That other person was seeping out, ready to explode. She forced herself to relax, let the real Alicia into play. It was getting harder. But there.

There she was.

Alicia crouched next to McCall. "Richard Hague is being

assaulted by a man who believes Richard killed his wife. Correct?"

"That's real clever, lovie. How'd you figure that out?"

"And this is taking place in your van."

"That's right too. Wow, are you psychic?"

"And this 'Alfie' person, he's the oriental gentleman you left with, along with Richard."

"Yes. Bloody hell!"

Alicia took hold of the cuffs and bent them upwards, which sent a bolt of pain up McCall's arm, forcing him to stand.

"These cuffs are great, aren't they, Murphy?" she said, walking Red out to the main store. "You get a guy in them and he's your slave forever. They twist the wrist in just the right place."

"Like Alfie," McCall said, now compliant. "He twisted me round and it hurt even more'n this."

"Hm. South-east Asian guy, likes twisting folk around." Passing the uniformed officers who were awaiting further instructions, she flipped the stud holding one of their batons and slid it out. "I might need this."

"Er, ma'am," said the constable, "I'm not sure..."

Murphy held out his hand to the other officer, who took his own baton and gave it to Murphy.

"Thank you, son," Murphy said. "I'll get this back to you."

Alicia drove the Vauxhall at an unsafe speed. Murphy sat in the back with McCall, sliding occasionally, but not hurting. Open countryside approached. Alicia swore she'd hurt this guy if he was bullshitting them.

As they left the city, Murphy radioed for backup, and Cleaver and Ndlove said they were en route. Three other cars checked in and Murphy ordered them into the area and await instruction once they knew the exact location.

"Hey," McCall said to Alicia as she pulled out of a skid, "you know how I'm being all cooperative and stuff?"

"What of it?"

"Any chance you could play a little Celine Dion?"

"I'm all out. I got some Maria Carey."

"Well ... she's o-*kay*. But she's no Celine. Nah, it's alright. I'll manage without." Outside the window, the snow eased, the passing scenery like white marshmallow.

He gave directions, claimed to be lost due to the snow, but as they whizzed by thick bunches of trees Alicia knew where they were heading.

"Eccup," she said. "They're at the reservoir."

"Jesus, she is *good*," McCall said.

He offered more specific directions. There was a small road coming up that led into the forest. They parked further on, past the narrow lane where Red McCall promised the van was located, and Murphy helped the bent PI out of the car while Alicia tramped through the snow and into the area of woodland. She carried the police baton flush to her arm, running in a crouch. She didn't plan what she was doing, but stayed low like she was taught on some course a gazillion years ago.

As the bare trees drew in tighter, she picked her way through the undergrowth. Shivered in the cold. The route grew even thicker, the going harder, scratching at her, but it came to a flush end where the road had been cut. She crouched and scanned the scene through a brown, leafless bush.

The van appeared dead from here, unoccupied. A shell. Then it moved slightly. Someone walking around inside.

Murphy cried out in pain, shouted something. Alicia turned to run back, but she didn't need to. Red McCall charged down the road, hands free, one with cuffs dangling. He laughed maniacally. Murphy pursued, limping badly, no way to catch up.

McCall yelled, "Hey, Alfie, look out! *Alfie!* The police are here!"

Alicia shot out of the trees. She intercepted McCall with a sharp rap from the baton across his shins. He tumbled, literally tumbling head over heels, and thumped to a halt in a cloud of snow. He struggled to find his feet, like an upended turtle, yelling for Alfie to get out of here. Alicia dropped on him quickly, pressed the baton to his windpipe—technically an illegal hold, but she figured she could get away with it.

She said, "Murphy, gimme a hand here."

But Murphy stood stock still. Alicia heard two footsteps crunch in the snow behind her. She turned, and froze.

The Asian man held a handgun, a six-shooter revolver. He closed the van door from which he'd climbed, and walked towards them. "Now this piece of shit is the best gun I could get hold of in your stupid country, but I think I can hit you from here. Ruger, six-shooter. Old, but accurate. Now, why don't you get off my buddy there and uncuff him. Then we'll have a think about what to do next."

Chapter Thirty-Two

MCCALL INSISTED ON DRIVING. He used his left hand to steer and his right to hold the gun Alfie had given him, rested it on his lap and aimed across his body towards his passenger, the cutest Cute Blondie Copper he ever did see. Well, it was technically McCall's gun, since he paid for it and had yet to receive any sort of remuneration from Alfie. Unless you included a pub lunch and a sore arm. Which he definitely did not.

This, however, this might go some way to making up for it.

Cute Blondie Copper sat, strapped in, grasping the seat itself as McCall sluiced the Vectra through the snow. There was nothing to worry about, though, not now he had Celine back on the air.

The car's back end slid out like a cat's arse. McCall compensated, turned into the skid, and righted it. He could only tell they were on the road because of the mounds that passed for walls either side.

Cute Blondie Copper's partner, who McCall had kicked real good in the knee, was in the back, now bound with the cuffs Red had slipped thanks to a universal key he picked up when kitting out Alfie's torture-board.

Not so dumb after all, eh?

McCall even sat the dour copper behind Cute Blondie Copper so he could keep an eye on him.

It was getting dark but the snow had slowed to a dandruff shower from heaven. Pretty in the headlights.

Cute Blondie Copper moved.

"Stop it!" McCall yelled, showing her the Ruger again. "I was in the Marines, babe. Don't think I don't know how to use this."

Actually, McCall didn't have the first clue how to use it. All guns are different. He'd handled a Magnum, a Baretta, an SA80 machine-gun, but never a Ruger. Still, it was fairly simple; he'd figure it out. He enlisted in the Marines *to Be the Best* and to kill foreign baddies, but never shot a single soul. Three years in and all he managed was to get bloody cold a lot more bloody often than he felt was right, and he moaned and moaned, and suggested maybe they should go off and start their own war, to ensure their wages weren't wasted. His friends laughed, but he was serious. This was all pre-9/11. If he'd still been around after the World Trade Centre got turned to dust, boy would those Arab dicks have got a shock. He'd have been all over them. "Medieval" wouldn't cut it.

"You have to let us go," Cute Blondie Copper said. Yet again. "Red, come on. There's more at stake here."

"Tell you what," McCall said. "You come up with something more original than that and I might consider letting you go, the next village we come to."

"Richard Hague has information we need. Two girls are going to die."

"Yeah, you said that already too. Stop fidgeting. You're making me nervous."

She sat still, pouting. Heh-heh. She sure looked good enough to eat, this one. McCall thought maybe there was a stirring in his trousers, but it was a false alarm. Not that he'd do anything like that to a girl, no. He wasn't that sort of guy. Even if he managed a stiffy.

Damn, he'd better get paid soon. He had another date planned with Deirdre from the bookies on Saturday, and she'd indicated that this was it, this was the night. *The* night. If he missed out on that he'd be *well* pissed off.

"You're not going to shoot us, Red," the moustache-man said from behind. "Even your boss said not to."

"Unless I had to," McCall corrected, waving the gun. "He told me what he was doing is more important than you two. That a hundred families have been torn a new arsehole by your witness friend back there."

"Bullshit," Cute Blondie Copper said.

The curse sounded so dumb coming from her. You'd expect nothing but sugar and kindness from that little mouth.

"Nah," McCall said. "One hundred. I mean I knew the fella was one evil dick but a *hundred*? Man, that takes some doing."

Cute Blondie Copper pouted again. She reminded McCall of a hooker he used to know, before his downstairs-troubles. Only eighteen, dressed like a schoolgirl all the time—hell, she probably *was* a schoolgirl—but she could suck a golf ball through a hosepipe if she put her mind to it. And boy, when he was on top...

"You're going to jail for this," Murphy said. "Unless you pull over right now."

"I'm not pulling over. Alfie said I gotta keep you busy until he's done. Then I can let you go."

"He's using you," Cute Blondie Copper said. "You know that don't you."

"Doesn't everyone use everyone? I'm an employee."

"You're a mug. He's going to kill our witness, then drive to the airport and go home. You'll not see a penny."

"Shut up! One more word and I'll plug you."

"My arse you will."

"Stop talking like that. You shouldn't talk like that. You should be nice and good."

She crossed her arms and stared out of the window, into the night closing around them. They were more sheltered now too, the trees either side taller and denser. The wind and the car's wake churned up misty snow flurries.

McCall's driving grew less erratic. He was unsure whether it was because his favourite Celine track—the one from the Titanic movie—was playing, or if it was because Cute Blondie Copper had stopped telling lies about his pal back in the van.

"Sod it," Cute Blondie Copper said suddenly.

She leaned over and grabbed the wheel.

"Hey, get off!" McCall cried, the car sliding sideways before he wrested control back.

"Alicia!" the copper in the back yelled.

McCall dropped the gun so he could fight her off better. He didn't want to hit her, not that schoolgirl face, but he needed her off him. He shoved her against the passenger door, regained control, going straight again, but she was on him once more.

"Alicia, stop it," the guy said.

"Yeah, stop it," said McCall.

Cute Blondie Copper's face sort of changed then. Like she was turning into a werewolf or something. A snarl, a grimace, screwing her nose right up, fangs bared. She gripped the steering wheel with a strength that shocked McCall, and turned it so hard that he had to let go. The car shot sideways, airborne for some reason, a tree hurtling towards them.

And in the split second between the car leaving the road and making head-on contact with the tree, McCall's brain managed to throw out one thought:

That's okay. This baby has airbags.

Chapter Thirty-Three

RICHARD'S WRISTS screamed in pain. He, however, did not. He made eye contact with Alfie Rhee and did not at any time break away. Alfie wanted to know why he did it, all of it, and Richard could not tell him. For the first time in his life he questioned the wisdom of his desires, or more specifically the wisdom of acting upon them. No, it was no problem taking lives. And looking at the corruption all around the world, the con artists masquerading as holy men, taking money from followers of magicians and sorcerers, as bad if not worse than anything Richard had ever done.

God is good. But then He destroys your life.

Allah will save you. Then He smites your entire country.

Buddha is just and fair. Where is he when you really need him?

Dead people feel nothing. It's the manner of the death that truly matters.

He tried to make Alfie see this. But in between threats and cursing, Alfie did make a couple of points that Richard found worth considering. Like: *but why take the life in the first place?*

Richard always thought of life as silly. Death was the end of that silliness. But why should you die? You live a miserable life (most people do; Richard was rather happy with his, thank you very much) and then you leave this life begging for a little more of it. So wasn't that the painfully simple answer to the meaning of life? *Your* life needs to matter to someone else. Like Richard's life now mattered to Katie.

"What are you thinking?" Alfie said. "Right now, what was the last coherent thought in that diseased mind of yours?"

"I just solved the meaning of life," Richard said. He pulled on the cuffs again, his wrists too thick to slip through, deep red welts that he could not see forming where they bit into him. "You want to know what it is?"

Alfie snorted. "Sure. Go on."

"Let me ask you this first. Have you moved on from Stacy? Started dating again?"

"Let *me* ask *you* this. Is that all the weapons you have?"

He referred to the knife case Richard was carrying when they picked him up, held open by Alfie's bone saw, the collection on show: the stiletto, the combat knife, the over-sized hunting blade, the bayonet; two throwing knives, a flick knife he took from the body of a drug dealer in Calumet City, one he didn't actually intend to kill and didn't count amongst his one-hundred; but this guy was pushing crack on high *school kids*. The final knife was one he saved for special occasions. He told Alfie this when he opened the case, and Alfie still held it now, waving it around like a conductor. It was two inches wide at the hilt, tapering slowly along twelve inches to a good sharp point. The handle was covered in cured leather, allowing excellent grip until you got too sweaty, and then it became the least effective of all the knives. But it was perfectly weighted, sharp enough to remove a human limb—with the right pressure and technique

—and the sentimental value glowed around it; the first weapon he ever used on a human being.

"I have a wider selection at home," Richard said, the pain in his wrists so constant it was beginning to feel good now. "But these are my favourites."

Alfie didn't seem to know what to do next, bless him. This man *could* kill, but took no pleasure in it. Even with the person responsible for his wife's death at his mercy, he still wasn't ready. Not in cold blood anyway.

"And you think that's acceptable?" Alfie said.

Asking him that a few days ago, Richard would have simply shrugged and stabbed Alfie in the heart.

Is that acceptable?

"Not in general, no," Richard answered. "But then in general, people are stupid. They believe in whatever their parents or priests tell them. They're wrong."

"So you come from nothing and return to nothing. That's your take on life? That it don't matter someone might cure cancer or AIDS if you let them live?"

Richard almost laughed. "You think your wife would have cured AIDS?"

"No. But she'd have brought my child into the world. That ain't gonna happen now."

"Oh come on, what are you? Forty-five? Fifty at the most? And still in great shape. You could land yourself a thirty-year-old. My girlfriend's thirty-two and that's more than young enough to have a kid." Referring to Alicia as his girlfriend felt both good and sad. When she discovered the truth about him, it was likely she'd end it.

Alfie swung the knife. He swung it back, harder and faster, producing a *swish* noise through the air. "I swore I'd not look at another woman until Stacy's killer had been brought to justice."

"Justice? You think *this*..." He rattled the cuffs again. "Is justice?"

"Not yet. Not yet."

Richard wished he'd get on with it. If he was going to die, which he doubted, he was going to die. But that was probably part of Alfie's plan—to make him suffer before turning him in.

"You were going to tell me your take on the meaning of life."

"Oh yes." Richard thought back to his conclusions. "I think you have to mean something to someone. If you can influence another's life in a positive fashion, your life is worth living. If you cannot, you should die."

"And you offer what, exactly? Whose life do you influence?"

"My daughter's."

Alfie turned from him. His forehead leaned on the side of the van, the knife tapping on metal. He knelt down and rested the blade on Richard's cheek, played with the flesh a little, moving it with the point. Then he poked the skin next to Richard's left eye. The fine tip blurred his vision.

"Fine, you got me. You're right. I can't let your daughter die. So yeah, I'll get you the phone. But you try anything, I *will* finish you."

When Alfie opened the door, the cold air blew in and didn't leave. Richard heaved at the cuffs, sure now that he'd drawn blood. His muscles ripped to maximum effort, bulging his clothing. He held in a cry of pain as one of the hooks through which the cuffs were linked shifted ever so slightly.

Alfie came back, an old Nokia in hand. "What's the number?"

Richard told Alfie to fish in his wallet—lying next to his knife case—for Alicia's card. Alfie read the number, dialled, and listened.

"It's busy," he said. "Any others?"

"You don't want to dial nine-nine-nine do you?"

Alfie gave a *wadda you think* look.

"Okay, try this one."

He gave Alfie a telephone number, the first one that came into his head, one he only remembered because it was the first he dialled the day Katie didn't come home, the one he dialled constantly for six hours until he called the police. The person on the other end picked up.

Alfie pressed the phone to Richard's ear.

"Brian? Hi, it's Richard here, Katie's dad."

Brian took a breath. "Oh, God. Any news? Please don't say she's—"

"No, nothing like that. Brian, listen. I know how much you care for my daughter, and I know how much grief I've given her over it. But if you can do this one thing for me, I promise I'll never doubt you as a human being again."

Alfie's line of sight was Richard's face, watching for tricks, for codes. But the phone call contained no codes. Richard's hand curled around the loop screwed into the board, the hook that had shifted that tiny bit while Alfie was out.

"Okay, Mr. Hague," Brian said. "What do I have to do?"

"I need you to call Glenpark police station, and get connected to either Detective Sergeant Alicia Friend or a Detective Inspector Murphy. Not sure of his first name."

His grip tightened and twisted, side to side, side to side, pulling upwards slowly and quietly. There was give here. It moved.

"Yes, Mr. Hague. What do I tell them?"

The hook ground out of its housing, an unnoticeable noise thanks to the talking inside and the wind out. Now Richard had a decision to make.

"Tell them that I know where Katie is. Tell them it doesn't matter how I know, but tell them."

Brian got excited. "Where? Where is she?"

Alfie wasn't a bad person. But nor was he useful to anyone. According to Richard's new vetting system for victims, that made Alfie a viable target. The screw end of the hook would go nicely in the man's neck.

"She's at an estate..."

"Wait, let me get a pen."

While Brian rummaged for a pen, Richard concluded that some compromise was required. Alfie didn't deserve to die, at least he didn't until he captured Richard, but Richard did not trust the voice on the end of the phone. Maybe he simply hated Brian for what he did to Katie—what all fathers do not think of around their daughters—or maybe it was because Brian lost her once and may do so again. Only one thing was certain: Richard had to do it himself.

He swung the three-inch hook. It sunk into Alfie's chest, but missed the heart. Some resistance; not as sharp as he'd hoped. But it went in. He slammed Alfie against the side, pushing harder, making sure it gouged as deep as possible.

Alfie screamed.

Then Richard yanked out the barb, leaving a ragged, bloody hole—no point in having a wound closed up, after all.

Alfie shrieked. His hand flew to the hole between his shoulder and pectoral muscle. He slid down the side and sat on the floor, while Richard took advantage of his lack of bearings and tipped him over. He fished in Alfie's back pockets and found the handcuff key.

"Think yourself lucky, Alfie," Richard said. "A week ago—hell, a day ago—I'd have stuck that in your neck just to see the look in your eyes."

Richard freed himself, and decided not to kill Alfie. He reached to open the door, but Alfie lunged at him, blood gushing from his torso. "You are *not* getting away."

They both went down and Richard threw an elbow. Alfie blocked and countered with a painful jab to the kidney. Richard tried a punch, from a good position this time, aimed right at the wound. The block came faster than he expected and Alfie's other hand pushed his elbow up, his wrist going down, and he lost all balance.

Richard had size and strength, but this guy had the moves. He kicked free and grabbed for something, anything, to use as a weapon, locating his knife case. He pulled out the first blade he came to—the bayonet—and slashed at Alfie as he attacked. Alfie stepped back, but in the small space Richard was too fast. He'd seen in movies where these martial artists disarm skilled knifemen barehanded, but it was all rubbish, not with a *really* skilful knifeman.

He thrust an intentionally clumsy blow, and Alfie— predictably—shifted his weight for the jab to the wrist. But Richard was ready. He simply switched the direction of the blade, spinning it as if on an axis, and Alfie embedded his own hand around it.

Alfie's eyes widened and another pain-filled cry would have escaped, but Richard punched him in the mouth. He went down. More than conscious, but beaten.

Richard knelt before him, hand gripping the man's throat, bayonet held away to prevent it being stolen. He pushed his face right up to Alfie's.

"You tried to kill my daughter. You did it because I was misguided enough to kill your wife, but that's no excuse. Katie may already be dead."

Alfie's hand flailed weakly on Richard's shoulder, and he was losing blood through the chest wound.

"I can finish it quickly for you." Richard raised the bayonet, both men now covered in Alfie Rhee's blood. "Say the word,

Alfie. It'll be quick." He readied himself to stab down hard into Alfie's chest, should he give permission.

Then the back doors flew open and Alicia stood there, shivering like a rosy-cheeked angel in the snow, aiming a gun right at Richard's head.

Chapter Thirty-Four

"STOP BEING SUCH A BABY," Alicia said.

Alfie Rhee, seated on the van's back step, winced again as Alicia held the small painful hole in his chest closed and applied a dirty rag she found on the floor of the van. He checked Richard Hague was still cuffed to one of the three loops that remained intact, aware that the man's knives were still close by. The gun, *Alfie's* gun, was in easy reach. He could end it all right now. Do Hague and persuade the blonde weirdo to call it self-defence. She'd go for it, right?

"It'll get infected," he said in between short sharp breaths.

"Infection they can treat. You bleed out or collapse in the snow, you die. Got it?"

"Sure, whatever. *Ow!*"

"Right. Hold that." She pressed the rag on the wound. "It's not as deep as it looks. But the hand needs treating ASAP."

"So you taking me to a hospital now?"

"Not exactly."

She tossed the handcuff key to the killer, who caught it, sorta confused, sorta frightened. The Alicia chick pointed the gun and said, "Okay, unlock the crank around the hook but keep the other round your wrist."

"What the hell you doing?" Alfie demanded.

"Move." She pushed Alfie in the direction of the road.

Up the narrow track, the trees' white beauty felt somehow vulgar in this setting. The main road cut across the top. His teeth began to chatter. Drops of blood stained the snow by his feet.

"The police know our approximate location," Alicia said. "They're zeroing in on my phone, but reception is sketchy. Go to the end, turn right. Walk for about half an hour, you find your friend Red since that's where he's heading. Ambulance and police assistance will find you soon."

Alicia didn't think she'd fallen unconscious after the crash. The passenger airbag worked a treat, deflated so she could climb out if she chose. Her bones ached. She'd felt for her head. Still on. But thumping. The driver had smashed into the steering column, nose crumpled and bloody, arms limp by his sides. But he had a pulse.

A grunt from the back seat told her Murphy was alive but hurt. She found her phone and unlocked it. One bar of service. She dialled.

"You can hear me okay?" she said after identifying herself.

"Yes," the operator replied.

She gave details of the accident, the victims, their location, and climbed in back to check on Murphy. He rested his head on the side of the car, staring blankly at Alicia, trying to speak.

"Help's coming," Alicia told him.

Murphy closed his eyes.

"I need to go somewhere first, though. I'll leave the phone in the car. They can track the signal."

Murphy's eyes opened. His head shuddered as if to say, "No."

She pulled the back seat down to access the boot, found a blanket and wrapped it around Murphy. There was nothing more she could do for him.

She said, "I have to go."

Outside, her breath clouded. Snow crunched under her. The car's front end was a mess. The bonnet buckled right up, glass on the ground, twisted metal jutting from all angles. Steam pouring. The windscreen was shattered but somehow the windows were intact.

Alicia climbed onto the hot bonnet and swept the tiny diamonds of glass from where she needed to lie. She checked McCall was still unconscious and, with her legs in the air, hung upside down in the driver's foot well, feeling about, head ringing, every last bone aching, wanting to let go, head to the hospital and rest. But then she found it.

Back out in the open, she looked the gun over with a mixture of excitement and fear. She'd never held a real one outside her obligatory gun courses, and they were lightweight professional pieces in a closed, sterile environment. Easy to handle. Easy to shoot at targets. This was so much heavier than she'd expected, so metallic-smelling and cold. Wielded so easily in movies, it took both thumbs to pull back the hammer.

She checked on Murphy one last time, then set off, wearing only her trouser suit, determined to find answers. Was Richard really a killer? McCall surely exaggerated when he said a hundred victims; no one would believe that. But she also needed to know how much was a lie. Was last night only to pump her for information, or had he felt something more? And if everything was true, if everyone knew this impossible thing about Richard Hague, how had she not seen it too? She was never wrong

(wink)

but now she was. Maybe. And if she was wrong about this, how the hell could she go on doing this job? A real person would see it. A real person would know.

So who was Alicia Friend? A person? A detective?

Or just ... nobody?

"Where the hell are you going?" Alfie demanded.

The Alicia chick turned to Richard, now free of the board. "Come on. I'm no expert with guns, but you can take a chance on this thing working if you like. I'll pull the trigger and either you get to add me to your tally, or your brain goes bye-bye."

"I won't hurt you," Richard said. "I mean that. I swear on everything I hold—"

"Save it. Get in the front. You." To Alfie she said, "Keys."

Alfie tossed her the keys. She unlocked the front passenger door and Richard climbed in. Jesus, the bitch was gonna do him herself!

"Phone too, please."

Alfie was going to argue, but the way things had gone he passed it to her without a word.

"You know," he said. "I'm the good guy here. You shouldn't be treating me like this."

She strode closer, lifting her feet high out of the snow with each step, gun at her side. "You kidnapped a man, tied him to the floor, no doubt planning on murdering him."

That was unfair. He was about to protest but she beat him to it.

"He may be what you all think he is, but you can't do that to a person. Besides, I need him more than you do. Now get going. The faster you walk, the warmer you'll stay."

"I gotta walk through the goddamn snow to get treatment?"

She opened the driver's door, trained the gun inside, said to Alfie, "I'm five-foot three, weigh seven stone six. Sorry, a hundred and four pounds. I walked out of a car accident and managed it wearing less than you. *Stop* being such a *baby.*"

As she climbed inside, Alfie hoped she might change her mind. Then the engine fired and the wheels span in the snow. She stopped revving. Tried again. The engine idled. The window wound down. The limey detective's head popped out.

"Give us a push, love."

Once free from the small drift, Alicia gave Alfie the thumbs up and drove to the end of the track, turned left. She was just glad for the warmth now provided by the heaters. The walk had been excruciating. Her feet were totally numb and her fingers were actually worse; they *burned*. If Richard had attacked when she opened the door, she'd probably be dead. Now, having secured the situation, she'd made a choice, probably a bad one, but it was made. They were headed for the Windsor estate.

"I assume that's where we need to be," she said to Richard.

He was cuffed to the door handle, right hand across his waist, secured on his left side so he couldn't grab her. His seatbelt was also fastened. Alicia held the gun, cocked, wedged under her thigh. The safety was on, but it still made her nervous.

"Yes," Richard said. "But we can't do it alone. I was coming to tell you when that Alfie guy jumped me. I wanted to free her myself but it's too much. Too hard."

"You mind telling me what you're talking about? It's a late-middle aged man and his psycho son who he keeps upstairs like Mrs. Rochester."

Richard didn't ask who that was, which pleased her for a split second. He said, "And the dogs."

"There are no dogs."

"Wellington said there were. Dobermans, patrolling. Said I'd never get in there without being torn to pieces."

"There are no Dobermans. He was either lying or the dogs were there when Welly last visited, but definitely not any more. Henry and his butler have it all on to keep a bunch of caged birds. And I didn't see any dogs when I was up there."

"You sure?"

"I'm surprised you don't shag me and get the information through pillow talk."

"It wasn't like that."

"Shut up."

She dialled a number on the phone she took from Alfie. She cursed that she remembered virtually no numbers any more. At school, she knew all her friends and about a dozen boys' numbers off by heart. Now she had to call in to the station, identify herself, and ask to be connected to Sergeant Ball. It took over a minute.

"Cold?" she said.

"I was. I turned the engine on. Don't care if they see me now."

"Fine. I need you to go inside and chat to Henry Windsor." She explained that the girls were somewhere in the grounds and that in all likelihood it was James that was holding them. "If anything happens, if James shows up, gets violent, you run. Understand? You *run*."

"Hey, I can handle myself."

"This kid can crush your head like a ripe plum. You run. Promise?"

"Okay, I promise."

She hung up. "Okay, Richard, I don't want any talk about last night, or bodies in drains or anything that does not relate to what I'm doing here. Understood?"

"Yes."

"I think I know what's going on. I need you to fill in the blanks. What did Welly tell you?"

"Welly?"

"Wellington. John Wellington."

"Please, Alicia, let me explain everything."

She left one hand on the wheel, picked up the gun and pointed it at Richard's head again. She forbade herself to cry. "My name is Detective Sergeant Friend. You do not call me Alicia *ever again.*"

A tear rolled down his cheek and Alicia couldn't bear to think about it. The man was a complete psychopath. And by "complete" she didn't mean devoid of humanity. Everyone who kills either for a living or enjoyment is a *socio*path, someone who has no empathy for their victims. But a *psycho*path will hide inside a shell, a cleverly constructed camouflage, designed to allow that person to blend into society. He knows he is different, that his thought processes are not like those of everyone else. But he also knows he is right, that everyone else is wrong, that their misguided way of life exists to supplement his. He is the centre of the universe. But a psychopath's false self, his outer skin, will fade after time, his madness spiralling to an often violent conclusion. Usually it slips along the way, this camouflage, allowing psychiatrists and psychologists a glimpse of what lies beneath.

Richard's camouflage was that of a loving husband and father, now widower, then lover; a kind, special man who deserved happiness. And Alicia had been only too willing to oblige.

No. By "complete", Alicia didn't think of it as a random

adjective to describe the man beside her. She meant "absolute." She meant "flawless."

Perfect.

And to produce a tear on cue, that would have been no problem for someone like him.

She put the gun back under her thigh. "Now talk."

And talk he did.

Chapter Thirty-Five

BALL'S CAR rolled up the driveway. Due to the abundance of pine trees and other non-deciduous foliage, it was largely untroubled by the weather, but when he came to the end, where the path to the house began, he had to get out and walk. It was only a ten-foot path, but he pulled on his bigger coat anyway.

Inside this place, he told himself, was someone in a lot of trouble. There was also a guy twice his size, able to "crush his head like a ripe plum." And DS Friend wanted him to go act as a delaying tactic. He assumed there was a lot of backup on its way: ARV, paramedics, the works. She must've got that warrant after all. Good girl.

But in the meantime, he was Katie and Siobhan's only hope. *The hero?*

In younger days he'd done a little undercover work, which was similar to how he felt now. He had played a drugs mule, a john, a vagrant acting as bait for kids who liked to set fire to vagrants. That was the worst one. Knowing that if this gang were to select him, and something went wrong, he'd be beaten, doused in fuel, then set alight.

As he walked up the short path to the towering front door,

Ball felt that same sensation, that this thing he was doing might make him a hero, but not in the sense he'd hoped. At least, unlike last time, his wife didn't give a shit about him anymore. He needn't worry about her.

He rang the bell.

He stamped his feet to stay warm.

Nothing.

He stamped his feet some more.

Rang the bell again.

Noises came from within. He couldn't tell what it was, just that they got steadily louder. No, not louder. *Nearer.*

Some suited guy in a wheelchair answered. "Can I help you?"

Ball showed him his ID. "I need a word with your, er, master."

The crippled guy rolled his eyes and backed up, and without a word he trundled into a cavernous anteroom with a huge Christmas tree. Ball stepped inside and closed the door, and the butler disappeared into one of the doors. He emerged seconds later, rolled up to Ball, and said, "My 'master' will see you now."

Ball went into the room as directed. The man he'd only seen in file pictures, Henry Windsor, stood posed beside the fireplace wearing a ridiculous padded green smoking jacket, of the sort comedians wear when imitating stupid rich folk.

"Good evening officer," he said. "What an unexpected pleasure."

"I need to talk to you about a few things," Ball said, overheating in his winter coat.

"A few things?"

"Well, one thing specifically. James. Your son."

The butler rolled halfway in the room. "Is there anything else, sir?"

"No," Windsor replied. "That will be all, Lawrence."

The butler nodded his head respectfully, backed out, and closed the door.

"Now," Windsor said, sitting in an impressive-sized armchair, legs crossed. "My son..?"

Sergeant Ball told him how much the police knew, and urged him to stop lying.

Henry Windsor said the word, "Preposterous." He repeated it several times, shaking his head with each utterance.

"I assure you it is not," Ball said.

"It is preposterous I tell you. James is in India, distributing Tanya's money to the poor. He's an idiot."

Okay, maybe daddy really believed it. But Ball had to keep him talking, and the half-hour grilling he'd set upon the man was starting to grow cold.

"So, let's talk about Tanya's money," Ball said.

"Am I being accused of something, Detective?"

"I'm a sergeant."

"Well, *sergeant*. Am I?"

"Not at all."

"Then I don't see the need to discuss money."

"You don't have a hell of a lot do you? You're technically rich but it's mostly in property and businesses, right?"

Henry Windsor reached in a desk drawer for a box of cigars and offered one to Ball, who accepted. Thick, eight inches, smelled divine. He hadn't smoked a cigar in years.

They lit up, puffing exuberantly.

"My money," Windsor said. "I still have substantial liquid assets from the sale of land to a developer. I made the sale a year or so before Tanya's parents tragically passed on. Tanya's money was a luxury when it came, one she insisted on bandying about. Enough for her to live the life of a royal if she chose—yachts, mansions, a small island if she desired. She lavished gifts on those close to her, even myself whom she saw as a ... disciplinarian compared to her own father. But she knew I didn't *have* to take her in, and she knew I knew nothing about the money she was to inherit."

"This was from her family's business assets?"

"And an enormous insurance pay-out after the crash."

Ball racked his brain for where to go next. He held the cigar aloft, pretending to examine it, appreciate it, while he searched for another angle. "And James was heir to her fortune."

"She was good for him. After his mother died, James went off the rails a bit. No doubt you know about the problems with the RSPCA."

"*Problems*, yeah."

Windsor stood and ambled over to the mantelpiece. He carefully took down a photograph and passed it to Ball. The frame was A4 sized and heavy enough to be silver. A boy of around six, a girl of eight, and two women, both about forty. All four hugged in front of a sunny landscape, hills like the ones surrounding the estate in the background. One woman was blonde and slim, while the other had dark hair, with a bigger frame, and pretty face.

"That's Jimmy there," Henry said. "Before he got in with a bad crowd. We had to send him to a ... comprehensive school." He shuddered. "We were waiting for the sale of our section of Roundhay Park to go through. After that, I was able to put him in a proper school."

Ball examined the photo again. "Who are the others?"

"My wife Paula is the one with Jimmy. The others are Tanya and her mother."

"How did James's mother die?" Ball asked.

"An accident. On a shoot. I used to keep pheasants wild on the estate. A gun went off and my wife was standing in its path."

Ball had a thought. "It wasn't Jimmy's gun was it?"

Windsor puckered up an indignant face. "No! It was not.

Someone left theirs unattended and it fell over. It went off. At least fifteen witnesses—"

"But was Jimmy there?"

Windsor sighed, the anger leaving his face. "Sadly, yes. He didn't see the gun fire, but he watched his mother die."

Ball returned the photograph to the mantelpiece. The sadness in Windsor sounded genuine. Then he twigged what it was that bothered him about the picture. "They were both beautiful women. Your wife, your sister-in-law."

"Indeed they were. Yes."

"What was Tanya's mother called?"

Henry sighed. "Rachel. Her name was Rachel."

Chapter Thirty-Six

NO STARS, no moon. The road was a blanket of white, head-lights cutting bright columns through the dark. Theirs were the first tracks and it was hard going. Alicia found controlling the van difficult. She was as close to the wheel as she could get but it was still a tippy-toe operation.

"Wellington claimed he didn't know at first," Richard said. "But later, he sort of guessed it. After the first week, he was sleeping with the Carmichael girl—called something else then, I can't remember."

"Collins. She was Hillary Collins then."

"She was looking for a sugar daddy, someone fairly well-off who'd be dead by the time she was middle-aged. At least that's what he told me."

"Stick to the task at hand."

"This *is* the task at hand. When the police put pressure on James Windsor over Tanya's disappearance, Henry had to protect his son. The family name was at risk, after all. Even when Henry tried blackmailing Wellington, a respectable police officer shagging a witness—"

"Keep on topic." She couldn't bear to hear Richard talk about S.E.X.

"Henry ordered Wellington to leave his son alone. Said he knew things looked kind-of bad, but insisted Wellington was doing nothing wrong. As far as Henry was concerned, James was *innocent*. Keep away, and Wellington's superiors wouldn't hear about his ... indiscretion. He also sweetened the deal with a pile of cash."

"Let me guess. Wellington didn't want it but Hillary persuaded him."

"On the actual money, Al—um, Detective. But Wellington never suspected murder. He figured they bought her off after some assault, hid her away in the tropics or something."

"So he knew pretty much from the beginning about Paavan, about running away to uni. All that. But why did they both want her to stay at home so badly?"

"It all came out when Wellington couldn't look the other way anymore. He was under pressure from above, and he no longer cared about the money, and he'd take his chances over Hillary. He wanted the disappearance solved. He insisted they tell him what happened."

"Are you stalling?" Alicia said. "Out with it!"

"James broke down, said how much he loved Tanya, how he couldn't see her leave with some dirty foreigner, and ruin her life. Henry agreed, suggested she was mentally ill."

Alicia thought it through. Nothing she hadn't figured out. But she had no proof. "So how did they stop Wellington from blowing the whole thing?"

"They told him Tanya was already dead."

They were approaching the estate. About five minutes away on a normal day. Probably ten tonight.

"Henry was very persuasive. He said it was an accident. That Tanya fell down some stairs whilst trying to escape their intervention. His word, apparently. They were holding her in the old air raid shelter, and when James tried to stop her ... tragedy struck."

"Doesn't explain it. One: the air raid shelter was converted to a garage years before Tanya disappeared. And two: he's a police officer. Before he learned about the kidnapping he was prepared to lose his job and everything. When he heard it was murder, that should have motivated him even more."

Richard looked sternly at her. "Hillary."

"Of course. They threatened her. Like you did."

"Two months after meeting her, and he was ready to settle down with a girl half his age."

"Wellington was fifty-nine, she was twenty-one. Nearer a third."

Richard smiled. "At least I'm less than twenty years older than you."

Alicia shot him a look that needed no words.

Richard said, "Left his wife of thirty years for Hillary, so he didn't want to lose that, his pension, *and* his reputation."

"So he called the case an unsolved, got it signed off by his boss, and took early retirement. And, what, someone better came along for Hillary?"

"Her parents are self-made millionaires and didn't believe in hand-outs. Unfortunately, Hillary grew up surrounded by society kids, so when Julian Carmichael expressed his disappointment that Hillary was spoken for, she broke up with merely well-off Mr. Wellington and took up with stinking-rich Mr. Carmichael."

"Nice girl. Okay, what else?"

"That's about it. As far as Wellington knew, Tanya was dead, his hands were tied, and that was the end of it. He doesn't know about the current girls. I assume they're in the same place."

"A place that doesn't exist."

"And isn't patrolled by dogs."

Alicia let the information run through her mini-computer. An army nut, fantasies of imprisonment, hence the animal traps. Compelled to watch them fight. Even attaches razors to some of them.

"James Windsor," Alicia said. "How much did Welly say?"

"He loved to play army, got really into weapons and combat. Once, he showed Wellington a picture, from Iraq or Kuwait or somewhere. Two American soldiers, captured, fighting one another in a cage, with enemy guns trained on them."

And with that simple image, Alicia knew everything. What James was doing to the girls, why Henry remained adamant he was out of the country. Yet she still didn't know where to look. She'd *been* in the old shelter. There was nothing down there but nice old cars.

"James is pairing the girls off," Alicia said, working the data, spitting it out to help clarify. "He's acting out fantasies he's had since childhood, and the prospect of losing Tanya to Paavan was too much." She wondered how much pain the lad felt as his favoured competitor was killed by Katie. She wondered how Katie had summoned such courage, and how on Earth she would ever recover. "You trained Katie to fight, didn't you?"

"Of course. Why do you think I'm doing all this?"

"To keep her safe, right?"

"Yes."

"That age-old refrain of men with control issues."

"I'm protecting my *daughter*." It sounded almost like a growl, his teeth bared, and Alicia instinctively pressed herself against the door. He must have sensed the slip in his mask, as he took some deep breaths before resuming his act of normalcy. "All parents protect their young. It's our duty."

"To keep her under your control."

"I prepared her for the real world. You know how many

young girls get raped? You know how many get beaten up by real monsters?"

Dissociating himself from other killers. Thinks he's special. Bloody typical.

"Of all the killers in the world, I get stuck with a textbook case of psychotic megalomania."

"She has never been hurt, never been assaulted, never got into a situation she couldn't control. She doesn't go home high with strange guys or flash her knickers at horny drunks—"

"Now you're into victim-blaming too?"

"No. Not blame. Control. Giving *her* control. Over her own life. And it worked. She was never in trouble at school, never dumb enough to get herself pregnant—"

"If she had got pregnant you'd have forced her into an abortion, I suppose?"

They crested the hill and the Windsor estate unfolded before them like a fairy-tale landscape.

"I would have strongly urged her to, yes. It would be the responsible thing to do."

"Because having a baby so young would ruin her life."

"Yes."

"All my study, and I still don't understand a society that demonises teen mums, those under eighteen especially. We terrify them into believing the nonsense that you can't have a life *and* a child, that your life automatically ends with childbirth. If teen mums received support instead of judgment and parental disappointment, sympathy instead of being harangued in the newspapers, perhaps those that Murphy bangs on about wouldn't live the lives they did; perhaps they'd know there was more to life, and society would be a better place."

Perhaps, perhaps, perhaps.

"Alicia, what are you talking ab—"

"He's testing them," she said, back on topic. "Making them

fight to the death. It's the ultimate control. Getting them to do your bidding like that. If Tanya was as perfect as James thought, she'd win every time."

Richard's left hand remained in view, on his lap.

"How many people did you kill to get this far?" Alicia asked. "To *protect* Katie."

He thought for a moment. "After the prostitute? Just the one, actually."

"Doyle."

Richard nodded.

The van entered the little Windsors' long driveway. She switched the lights off and pulled over to the side and turned off the engine. Nothing lay ahead except a dark gauntlet of trees.

Alicia said, "But you didn't get much further. You didn't get to Paavan."

"You got there first."

"And when you asked me about the case, all that was so you could get to her first? Deal with him yourself."

"You didn't ask about the others. The ones from before."

"I don't want to know." She opened the door and placed a foot on the step.

"I take it I'm not coming with you," Richard said.

"You take it right."

"That gun. Once you release the safety it's ready to fire. Point, and squeeze the trigger. Don't pull. Ease your finger tighter. It's not a professional weapon, so there'll be a strong recoil. Aim for the chest. The head's a more lethal shot, but the chest's the biggest target." He used his free hand to make a gun, pressed his thumb like a hammer. "Then when he's down you can shoot him in the head."

Alicia stepped on the crunchy snow, hand freezing on the gun, terrified of having to use it. She almost thanked this man she thought she'd known. Instead, she tried to read if the shame in his eyes was genuine, or another facet of his camouflage.

"By the way, you're under arrest for the murders of Melanie Sykes and Doyle Underwood. Amongst other things." She read him his rights, slammed the door closed, and started up the drive.

Shivering, under a moonless sky, tramping headlong into dark grounds holding an evil she had never dreamt possible, Alicia Friend removed the pink scrunchies, shook the pigtails out of existence, and let her hair fall dead around her.

Chapter Thirty-Seven

KATIE COULDN'T EVEN TRY to fight him off now. Her breathing was steady but her throat was still not right. Air was getting in but only through a small gap. And she wanted to fight. She wanted to fight so much. He held her in his arms like a baby.

He entered silently several minutes earlier, locked the door again, and came down the stairs. The sword he'd promised Siobhan never materialised. It was still the mallet. Katie wondered what he would have done had Siobhan shot her as he asked. But Katie was still his First—it was the rule, he said—and he wanted her to hold the rubber mallet, pleading with her to take it, accept his gift, to destroy the Second, so he could bring her a final test. But Katie couldn't even hold the tool.

She had managed to raise her arms onto the sides of the bath, held there by her elbows. She extended her neck as high as she could, levering her lungs open with her arms high-up, and begun to breathe as near to normal as she had in a long time. But when she refused to take the mallet, he grew angry, accusing her of more trickery, more betrayal, betraying him again and again. When it was clear she wasn't faking, he pulled her from the bath and held her tightly.

"I'm so sorry, Rachel," he said over and over. "I'm so sorry. I never meant this. I don't want to lose you again."

Katie would have told him to piss off if she'd had the strength, but she felt like a rubber doll, unable to move a single limb more than a few floppy inches at a time.

Siobhan wept in the corner farthest from them. The man continued to stroke Katie's hair, apologising to her for how everything had turned out.

The gun sat heavily in Alicia's jacket pocket, another set of handcuffs in the opposite one. She felt like a cowboy carrying his own saddlebags. She peeked through the large brass letterbox and heard voices. One of them was Ball. Good. She'd not sent him to his death.

Alicia rang the bell and Henry himself answered. He looked her up and down. She did the same to him: a pompous middle aged man feigning respectability. He might not have killed his niece, but he was equally as responsible as James. She briefly wondered what he thought of her tattered clothes and jacket, sopping wet trouser legs, and a once-white blouse now stained with small amounts of Alfie Rhee's blood and a good deal of her own sweat. Her face was probably filthy, and her hair ragged, curly in places where the silly pigtails hung. She was so tired from the walking and the cold that she could fall asleep right there in the hall.

And she was not smiling.

"Come in, Detective," Henry said. "Your colleague is already here. And, might I add, a sight better dressed."

She followed him into the same over-the-top study she'd

been in before, and Ball greeted her with, "What the hell happened to you?"

"I'll tell you later," she said. "I need Henry here to take us to Katie and Siobhan."

He reacted like a rooster bristling his feathers, inhaled to plump up his chest. Opened his mouth to utter a denial.

"Save it, Henry." Alicia produced the gun.

Ball backed up, fell onto the chaise-longue. Henry came up against the mantelpiece.

Alicia could have asked a few questions, run him in circles, tripped him up on the inconsistencies. She'd run it through her head on the walk up the drive, even had a plan of attack. But she was sick of doing that. Sick of the games, the subterfuge. Focus on getting the girls, she told herself. Arrest the bad guy, then go home and have a good long bath, and unload this whole shitty week on Roberta's broad shoulders. It's what friends are for, after all.

Alicia pulled the trigger. A bang rang out, far louder than she'd expected, and the PC monitor on Henry's desk imploded. Richard wasn't kidding about the recoil, but she was sure she made it look bad-ass.

"Jesus!" Ball cried, skittering further away.

Henry's eyes widened. "How *dare* you? This is not allowed!"

She'd found Henry Windsor unpleasant and fake at first. Then she'd disliked him, the caged birds setting off that emotion. Then she'd grown to fear him, that anyone could be as cold and calculating as this. But since discovering the truth about Richard, someone she'd thought of as a wonderful human being, like Murphy and his scum-sucking mingers, now Alicia found the man *boring*.

"The next one," she said, "goes in your knee."

He shut up.

"Alicia..." Ball said cautiously.

Using her first name, putting her at ease, building rapport. Rubbish trick.

"Please," Ball said. "Let me call in. We need more help out here. I don't suppose you got that warrant in the end."

"No. This prick has too many pals. It ends. And I won't implicate anyone else in this. I just want the girls safe."

"Then we need back up. There's no way we'll search the grounds alone."

"That's why he's going to tell me where they are."

"I don't know, I swear it!" Henry said.

Another shot and a bullet tore through Henry's left thigh. He went down, clutching the wound, surprisingly not making much noise.

Alicia's ears rang.

"*Please*, Alicia," Ball said. "This isn't right. Let me call in."

She considered it. They might need help soon. "Fine. Do it. Call in."

"My mobile's in the car."

"Use that one."

Ball edged past Alicia, hands up. Her eyes followed him but the gun remained on Henry. He went for the phone on the table next to the door.

"It's dead," he said, replacing the receiver.

"Oh, dear God," Henry said, straining to stem the flow. "We have to get out of here."

He pulled himself up, gingerly trying his leg. It wouldn't support him.

"We're going nowhere," Alicia said. "Where are the phone lines controlled from?"

"The garage. The underground garage."

The old air-raid shelter. It was open, light, the only places to hide being behind cars. If that's where the phones were cut, it might still be worth checking out.

"Walk," she said.

"I can't."

"Then hobble. It's a good clean wound. Can't hurt that much."

He gestured to an umbrella stand. She tossed him a walking stick. He tested it. He'd move, but slowly. Blood seeped from the bullet hole.

Alicia took Ball's tie from him, the gun in her armpit, then knelt and tied it around Henry's leg.

"Now," she said, pointing the gun again. "Take us to James."

"He's not here I tell you," Henry said.

"We'll see."

When the second shot rang out, Richard's heart jumped. It was too long after the first. He was glad when he heard that one, readying himself for Katie running down the drive into his arms, the killer, this James lad, either being led in handcuffs or dragged out on a gurney. If still alive, Richard decided to kill him anyway. Alicia's actions were illegal, totally reckless. Richard knew he'd never see the outside world again, not after tonight, so what did extinguishing one more undesirable matter? Better to see him finished for good than escape on technicalities.

But the second shot could have meant anything.

He put his free left hand against the door, and with his cuffed right he gave a good solid yank. The handle snapped away immediately. He could have done this at any time, but Alicia needed to feel safe, that he could not harm her. And he never would. He'd die first.

Although no longer attached to the van, the cuffs were still locked on his wrist, but there was no time to deal with that. He climbed out and opened the rear door. His knives were still there.

Alicia confiscated them as evidence. He opened it and picked up the hunting knife. He weighed it in his hand, holding it up to what he thought would be moonlight, but the clouds hid all light away. It didn't feel right. It was the most effective of them all, the messiest too, but he needed something else. His special occasion knife still lay on the van's floor, where Alfie dropped it. The leather grip, the perfectly honed blade. Yes. This was the one.

He closed the door and ran into the woods, avoiding the drive in case of cameras. He needed to be sure Alicia wasn't screwing this up, that Katie would be free, that the person responsible was punished.

The woods ended and Richard squatted at the periphery. Trees were dotted all around the enormous house, before once again becoming forest. He ducked lower as Alicia led a man in a green smoking jacket at gunpoint, the man limping badly on a walking stick. One of the detectives followed, the one with the beard. The fat man ducked into his car, only to come back, shrugging, disappointed. He had a stick of some sort though. They all followed the vague outline of a path, circling around the back of the house. The limping man shouted, "What do I have to do to convince you? He is not here!"

Richard, skirting close to the cover of trees, stalked after them.

Alicia was beginning to believe him, or at least believe that Henry believed it. When they discovered his son umpiring a human cockfight, she wondered how surprised the man would be. The fact that Ball's phone had no reception, and the radio too, meant they were all alone. The only means of communication was the phone Alicia left in the van, which would have to be driven to higher ground to work. And she didn't want Ball risking a meeting with Richard. Not armed only with the baton he carried in the car.

They rounded the house, arrived at the entrance to the garage. Henry inserted the key and turned. When they'd first visited, the roller-door simply opened and they stepped inside. This time, the lift had to rise to get here.

Alicia explained to Ball the size of the room, the cars. When the lift door opened, Ball gave it the once over, whistled as if impressed. Alicia and Henry got in, Alicia stopping Ball.

"If I'm not out in ten minutes," she said, "go and get help. There's a van at the bottom of the drive. Be careful of the man inside. He's cuffed but dangerous."

"You might need help now," Ball said. "Down there."

"I need someone to watch my back. I need a guard."

Henry pressed the down button. The shutter closed, Ball ducking for one last look at them.

Silently, the lift descended.

Henry leaned on the wall, resting his leg. Alicia checked he wasn't about to jump her or something. She was dying to ask but didn't dare. If he replied how she thought he would, it was not even worth considering. It might make her complacent.

The door opened to the glare of the underground garage. Cars gleamed, the X-Type retaining pride of place in the centre. Pictures stared in from the walls. It was silent but for the hum of the lights.

She asked the question anyway. "Do you really believe James isn't responsible?"

"He can't be," Henry said. "It isn't possible."

"Where is he? Where could he hide down here?"

"He couldn't."

Alicia stepped out into the space. She pointed the gun ahead of her, as she'd seen ARV folk do, though she hadn't a clue how she'd react if the young man came at her. Could she do it? Kill a fellow human being?

She lay on the floor and scanned under the cars. Nothing.

"I'll check the phone lines," Henry said, hobbling towards a case the size of a bedside cabinet next to a mounted life-sized photo of a Ferrari Testarossa.

As he fiddled with the cabinet, Alicia examined each car. She needed a sign, something. Blood would have been a good start. But the only blood here was the footprints that formed each time Henry took a step. She was beginning to regret shooting him. It was unnecessary.

"You're sure there's nothing else down here?" Alicia said. "Nowhere else to hide?"

The lift door rattled in the echoing space. Both jumped, startled. Then it began to rise. Ball, she supposed, getting cold or worried. *But stay alert, Alicia. Don't assume anything.*

Recovering from the shock, Henry said to her, "No. The only other thing down here is the old bathroom. And we bricked that up when this place was built."

Alicia scanned the walls. "Where? Where is it?"

"They've been cut," Henry said, finishing his assessment. "Someone cut them."

"*Where?*" she said again, now approaching him as menacingly as she could. "Where was the bathroom?"

"Oh, over there." He pointed at another car picture, this one a Land Rover going vertically up a mountain, again life-sized. "We hung that photograph over it."

During the last few days, Alicia had often wondered if there was more at work here, more than a series of murders. But nothing she had seen prepared her for what followed.

On Henry's words, *We hung that photograph over it*, the framed picture moved. It shuddered and then shifted slightly forward. Then, on a hinge at the left-hand side, it swung open to reveal a pitch black doorway, gaping like a hole in the world.

Alicia aimed the gun into the blackness. "James?"

"It's not James," Henry said. "It can't be him."

"Quiet. James? This is the police. I'm armed. Come out with your hands over your head."

Henry shook his head. In denial. A father's denial. "It isn't him. It isn't."

"How can you be so sure?"

"I just am."

She could hear movement down there, in the black pit. "James? Come on out. Let them go."

"It isn't James, I know it isn't."

Alicia's frustration outran her fear. "How the hell can you be so sure?"

The gunshot from inside the doorway flashed and then boomed, and a red cloud burst from Henry's chest. He stood upright a moment. The blood seeped from the entry wound, a little to the right of his heart, and Henry Windsor fell flat on his face.

"He knows it isn't James," came a familiar voice from within the darkness, "because he watched as I garrotted him."

And the man who'd seemed so harmless, so overweight and benign, Lawrence—*the butler*—emerged, aiming a gun straight down Alicia's throat.

Chapter Thirty-Eight

HOLDING an automatic pistol firm in one hand, he emerged from the black dressed like a soldier. Lawrence, the butler Tanya had brought with her when she came to live with James and his parents, the man who served her mother and father, the cripple, now not so crippled, striding confidently out into the garage, dressed all in black, like some special ops guy in an 80s action movie.

"James was a sick child," Lawrence said. "His mother ... his sweet mother ... killed like that ... then Tanya's too ... Rachel ... such a senseless death."

Sad as he looked, it was his size that struck Alicia. Sat in the wheelchair he appeared overweight, the way Alicia would expect Ball or Cleaver to look in the same position. But it was muscle. He must have been about late fifties, but he'd kept all his size, slouched to hide it. Ex-army, a good aim no doubt; he had to be to shoot Henry from his angle. And now he threatened Alicia at gunpoint.

But she was not exactly helpless.

"I know what you're thinking," he said. "You have a gun. I have a gun. But I've taken bullets before. Have you? Do you know what to expect? A thump in the chest, then burning as the little metal pellet tears through muscle and bone, bursting out the other side, leaving an exit wound the size of my fist."

She raised the weapon, eyes on his legs. "So the physio Tanya paid for was more effective than you let on."

"A necessary ruse," he said. "Tanya's fund paid for several operations during my time here, and continued my treatment even after she was taken. Including the physio. Poor old Henry had no idea of the progress I'd made."

The blood from Henry's chest reached her feet. He gasped for breath. With no idea how badly the man was hurt, she stepped to the side, holding the gun out, trying not to shake.

She said, "James?"

"He was an animal." The man was not shouting, but the undertones in his voice were pure anger.

"None of you wanted Tanya to leave you. With Henry it was because of the money. You and James, you *wanted* her here."

"Clever girl. And what else?"

"You were hurt. In Iraq. The Republican Guard made you fight amongst yourselves, made bets, like James did with the animals. He did that because of the stories you told him."

"I cared for the boy. But he thought my injuries were 'cool', that my barbaric stories were, in his words, 'awesome'. Tanya's father was part of the brigade that rescued me and brought me back to reality. I served on as a cook, but this had been my profession before the war and provided for me, enabled me to go back to it. He was a good man, Peter Windsor. A good man who married a woman of such compassion ... I just can't say." He had made ground on Alicia without her noticing. Now he was too close. "But James and his father were fools. I told James about the reality of war, showed him my scars."

"But he thought that was even cooler, right?"

"You *are* clever."

"What did he do?" Alicia said, focusing on her fingers. *Squeeze, don't pull.* "It was Tanya, wasn't it? He did something to her."

"When Tanya fled, James said he killed her. That was never the plan."

"No. You wanted her to see sense. To keep her here. To make her happy. Do what you thought her parents wanted, those people you admired so much."

"Right again."

"And when he said that, you flipped. You loved Tanya and you killed James."

"No. Actually, I was very sad. James said it was an accident, and his father believed it. I went to retrieve the body, from down here, right where Henry's lying now. And she was alive. But only just."

Alicia computed the possibilities, came up with one. "She'd been raped, hadn't she?"

"James raped his own cousin. The daughter of the most wonderful woman in the world. The embodiment of her mother. And yes, in front of his father, I killed James. Did the old piano wire stuff."

"Her mother ... you were in love with Tanya's mother."

"I would never have moved on her. No. Peter Windsor was more than worthy."

"And you wanted to keep Tanya safe, do what was right by her, even if that meant—"

"Don't judge me like that. Don't judge me at all."

"It was like James raped the love of your life, that all your efforts were for nothing. You killed James, and buried him ... where? In Tanya's grave? No. Not there. The *aviary*."

"Ironic, don't you think?"

Not as ironic as the conclusion to this case, Alicia thought. *The frigging* butler *did it.*

She said, "That's why Henry was so confident James wasn't down here."

Lawrence chuckled. "Now how about you give me the gun? Then you can come see the girls."

Alicia readied herself. The slightest twitch. His thumb going half a millimetre either way, a tendon bulging, and she would *squeeze-not-pull* the trigger.

The trigger.

"It was Rachel dying," she said. "That was what triggered your psychosis."

"Don't you analyse *me*."

"You lost the love of your life, and idealised Tanya as her replacement. Her embodiment. It was a benign psychosis at first, a form of depression, but when James did that to her—to *Rachel* in your eyes—you snapped."

"I said don't *do* that."

A clattering noise from behind.

She glanced sideways for a split second, a heartbeat, but it was enough. The gun was gone, her shoulder flared in pain, and Lawrence held her against himself, a slab of a hand around her neck. The roller door of the lift rumbled upwards. Lawrence aimed the gun.

And Richard stepped into the garage's glare.

"Richard, look out!" Alicia cried.

The gun boomed and hot air crackled all around, sulphur stinging Alicia's nose. Another shot and, somewhere, glass shattered. So close to her ear, it almost deafened her.

Through the smoke, she saw the E-type's windscreen was gone.

Lawrence breathed hard through his nose, sounding like some threatened beast. In a sense, he was. But Richard was unarmed, or at best he'd retrieved a knife. He was also still wearing the cuffs.

Then something hit her: where was Ball?

Upstairs, in the freezing snow, Sergeant Ball stirred. He wasn't sure where he was, only that his jaw hurt like hell. He remembered Alicia and a gun, and being ordered to stand guard while she led some comedian into a lift large enough for a car. Cars. That's where they were headed. Down in a lift to see some cars.

He also remembered hearing soft footsteps, that he was afraid of something, of some*one*. When he spun he was afraid that it might be that person, that he was in trouble. He caught a glimpse of who hit him, and it wasn't who he thought it was going to be. Instead, it was the father of one of the girls.

The ground was so cold. But his head span and he didn't want to get up, not until he thought this through.

Then he remembered something else too. It was the same father who was wanted in connection with two murders. The same father who appeared before the cameras and claimed his daughter was the most precious thing in the world.

Jesus!

The guy did his own daughter!

It was the same old story. The grieving relative, appealing for their return.

The bastard.

How had DS Friend not spotted it? How? She was one of those head-doctor types, some smart arse with a degree. It was her job to interpret press conferences, finger the guy, the mother, the boyfriend.

And he'd knocked Ball unconscious.

Ball sat up, still dizzy, but coherent. He stood, finding the key that Henry used to open the lift. He was sure that's where Katie Hague's dad had gone. *There it is.*

Shit.

The key was in the mechanism but it had been snapped off. No way to turn it, not without the right tools.

He thought back to his orders.

Go get help if I'm not out in ten.

Well, he'd been unconscious for ... how long? He couldn't tell. Forget it.

He stumbled a little at first, regaining balance, checking which way up the world was, and ran drunkenly towards where Alicia said a van was parked. It was her only chance.

Lawrence pulled Alicia backwards. She dug her heels in, but the floor was polished stone. No grip.

"Richard, get out!" she yelled. "Get help!"

He didn't reply.

Lawrence held Alicia tighter as he backed up. "Your daughter's going to die. So's your girlfriend. Come on out."

"I'm *not* his girlfriend," Alicia said.

"I've seen him on television. And you. The way you act together. Fawning over him."

She hadn't thought one little thing of the press conference. She'd offered Richard her hand, both of them. She was comforting him. But she knew how it might look now.

Through the fear and the desperate sorrow at failing so badly, Alicia sensed an emotion she hated, a sentiment she had never succumbed to before: self-pity. Even if she lived, even if they all walked out of here right now, there would be an inquiry. She'd be found out. It was the end for her as a police officer. No matter what plaudits her track record exuded. If this lunatic could spot it, a skilled PSD officer certainly would.

They were through the doorway, into the darkness. She saw the garage getting smaller, the bright lights receding. She hoped to see Richard once more, bounding forward, dodging the bullets like a superhero, the man for whom she fell so hard returning for one last noble feat.

Lawrence lifted her off the ground and tossed her aside. She didn't hit the floor when she expected to. That came shortly after. Then she hit it again, and again. Stairs. She curled into a ball, elbow striking stone as she protected her head. A rib snapped.

She stopped.

Gazed back up from where she'd fallen. Lawrence the butler stood silhouetted against the glare. Then the shape of his arm reached up, pulled the door shut with a small hiss, and everything turned absolutely black.

Chapter Thirty-Nine

"*NO!*"

Richard watched helplessly as the door closed.

He had observed the man's movements, retreating towards the door leading who-knows-where, and he predicted what would happen. So he'd snuck around the cars—the Jags, the Mercs, the Bentley—and pressed himself against the wall, out of the guy's line of sight. He gripped the knife, its softness reassuring in his palm. He was ready to surprise the camouflage-dressed nutter with a head-on assault, when the door swung shut, replaced by a picture of a Land Rover going sideways up a mountain.

Now he experienced a falling sensation, his feet turning to stone, his thoughts swirling too fast to understand. For the first time in his life, Richard Hague was panicking.

Katie was down there, he was sure, and the other girl. And, of course, Alicia. He heard her cry out before the door closed and cut her off.

He was sweating. His hand moistening the knife. He wiped his palms on his trousers.

The first thing he did reaped no rewards: he tried the picture frame. He dug his fingers behind the frame, set his foot against the wall, and heaved. The picture flew off the wall, clattering to the ground. Flush to the pristine clean wall, a cast-iron door blocked his way, locked by a keypad, its numbers raised so he could not repeat the trick that accessed the Priceway store in Bridlington. There were no gaps, no holes, no opening of any kind. Even his knife wouldn't find leverage.

He searched for something to use. But what? On a work bench he found screwdrivers, a wrench, even a crowbar. He tried jimmying the door, but it was solid.

She's going to die.

She's going to die.

It's all my fault.

They're dead, and it's all my fault.

But when he comes out, I'll be waiting. I'll gut him like he's nothing. My knife'll take his skin off and I'll burn it in front of him while he dies. I'll ram my fist down his neck. I'll—

—ram.

What the hell am I thinking? How stupid can one guy be?

Okay, Richard, get a grip. Think. How can you make this work?

The lights came on and Alicia blinked. She was half blind, half deaf. Lawrence spoke to a girl on the floor. She was curled up like a baby, dark hair matted and filthy, crying, with the butler coaxing her back to normality. It was *Siobhan*.

Where was Katie?

Nothing here but white tiles with a small puddle of dried blood, a hose, a bath. Was she dead already?

A hand! A hand hung out of the bath.

"Katie?"

The hand moved.

"No talking!" Lawrence shouted. "No talking until I say so."

Alicia sat up. Her right elbow ached like hell, and her ribs were agony. Broken, and she knew it. Her arm just about worked, but it'd swell and bruise. She focussed on Lawrence as he helped Siobhan to her feet. And Katie was alive too. Her cause wasn't lost after all.

"Let us go and you might still qualify for mental incapacity," Alicia lied. "I could tell the judge you can't stand trial."

Lawrence sat the girl in a chair, at first seeming not to hear Alicia, but then he stormed over. He lifted her to her feet, as easily as picking up a bag of apples, and yelled in her face, "*I am not insane! I'm upset.*"

"About Tanya, I know. You wanted to prove she loved you. You made her kill for you."

"*You don't understand.*"

She maintained a calm and soothing voice, using his first name, rubbish trick or not. "Lawrence, I do understand. She was hurt, needed nurturing back to health. You killed the person who hurt her, and then you took care of her."

"Stop it."

"Henry thought both of them were dead, didn't he? That's why he was so shocked when Tanya showed up."

He led Alicia roughly to a chair opposite Siobhan. "You can fight on behalf of Katie."

"Let me see Katie. She needs help."

"*You* will fight on behalf of *Katie.*" He held out a rubber mallet. "Take it. You will be my First."

"You wanted Tanya to kill for you like you killed for her. Isn't that right, Lawrence? Isn't that right?"

He closed his eyes, containing his anger. "If you win, Katie lives. If you die, Katie dies."

"I'm not fighting Siobhan for you."

He thrust the mallet forward, hand trembling. "Take the damn hammer!"

"No."

"Take it."

"No."

He gripped Alicia's hand and jammed the tool in it, closing her fingers. She tried to open them but he was too strong. As soon as he let go, the automatic gun came out, the six-shooter Ruger wedged in the back of his trousers. He cocked the weapon and aimed it at Siobhan.

He said, "You drop that and I'll shoot her right now."

Alicia held on to the hammer. "Let me see Katie."

"No. You'll see her if you live."

"But I'm not going to fight."

"You're no Rachel, Detective. You don't even look like her. But you have her fire, her intelligence. You must have to find me like this. You can fight for her. You *will* fight for her." He addressed Siobhan. "You know the rules, honey. You fight until one of you dies."

"And you didn't expect Tanya to die, did you," Alicia said.

That froze him right where he was.

"You thought you'd nursed her back to health. Better than that, you physically improved her, trained her to fight, wanted her to prove her skill, even though she was damaged … emotionally. So you found Pippa Bradshaw, someone you could keep as a replacement just in case Tanya wasn't as strong as you hoped. But when she wouldn't fight, when neither of them would fight, you killed Pippa yourself. Didn't you, Lawrence? You murdered her as an example. One punch. Then made Tanya disfigure the body."

"They wouldn't obey. They didn't understand. Like you."

"But when you brought Hayley along, you'd scared Tanya so much that she did it for you. She beat Hayley and you promised to free her if she killed for you. But you didn't. You brought Katie instead."

"I needed to see it wasn't a fluke. I needed another Second. Tanya—*Rachel*—was my First..."

"Rachel was Tanya's mother, Lawrence. She died long ago. I know you must have loved her dearly, but Tanya didn't have to pay like this. Nor Hayley or Pippa."

"You have to fight now."

"We're not going to fight."

"Oh no?" He fired the gun in the air, the bang filling the room.

Alicia closed her eyes at the noise, and when she opened them, Siobhan was running at her. She leapt on Alicia, clawing and scratching for the mallet. Alicia held it away and received a thump to the face. Not a controlled hit, just panic and anger. Siobhan gripped Alicia's hair and pulled her head up, whacking it back down on the tiles. White pain flashed. Dull thuds around her skull.

"Come on, fight back," Lawrence urged.

Alicia dropped the mallet and got hold of Siobhan's wrists. But the girl was panicking, making her strong—stronger than Alicia. She kept hold of Alicia's hair, but was not banging anything off the ground. Alicia retracted her legs, tucked them under Siobhan's armpits, then extended quick and hard. Siobhan shot into the air and across the room.

Alicia got to her feet, and Siobhan was coming back at her. Alicia parried and flipped Siobhan over, sending her across the floor again. Unfortunately, she landed right next to the mallet. She scrambled up, swinging at Alicia, a snarl to her face, hate in her eyes. It wasn't Alicia she was fighting, not in her mind, not deep down; it was Lawrence.

Alicia backed up too far. She hit a chair, lost her balance and landed on her back. Siobhan was on her in a second. She straddled Alicia, knees pinning her arms, the injured elbow now agony. Siobhan raised the mallet with both hands, the lethal blow prepared.

"Please," Alicia said. "You do this, and he wins."

Siobhan wavered. Breathing. Breathing steadily. Eyes wide and locked with Alicia's.

"But I live," she replied, and swung down.

Horrendous thunder exploded from one corner of the room. Metal on stone boomed out, dust billowing. Huge chunks of masonry rumbled to the floor, smashing tiles. Rocks flew, fragments landing on the grappling women, and debris tumbled and cracked. Siobhan scrambled off Alicia, screaming, hands over her head, the mallet still in her hands. Lawrence shielded himself from the stone shards, pointed his gun upwards. Fired once, twice. Alicia pushed away, right up against the wall. She could reach the bath.

It was like a bomb had exploded.

ARV backup? This quickly?

When the dust mostly settled it became clear what had happened. The battered nose of an E-type Jaguar jutted through the doorway at the top of the stairs, the door now non-existent. Stone from the wall itself had caved inwards and was still crumbling.

Lawrence aimed his gun, motionless in the eddying dust.

Another crash sounded to the left, the wall bending in but not collapsing. Lawrence instinctively turned to it. And as he did, out of the smoke and ruins, Richard Hague launched himself off the bonnet of the Jaguar. Lawrence loosed off two clumsy rounds, but Richard landed on him, knife in hand, slashing away.

Richard's face, Alicia noticed, was not that of a blood-crazed maniac; he was *concentrating*. Keeping the gun-hand at bay, meticulous attention to his own weapon. His expression ... *neutral*.

Alicia heaved herself up, looked in the bath.

Katie Hague could hardly breathe. Her lips were blue and her eyes were wide and scared. It sounded like she was inhaling through a straw.

Asthma. Richard said she was asthmatic. The dust in the air was killing her!

Richard and Lawrence squared off, like boxers now. Lawrence bled from cuts to his face and chest, and a defensive wound to his arm. Richard still wielded the knife, but Lawrence was unarmed. Unless...

"He's got another gun!" Alicia said.

But it was too late. He was far enough away to whip the gun out and point it, cocked, ready to go, before Richard could even move. Instead of shooting Richard, however, he pointed the weapon at Alicia.

"Right," Lawrence said. "Let's see what you're really made of."

It took several minutes to set up the scene as the killer wanted it. He made Richard drop the knife on the floor and slide it over. Lawrence caught it under his foot and held it there. Then the military nut retrieved his own weapon. This was the scenario Richard had envisaged all along. Him and this man. Face to face. But it wasn't working quite as he hoped.

The pop star girl wept in the corner, shaking her head and pleading not to be hurt. Alicia was made to crouch on her knees and look at the floor, like a Catholic schoolgirl. Katie—*Jesus, Katie!*—lay in a bath, taking fast, tiny breaths. She saw Richard, her eyes dancing with hope.

And Lawrence trained his gun on Katie.

"Go over there," he said to Richard. "Face your two girls."

Richard complied. He stood two feet away from his daughter.

Unable to touch her, hug her, help her. He couldn't see what Lawrence was doing.

Metal sounded, tinkling on tile. Then a snap. Then something slid along the floor, halting by his foot.

"Pick it up in your right hand," Lawrence said.

The butler moved to Richard's left, stood near the rubble-covered stairs. He'd be able to see everything from here, even the last girl, rocking and crying in the far corner. His gun was aimed at Richard.

"I said, pick it up in your right hand."

Richard slowly bent down and took the object. He knew what it was.

The Ruger.

"There's one bullet in there," Lawrence said. "So here's the deal. You shoot one of your girls in the head, and the other will live. You're not fast enough to turn the gun on me. I'll shoot you dead, then do *both* your girls."

Richard assessed them both. Katie would be dead soon anyway, and Alicia had arrested him once. There's no way she could forgive him. No redemption. Katie would find out about him, and he'd lose her too. No one wants a killer for a dad, no matter how justified his reasons.

"Choose, you bastard. And choose quickly." He took one step forward.

Richard put the barrel against Alicia's head. He said, "You do believe when I say I love you. Don't you?"

Alicia nodded.

"And you understand I *stopped*. I stopped killing people. I only started again when Katie was taken. You understand that?"

That cute little nod, the lilt of her head, her hair falling about her. "Something triggered your psychosis again. I understand."

"Not 'psychosis.' I need..." He couldn't put it in words. "I don't know ... something to occupy me ... Katie was that person—"

"*Do it!*" Lawrence ordered, stepping closer behind them.

Richard said, "You must know that I mean it when I say I'm sorry."

She held back tears in her eyes. She mouthed, "Do it."

It was a strange sort of serenity that swept over him as he made the decision. Not sadness as such. A necessity, like concluding a business deal or pushing a stiletto knife into a vagrant's heart.

"Have a good life," Richard said, and put the gun against the side of his own neck, and pulled the trigger.

When the pin struck the primer in the solitary bullet, a brilliant amount of heat erupted in under a tenth of a second. The primer burst aflame, the expanding pressure propelling the bullet out through the barrel and into Richard's soft skin. This broke under the force and speed of the little piece of spinning metal, and burnt the epidermis black with the heat. The bullet crashed through his flesh, grazed his trachea, narrowly missed his spinal cord, and splashed through his carotid artery on the way out the other side.

It was a gamble. And it paid off.

The bullet continued to travel, virtually in a straight line, although all bullets kind-of wobble in mid-air, especially after chewing through a human neck. This bullet, slowed by the obstacle, managed to find a second target, albeit with less impact than a pure shot.

It landed, and stuck, in Lawrence's left lung.

.   .   .

Lawrence staggered and dropped the gun, and Alicia was up on her feet. Richard fell to the floor, his blood spilling in a gushing river across the tiles. She dashed to him, unable to stem the flow. And she still wanted to—she still *had* to save him.

The butler collapsed against the wall, but the gun had landed close by, and the killer still possessed enough strength to stand upright. He was confused, but the shock was leaving him and he focussed around the room.

Alicia had decisions to make and her brain wasn't fast enough. She couldn't carry Katie. Siobhan was in a panic. She could run, say she was getting help, but that would be like executing them herself.

Richard's eyes were still alive, but he gasped like a beached fish. Reaching towards Katie. No. Not Katie. His knife.

Lawrence gained his bearings now and searched for his gun. No ranting, just looking, treading like some hulking ape. Alicia's instinct was still to run, up the stairs, over the car, and out, into the world above. But she wouldn't leave these girls.

Noises from above.

She could hear them now, shouting, metal clanging, and suddenly she was crying herself. The relief, that help was here at last.

Lawrence located the gun. Now he was trying to bend down. It wasn't easy. Blood bubbled and spilled from his chest with every movement.

Alicia yelled, "*We're in here!*" but the banging and clanging and shouting persisted with no progress.

They couldn't get in.

Lawrence, moving so his wound didn't rip further, touched his fingers to the pistol.

Katie stared blankly at the ceiling, her breathing no more than a jerky movement of her mouth.

Then Lawrence grasped the gun. Unsteadily, he aimed at

Alicia. He was trained for this. Even weakened, he would easily kill her.

Alicia hated the next bit. She'd only ever learned the minimum about guns as her job demanded; she always thought she'd never be able to kill. If it ever came down to "him or me" it would probably be her. But after everything—the girls, the American, the bodies in pipes, and hostage-taking—after everything that happened in the past week, Alicia was not prepared to allow one more bad-guy to get away with it.

She ducked to the side as Lawrence made his first shot. He was too weak to move fast, but he could still move.

More urgency sounded from upstairs, shouting growing louder, clanging harder.

They would still be too late. Far too late. So in one fluid movement, of pumping legs, and swinging arms, of ribs screaming for her to *stop, rest, get better*, Alicia charged forward, swept up Richard Hague's knife, and leapt over the bath. She landed on Lawrence, her damaged arm hooked around his neck. With all the strength she could muster, she slammed the knife down, and plunged the blade deep into the man's chest. It stopped close to the hilt, oozing red.

She had hit him square in the heart.

Lawrence dropped the gun, eyes wide in surprise, looking at the knife as if he'd never seen one before. His lips drew back, baring his teeth, eyes morphing from confusion to realisation to anger, fingers feeling upwards, inwards, unable to reach this monstrous object protruding from him. The butler's motion slowed. He growled, even the growl slower than normal speed, but that may have been Alicia's perception rather than reality.

Then, simply, he keeled over. And died.

Chapter Forty

THE ROOM deep inside Sheerton police station was supposed to offer comfort to the bereaved. It was called the Family Room. It held one person. And her family was not with her.

Sat on the table, her cuts tended, her clothes were gone, replaced by a towelling tracksuit normally worn by prisoners. The touch of a brief physical exam still lingered. Her left arm was bandaged and held in a sling, not broken, but hurting, and binding around her ribs, an injection staving off the pain. Inside, she replayed this night.

The gun, the knife, the car crashing through a wall to her rescue. And the initial resistance of a blade on a human being, then the give of splitting bone, and finally the easy slice as it cut through the meat of Lawrence's heart.

They broke through thirty seconds later to the sight of DS Alicia Friend desperately trying to hold closed a bullet-wound to the neck of the killer who lay on the floor beside her. She had already helped Katie from the bath and lay her next to her father. Where, although neither could talk to the other, plenty was said before Richard closed his eyes and ceased to move. He even managed a smile.

For Alicia, the next hour was like sitting in the centre of a storm. Everything going on around her existed in another realm. Paramedics stormed the old bathroom. Alicia directed them to Katie and they possessed the right equipment to save her. She responded quickly and the first thing she did was cry. She said, "Dad, what the..." but she needed more oxygen. As soon as she was strong enough, the paramedics carried her out.

Ball crouched beside Alicia, asking if she was alright, explaining they couldn't get through the lift, that he was sorry, so sorry they hadn't arrived sooner. She heard his words, but they were tinny, as if being spoken from inside a metal box. Even Richard's occasional feeble judder hardly registered.

Other officers tried to tempt Siobhan back from the depths of her corner, out into the real world, but she screamed and wouldn't let anyone near her. An indeterminate time later, presumably once Katie was stable, the paramedics returned and sedated her.

Eventually, Sergeant Ball persuaded Alicia to let go of Richard's wound, stand up, and let the paramedics take over. It was only when she looked down that she realised she had been sitting in a lake of Richard Hague's blood.

And now she recalled herself. Her choices. Her decision to abandon the job she'd worked so hard at, the job that had battled against her true personality, that would not let her be who she wanted to be. The job had won.

She barely sensed the door open, nor the man enter. He wore a pristine police uniform, silver buttons gleaming in the meagre light, his grey hair flat to his head, as if he'd gotten ready in a hurry but still wanted to look smart. He stood before her, arms by his side. She did not look up.

"Alicia?" he said.

She moved her head, to face away from him, but winced, a pain she had not detected before, shooting through her neck.

She turned back, catching the man's eye. Then she was unable to look away.

"Graham," she said. "Sir."

"You saved them," Rhapshaw said.

Alicia nodded.

He said, "Katie and Siobhan are sedated but healthy. Katie will need some more medical care, but Siobhan should be out in a couple of days." A slight chuckle, then, "Even Henry Windsor survived somehow. The way he fell seemed to stem the wound. He should recover."

Alicia nodded again.

Rhapshaw sighed deeply. "I'm glad you're okay, Alicia."

"Me too," she said. "Glad. Very glad I'm okay."

"Murphy was asking for you. Whiplash, bruised ribs, a little grumpy you left him. Seems to understand, though."

"Sergeant Ball? He was bleeding."

"They're keeping him in overnight in case of concussion." He smiled awkwardly. "His wife showed up, started crying. Told him never to do anything like that ever again. I couldn't tell if he was happy or scared by that."

Alicia found a smile of her own. It faded quickly. She didn't want to ask about the final man in that basement.

Rhapshaw didn't need prompting.

He said, "Richard Hague died twice on the way to the hospital. If he sees out the night, they'll be surprised."

Alicia tried not to feel anything about that. To her shame, she failed. Relief that he wasn't dead; sad that he would be soon.

She said, "I'll have my resignation to you ASAP. Once the doctors clear me."

"You wouldn't go to the hospital. Why?"

"I didn't want to see them. Ball. Katie. Murphy. I didn't want to see anyone."

"Come on. Let me take you to St James's. The others are at the General."

She shook her head again. "I just need some rest."

Rhapshaw unbuttoned his jacket and sat on a chair, looking up at Alicia. "I spoke to someone else at the hospital. One Alfie Rhee? He's willing to play his part in the enquiry. Says he knows what it's like when an officer has to go outside the usual procedures."

"I'm resigning, Graham. I can't stay after what I've done."

"You used an illegal weapon in a high-stress situation. Your life was threatened. The lives of two girls were at stake. I'm sure the bullet to Mr. Windsor's thigh was an accidental discharge due to your lack of experience with firearms."

"Yeah," she said with a humourless chuckle. "That'll be it."

"About the only concrete thing you did wrong was to enter the Windsor estate without a warrant. But since the proprietor is at death's door, and likely to be charged with conspiracy if he wakes up, there's no one to press charges but the CPS. You can get away with a formal reprimand."

The consideration she gave lasted a heartbeat, maybe two. Carry on as before. Be herself again, return to that cute-as-sin kitten-eyed girl—*her true self*—solving crimes that the men found too hard. Getting a kick out of seeing their faces when she opened her mouth for the first time. That shock, that disbelief that *she* was one of the best, one of the most successful, that *she*, this little girl, was going to be in charge. Murphy the latest.

Could she go back to that person? Or would she turn into one of those bitches, trying to prove herself in all the wrong ways?

"Alicia?" Rhapshaw said. "You still with me?"

"Will you drive me home?"

He smiled, nodded. He presented a carrier bag, opened it,

and removed some of Alicia's clothes. "I stopped by your place on the way up. Your flatmate's waiting for you."

"It's a school night."

"She'll phone in sick tomorrow."

"She's a good friend."

"I can see why you two get along. She's some lady, that Roberta."

"She's special." Alicia realised that thinking of Robbie was keeping her going, the prospect of crying into her considerable bosom the one thing she wanted more than anything else. She hopped onto the floor and held up the "Men are for here for a good time, not a long time" sweatshirt.

"Sir?"

"Yes?"

"Are you going to watch me change, or will you wait outside?"

One thing Rhapshaw had not brought with him was a coat. So while he retrieved the car and brought it around the back, Alicia sat in the rear foyer. The door outside was discreet, and no reporters lurked.

Sat on the single seat, legs up, arms hugging her knees, Alicia heard voices. A woman and a man.

"Where are we going?" the man asked.

"Home, Freddie, we're going home."

Closer, the man said, "Back to my pipe? My well?"

"No, baby, home. *Our* home."

"But we don't love me anymore."

"We?" the woman said.

"You hate me. I don't like me either."

"Don't talk like that, Freddie."

They came into view. A woman in her forties and a man with a bushy beard and smart suit.

"But Brenda," the man protested, "you threw me out. You told me never to come back. And then Jodie didn't want me anymore either..."

"Honey, I was angry. I didn't mean it. Oh, you silly thing."

The woman kissed him on the lips, a sloppy one. Alicia couldn't help but feel something good was happening. She was unsure what, exactly, but the numbness in her chest began to ease.

As they passed, both acknowledged her with a smile and a nod of the head. The man said, "She was in the papers! The one sat with the man from my well."

"Honey," the woman said, stroking his beard. "We'll get it all sorted out. Come home for a little while, and if you still want to go back to your well, then we'll go back together. Okay?"

The man thought for a moment. "Okay," he said, and opened the door, put his arm protectively around his wife as the cold air rushed in, and led her outside. The last thing Alicia heard before the door clicked shut was, "I think you'll like my well. It's sheltered ... lots of fresh air..."

Then they were gone. And the flicker of a smile played at the corners of Alicia's cute little mouth.

Epilogue

THE SNOW CRUNCHED UNDERFOOT, cold air not biting but caressing the skin, like winters folk remember from those "better" times. Even the sun radiated brighter than it had not so long ago.

Donald Murphy had been out of the hospital for almost two weeks when he decided to visit Alicia Friend. Her resignation still hung in limbo, neither she nor the Serious Crime Agency willing to back down. His neck still hurt, but he'd taken off the brace. The last thing he needed was Ms. Friend telling him what a sissy he was.

He'd called her four or five times, the conversations always short, stilted affairs, like a divorced couple discussing their kids. In their latest he told her in bullet points about the latest fallout: as soon as he got threatened with a long stint in a tough prison, Red McCall made a deal for a softer sentence and sang loud and clear, and DCI Chambers' involvement with Alfie Rhee came out along with her expensive poker addiction.

But Murphy didn't like those unnatural chats. He felt they'd grown closer than that, despite leaving him in the wreck of a car in the snow. He knew he'd have done the same if it meant finding Katie and Siobhan. Both of whom were doing fine. Physically, at any rate. He spent time with Katie, explaining what he knew about her sick father—and he meant "sick" in the medical term, not as an insult, although what he said away from the girl was vastly different. He couldn't understand why Richard Hague did what he did, only that Katie's existence changed him. Was it possible to be two different people? To change so absolutely?

Maybe one day he would wake up and tell them.

Richard Hague had died three times in total. Twice in the ambulance and once on the operating table. His life was now one of perpetual darkness, unlikely he'd ever wake up. Brain dead, they said, but Katie pleaded for him to remain alive. She wanted answers. She *needed* answers.

Murphy remembered describing Susan's father as a psychopath when he brought her home late one night and the old man chased him with a cricket bat. That was another time though. Back then, the idea of so much death in one place was unthinkable. Now, the papers ate it up for a week or so, laid Alicia's apartment to siege, then got bored and moved on. A few people did follow-ups, the scumbag Clancy demanding a witch hunt, but when another tabloid scooped a politician's gay affair, the others—including Clancy— had to follow.

Now Murphy needed to persuade Alicia to take a little more time deciding her future.

Alicia's apartment block was fairly new, rising from the rubble of an old factory, as did many of the housing developments nearby. From the street, Murphy accessed the building without passing a barrier—no need here; this was a nice neighbourhood.

He was out of his work clothes, still on sick leave himself, and the jeans he hadn't worn for a year seemed to have shrunk. He climbed the stairs, the effort once again reminding him to get more exercise.

Number thirty-eight.

He had rehearsed a little speech, about how special Alicia was, how they wouldn't have made the connections they did without her little computer of a brain. That, had she been another hard-arsed officer with a point to prove, Murphy wouldn't have liked her half as much as he finally admitted he did. He remembered something she'd said when they first met: *I'll just be myself. You'll fall in love with me and your change will happen all by itself.* He looked at his jeans, stroked the area of skin formerly occupied by his moustache.

"The cow," he said, and rang the bell.

Nothing for a long moment. Then the sound of running from inside, and Alicia answered in a rush. "Oh, hi! Sorry, I was in the loo. What are you doing here?"

She wore tracky bottoms and a Leeds United shirt, her hair in a ponytail. No makeup. Her eyes held more weight than when they first met.

She said, "I heard they were finally able to arrest Henry Windsor."

"Nice greeting," he said. "I'm fine, how are you?"

"Sorry. You look fine, so I figured you were. *Love* the top lip."

Murphy shrugged his coat higher. "Cold out."

"Oh, right. Come on in."

He stepped inside. The Christmas decorations were a little over the top, but he expected no less. "They found James's body last week and arrested Henry yesterday. Took some doing. Perverting the course of justice, bribing a police officer. They won't make it stick that he was accomplice to Lawrence, though."

"His lawyers will say he was being threatened. That he was a victim as much as the girls."

"Could use that defence about bribing Wellington too."

"He might just plead. There's a lot of guilt in that man."

Murphy didn't expand on that. *No more shop talk.* "No Roberta?"

"She flew out to see her parents in New York. She's staying there for Christmas and New Year."

"And you?"

"I'm popping over to my dad's tomorrow. You?"

He shrugged. "My niece invited me over. Darla has a new boyfriend she wants me to meet. Can't imagine who that is. I can hardly wait."

Alicia stood still, hands in pockets. He'd seen this before. Officers so traumatised they couldn't bear to be around others from the job. But Alicia didn't seem the type to be traumatised. She was too focused. Yeah, he thought that. He knew the dizzy stuff was an act, who she *wanted* to be. Even if *she* didn't see it.

"I'm taking you for lunch," he told her. "Not a request."

She looked into the apartment, somewhere beyond Murphy.

"Come on," Murphy said. "You can go like that if you want, but I'll have to take you somewhere they think 'classy' means pictures of dogs playing snooker." He pulled a green paper crown out of his pocket, one he took from a Christmas cracker. Placed it on his head. "It's Christmas Eve, Alicia."

A smile cracked on her face and Murphy felt himself mirror her. Her smile grew into a little laugh.

"Well," she said, "I suppose I'd better make a little effort."

She dressed quickly and skipped from the bedroom in beige trousers, a smart top, and flashing Santa Claus earrings. And when she slipped into her coat, she produced a sprig of mistletoe. Murphy bent down to accept the peck on the lips, felt a happiness he'd forgotten some time ago, and found himself hoping Alicia would find a nice man soon.

God, that made him feel old. Wishing a beautiful young woman a decent life rather than yearning to reverse his years, say, twenty of them.

With Alicia twittering about the nice new pub down the road, Murphy led her outside. The door closed, leaving the apartment empty.

And within the empty apartment, Alicia and Robbie's decorations sparkled in the rays of sunlight through the windows. But no one was left to see them. Each room held a different array of tinsel, foil and lights. The living room, of course, was the most extravagant, with dancing reindeer and tree bulbs winking on and off. The only room to escape such adornments was the bathroom. Alicia had tried it one year, but as soon as it steamed up, the shiny rows of paper flopped to the floor.

It was in this room, however, that a foreign object remained. Alicia had been attending to it moments before Murphy called round. She put off using it until Robbie was away, and then again until she had a sherry or three inside her.

And here, perched on the edge of her bath, as Alicia sat opposite her friend in the pub ordering the Christmas special, a lonely pregnancy kit held onto its answer, and would wait patiently for her to return.

In Black In White

Meet Detective Sergeant Alicia Friend: cop, analyst, cutie-pie.

She acknowledges she is an irritating person to have around at first but, when given a chance, all her colleagues fall in love with her. She can't explain it, but it's how she works, how she gets her best results.

And it is exactly how she must work when a British diplomat is murdered on US soil, and the UK Ambassador orders her to observe the FBI's investigation.

Soon, the murders expand to encompass a wider victim profile, each confessing their politically-motivated lies on camera, and Alicia shows why her superiors overlook her quirks, and consider her one of the best minds in her field.

Drafting in her old partner, Alicia imposes her personality on the investigation, and expands the focus from a politically-charged arena to the madness of a psychopath who cannot seem to stop.

Note from the Author

I just wanted to say a huge thank you for buying this book. If you've made it this far, I hope I am not being too presumptuous in assuming you enjoyed it. I also hope it means you will be happy to leave me a review.

Reviews are the lifeblood of up-and-coming authors, and as someone who is striving to make this a career, positive feedback on retailers, can mean the difference between an undecided reader hitting 'buy' and moving on to the next writer. If you have time, I would be truly grateful for an endorsement, no matter how brief.

*If you would like to be kept up to date with forthcoming developments, you can sign up at www.addavies.com/newsletter, where I will be initiating **free previews**, sharing news, even **giving away books** ... but I will only contact you when I have something to say. You won't be spammed with nonsense, and your email address will NEVER be shared with third parties.*

Once again, thank you for buying this book – it really does make me happy to think I've brought even a small amount of pleasure to a stranger through my words.

A.D. Davies

www.addavies.com

Novels by A. D. Davies

Moses and Rock Novels:

Fractured Shadows

No New Purpose

Persecution of Lunacy

Adam Park Thrillers:

The Dead and the Missing

A Desperate Paradise

The Shadows of Empty men

Night at the George Washington Diner

Master the Flame

Under the Long White Cloud

Alicia Friend Investigations:

His First His Second

In Black In White

With Courage With Fear

A Friend in Spirit

To Hide To Seek

A Flood of Bones

To Begin The End

Standalone:

Three Years Dead

Rite to Justice

The Sublime Freedom

Shattered: Fear in the Mind

Co-Authored:

Project Return Fire – with Joe Dinicola

Lost Origins Novels:

Tomb of the First Priest

Secret of the Reaper Seal

Curse of the Eagle Plague

The Dead and the Missing

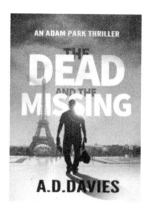

A missing girl. An international underworld. A PI who will not quit.

Adam Park is an ex-private investigator, now too wealthy to need a job. But when his old mentor's niece rips off a local criminal and flees the UK, his life of surfing and travel comes to an abrupt end.

Using cutting-edge technology, Adam tracks the young woman and her violent boyfriend through the Parisian underground where he learns of a brutal criminal enterprise for whom people are just a business commodity.

But when the men who run this enterprise feel threatened by his investigation, Adam is propelled to more dangerously-exotic locales, where he must fight harder than ever before.

To return the girl safely and protect the ones he loves, Adam will need to burn down his concepts of right and wrong; the only path to survival is through the darkest recesses of his soul.

Three Years Dead

When a good man ... becomes a bad cop ... but can't remember why...

Following an attempt on his life, Detective Sergeant Martin Money wakes from a week-long coma with no memory of the previous three years. He quickly learns that corrupt practices got him demoted, violence caused his wife to divorce him, and his vices and anger drove his friends away one by one. On top of this, the West Yorkshire Police do not seem to care who tried to kill him, and he is offered a generous pay-out to retire.

But with a final lifeline offered by a former student of his, Martin takes up the case of a missing male prostitute, an investigation that skirts both their worlds, forcing him back into the run-down estates awash with narcotics, violence, and sex, temptations he must resist if he is to resume his life as the good man he remembers himself to be.

To stay out of jail, to punish whoever tried to kill him, and to earn his redemption, Martin attempts to unravel the circumstances of his assault, and—more importantly—establish why everyone from his past appears to be lying at every turn.

The ancient world is not what we thought...

Tomb of the First Priest

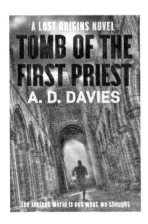

Freelance treasure hunter Jules has finally located the bangle stolen from his dying mother, an artifact that may unravel a centuries-old secret: the location of the Tomb of the First Priest.

But when a reclusive billionaire beats him to the artifact, Jules has no choice but to join forces with an institute of unconventional archaeologists who reveal to him clues penned two thousand years ago, and who claim the bangle holds properties that science cannot explain. And Jules appears to be the only person who can activate them.

As both parties race to decipher the bangle's origins, they uncover a trail meant only for the holiest of men, leading to an apostle's manuscript, the hunt for a tomb alleged to conceal great power, and a breathless, globe-trotting adventure that threatens to destroy them all.

Printed in Great Britain
by Amazon

79624771R00226